THE WORLD'S CLASSICS

LADY ANNA

ANTHONY TROLLOPE (1815–82), the son of a failing London barrister, was brought up an awkward and unhappy youth amidst debt and privation. His mother maintained the family by writing, but Anthony's own first novel did not appear until 1847, when he had at length established a successful Civil Service career in the Post Office, from which he retired in 1867. After a slow start, he achieved fame, with 47 novels and some 16 other books, and sales sometimes topping 100,000. He was acclaimed an unsurpassed portraitist of the lives of the professional and landed classes, especially in his perennially popular *Chronicles of Barsetshire* (1855–67), and his six brilliant Palliser novels (1864–80).His fascinating *Autobiography* (1883) recounts his successes with an enthusiasm which stems from memories of a miserable youth. Throughout the 1870s he developed new styles of fiction, but was losing critical favour by the time of his death.

STEPHEN ORGEL is the Jackson Eli Reynolds Professor of Humanities at Stanford University. His books include *The Jonsonian Masque*, *The Illusion of Power*, and, in collaboration with Sir Roy Strong, *Inigo Jones: The Theatre of the Stuart Court*. He has edited Ben Jonson's masques, Christopher Marlowe's poems and translations, and Shakespeare's *The Tempest* for the Oxford Shakespeare.

THE WORLD'S CLASSICS

ANTHONY TROLLOPE

Lady Anna

Edited with an Introduction by
STEPHEN ORGEL

Oxford   New York

OXFORD UNIVERSITY PRESS

Oxford University Press, Walton Street, Oxford OX2 6DP

Oxford New York Toronto
Delhi Bombay Calcutta Madras Karachi
Petaling Jaya Singapore Hong Kong Tokyo
Nairobi Dar es Salaam Cape Town
Melbourne Auckland

and associated companies in
Berlin Ibadan

Oxford is a trade mark of Oxford University Press

Introduction, Note on the Text, Select Bibliography,
Explanatory Notes © Stephen Orgel 1990
Chronology © N. J. Hall, 1991

First published 1984
First issued as a World's Classic paperback 1990
Reprinted 1992

British Library Cataloguing in Publication Data

Trollope, Anthony 1815–1882
Lady Anna. — (The World's classics)
I. Title   II. Orgel, Stephen 1933–   III. Series
823'.914[F]
ISBN 0-19-282134-2

Library of Congress Cataloging in Publication Data

Trollope, Anthony, 1815–1882.
Lady Anna/Anthony Trollope: edited with an introduction by
Stephen Orgel.
p.   cm. — (The World's classics)
Reprint. Originally published: London: Chapman and Hall, 1874
Includes bibliographical references.
I. Orgel, Stephen.   II. Title.   III. Series.
PR5684.L3   1990   823'.8—dc20   90-30827
ISBN 0-19-282134-2

Printed in Great Britain by
BPCC Hazell Ltd.
Aylesbury, Bucks

CONTENTS

ACKNOWLEDGEMENTS

It is a pleasure to acknowledge two experts who have been especially helpful to this amateur: Peter Edwards of the University of Queensland, and my Stanford colleague Robert Polhemus. This edition was done, as *Lady Anna* was written, on a trip to Australia. For assistance less material but equally indispensible, I am grateful to my friends Ruth Blair and Adrian Kiernander.

S. O.

INTRODUCTION

Lady Anna was composed in 1874, on board ship during the Trollopes' eight-week voyage to Melbourne to visit their elder son Frederic, who had emigrated to Australia as a sheep-farmer. Trollope had left with his publisher the manuscripts of two of his richest and ultimately most successful novels, *The Eustace Diamonds* and *Phineas Redux*; in the next two years he was to write *The Way We Live Now*, for modern readers probably his greatest work, and the penultimate volume of the Palliser series, *The Prime Minister*. Against such competition, *Lady Anna* has invariably been seen as a disappointment. But few novels, by Trollope or anyone else, will stand comparison with Trollope at his best, and if we can resist the invidious contrast we shall find in *Lady Anna* a complex and often powerful work, and a remarkable index to his changing social and political sensibility.

Like most Trollope novels, *Lady Anna* is about marriage; but the subject is treated with an unusually single-minded intensity, and the plot involves, for the central character, an almost pathological limitation of the already meagre options normally open to Trollope's women. Lady Anna's tragedy is determined in the previous generation; it is the story of her mother's attempt to force her to marry against her will, but it is in the mother's story that Trollope's greatest passion is invested. In its treatment of Anna's mother, the novel, in fact, constitutes one of the most detailed of Trollope's studies of that classic Victorian exemplum, the poor but well-born girl who marries solely for money and position. In a sense *Lady Anna* extends the issues of a story like *The Claverings*, or like that of Lady Laura Standish in *Phineas Finn*, into the next generation, imagining the effects of such marriages on the children; and it is in this respect that the central figure is not the titular heroine but her mother, the Countess Lovel. She was a poor girl from a good family, who married the Earl Lovel, though she did not love him and, as it rapidly turns out, scarcely knew him. Shortly after the birth of their daughter Anna the earl reveals himself as a scoundrel, turning his wife and child out of his house and asserting that they are not even legally married—he already has a wife living in Italy. The novel records the countess's lifelong attempt to justify her claim to her title, and to prove the legitimacy of her daughter. Though she is ultimately successful, the cost in human terms is terrible, and most terrible for Anna.

Anna has been raised in poverty, but also as the daughter of an earl. There is clearly a good deal of autobiography in this for Trollope, the child of impoverished gentry, the day-boy at Harrow suffering the jeers of his classmates for his poor clothes and mud-stained shoes. During her years of litigation, the countess is supported by her one loyal friend Thomas Thwaite, a tailor of radical political leanings, who places all his efforts, and ultimately all his money, at her disposal. Anna grows up with his son Daniel as her guide and playmate, grows to love him, and promises to marry him. The engagement is, of course, concealed from their parents.

It becomes increasingly apparent that the countess will succeed in her claim to be the earl's widow, and her daughter will thereby be acknowledged as the legitimate heir to her father's estate. This is a blow to the family of the new earl, Anna's cousin, a young man of charm and sensibility who has been made poor by his uncle's excesses and financial chicanery. The lawyers on both sides observe that all the family's problems will be resolved if the cousins fall in love, and the heir to the old earl's fortune marries the heir to his title. This arrangement seems to the countess the resolution of her dreams. The young man undertakes his wooing with a will, and does in fact find himself deeply attracted to Anna, who, in her turn, is genuinely moved by his grace, intelligence, and good nature. There is the story's dilemma: should Anna, to satisfy her family ties, the demands of her heritage, and her growing fondness for the young earl, transfer her love from Daniel, who is now a journeyman tailor, to her cousin; or in more human terms—

terms that Trollope rarely allows the novel to take seriously—can Anna permit herself to change her mind?

That she will not do so is, of course, a forgone conclusion. Trollope describes the novelistic problem he set himself in a letter to his friend Lady Wood, written when twelve of the book's forty-eight chapters had appeared in the *Fortnightly Review*, and readers were already pressing for Anna to be allowed to marry the earl:

> Of course the girl has to marry the tailor. It is very dreadful, but there was no other way. The story originated in my mind by an idea I had as to the doubt which would (or might) exist in a girl's mind as to whether she ought to be true to her troth, or true to her lineage, when, from early circumstances the one had been given in a manner detrimental to the other—and I determined that in such a case she ought to be true all through. To make the discrepancy as great as possible I made the girl an earl's daughter, and the betrothed a tailor. All the horrors had to be invented to bring about a condition in which an earl's daughter could become engaged to a tailor without glaring fault on her side.[1]

It will be noted here that, without the mitigating presence of 'horrors', aristocratic girls who fall in love with tailors are to be considered gravely culpable. Trollope forcefully defends himself against his readers' disapproval in the *Autobiography*:

> It was my wish of course to justify her in doing so [i.e. marrying the tailor], and to carry my readers along with me in my sympathy with her. But everybody found fault with me for marrying her to the tailor. What would they have said if I had allowed her to jilt the tailor and marry the good-looking young lord? How much louder, then, would have been the censure! The book was read, and I was satisfied. If I had not told my story well, there would have been no feeling in favour of the young lord. The horror which was expressed to me of the evil thing I had done, in giving the girl to the tailor, was the strongest testimony I could receive of the merits of the story.[2]

[1] *The Letters of Anthony Trollope*, 2 vols., ed. N. John Hall (Stanford, 1983), ii. 589–90; spelling and punctuation have been normalized.

[2] Anthony Trollope, *An Autobiography* (Oxford World's Classics, 1980), p. 347.

These accounts of the novel are particularly interesting because to a certain extent they misrepresent the book's moral dilemma. To put it in the simplest terms, Anna cannot change her mind not because her troth and her lineage are in conflict, but because a rigid constancy is the normal condition imposed on women in Trollope. There is in fact nothing unusual about Anna's situation: the books are full of far more extreme cases, of girls who give their hearts in ignorance, or even through outright deception on the fiancé's part, but are not therefore justified in transferring their affections to another man. The most thorough-going treatment of the situation is in *The Small House at Allington*, in the love of Lily Dale for Adolphus Crosbie. The lover in this case is demonstrably a cad and a liar, but Lily to the end, even years later, refuses the comforts of a marriage to her doggedly faithful admirer Johnny Eames. There is, moreover, no implication here that, had Trollope allowed her to accept Johnny, the reading public would have been horrified. On the contrary, the novel continually teases us with the possibility that Lily will finally consent to be happy; and, indeed, nothing in *The Small House at Allington* precludes a happy ending. *Can You Forgive Her?*, as the title suggests, poses the question almost abstractly: is breaking an engagement, whatever the circumstances, unforgivable? If in this case it is not, that is only because Alice Vavasor ends up on the third try with her original lover.

Behind the plot of *Lady Anna* is a large, unanswered, and very Trollopian question: men, even Trollope's heroes, occasionally change their minds about whom they will marry; why is it so overwhelmingly important that women not change their minds, and that, if they do, they suffer for it, whereas the men simply move on—the case, for example, of Lady Mabel Grex and Frank Tregear in *The Duke's Children*? Why is this sort of female constancy a virtue, whereas the idea of women truly knowing their own minds is not? Why is Lily Dale not allowed to decide that her judgement was mistaken merely because she was deceived, and to set aside her erroneous choice? Why is the manifest dishonesty of her lover not exculpatory? In fact, for generations of readers, it *has* been exculpatory; Johnny's bafflement that Lily will not have him at last is dramatically justified. Trollope in *Lady Anna* set himself a perfectly characteristic problem, though in many ways its solution, as in the case of Lily Dale, went against all his human instincts. The novel actually makes a good case against its predetermined conclusion—the same case that five years later Meredith was to argue with such exhaustive tenacity in *The Egoist*.

Trollope is, moreover, perfectly clear about the fact that the issue is not a social but a novelistic one—that the constraints on Anna's choice are not those of Victorian society. When Daniel goes for advice to his father's friend, the old radical poet modelled on Southey, he is told that he is unreasonable to expect Anna to remain true to her vows, that 'we tell of a constancy in love which is hardly compatible with the use of this as yet imperfect world. Look abroad, and see whether girls do not love twice, and young men thrice' (p. 272). If this is bad advice, it is bad only in the context Trollope has created, and it indicates the extent to which the novel is willing to acknowledge that its heroine is being held to a standard that its readers are not expected to observe.

What then is this book about? To say it is about marriage scarcely defines it: why, in Trollope's world, do women marry? Josephine Murray in becoming the Countess Lovel has looked above her station and married without love; Trollope early in the novel accuses her of marrying merely to be a countess, but, in fact, she is not represented as having accepted the earl for his money or his position. He is said to be charming—even seductively so, though there is no implication that she is seduced—but she is aware that he has no society and an unimpressive house. Nothing about his life dazzles her, and all she is said to find attractive in her prospects is the landscape. Nevertheless, she is fully prepared to be everything the earl requires in a wife. Unquestionably she knows too little about his true character to make a rational choice; but in fact she knows as much as most women in Trollope's world ever know about their prospective husbands. Marriages, even those with no financial or social disabilities, are almost inevitably based on a profound ignorance: the case is brilliantly analysed in *He Knew He Was Right*. Josephine Murray is from a good family, but she has an ineffectual father, no dowry, and only distant relatives; she looks about her, weighs her options, and makes her decision. Trollope no doubt loads the case by making the earl a charming monster, but, like many women in Trollope—even many sensible women—she marries essentially for security. The line between the sensible and the cynical in this world is a very fine one. In one respect she reaps the reward of her coldness of heart, her willingness to marry the monster without even being in love with him (unlike Lily Dale, she knows something about the bargain she is making); but how would the case be different if she had loved him? There are very few women in Trollope of whom it can be said that they get what they deserve.

The novel's tragic force derives from the way the countess tries to use her daughter to right the wrongs that have been done to her, forcing Anna to marry another unloved Earl Lovel. But even this is not presented as a battle between social pressure and true love: Trollope makes it clear that Anna's marriage to Daniel Thwaite is, in its way, no less constrained. 'If Lady Anna asked for release,' Daniel tells himself, 'she should be released. But not till she had heard his words. How scalding these words might be, how powerful to prevent the girl from really choosing her own fate, he did not know himself' (p. 118). There are many moments like this in the book, and they pose the largest question of whether women in the society Trollope imagines really have any power of choice at all; and, if they do, and they exercise it, whether it is not bound to be wrong.

Such issues are intimately related to the radical political background within which the story is set. The action takes place in the 1830s; the first Reform Bill is still news. Charles Kingsley's *Alton Locke* (1850) had created a revolutionary poet–tailor to plead the Chartist cause in a nearly contemporary setting; if Trollope's radical tailors owe something to Kingsley, *Lady Anna*'s pre-Victorian setting is not merely the stuff of historical romance. It reflects the intense debate throughout the 1860s over class barriers, privilege, and, especially, voting rights, culminating in the Hyde Park riot of 1866 and the ultimate passage of the second Reform Bill of 1867, which, though far from a universal franchise, did give representation to a much larger segment of the working classes and significantly altered the balance of parliamentary power. Trollope was a staunch Liberal, but his decision to make his Liberal Prime Minister a Duke of Omnium is a clear index to his ambivalence about the social movement of the age. (George Eliot's equally ambivalent *Felix Holt the Radical*, with a far more active and idealistic political hero than Daniel, disarmed by an even more melodramatic and unlikely plot, had appeared in 1866.) Anna grows up in Keswick, in Cumberland, in the northern Lake District, a mining and manufacturing town, but also known for its scenic beauty and its association with the Romantic poets. Southey retired to Keswick after his defection from the radical cause; and the scene in which Daniel receives the old poet's disappointing advice reflects the Victorian Liberal's sense of the inevitable failure of the older generation's brand of radicalism—by the time Trollope was writing, a Radical was merely a progressive Liberal, hardly a revolutionary.

Trollope's presentation of radical politics is not wholly unsympathetic, though he clearly has far more affection for the quixotic idealism of Thomas Thwaite than for the more impersonal and singularly charmless politics of his son. The fact that a radical can devote all his resources to a just cause, even if the cause ultimately upholds the interests of the class system, indicates a true nobility of spirit. Thomas Thwaite's support for the countess is impractical and self-defeating, and the price of vindicating her title and making Anna a lady is the destruction of his own son's prospects in the honest craft he has been trained for. These matters are often remarked upon in the novel, and even with some bitterness, but they constitute nevertheless, overall, another point in the old tailor's favour. Those aspects of radicalism that promise any genuine change in the social structure seem only ominous to Trollope.

Indeed, the radical Daniel is a particularly unpromising figure, even as a lover. His father's politics are an aspect of his individuality, full of independence, courage, and even, when he strikes the earl in a righteous rage, of old-fashioned chivalry, but Daniel's radicalism is much more pro-grammatic, a matter of generalized, if fervent, assurances that things must someday, somewhere, be better. He is neither attractive nor gracious; nothing in Trollope's account of him is designed to make readers feel that Anna's fate is in any way a romantic one. At moments Trollope even looks through the idealism of his politics to see it as a function of a positively unsavoury character:

He was ambitious, discontented, sullen, and tyrannical. He hated the domination of others, but was prone to domineer himself. He suspected evil of all above him in rank, and the millennium to which he looked forward was to be produced by the gradual extirpation of all social distinctions. (p. 215)

Nor is he even allowed to be physically prepossessing: 'Daniel Thwaite was a dark brown man, with no tinge of ruddiness about him, a thin spare man, almost swarthy, whose hands were as brown as a nut, and whose cheeks and forehead were brown' (p. 38). If we put this together with the talk, late in the novel, about the impossibility of washing blackamoors white (pp. 492–3) we shall have a sense of the intensity of Trollope's ambivalence about the husband he is obliging Anna to choose. Indeed, the fact that Anna's choice is limited to the sole alternatives of her childhood sweetheart and her aristocratic cousin says much about the limitations of the novel as a whole. Such a choice, in a very real sense, is no choice at all.

Yet there are moments when Trollope allows other possibilities to enter the story. Perhaps the most striking comes when Anna's marriage to Daniel has at last been agreed upon and the lawyers, observing that Daniel has invariably insisted that her money means nothing to him, propose to give Anna control of her inheritance in her own right. This in fact would make Anna independent in a way that few Victorian wives could ever be, and it would certainly permit her a kind of self-determination unthinkable for most of Trollope's heroines. It is, in its way, as utopian a proposal about marriage as we shall find in Trollope. But Daniel rejects the proposal immediately and indignantly: ' "I'll have nothing to do with such a settlement. . . . When she is my wife her property shall be my property. . . . I don't want my wife to have anything of her own before marriage," said he; "but she certainly shall have nothing after marriage,—independent of me" ' (p. 483). And an authorial voice ironically observes, 'For a man with sound views of domestic power and marital rights always choose a Radical!' The limits of utopian democracy are women.

This aspect of Anna's situation is simply taken for granted in the novel; it is not presented as part of the problem. But Daniel's attitude is merely a benign version of the monstrous old earl's behaviour to Anna's mother. Husbands protect their wives or abuse them, but they are empowered to do either; very little authority inheres in the wife's position. Daniel is not mercenary, but in practice his attitude towards the money he scorns is identical with that of Anna's alternative suitor, the young earl. If Lovel has good arguments about why she should prefer him to the tailor, they are good only because Anna is rich. Whether he loves her or not, the money is crucial: she is nothing to him without it. This is represented as a telling point in Daniel's favour, but what is Anna to Daniel besides her money? She is to be the mother of his children and their educator in the principles of utopian democracy (p. 250), his rest and comfort in his labours, 'affectionate, self-denying, and feminine' (p. 29). If we consider why self-denial is essential and what the meaning of 'feminine' is here, we shall see why Daniel is not the solution but the problem.

Trollope repeatedly formulates Anna's dilemma as a choice between two kinds of obligations; he rejects the obligation of class and lineage, but, as we have seen, only because there are extraordinary mitigating circumstances. The novel consistently defines the problem in the terms Daniel uses to himself: 'that it was natural that she should transfer to another the affection that she had once bestowed upon him, because that other was a lord, he would not allow' (p. 274). But as Trollope presents the matter dramatically, this is not the choice Anna is being offered. She is being tempted to imagine another kind of life, to change her mind in the fullest sense of the phrase, not merely to accede to the implications of her origins, whatever these may be determined to be, but to move beyond them. It is impossible not to be struck with how reductive a concept marriage has become here. Anna is trapped in either case, since it is assumed that she can only marry, and that she must marry one of only two suitors. She herself says that the appropriate solution is for her to die.

Why *is* Daniel the only solution? In another of those moments when Trollope imagines an alternative, and happier, ending, the genial Solicitor-General Sir William Patterson urges the Earl Lovel, Anna's now definitively rejected suitor, to accept his cousin and her working-class husband fully into the family. In fact, Lovel owes Anna a great deal, since she has rescued him from poverty—and from the necessity of marrying for money—by giving him half her inheritance. Moreover, Sir William continues,

I am much mistaken if you will not owe much to him. Accept them both, and make the best of them. In five years he'll be in Parliament as likely as not. In ten years he'll be Sir Daniel Thwaite,—if he cares for it. And in fifteen years Lady Anna will be supposed by everybody to have made a very happy marriage. (p. 437)

This is a reasonable and comfortable scenario, and not at all improbable given the parliamentary politics of the 1870s. That it shows Daniel being co-opted by the establishment is not necessarily a point against it; Sir William imagines Daniel making his peace with a social system that Trollope on the whole admires.

The novel in fact goes to some lengths to rescue the class

system from Daniel's shallow contempt. 'His eyes saw merely the power, the privileges, the titles, the ribbons, and the money;—and he hated a lord'; but 'he had been unable as yet to catch a glimpse of the fact that from the ranks of the nobility are taken the greater proportion of the hard-working servants of the State' (p. 306). And late in the novel Sir William Patterson produces eloquent arguments in defence of a concept of natural aristocracy, which Daniel concedes to be unanswerable—at least by himself. There is nothing disingenuous in Trollope's procedure here, but, despite the often reiterated conviction that Anna must be true to her promise, it is clear that, in rejecting her lineage, she is rejecting everything.

The dream of freedom is Daniel's; Anna has no part in it. It can be pursued only in a new society; the novel ends with the couple setting sail, like Trollope's son Fred, and Trollope himself writing their story, for Australia. Of course, if Sir William is correct, Australia will be very like England in a generation or two; but Trollope's admiration for democratic systems based on egalitarian ideals, while not unmixed, was genuine and often enthusiastic. Observing in the *Autobiography* that Americans are at times 'too prone to prove by ill-concealed struggles that they are as good as you', he nevertheless continues, 'whereas you perhaps have been long acknowledging to yourselves that they are much better'.[3] The freedom represented by America or Australia promises a great deal in Trollope, a world where a John Caldigate (in the novel named for him, written in 1878) or Paul Montague (in *The Way We Live Now*)—or Fred Trollope—those heroes of the impecunious gentry, can realize ambitions that would only be stifled in England. But the result is rarely what the protagonists hope for. Though Caldigate makes his fortune in the Australian gold fields, he pays dearly for it; Paul Montague's America makes him rich only in experience; Fred (as Trollope pointedly informs his readers) is an unsuccessful sheep-farmer.

[3] Anthony Trollope, *An Autobiography* (Oxford World's Classics, 1980), p. 316.

Egalitarian society is, moreover, full of unanticipated dangers, the greatest of which is precisely the danger that Trollope guards so strongly against in *Lady Anna*: the liberation of women. Paul Montague's wooing of the patient, unpretentious, altogether admirable Hetta Carbury is interrupted by the appearance of an American lover from his past, a Mrs Winifred Hurtle. She is everything Hetta is not: vibrant, beautiful, passionate, above all sexually experienced, and Paul has proposed marriage to her, and subsequently abandoned her. That she is ill-used by him there is no question; but his behaviour to her is excused by the same mitigating circumstances that Lily Dale will not allow to excuse herself: his ignorance of her past and the dubiousness of her character. She has been married and calls herself a widow; it later transpires that her husband may be alive, but she is in any case divorced from him; she admits to having shot a man in Oregon, but insists that it was in self-defence. A similarly dangerous woman, a Mrs Euphemia Smith, beautiful, passionate, and sexually alive appears from John Caldigate's Australian past shortly after his marriage. They had lived openly together in the gold fields, and she produces evidence that he has not merely made promises to her but has actually married her. Caldigate is duly convicted of bigamy and imprisoned, though he is eventually exonerated.

Such women are represented as predatory, destructive, and powerfully, dangerously attractive. That their men have used them badly is not in question, though Mrs Smith is willing to perjure herself to obtain what she conceives to be justice. But what is most dangerous about them is not any incidental criminal activity, which may or may not be involved; it is their assumption of their rights and entitlements—the fact, in short, that they behave like men. Trollope, indeed, in an extraordinarily revealing moment, makes this charge explicit in the case of Mrs Hurtle:

He could not say that she had not washed herself clean;—and yet, from the story as told by herself, what man would wish to marry her? She had seen so much of drunkenness, had become so handy with pistols, and had done so much of a man's work, that any ordinary man might well hesitate before he assumed to be her master.[4]

Trollope's admiration for American women is expressed openly and wholeheartedly in the *Autobiography*. Mrs Hurtle is the dark side of that admiration; it is not only to the fictional Daniel Thwaite that the limits of utopian democracy are women.

Such figures are obviously versions of the Countess Lovel. She has been in her way the one liberated woman in the book, making her own marriage, establishing her title and her rights, managing her daughter, even attempting to murder Daniel Thwaite to defend her cause. If Lady Anna is trapped by the assumptions of a patriarchal system, it is her mother who most powerfully embodies the patriarchy. Nor is her passion hers alone; though Trollope insists that Anna must be true to her word, the counter-arguments are repeated throughout the book with an unvarying and compulsive energy that does not come from the countess. Trollope's loyalties are powerfully divided, and his convictions and demands are as compelling and peremptory here as those of either of his heroines.

---

[4] *The Way We Live Now* (Oxford World's Classics, 1982), pp. 446–7.

NOTE ON THE TEXT

Lady Anna first appeared as a serial in the *Fortnightly Review* from April 1873 to April 1874; it was published in book form in two volumes in May 1874, and again the same year in a one-volume edition with some minor changes in punctuation. This was the basis of the Oxford World's Classics text issued in 1936, which has been reproduced here.

SELECT BIBLIOGRAPHY

Lady Anna has received relatively little critical attention. The following books contain the most interesting extended discussions: Robert Tracy, *Trollope's Later Novels* (Berkeley, California, 1978); R. D. McMaster, *Trollope and the Law* (London, 1986).

There are valuable brief remarks on *Lady Anna* in the following: James Kincaid, *The Novels of Anthony Trollope* (Oxford, 1977); P. D. Edwards, *Anthony Trollope: His Art and Scope* (Brighton, 1978); Geoffrey Harvey, *The Art of Anthony Trollope* (London, 1980).

The following general studies provide important contexts for *Lady Anna*: Robert Polhemus, *The Changing World of Anthony Trollope* (Berkeley, California, 1968); Ruth apRoberts, *Trollope: Artist and Moralist* (London, 1971; in US entitled *The Moral Trollope*); Coral Lansbury, *The Reasonable Man* (Princeton, 1981); Shirley Robin Letwin, *The Gentleman in Trollope* (London, 1982); Walter Kendrick, *The Novel Machine: The Theory and Fiction of Anthony Trollope* (Baltimore, 1980).

A CHRONOLOGY OF
ANTHONY TROLLOPE

Virtually all Trollope's fiction after *Framley Parsonage* (1860–1) appeared first in serial form, with book publication usually coming just prior to the final instalment of the serial.

1815   (24 Apr.) Born at 16 Keppel Street, Bloomsbury, the fourth son of Thomas and Frances Trollope.
(Summer ?) Family moves to Harrow-on-the-Hill.

1823   To Harrow School as a day-boy.

1825   To a private school at Sunbury.

1827   To school at Winchester College.

1830   Removed from Winchester and returned to Harrow.

1834   (Apr.) The family flees to Bruges to escape creditors.
(Nov.) Accepts a junior clerkship in the General Post Office, London.

1841   (Sept.) Made Postal Surveyor's Clerk at Banagher, King's County, Ireland.

1843   (mid-Sept.) Begins work on his first novel, *The Macdermots of Ballycloran*.

1844   (11 June) Marries Rose Heseltine.
(Aug.) Transferred to Clonmel, County Tipperary.

1846   (13 Mar.) Son, Henry Merivale Trollope, born.

1847   *The Macdermots of Ballycloran*, published in 3 vols. (Newby).
(27 Sept.) Son, Frederic James Anthony Trollope, born.

1848   *The Kellys and the O'Kellys; or Landlords and Tenants* 3 vols. (Colburn).
(Autumn) Moves to Mallow, County Cork.

1850   *La Vendée; An Historical Romance* 3 vols. (Colburn).
Writes *The Noble Jilt* (A play, published 1923).

1851   (1 Aug.) Sent to south-west of England on special postal mission.

1853   (29 July) Begins *The Warden* (the first of the Barsetshire novels).

(29 Aug.) Moves to Belfast as Acting Surveyor.

1854 (9 Oct.) Appointed Surveyor of Northern District of Ireland.

1855 *The Warden* 1 vol. (Longman).
Writes *The New Zealander*.
(June) Moves to Donnybrook, Dublin.

1857 *Barchester Towers* 3 vols. (Longman).

1858 *The Three Clerks* 3 vols. (Bentley).
Doctor Thorne 3 vols. (Chapman & Hall).
(Jan.) Departs for Egypt on Post Office business.
(Mar.) Visits Holy Land.
(Apr.–May) Returns via Malta, Gibraltar and Spain.
(May–Sept.) Visits Scotland and north of England on postal business.
(16 Nov.) Leaves for the West Indies on postal mission.

1859 *The Bertrams* 3 vols. (Chapman & Hall).
The West Indies and the Spanish Main 1 vol. (Chapman & Hall).
(3 July) Arrives home.
(Nov.) Leaves Ireland; settles at Waltham Cross, Hertfordshire, after being appointed Surveyor of the Eastern District of England.

1860 *Castle Richmond* 3 vols. (Chapman & Hall).
First serialized fiction, *Framley Parsonage*, published in the *Cornhill Magazine*.
(Oct.) Visits, with his wife, his mother and brother in Florence; makes the acquaintance of Kate Field, a 22-year-old American for whom he forms a romantic attachment.

1861 *Framley Parsonage* 3 vols. (Smith, Elder).
Tales of All Countries 1 vol. (Chapman & Hall).
(24 Aug.) Leaves for America to write a travel book.

1862 *Orley Farm* 2 vols. (Chapman & Hall).
North America 2 vols. (Chapman & Hall).
The Struggles of Brown, Jones and Robinson: By One of the Firm 1 vol. (New York, Harper—an American piracy; first English edition 1870, Smith, Elder).
(25 Mar.) Arrives home from America.
(5 Apr.) Elected to the Garrick Club.

1863   *Tales of All Countries*, Second Series, 1 vol. (Chapman &
        Hall).
        Rachel Ray 2 vols. (Chapman & Hall).
        (6 Oct.) Death of his mother, Mrs Frances Trollope.

1864   *The Small House at Allington* 2 vols. (Smith, Elder).
        (12 Apr.) Elected a member of the Athenaeum Club.

1865   *Can You Forgive Her?* 2 vols. (Chapman & Hall).
        Miss Mackenzie 1 vol. (Chapman & Hall).
        Hunting Sketches 1 vol. (Chapman & Hall).

1866   *The Belton Estate* 3 vols. (Chapman & Hall).
        Travelling Sketches 1 vol. (Chapman & Hall).
        Clergymen of the Church of England 1 vol. (Chapman & Hall).

1867   *Nina Balatka* 2 vols. (Blackwood).
        The Claverings 2 vols. (Smith, Elder).
        The Last Chronicle of Barset 2 vols. (Smith, Elder).
        Lotta Schmidt and Other Stories 1 vol. (Strahan).
        (1 Sept.) Resigns from the Post Office.
        Assumes editorship of *Saint Pauls Magazine*.

1868   *Linda Tressel* 2 vols. (Blackwood).
        (11 Apr.) Leaves London for the United States on postal
        mission.
        (26 July) Returns from America.
        (Nov.) Stands unsuccessfully as Liberal candidate for
        Beverley, Yorkshire.

1869   *Phineas Finn; the Irish Member* 2 vols. (Virtue & Co).
        He Knew He Was Right 2 vols. (Strahan).
        Did He Steal It? A Comedy in Three Acts (a version of *The Last
        Chronicle of Barset*, privately printed by Virtue & Co).

1870   *The Vicar of Bullhampton* 1 vol. (Bradbury, Evans).
        An Editor's Tales 1 vol. (Strahan).
        The Commentaries of Caesar 1 vol. (Blackwood).
        (Jan.–July) Eased out of *Saint Pauls Magazine*.

1871   *Sir Harry Hotspur of Humblethwaite* 1 vol. (Hurst & Blackett).
        Ralph the Heir 3 vols. (Hurst & Blackett).
        (Apr.) Gives up house at Waltham Cross.
        (24 May) Sails to Australia to visit his son.
        (27 July) Arrives at Melbourne.

1872   *The Golden Lion of Granpere* 1 vol. (Tinsley).

(Jan.–Oct.) Travelling in Australia and New Zealand.
(Dec.) Returns via the United states.

1873   *The Eustace Diamonds* 3 vols. (Chapman & Hall).
        Australia and New Zealand 2 vols. (Chapman & Hall).
        (Apr.) Settles in Montagu Square, London.

1874   *Phineas Redux* 2 vols. (Chapman & Hall).
        Lady Anna 2 vols. (Chapman & Hall).
        Harry Heathcote of Gangoil. A Tale of Australian Bush Life 1 vol.
        (Sampson Low).

1875   *The Way We Live Now* 2 vols. (Chapman & Hall).
        (1 Mar.) Leaves for Australia via Brindisi, the Suez Canal,
        and Ceylon.
        (4 May) Arrives in Australia.
        (Aug.–Oct.) Sailing homewards.
        (Oct.) Begins *An Autobiography*.

1876   *The Prime Minister* 4 vols. (Chapman & Hall).

1877   *The American Senator* 3 vols. (Chapman & Hall).
        (29 June) Leaves for South Africa.
        (11 Dec.) Sails for home.

1878   *South Africa* 2 vols. (Chapman & Hall).
        Is He Popenjoy? 3 vols. (Chapman & Hall).
        (June–July) Travels to Iceland in the yacht 'Mastiff'.
        How the 'Mastiffs' Went to Ireland 1 vol. (privately printed,
        Virtue & Co).

1879   *An Eye for an Eye* 2 vols. (Chapman & Hall).
        Thackeray 1 vol. (Macmillan).
        John Candigate 3 vols. (Chapman & Hall).
        Cousin Henry 2 vols. (Chapman & Hall).

1880   *The Duke's Children* 3 vols. (Chapman & Hall).
        The Life of Cicero 2 vols. (Chapman & Hall).
        (July) Settles at South Harting, Sussex, near Petersfield.

1881   *Dr Wortle's School* 2 vols. (Chapman & Hall).
        Ayala's Angel 3 vols. (Chapman & Hall).

1882   *Why Frau Frohmann Raised Her Prices; and Other Stories* 1 vol.
        (Isbister).
        The Fixed Period 2 vols. (Blackwood).
        Marion Fay 3 vols. (Chapman & Hall).
        Lord Palmerston 1 vol. (Isbister).

Kept in the Dark 2 vols. (Chatto & Windus).
(May) Visits Ireland to collect material for a new Irish novel.
(Aug.) Returns to Ireland a second time.
(2 Oct.) Takes rooms for the winter at Garlant's Hotel, Suffolk St., London.
(3 Nov.) Suffers paralytic stroke.
(6 Dec.) Dies in nursing home, 34 Welbeck St., London.

1883 *Mr. Scarborough's Family* 3 vols. (Chatto & Windus).
      The Landleaguers (unfinished) 3 vols. (Chatto & Windus).
      An Autobiography 2 vols. (Blackwood).

1884 *An Old Man's Love* 2 vols. (Blackwood).

1923 *The Noble Jilt* 1 vol. (Constable).

1927 *London Tradesmen* 1 vol. (Elkin Mathews and Marrat).

1972 *The New Zealander* 1 vol. (Oxford University Press).

Lady Anna

CONTENTS

CHAPTER XXV

CHAPTER XXVI

CHAPTER XXVII

CHAPTER XXVIII

CHAPTER XXIX

CHAPTER XXX

CHAPTER XXXI

CHAPTER XXXII

CHAPTER XXXIII

CHAPTER XXXIV

CHAPTER XXXV

CHAPTER XXXVI

CHAPTER XXXVII

CONTENTS

CHAPTER I

The Early History of Lady Lovel

WOMEN have often been hardly used by men, but perhaps no harder usage, no fiercer cruelty was ever experienced by a woman than that which fell to the lot of Josephine Murray from the hands of Earl Lovel, to whom she was married in the parish church of Applethwaite,—a parish without a village, lying among the mountains of Cumberland,—on the 1st of June, 181—. That her marriage was valid according to all the forms of the Church, if Lord Lovel were then capable of marrying, no one ever doubted; nor did the Earl ever allege that it was not so. Lovel Grange is a small house, surrounded by a small domain,—small as being the residence of a rich nobleman, lying among the mountains which separate Cumberland from Westmoreland, about ten miles from Keswick,* very lovely, from the brightness of its own green sward and the luxuriance of its wild woodland, from the contiguity of overhanging mountains, and from the beauty of Lovel Tarn, a small lake belonging to the property, studded with little islands, each of which is covered with its own thicket of hollies, birch, and dwarfed oaks. The house itself is poor, ill built, with straggling passages and low rooms, and is a sombre, ill-omened looking place. When Josephine Murray was brought there as a bride she thought it to be very sombre and ill-omened; but she loved the lakes and mountains, and dreamed of some vague mysterious joy of life which was to come to her from the wildness of her domicile.

I fear that she had no other ground, firmer than this, on which to found her hopes of happiness. She could not have thought Lord Lovel to be a good man when she married him, and it can hardly be said that she loved him. She was then twenty-four years old, and he had counted double as many years. She was very beautiful, dark, with large, bold, blue eyes, with hair almost black, tall, well made, almost robust, a well-born, brave, ambitious woman, of whom it must be acknowledged that she thought it very much to be the wife of a lord. Though our story will be concerned much with her sufferings, the record of her bridal days may be very short. It is with struggles that came to her in after years that we shall be most concerned, and the reader, therefore, need be troubled with no long description of Josephine Murray as she was when she became the Countess Lovel. It is hoped that her wrongs may be thought worthy of sympathy,—and may be felt in some sort to atone for the ignoble motives of her marriage.

The Earl, when he found his bride, had been living almost in solitude for a twelvemonth. Among the neighbouring gentry in the lake country he kept no friendly relations. His property there was small, and his character was evil. He was an English earl, and as such known in some unfamiliar fashion to those who know all earls; but he was a man never seen in Parliament, who had spent the greater part of his manhood abroad, who had sold estates in other counties, converting unentailed acres into increased wealth, but wealth of a kind much less acceptable to the general English aristocrat than that which comes direct from the land. Lovel Grange was his only remaining English property, and when in London he had rooms at an hotel. He never entertained, and he never accepted hospitality. It was known of him that he was very rich, and men said that he was mad. Such was the man whom Josephine Murray had chosen to marry because he was an earl.

He had found her near Keswick, living with her father in a pretty cottage looking down upon Derwentwater,—a thorough gentleman, for Captain Murray had come of the right Murrays;—and thence he had carried her to Lovel Grange. She had brought with her no penny of fortune, and no settlement had been made on her. Her father, who was then an old man, had mildly expostulated; but the ambition of the daughter had prevailed, and the marriage was accomplished. The beautiful young woman was carried off as a bride. It will be unnecessary to relate what efforts had been made to take her away from her father's house without bridal honours; but it must be told that the Earl was a man who had never yet spared a woman in his lust. It had been the rule, almost the creed of his life, that woman was made to gratify the appetite of man, and that the man is but a poor creature who does not lay hold of the sweetness that is offered to him. He had so lived as to teach himself that those men who devote themselves to their wives, as a wife devotes herself to her husband, are the poor lubberly clods of creation, who had lacked the power to reach the only purpose of living which could make life worth having. Women had been to him a prey, as the fox is a prey to the huntsman and the salmon to the angler. But he had acquired great skill in his sport, and could pursue his game with all the craft which experience will give. He could look at a woman as though he saw all heaven in her eyes, and could listen to her as though the music of the spheres was to be heard in her voice. Then he could whisper words which, to many women, were as the music of the spheres, and he could persevere, abandoning all other pleasures, devoting himself to the one wickedness with a perseverance which almost made success certain. But with Josephine Murray he could be successful on no other terms than those which enabled her to walk out of the church with him as Countess Lovel.

She had not lived with him six months before he told her that the marriage was no marriage, and that she was—his mistress. There was an audacity about the man which threw aside all fear of the law, and which was impervious to threats and interference. He assured her that he loved her, and that she was welcome to live with him; but that she was not his wife, and that the child which she bore could not be the heir to his title, and could claim no heirship to his property. He did love her,—having found her to be a woman of whose company he had not tired in six months. He was going back to Italy, and he offered to take her with him,—but he could not, he said, permit the farce of her remaining at Lovel Grange and calling herself the Countess Lovel. If she chose to go with him to Palermo, where he had a castle, and to remain with him in his yacht, she might for the present travel under the name of his wife. But she must know that she was not his wife. She was only his mistress.

Of course she told her father. Of course she invoked every Murray in and out of Scotland. Of course there were many threats. A duel was fought up near London, in which Lord Lovel consented to be shot at twice,—declaring that after that he did not think that the circumstances of the case required that he should be shot at any more. In the midst of this a daughter was born to her and her father died,—during which time she was still allowed to live at Lovel Grange. But what was it expedient that she should do? He declared that he had a former wife when he married her, and that therefore she was not and could not be his wife. Should she institute a prosecution against him for bigamy, thereby acknowledging that she was herself no wife and that her child was illegitimate? From such evidence as she could get, she believed that the Italian woman whom the Earl in former years had married had died before her own marriage. The Earl declared that the Countess, the real Countess, had not paid her debt to nature, till some months after the little ceremony which had taken place in Applethwaite Church. In a moment of weakness Josephine fell at his feet and asked him to renew the ceremony. He stooped over her, kissed her, and smiled. 'My pretty child,' he said, 'why should I do that?' He never kissed her again.

What should she do? Before she had decided, he was in his yacht sailing to Palermo;—sailing no doubt not alone. What should she do? He had left her an income,—sufficient for the cast-off mistress of an Earl,—some few hundreds a year, on condition that she would quietly leave Lovel Grange, cease to call herself a Countess, and take herself and her bairn,—whither she would. Every abode of sin in London was open to her for what he cared. But what should she do? It seemed to her to be incredible that so great a wrong should befall her, and that the man should escape from her and be free from punishment,—unless she chose to own the baseness of her own position by prosecuting him for bigamy. The Murrays were not very generous in their succour, as the old man had been much blamed for giving his daughter to one of whom all the world knew nothing but evil. One Murray had fired two shots on her behalf, in answer to each one of which the Earl had fired into the air; but beyond this the Murrays could do nothing. Josephine herself was haughty and proud, conscious that her rank was greater than that of any of the Murrays with whom she came in contact. But what should she do?

The Earl had been gone five years, sailing about the world she knew not where, when at last she determined to institute a prosecution for bigamy. During these years she was still living at the Grange, with her child, and the Courts of Law had allotted her some sum by way of alimony till her cause should be decided; but upon this alimony she found it very difficult to lay her hands,—quite impossible to lay her hands upon the entirety of it. And then it came to pass that she was eaten up by lawyers and tradesmen, and fell into bad repute as asserting that claims made against her, should legally be made against the very man whom she was about to prosecute because she was not his wife. And this went on till further life at Lovel Grange became impossible to her.

In those days there was living in Keswick a certain Mr. Thomas Thwaite, a tailor, who by degrees had taken a strong part in denouncing the wrongs to which Lady Lovel had been subjected. He was a powerful, sturdy man, with good means for his position, a well-known Radical in a county in which Radicals have never been popular, and in which fifty years ago they were much rarer than they are now. At this time Keswick and its vicinities were beginning to be known as the abodes of poets, and Thomas Thwaite was acquainted with Southey and Wordsworth. He was an intelligent, up-standing, impulsive man, who thought well of his own position in the world, and who could speak his mind. He was tall, massive, and square; tender-hearted and very generous; and he hated the Earl of Lovel with all his heart. Once the two men had met since the story of the Countess's wrongs had become known, and the tailor had struck the Earl to the ground. This had occurred as the Earl was leaving Lovel Grange, and when he was starting on his long journey. The scene took place after he had parted from his Countess,—whom he never was to see again. He rose to his feet and rushed at the tailor; but the two were separated, and the Earl thought it best to go on upon his journey. Nothing further was done as to the blow, and many years rolled by before the Earl came back to Cumberland.

It became impossible for the Countess and her daughter, the young Lady Anna as she was usually called, to remain at Lovel Grange, and they were taken to the house of Mr. Thwaite, in Keswick, as a temporary residence. At this time the Countess was in debt, and already there were lawsuits as to the practicability of obtaining payment of those debts from the husband's estate. And as soon as it was determined that the prosecution for bigamy should be instituted, the confusion in this respect was increased. The Countess ceased to call herself a countess, as she certainly would not be a countess should she succeed in proving the Earl to have been guilty. And had he been guilty of bigamy, the decree under which alimony was assigned to her would become void. Should she succeed, she would be a penniless unmarried female with a daughter, her child would be unfathered and base, and he,—as far as she could see,—would be beyond the reach of punishment. But, in truth, she and her friend the tailor were not in quest of success. She and all her friends believed that the Earl had committed no such crime. But if he were acquitted, then would her claim to be called Lady Lovel, and to enjoy the appanages of her rank, be substantiated. Or, at least, something would have been done towards substantiating those claims. But during this time she called

herself Mrs. Murray, and the little Lady Anna
was called Anna Murray.

It added much to the hardship of the woman's
case that public sympathy in distant parts of the
country,—up in London, and in southern counties, and even among a portion of the gentry in
Cumberland and Westmoreland,—did not go
with her. She had married without due care.
Some men said,—and many women repeated
the story,—that she had known of the existence
of the former wife, when she had married the
Earl. She had run into debt, and then repudiated her debts. She was now residing in the
house of a low radical tailor, who had assaulted
the man she called her husband; and she was
living under her maiden name. Tales were told
of her which were utterly false,—as when it was
said that she drank. Others were reported which
had in them some grains of truth,—as that she
was violent, stiff-necked, and vindictive. Had
they said of her that it had become her one
religion to assert her daughter's right,—per fas
aut nefas,—to assert it by right or wrong; to do
justice to her child let what injustice might be
done to herself or others,—then the truth would
have been spoken.

The case dragged itself on slowly, and little
Anna Murray was a child of nine years old
when at last the Earl was acquitted of the criminal charge which had been brought against him.
During all this time he had been absent. Even
had there been a wish to bring him personally
into court, the law would have been powerless
to reach him. But there was no such wish. It
had been found impossible to prove the former

marriage, which had taken place in Sicily;—
or if not impossible, at least no adequate proof
was forthcoming. There was no real desire that
there should be such proof. The Earl's lawyers
abstained, as far as they could abstain, from
taking any steps in the matter. They spent what
money was necessary, and the Attorney-General
of the day defended him. In doing so, the
Attorney-General declared that he had nothing
to do with the Earl's treatment of the lady who
now called herself Mrs. Murray. He knew nothing of the circumstances of that connection,
and would not travel beyond his brief. He
was there to defend Earl Lovel on a charge
of bigamy. This he did successfully, and the
Earl was acquitted. Then, in court, the counsel
for the wife declared that his client would again
call herself Lady Lovel.

But it was not so easy to induce other people
to call her Lady Lovel.

And now not only was she much hampered
by money difficulties, but so also was the tailor.
But Thomas Thwaite never for a moment slack-
ened in his labours to make good the position
of the woman whom he had determined to
succour; and for another and a longer period of
eight years the battle went on. It went on very
slowly, as is the wont with such battles; and
very little way was made. The world, as a rule,
did not believe that she who now again called
herself the Countess Lovel was entitled to that
name. The Murrays, her own people,—as far
as they were her own people,—had been taught
to doubt her claim. If she were a countess why
had she thrown herself into the arms of an old

tailor? Why did she let her daughter play with
the tailor's child,—if, in truth, that daughter
was the Lady Anna? Why, above all things,
was the name of the Lady Anna allowed to be
mentioned, as it was mentioned, in connection
with that of Daniel Thwaite, the tailor's son?

During these eight weary years Lady Lovel,
—for so she shall be called,—lived in a small
cottage about a mile from Keswick, on the road
to Grassmere and Ambleside, which she rented
from quarter to quarter. She still obtained a
certain amount of alimony, which, however,
was dribbled out to her through various sieves,
and which reached her with protestations as to
the impossibility of obtaining anything like the
moderate sum which had been awarded to her.
And it came at last to be the case that she hardly
knew what she was struggling to obtain. It was,
of course, her object that all the world should
acknowledge her to be the Countess Lovel, and
her daughter to be the Lady Anna. But all the
world could not be made to do this by course
of law. Nor could the law make her lord come
home and live with her, even such a cat and
dog life as must in such case have been hers.
Her money rights were all that she could demand;—and she found it to be impossible to
get anybody to tell her what were her money
rights. To be kept out of the poorhouse seemed
to be all that she could claim. But the old tailor
was true to her,—swearing that she should even
yet become Countess Lovel in very truth.

Then, of a sudden, she heard one day,—that
Earl Lovel was again at the Grange, living there
with a strange woman.

CHAPTER II

The Earl's Will

NOT a word had been heard in Keswick of the proposed return of the old lord,—for the Earl was now an old man,—past his sixtieth year, and in truth with as many signs of age as some men bear at eighty. The life which he had led no doubt had had its allurements, but it is one which hardly admits of a hale and happy evening. Men who make women a prey, prey also on themselves. But there he was, back at Lovel Grange, and no one knew why he had come, nor whence, nor how. To Lovel Grange in those days, now some forty years ago, there was no road for wheels but that which ran through Keswick. Through Keswick he had passed in the middle of the night, taking on the post-horses which he had brought with him from Grassmere, so that no one in the town should see him and his companion. But it was soon known that he was there, and known also that he had a companion. For months he resided thus, and no one saw him but the domestics who waited upon him. But rumours got abroad as to his conduct, and people through the county declared that Earl Lovel was a maniac. Still his property was in his own control, and he did what it listed him to do.

As soon as men knew that he was in the land, claim after claim was made upon him for money due on behalf of his wife, and loudest among the claimants was Thomas Thwaite, the tailor. He was loudest and fiercest among the claimants, but was loud and fierce not in enmity to his old friend the Countess, but with a firm resolve to make the lord pay the only price of his wickedness which could be exacted from him. And if the Earl could be made to pay the claims against him which were made by his wife's creditors, then would the law, so far, have decided that the woman was his wife. No answer was made to any letter addressed to the Earl, and no one calling at the Grange could obtain speech or even sight of the noble owner. The lord's steward at the Grange referred all comers to the lord's attorneys in London, and the lord's attorneys simply repeated the allegation that the lady was not the lord's wife. At last there came tidings that an inquiry was to be made as to the state of the lord's health and the state of the lord's mind, on behalf of Frederic Lovel, the distant heir to the title. Let that question of the lord's marriage with Josephine Murray go as it might, Frederic Lovel, who had never seen his far-away cousin, must be the future earl. Of that there was no doubt;—and new inquiries were to be made. But it might well be that the interest of the young heir would be more deeply involved in the marriage question than in other matters concerning the family. Lovel Grange and the few mountain farms attached to the Cumberland estate must become his, let the frantic Earl do what damage he might to those who bore his name; but the bulk of the property, the wealth of the Lovels, the great riches which had enabled this mighty lord to live as a beast of prey among his kind, were

at his own disposal. He had one child certainly,
the Lady Anna, who would inherit it all were
the father to die intestate, and were the marriage
proved. The young heir and those near to
him altogether disbelieved the marriage,—as
was natural. They had never seen her who now
called herself the Countess, but who for some
years after her child was born had called herself
Mrs. Murray,—who had been discarded by her
own relations, and had taken herself to live
with a country tailor. As years had rolled by
the memory of what had really occurred in
Applethwaite Church had become indistinct;
and, though the reader knows that that marriage
was capable of easy proof,—that there would
have been but little difficulty had the only
difficulty consisted in proving that,—the young
heir and the distant Lovels were not assured
of it. Their interest was adverse, and they were
determined to disbelieve. But the Earl might,
and probably would, leave all his wealth to a
stranger. He had never in any way noticed his
heir. He cared for none that bore his name.
Those ties in the world which we call love, and
deem respectable, and regard as happy, because
they have to do with marriage and blood rela-
tionship as established by all laws since the days
of Moses, were odious to him and ridiculous in his
sight, because all obligations were distasteful to
him,—and all laws, except those which preserved
to him the use of his own money. But now there
came up the great question whether he was mad
or sane. It was at once rumoured that he was
about to leave the country, and fly back to Sicily.
Then it was announced that he was dead.

And he was dead. He had died at the age of sixty-seven, in the arms of the woman he had brought there. His evil career was over, and his soul had gone to that future life for which he had made it fit by the life he had led here. His body was buried in Applethwaite churchyard, in the further corner of which long, straggling valley parish Lovel Grange is situated. At his grave there stood no single mourner;—but the young lord was there, of his right, disdaining even to wear a crape band round his hat. But the woman remained shut up in her own chamber,—a difficulty to the young lord and his lawyer, who could hardly tell the foreigner to pack and begone before the body of her late—lover had been laid in the grave. It had been simply intimated to her that on such a date,—within a week from the funeral,—her presence in the house could not longer be endured. She had flashed round upon the lawyer, who had attempted to make this award known to her in broken French, but had answered simply by some words of scorn, spoken in Italian to her waiting-maid.

Then the will was read in the presence of the young earl;—for there was a will. Everything that the late lord had possessed was left, in one line, to his best-beloved friend, the Signorina Camilla Spondi; and it was stated, and very fully explained, that Camilla Spondi was the Italian lady living at the Grange at the date on which the will was made. Of the old lord's heir, the now existing Earl Lovel, no mention was made whatever. There were, however, two other clauses or parts in the will. There was a schedule giving in detail the particulars of the property left to Camilla Spondi; and there was a rambling statement that the maker of the will acknowledged Anna Murray to be his illegitimate daughter,—that Anna Murray's mother had never been the testator's legitimate wife, as his real wife, the true Countess Lovel, for whom he had separately made adequate provision, was still alive in Sicily at the date of that will,—and that by a former will now destroyed he had made provision for Anna Murray, which provision he had revoked in consequence of the treatment which he had received from Josephine Murray and her friends. They who believed the statements made in this will afterwards asserted that Anna had been deprived of her inheritance by the blow with which the tailor had felled the Earl to the earth.

To Camilla Spondi intimation was given of the contents of the Earl's will as far as they concerned her; but she was told at the same time that no portion of the dead man's wealth would be placed in her hands till the courts should have decided whether or no the old lord had been sane or insane when he signed the document. A sum of money was, however, given her, on condition that she should take her immediate departure;—and she departed. With her personally we need have no further concern. Of her cause and of her claim some mention must be made; but in a few pages she will drop altogether from our story.

A copy of the will was also sent to the lawyers who had hitherto taken charge of the interests of the repudiated Countess, and it was intimated that the allowance hitherto made to her must now of necessity cease. If she thought fit to prosecute any further claim, she must do so by proving her marriage;—and it was explained to her, probably without much of legal or precise truth in the explanation, that such proof must include the disproving of the assertion in the Earl's will. As it was the intention of the heir to set aside that will, such assurance was, to say the least of it, disingenuous. But the whole thing had now become so confused that it could hardly be expected that lawyers should be ingenuous in discussing it.

The young Earl clearly inherited the title and the small estate at Lovel Grange. The Italian woman was primâ facie heiress to everything else,—except to such portion of the large personal property as the widow could claim as widow, in the event of her being able to prove that she had been a wife. But in the event of the will being no will, the Italian woman would have nothing. In such case the male heir would have all if the marriage were no marriage;— but would have nothing if the marriage could be made good. If the marriage could be made good, the Lady Anna would have the entire property, except such portion as would be claimed of right by her mother, the widow. Thus the Italian woman and the young lord were combined in interest against the mother and daughter as regarded the marriage; and the young lord and the mother and daughter were combined against the Italian woman as regarded the will;—but the young lord had to act alone against the Italian woman, and against the mother and daughter whom he and his friends regarded as swindlers and impostors. It was for him to set aside the will in reference to the Italian woman, and then to stand the brunt of the assault made upon him by the soi-disant wife.

In a very short time after the old Earl's death a double compromise was offered on behalf of the young Earl. The money at stake was immense. Would the Italian woman take £10,000, and go her way back to Italy, renouncing all further claim; and would the soi-disant Countess abandon her title, acknowledge her child to be illegitimate, and go her way with another £10,000;—or with £20,000, as was soon hinted by the gentlemen acting on the Earl's behalf? The proposition was one somewhat difficult in the making, as the compromise, if made with both, would be excellent, but could not be made to any good effect with one only. The young Earl certainly could not afford to buy off the Italian woman for £10,000, if the effect of such buying off would only be to place the whole of the late lord's wealth in the hands of his daughter and of his daughter's mother.

The Italian woman consented. She declared with Italian energy that her late loving friend had never been a day insane; but she knew nothing of English laws, and but little of English money. She would take the £10,000,—having had a calculation made for her of the number of lire into which it would run. The number was enormous, and she would take the offer. But when the proposal was mentioned to the Countess, and explained to her by her old friend, Thomas

Thwaite, who had now become a poor man in her cause, she repudiated it with bitter scorn,—with a scorn in which she almost included the old man who had made it to her. 'Is it for that, that I have been fighting?' she said.

'For that in part,' said the old man.

'No, Mr. Thwaite, not for that at all; but that my girl may have her birth allowed and her name acknowledged.'

'Her name shall be allowed and her birth shall be acknowledged,' said the tailor, in whose heart there was nothing base. 'She shall be the Lady Anna, and her mother shall be the Countess Lovel.' The estate of the Countess, if she had an estate, then owed the tailor some five or six thousand pounds, and the compromise offered would have paid the tailor every shilling and have left a comfortable income for the two women.

'For myself I care but little,' said the mother, taking the tailor's hand in hers and kissing it. 'My child is the Lady Anna, and I do not dare to barter away her rights.' This took place down at the cottage in Cumberland, and the tailor at once went up to London to make known the decision of the Countess,—as he invariably called her.

Then the lawyers went to work. As the double compromise could not be effected, the single compromise could not stand. The Italian woman raved and stamped, and swore that she must have her half million of lire. But of course no right to such a claim had been made good to her, and the lawyers on behalf of the young Earl went on with their work. Public sympathy as a matter of course went with the young Earl. As against the Italian woman he had with him every English man and woman. It was horrible to the minds of English men and English women that an old English Earldom should be starved in order that an Italian harlot might revel in untold riches. It was felt by most men and protested by all women that any sign of madness, be it what it might,—however insignificant,—should be held to be sufficient against such a claimant. Was not the fact that the man had made such a will in itself sufficient proof of his madness? There were not a few who protested that no further proof could be necessary. But with us the law is the same for an Italian harlot and an English widow; and it may well be that in its niceties it shall be found kinder to the former than to the latter. But the Earl had been mad, and the law said that he was mad when he had made his will,—and the Italian woman went away, raging, into obscurity.

The Italian woman was conquered, and now the battle was open and free between the young Earl and the claimant Countess. Applications were made on behalf of the Countess for funds from the estate wherewith to prove the claim, and to a certain limited amount they were granted. Such had been the life of the late Earl that it was held that the cost of all litigation resulting from his misdeeds should be paid from his estate;—but ready money was wanted, immediate ready money, to be at the disposal of the Countess to any amount needed by her agent, and this was hardly to be obtained. By this time public sympathy ran almost entirely

with the Earl. Though it was acknowledged that
the late lord was mad, and though it had become
a cause of rejoicing that the Italian woman had
been sent away penniless, howling into obscurity,
because of the old man's madness, still it was
believed that he had written the truth when
he declared that the marriage had been a mock
marriage. It would be better for the English
world that the young Earl should be a rich man,
fit to do honour to his position, fit to marry the
daughter of a duke, fit to carry on the glory of
the English peerage, than that a woman, ill
reputed in the world, should be established as
a Countess, with a daughter dowered with tens
of thousands, as to whom it was already said
that she was in love with a tailor's son. Nothing
could be more touching, more likely to awaken
sympathy, than the manner in which Josephine
Murray had been carried away in marriage,
and then roughly told by the man who should
have protected her from every harshly blowing
wind of heaven, that he had deceived her and
that she was not his wife. No usage to which
woman had ever been subjected, as has been
said before, was more adapted to elicit compassion and energetic aid. But nineteen years
had now passed by since the deed was done,
and the facts were forgotten. One energetic
friend there still was,—or we may say two, the
tailor and his son Daniel. But public belief ran
against the Countess, and nobody who was anybody in the world would give her her title. Bets
were laid, two and three to one against her;
and it was believed that she was an impostor.
The Earl had all the glory of success over his

first opponent, and the loud boasting of self-confident barristers buoyed up his cause.

But loud-boasting barristers may nevertheless be wise lawyers, and the question of a compromise was again mooted. If the lady would take thirty thousand pounds and vanish, she should have the money clear of deduction, and all expenses should be paid. The amount offered was thought to be very liberal, but it did not amount to the annual income that was at stake. It was rejected with scorn. Had it been quadrupled, it would have been rejected with equal scorn. The loud-boasting barristers were still confident; but——. Though it was never admitted in words still it was felt that there might be a doubt. What if the contending parties were to join forces, if the Countess-ship of the Countess were to be admitted and the heiress-ship of the Lady Anna, and if the Earl and the Lady Anna were to be united in holy wedlock? Might there not be a safe solution from further difficulty in that way?

CHAPTER III

Lady Anna

THE idea of this further compromise, of this something more than compromise, of this half acknowledgement of their own weakness, came from Mr. Flick, of the firm of Norton and Flick, the solicitors who were employed in substantiating the Earl's position. When Mr. Flick mentioned it to Sir William Patterson, the great barrister, who was at that time Solicitor-General* and leading counsel on behalf of Lord Lovel, Sir William Patterson stood aghast and was dismayed. Sir William intended to make mincemeat of the Countess. It was said of him that he intended to cross-examine the Countess off her legs, right out of her claim, and almost into her grave. He certainly did believe her to be an impostor, who had not thought herself to be entitled to her name when she first assumed it.

'I should be sorry, Mr. Flick, to be driven to think that anything of that kind could be expedient.'

'It would make sure of the fortune to the family,' said Mr. Flick.

'And what about our friend, the Countess?'

'Let her call herself Countess Lovel, Sir William. That will break no bones. As to the formality of her own marriage, there can be no doubt about that.'

'We can prove by Grogram that she was told that another wife was living,' said Sir William.

Grogram was an old butler who had been in the old Earl's service for thirty years.

'I believe we can, Sir William; but——. It is quite clear that we shall never get the other wife to come over and face an English jury. It is of no use blinking it. The gentleman whom we have sent over doubts her altogether. That there was a marriage is certain, but he fears that this woman is not the old Countess. There were two sisters, and it may be that this was the other sister.'

Sir William was a good deal dismayed, but he recovered himself. The stakes were so high that it was quite possible that the gentleman who had been sent over might have been induced to open his eyes to the possibility of such personation by overtures from the other side. Sir William was of opinion that Mr. Flick himself should go to Sicily. He was not sure that he, Sir William, her Majesty's Solicitor-General, would not make the journey in person. He was by no means disposed to give way. 'They tell me that the girl is no better than she should be,' he said to Mr. Flick.

'I don't think so bad as that of her,' said Mr. Flick.

'Is she a lady,—or anything like a lady?'

'I am told she is very beautiful.'

'I dare say;—and so was her mother before her. I never saw a handsomer woman of her age than our friend the Countess. But I could not recommend the young lord to marry an underbred, bad girl, and a bastard who claims to be his cousin,—and support my proposition merely on the ground of her looks.'

'Thirty-five thousand a year, Sir William!' pleaded the attorney.

'I hope we can get the thirty-five thousand a year for our client without paying so dear for them.'

It had been presumed that the real Countess, the original Countess, the Italian lady whom the Earl had married in early life, would be brought over, with properly attested documentary evidence in her pocket, to prove that she was the existing Countess, and that any other Countess must be either an impostor or a deluded dupe. No doubt the old Earl had declared, when first informing Josephine Murray that she was not his wife, that his real wife had died during the few months which had intervened since his mock marriage; but it was acknowledged on all sides, that the old Earl had been a villain and a liar. It was no part of the duty of the young Earl, or of those who acted for him, to defend the character of the old Earl. To wash that blackamoor white, or even to make him whity-brown, was not necessary to anybody. No one was now concerned to account for his crooked courses. But if it could be shown that he had married the lady in Italy,—as to which there was no doubt,—and that the lady was still alive, or that she had been alive when the second marriage took place, then the Lady Anna could not inherit the property which had been freed from the grasp of the Italian mistress. But it seemed that the lady, if she lived, could not be made to come. Mr. Flick did go to Sicily, and came back renewing his advice to Sir William that Lord Lovel should be advised to marry the Lady Anna.

At this time the Countess, with her daughter, had moved their residence from Keswick up to London, and was living in very humble lodgings in a small street turning out of the New Road, near the Yorkshire Stingo.* Old Thomas Thwaite had accompanied them from Cumberland, but the rooms had been taken for them by his son, Daniel Thwaite, who was at this time foreman to a somewhat celebrated tailor who carried on his business in Wigmore Street; and he, Daniel Thwaite, had a bed-room in the house in which the Countess lodged. The arrangement was not a wise one, as reports had already been spread abroad as to the partiality of the Lady Anna for the young tailor. But how should she not have been partial both to the father and to the son, feeling as she did that they were the only two men who befriended her cause and her mother's? As to the Countess herself, she, perhaps, alone of all those who interested themselves in her daughter's cause, had heard no word of these insinuations against her child. To her both Thomas and Daniel Thwaite were dear friends, to repay whom for their exertions with lavish generosity,—should the means to do so ever come within their reach, —was one of the dreams of her existence. But she was an ambitious woman, thinking much of her rank, thinking much even of the blood of her own ancestors, constantly urgent with her daughter in teaching her the duties and privileges of wealth and rank. For the Countess never doubted that she would at last attain success. That the Lady Anna should throw herself away upon Daniel Thwaite did not occur to her as a possibility. She had not even dreamed that Daniel Thwaite would aspire to her daughter's hand. And yet every shop-boy and every shop-girl in Keswick had been so saying for the last twelvemonth, and rumours which had hitherto been confined to Keswick and its neighbourhood, were now common in London. For the case was becoming one of the celebrated causes of the age, and all the world was talking of the Countess and her daughter. No momentary suspicion had crossed the mind of the Countess till after their arrival in London; and then when the suspicion did touch her it was not love that she suspected,—but rather an unbecoming familiarity which she attributed to her child's ignorance of the great life which awaited her. 'My dear,' she said one day when Daniel Thwaite had left them, 'you should be less free in your manner with that young man.'

'What do you mean, mamma?' said the daughter, blushing.

'You had better call him Mr. Thwaite.'

'But I have called him Daniel ever since I was born.'

'He always calls you Lady Anna.'

'Sometimes he does, mamma.'

'I never heard him call you anything else,' said the Countess, almost with indignation. 'It is all very well for the old man, because he is an old man and has done so much for us.'

'So has Daniel;—quite as much, mamma. They have both done everything.'

'True; they have both been warm friends; and if ever I forget them may God forget me. I trust that we may both live to show them that they are not forgotten. But it is not fitting that there should exist between you and him the intimacy of equal positions. You are not and cannot be his equal. He has been born to be a tailor, and you are the daughter and heiress of an Earl.'

These last words were spoken in a tone that was almost awful to the Lady Anna. She had heard so much of her father's rank and her father's wealth,—rank and wealth which were always to be hers, but which had never as yet reached her, which had been a perpetual trouble to her, and a crushing weight upon her young life, that she had almost learned to hate the title and the claim. Of course it was a part of the religion of her life that her mother had been duly married to her father. It was beyond a doubt to her that such was the case. But the constant battling for denied rights, the assumption of a position which could not be attained, the use of titles which were simply ridiculous in themselves as connected with the kind of life which she was obliged to lead,—these things had all become odious to her. She lacked the ambition which gave her mother strength, and would gladly have become Anna Murray or Anna Lovel, with a girl's ordinary privilege of loving her lover, had such an easy life been possible to her.

In person she was very lovely, less tall and robust than her mother had been, but with a sweeter, softer face. Her hair was less dark, and her eyes were neither blue nor bold. But they were bright and soft and very eloquent, and when laden with tears would have softened

the heart,—almost of her father. She was as
yet less powerful than her mother, both in body
and mind, but probably better calculated to
make a happy home for a husband and children.
She was affectionate, self-denying, and feminine.
Had that offer of compromise for thirty, twenty,
or for ten thousand pounds been made to her,
she would have accepted it willingly,—caring
little for her name, little even for fame, so that
she might have been happy and quiet, and at
liberty to think of a lover as are other girls. In
her present condition, how could she have any
happy love? She was the Lady Anna Lovel,
heir to a ducal fortune,—but she lived in small
close lodgings in Wyndham Street, New Road.
She did not believe in the good time coming
as did her mother. Their enemy was an undoubted Earl, undoubtedly owner of Lovel
Grange of which she had heard all her life.
Would it not be better to take what the young
lord chose to give them and to be at rest? But
she did not dare to express such thoughts to
her mother. Her mother would have crushed
her with a look.

'I have told Mr. Thwaite,' the mother said to
her daughter, 'what we were saying this morning.'

'About his son?'

'Yes—about his son.'

'Oh, mamma!'

'I was bound to do so.'

'And what did he say, mamma?'

'He did not like it, and told me that he did
not like it;—but he admitted that it was true.
He admitted that his son was no fitting intimate
for Lady Anna Lovel.'

'What should we have done without him?'

'Badly indeed; but that cannot change his duty, or ours. He is helping us to struggle for that which is our own; but he would mar his generosity if he put a taint on that which he is endeavouring to restore to us.'

'Put a taint, mamma!'

'Yes;—a taint would rest upon your rank if you as Lady Anna Lovel were familiar with Daniel Thwaite as with an equal. His father understands it, and will speak to him.'

'Mamma, Daniel will be very angry.'

'Then he will be very unreasonable;—but, Anna, I will not have you call him Daniel any more.'

CHAPTER IV

The Tailor of Keswick

OLD Thomas Thwaite was at this time up in London about the business of the Countess, but had no intention of residing there. He still kept his shop in Keswick, and still made coats and trousers for Cumberland statesmen.* He was by no means in a condition to retire from business, having spent the savings of his life in the cause of the Countess and her daughter. Men had told him that, had he not struck the Earl in the yard of the Crown at Keswick, as horses were being brought out for the lord's travelling carriage, ample provision would have been made by the rich old sinner for his daughter. That might have been so, or might not, but the saying instigated the tailor to further zeal and increased generosity. To oppose an Earl, even though it might be on behalf of a Countess, was a joy to him; to set wrong right, and to put down cruelty and to relieve distressed women was the pride of his heart,—especially when his efforts were made in antagonism to one of high rank. And he was a man who would certainly be thorough in his work, though his thoroughness should be ruinous to himself. He had despised the Murrays, who ought to have stuck to their distant cousin, and had exulted in his heart at thinking that the world would say how much better and truer had been the Keswick tailor than the well-born and comparatively wealthy Scotch relations. And the poets of the lakes, who had not as yet become altogether Tories,* had taken him by the hand and praised him. The rights of the Countess and the wrongs of the Countess had become his life. But he still kept on a diminished business in the north, and it was now needful that he should return to Cumberland. He had heard that renewed offers of compromise were to be made,—though no idea of the proposed marriage between the distant cousins had been suggested to him. He had been discussing the question of some compromise with the Countess when she spoke to him respecting his son; and had recommended that certain terms should, if possible, be effected. Let the money be divided, on condition that the marriage were allowed. There could be no difficulty in this if the young lord would accede to such an arrangement, as the marriage must be acknowledged unless an adverse party should bring home proof from Italy to the contrary. The sufficiency of the ceremony in Applethwaite Church was incontestable. Let the money be divided, and the Countess be Countess Lovel, and Lady Anna be the Lady Anna to all the world. Old Thomas Thwaite himself had seemed to think that there would be enough of triumph in such a settlement. 'But the woman might afterwards be bribed to come over and renew her claim,' said the Countess. 'Unless it be absolutely settled now, they will say when I am dead and gone that my daughter has no right to her name.' Then the tailor said that he would make further inquiry how that might be. He was inclined to think that there might be a decision which should be absolute, even though that decision should be reached by compromise between the now contending parties.

Then the Countess had said her word about Daniel Thwaite the son, and Thomas Thwaite the father had heard it with ill-concealed anger. To fight against an Earl on behalf of the Earl's injured wife had been very sweet to him, but to be checked in his fight because he and his were unfit to associate with the child of that injured wife, was very bitter. And yet he had sense to know that what the Countess said to him was true. As far as words went, he admitted the truth; but his face was more eloquent than his words, and his face showed plainly his displeasure.

'It is not of you that I am speaking,' said the Countess, laying her hand upon the old man's sleeve.

'Daniel is, at any rate, fitter than I,' said the tailor. 'He has been educated, and I never was.'

'He is as good as gold. It is not of that I speak. You know what I mean.'

'I know very well what you mean, Lady Lovel.'

'I have no friend like you, Mr. Thwaite;— none whom I love as I do you. And next to you is your son. For myself, there is nothing that I would not do for him or you;—no service, however menial, that I would not render you with my own hands. There is no limit to the gratitude which I owe you. But my girl is young, and if this burden of rank and wealth is to be hers,—it is proper that she do honour to it.'

'And it is not honourable that she should be seen speaking—to a tailor?'

'Ah,—if you choose to take it so!'

'How should I take it? What I say is true. And what you say is true also. I will speak to Daniel.' But she knew well, as he left her, that his heart was bitter against her.

The old man did speak to his son, sitting with him up in the bed-room over that which the Countess occupied. Old Thomas Thwaite was a strong man, but his son was in some respects stronger. As his father had said of him, he had been educated,—or rather instructed; and instruction leads to the power of thinking. He looked deeper into things than did his father, and was governed by wider and greater motives. His father had been a Radical all his life, guided thereto probably by some early training, and made steadfast in his creed by feelings which induced him to hate the pretensions of an assumed superiority. Old Thwaite could not endure to think that one man should be considered to be worthier than another because he was richer. He would admit the riches, and even the justice of the riches,—having been himself, during much of his life, a rich man in his own sphere; but would deny the worthiness; and would adduce, in proof of his creed, the unworthiness of certain exalted sinners. The career of the Earl Lovel had been to him a sure proof of the baseness of English aristocracy generally. He had dreams of a republic in which a tailor might be president or senator, or something almost noble. But no rational scheme of governance among mankind had ever entered his mind, and of pure politics he knew no more than the journeyman who sat stitching upon his board.

But Daniel Thwaite was a thoughtful man who had read many books. More's Utopia and Harrington's Oceana,* with many a tale written in the same spirit, had taught him to believe that a perfect form of government, or rather of policy, under which all men might be happy and satisfied, was practicable on earth, and was to be achieved,—not merely by the slow amelioration of mankind under God's fostering ordinances,—but by the continued efforts of good and wise men who, by their goodness and wisdom, should be able to make the multitude believe in them. To diminish the distances, not only between the rich and the poor, but between the high and the low, was the grand political theory upon which his mind was always running. His father was ever thinking of himself and of Earl Lovel; while Daniel Thwaite was considering the injustice of the difference between ten thousand aristocrats and thirty million of people, who were for the most part ignorant and hungry. But it was not that he also had not thoughts of himself. Gradually he had come to learn that he need not have been a tailor's foreman in Wigmore Street had not his father spent on behalf of the Countess Lovel the means by which he, the son, might already have become a master tradesman. And yet he had never begrudged it. He had been as keen as his father in the cause. It had been the romance of his life, since his life had been capable of romance;—but with him it had been no respect for the rank to which his father was so anxious to restore the Countess, no value which he attached to the names claimed by the mother and the daughter. He hated the Countess-ship of the Countess, and the ladyship of the Lady Anna. He would fain that they should have abandoned them. They were to him odious signs of iniquitous pretensions. But he was keen enough to punish and to remedy the wickedness of the wicked Earl. He reverenced his father because he assaulted the wicked Earl and struck him to the ground. He was heart and soul in the cause of the injured wife. And then the one thing on earth that was really dear to him was the Lady Anna.

It had been the romance of his life. They had grown up together as playmates in Cumberland. He had fought scores of battles on her behalf with those who had denied that she was the Lady Anna,—even though he had then hated the title. Boys had jeered him because of his noble little sweetheart, and he had exulted at hearing her so called. His only sister and his mother had died when he was young, and there had been none in the house but his father and himself. As a boy he had ever been at the cottage of the Countess, and he had sworn to Lady Anna a thousand times that he would do and die in her service. Now he was a strong man, and was more devoted to her than ever. It was the great romance of his life. How could it be brought to pass that the acknowledged daughter of an Earl, dowered with enormous wealth, should become the wife of a tailor? And yet such was his ambition and such his purpose. It was not that he cared for her dower. It was not, at any rate, the hope of her dower that had induced him to love her. His passion had grown and his purpose had been formed before the old Earl had returned for the last time to Lovel Grange,—when nothing was known of the manner in which his wealth might be distributed. That her prospect of riches now joined itself to his aspirations it would be an affectation to deny. The man who is insensible to the power which money brings with it must be a dolt; and Daniel Thwaite was not a dolt, and was fond of power. But he was proud of heart, and he said to himself over and over again that should it ever come to pass that the possession of the girl was to depend on the abandonment of the wealth, the wealth should be abandoned without a further thought.

It may be imagined that with such a man the words which his father would speak to him about the Lady Anna, suggesting the respectful distance with which she should be approached by a tailor's foreman, would be very bitter. They were bitter to the speaker and very bitter to him who heard them. 'Daniel,' said the father, 'this is a queer life you are leading with the Countess and Lady Anna just beneath you, in the same house.'

'It was a quiet house for them to come to;— and cheap.'

'Quiet enough, and as cheap as any, I dare say;—but I don't know whether it is well that you should be thrown so much with them. They are different from us.' The son looked at his father, but made no immediate reply. 'Our lot has been cast with theirs because of their difficulties,' continued the old man, 'but the time is coming when we had better stand aloof.'

'What do you mean, father?'

'I mean that we are tailors, and these people are born nobles.'

'They have taken our help, father.'

'Well; yes, they have. But it is not for us to say anything of that. It has been given with a heart.'

'Certainly with a heart.'

'And shall be given to the end. But the end of it will come soon now. One will be a Countess and the other will be the Lady Anna. Are they fit associates for such as you and me?'

'If you ask me, father, I think they are.'

'They don't think so. You may be sure of that.'

'Have they said so, father?'

'The Countess has said so. She has complained that you call her daughter simply Anna. In future you must give her a handle to her name.' Daniel Thwaite was a dark brown man, with no tinge of ruddiness about him, a thin spare man, almost swarthy, whose hands were as brown as a nut, and whose cheeks and forehead were brown. But now he blushed up to his eyes. The hue of the blood as it rushed to his face forced itself through the darkness of his visage, and he blushed, as such men do blush,—with a look of indignation on his face. 'Just call her Lady Anna,' said the father.

'The Countess has been complaining of me then?'

'She has hinted that her daughter will be

injured by your familiarity, and she is right. I suppose that the Lady Anna Lovel ought to be treated with deference by a tailor,—even though the tailor may have spent his last farthing in her service.'

'Do not let us talk about the money, father.'

'Well; no. I'd as lief not think about the money either. The world is not ripe yet, Daniel.'

'No;—the world is not ripe.'

'There must be earls and countesses.'

'I see no must in it. There are earls and countesses as there used to be mastodons and other senseless, over-grown brutes roaming miserable and hungry through the undrained woods,—cold, comfortless, unwieldy things, which have perished in the general progress. The big things have all to give way to the intellect of those which are more finely made.'

'I hope men and women will not give way to bugs and fleas,' said the tailor, who was wont to ridicule his son's philosophy.

The son was about to explain his theory of the perfected mean size of intellectual created beings, when his heart was at the present moment full of Anna Lovel. 'Father,' he said, 'I think that the Countess might have spared her observations.'

'I thought so too;—but as she said it, it was best that I should tell you. You'll have to marry some day, and it wouldn't do that you should look there for your sweetheart.' When the matter was thus brought home to him, Daniel Thwaite would argue it no further. 'It will all come to an end soon,' continued the old man, 'and it may be that they had better not move till it is settled. They'll divide the money, and there will be enough for both in all conscience. The Countess will be the Countess, and the Lady Anna will be the Lady Anna; and then there will be no more need of the old tailor from Keswick. They will go into another world, and we shall hear from them perhaps about Christmas time with a hamper of game, and may be a little wine, as a gift.'

'You do not think that of them, father.'

'What else can they do? The lawyers will pay the money, and they will be carried away. They cannot come to our house, nor can we go to theirs. I shall leave to-morrow, my boy, at six o'clock; and my advice to you is to trouble them with your presence as little as possible. You may be sure that they do not want it.'

Daniel Thwaite was certainly not disposed to take his father's advice, but then he knew much more than did his father. The above scene took place in the evening, when the son's work was done. As he crept down on the following morning by the door of the room in which the two ladies slept, he could not but think of his father's words, 'It wouldn't do that you should look there for your sweetheart.' Why should it not do? But any such advice as that was now too late. He had looked there for his sweetheart. He had spoken, and the girl had answered him. He had held her close to his heart, and had pressed her lips to his own, and had called her his Anna, his well-beloved, his pearl, his treasure; and she,—she had only sighed in his arms, and yielded to his embrace. She had wept alone when she thought of it, with a conscious feeling

that as she was the Lady Anna there could be
no happy love between herself and the only
youth whom she had known. But when he had
spoken, and had clasped her to his heart, she
had never dreamed of rebuking him. She had
known nothing better than he, and desired
nothing better than to live with him and to be
loved by him. She did not think that it could
be possible to know any one better. This weary,
weary title filled her with dismay. Daniel, as
he walked along thinking of her embrace, thinking of those kisses, and thinking also of his
father's caution, swore to himself that the difficulties in his way should never stop him in his
course.

CHAPTER V

The Solicitor-General makes a Proposition

WHEN Mr. Flick returned from Sicily he was very strongly in favour of some compromise. He had seen the so-called Italian Countess,— who certainly was now called Contessa by everybody around her,—and he did not believe that she had ever been married to the old Earl. That an Italian lady had been married to the old lord now twenty-five years ago, he did believe,—probably the younger sister of this woman,—and he also believed that this wife had been dead before the marriage at Applethwaite. That was his private opinion. Mr. Flick was, in his way, an honest man,—one who certainly would have taken no conscious part in getting up an unjust claim; but he was now acting as legal agent for the young Earl, and it was not his business to get up evidence for the Earl's opponents. He did think that were he to use all his ingenuity and the funds at his disposal he would be able to reach the real truth in such a manner that it should be made clear and indubitable to an English jury; but if the real truth were adverse to his side, why search for it? He understood that the English Countess would stand her ground on the legality of the Applethwaite marriage, and on the acquittal of the old Earl as to the charge of bigamy. The English Countess being firm, so far as that ground would make her firm, it would in reality be for the other side—for the young Earl—to prove a former marriage. The burden of the proof would be with him, and not with the English Countess to disprove it. Disingenuous lawyers —Mr. Flick, who though fairly honest could be disingenuous, among the number—had declared the contrary. But such was the case; and, as money was scarce with the Countess and her friends, no attempt had been made on their part to bring home evidence from Sicily. All this Mr. Flick knew, and doubted how far it might be wise for him further to disturb that Sicilian romance. The Italian Countess, who was a hideous, worn-out old woman, professing to be forty-four, probably fifty-five, and looking as though she were seventy-seven, would not stir a step towards England. She would swear and had sworn any number of oaths. Documentary evidence from herself, from various priests, from servants, and from neighbours there was in plenty. Mr. Flick learned through his interpreter that a certain old priest ridiculed the idea of there being a doubt. And there were letters, —letters alleged to have been written by the Earl to the living wife in the old days, which were shown to Mr. Flick. Mr. Flick was an educated man, and knew many things. He knew something of the manufacture of paper, and would not look at the letters after the first touch. It was not for him to get up evidence for the other side. The hideous old woman was clamorous for money. The priests were clamorous for money. The neighbours were clamorous for money. Had not they all sworn anything that was wanted, and were they not to be paid? Some moderate payment was made to the hideous, screeching, greedy old woman; some trivial payment—as to which Mr. Flick was heartily ashamed of himself—was made to the old priest; and then Mr. Flick hurried home, fully convinced that a compromise should be made as to the money, and that the legality of the titles claimed by the two English ladies should be allowed. It might be that that hideous hag had once been the Countess Lovel. It certainly was the case that the old Earl in latter years had so called her, though he had never once seen her during his last residence in Sicily. It might be that the clumsy fiction of the letters had been perpetrated with the view of bolstering up a true case with false evidence. But Mr. Flick thought that there should be a compromise, and expressed his opinion very plainly to Sir William Patterson. 'You mean a marriage,' said the Solicitor-General. At this time Mr. Hardy, Q.C., the second counsel acting on behalf of the Earl, was also present.

'Not necessarily by a marriage, Sir William. They could divide the money.'

'The girl is not of age,' said Mr. Hardy.

'She is barely twenty as yet,' said Sir William.

'I think it might be managed on her behalf,' said the attorney.

'Who could be empowered to sacrifice her rights?' said Mr. Hardy, who was a gruff man.

'We might perhaps contrive to tide it over till she is of age,' said the Solicitor-General, who was a sweet-mannered, mild man among his friends, though he could cross-examine a witness off his legs,—or hers,—if the necessity of the case required him to do so.

'Of course we could do that, Sir William. What is a year in such a case as this?'

'Not much among lawyers, is it, Mr. Flick? You think that we shouldn't bring our case into court.'

'It is a good case, Sir William, no doubt. There's the woman,—Countess, we will call her, —ready to swear, and has sworn, that she was the old Earl's wife. All the people round call her the Countess. The Earl undoubtedly used to speak of her as the Countess, and send her little dribbles of money, as being his Countess, during the ten years and more after he left Lovel Grange. There is the old priest who married them.'

'The devil's in it if that is not a good case,' said Mr. Hardy.

'Go on, Mr. Flick,' said the Solicitor-General.

'I've got all the documentary evidence of course, Sir William.'

'Go on, Mr. Flick.'

Mr. Flick scratched his head. 'It's a very heavy interest, Sir William.'

'No doubt it is. Go on.'

'I don't know that I've anything further to say, except that I'd arrange it if I could. Our client, Sir William, would be in a very pretty position if he got half the income which is at stake.'

'Or the whole with the wife,' said the Solicitor-General.

'Or the whole with the wife, Sir William. If he were to lose it all, he'd be,—so to say, nowhere.'

'Nowhere at all,' said the Solicitor-General.

'The entailed property isn't worth above a thousand a year.'

'I'd make some arrangement,' said Mr. Flick, whose mind may perhaps have had a not unnatural bend towards his own very large venture in this concern. That his bill, including the honorarium of the barristers, would sooner or later be paid out of the estate, he did not doubt; —but a compromise would make the settlement easy and pleasant.

Mr. Hardy was in favour of continued fighting. A keener, honester, more enlightened lawyer than Mr. Hardy did not wear silk* at that moment, but he had not the gift of seeing through darkness which belonged to the Solicitor-General. When Mr. Flick told them of the strength of their case, as based on various heads of evidence in their favour, Mr. Hardy believed Mr. Flick's words and rejected Mr. Flick's opinion. He believed in his heart that the English Countess was an impostor, not herself believing in her own claim; and it would be gall and wormwood to him to give such a one a moiety of the wealth which should go to support the ancient dignity and aristocratic grace of the house of Lovel. He hated compromise and desired justice,—and was a great rather than a successful lawyer. Sir William had at once perceived that there was something in the background on which it was his duty to calculate, which he was bound to consider,— but with which at the same time it was inexpedient that he should form a closer or more accurate acquaintance. He must do the best he could for his client. Earl Lovel with a thousand a year, and that probably already embarrassed, would be a poor, wretched creature, a mock lord, an earl without the very essence of an earldom. But Earl Lovel with fifteen or twenty thousand a year would be as good as most other earls. It would be but the difference between two powdered footmen and four, between four hunters* and eight, between Belgrave Square and Eaton Place. Sir William, had he felt confident, would of course have preferred the four footmen for his client, and the eight hunters, and Belgrave Square; even though the poor English Countess should have starved, or been fed by the tailor's bounty. But he was not confident. He began to think that that wicked old Earl had been too wicked for them all. 'They say she's a very nice girl,' said Sir William.

'Very handsome indeed, I'm told,' said Mr. Flick.

'And in love with the son of the old tailor from Keswick,' said Mr. Hardy.

'She'll prefer the lord to the tailor for a guinea,' said Sir William.

And thus it was decided, after some indecisive fashion, that their client should be sounded as to the expedience of a compromise. It was certain to them that the poor woman would be glad to accept, for herself and her daughter, half of the wealth at stake, which half would be to her almost unlimited riches, on the condition that their rank was secured to them,—their rank and all the privileges of honest legitimacy. But as to such an arrangement the necessary delay offered no doubt a serious impediment, and it was considered that the wisest course would be to propose the marriage. But who should propose it, and how should it be proposed? Sir William was quite willing to make the suggestion to the young Lord or the young Lord's family, whose consent must of course be first obtained; but who should then break the ice to the Countess? 'I suppose we must ask our friend, the Serjeant,' said Mr. Flick. Serjeant Bluestone was the leading counsel for our Countess, and was vehemently energetic in this case. He swore everywhere that the Solicitor-General hadn't a leg to stand upon, and that the Solicitor-General knew that he hadn't a leg. Let them bring that Italian Countess over if they dared. He'd countess her, and discountess her too! Since he had first known the English courts of law there had been no case hard as this was hard. Had not the old Earl been acquitted of the charge of bigamy, when the unfortunate woman had done her best to free herself from her position? Serjeant Bluestone, who was a very violent man, taking up all his cases as though the very holding of a brief opposite to him was an insult to himself, had never before been so violent. 'The Serjeant will take it as a surrender,' said Mr. Flick.

'We must get round the Serjeant,' said Sir William. 'There are ladies in the Lovel family; we must manage it through them.' And so it was arranged by the young Lord's lawyers that an attempt should be made to marry him to the heiress.

The two cousins had never seen each other. Lady Anna had hardly heard of Frederic Lovel before her father's death; but, since that, had been brought up to regard the young Lord as her natural enemy. The young Lord had been taught from his youth upwards to look upon the soi-disant Countess and her daughter as impostors who would some day strive to rob him of his birthright;—and, in these latter days, as impostors who were hard at work upon their project. And he had been told of the intimacy between the Countess and the old tailor,—and also of that between the so-called Lady Anna and the young tailor. To these distant Lovels, —to Frederic Lovel who had been brought up with the knowledge that he must be the Earl, and to his uncle and aunt by whom he had been brought up,—the women down at Keswick had been represented as vulgar, odious, and disreputable. We all know how firm can be the faith of a family in such matters. The Lovels were not without fear as to the result of the attempt that was being made. They understood quite as well as did Mr. Flick the glory of the position which would attend upon success, and the wretchedness attendant upon a pauper earldom. They were nervous enough, and in some moods frightened. But their trust in the justice of their cause was unbounded. The old Earl, whose memory was horrible to them, had purposely left two enemies in their way. There had been the Italian mistress backed up by the will; and there had been this illegitimate child. The one was vanquished; but the other——! Ah,—it would be bad with them indeed if that enemy could not be vanquished too! They had offered £30,000 to the enemy; but the enemy would not accept the bribe. The idea of ending

all their troubles by a marriage had never
occurred to them. Had Mrs. Lovel been asked
about it, she would have said that Anna Murray,
—as she always studiously called the Lady Anna,
was not fit to be married.

The young lord, who a few months after his
cousin's death had been old enough to take his
seat in the House of Peers, was a gay-hearted,
kindly young man, who had been brought home
from sea at the age of twenty on the death of
an elder brother. Some of the family had wished
that he should go on with his profession in spite
of the earldom; but it had been thought unfit
that he should be an earl and a midshipman at
the same time, and his cousin's death while he
was still on shore settled the question. He was
a fair-haired, well-made young lad, looking like
a sailor, and every inch a gentleman. Had he
believed that the Lady Anna was the Lady Anna,
no earthly consideration would have induced
him to meddle with the money. Since the old
Lord's death, he had lived chiefly with his
uncle Charles Lovel, having passed some two
or three months at Lovel Grange with his uncle
and aunt. Charles Lovel was a clergyman,
with a good living at Yoxham, in Yorkshire,
who had married a rich wife, a woman with
some two thousand a year of her own, and was
therefore well to do in the world. His two sons
were at Harrow,*and he had one other child, a
daughter. With them also lived a Miss Lovel,
Aunt Julia,—who was supposed of all the Lovels
to be the wisest and most strong-minded. The
parson, though a popular man, was not strong-
minded. He was passionate, loud, generous,

affectionate and indiscreet. He was very proud of his nephew's position as head of the family—and very full of his nephew's wrongs arising from the fraud of those Murray women. He was a violent Tory, and had heard much of the Keswick Radical. He never doubted for a moment that both old Thwaite and young Thwaite were busy in concocting an enormous scheme of plunder by which to enrich themselves. To hear that they had both been convicted and transported was the hope of his life. That a Radical should not be worthy of transportation was to him impossible. That a Radical should be honest was to him incredible. But he was a thoroughly humane and charitable man, whose good qualities were as little intelligible to old Thomas Thwaite, as were those of Thomas Thwaite to him.

To whom should the Solicitor-General first break the matter? He had already had some intercourse with the Lovels, and had not been impressed with a sense of the parson's wisdom. He was a Whig Solicitor-General, for there were still Whigs in those days,* and Mr. Lovel had not much liked him. Mr. Flick had seen much of the family,—having had many interviews with the young lord, with the parson, and with Aunt Julia. It was at last settled by Sir William's advice that a letter should be written to Aunt Julia by Mr. Flick, suggesting that she should come up to town.

'Mr. Lovel will be very angry,' said Mr. Flick.

'We must do the best we can for our client,' said Sir William. The letter was written, and Miss Lovel was informed in Mr. Flick's most discreet style, that as Sir William Patterson was anxious to discuss a matter concerning Lord Lovel's case in which a woman's voice would probably be of more service than that of a man, perhaps Miss Lovel would not object to the trouble of a journey to London. Miss Lovel did come up, and her brother came with her.

The interview took place in Sir William's chambers, and no one was present but Sir William, Miss Lovel, and Mr. Flick. Mr. Flick had been instructed to sit still and say nothing, unless he were asked a question; and he obeyed his instructions. After some apologies, which were perhaps too soft and sweet,—and which were by no means needed, as Miss Lovel herself, though very wise, was neither soft nor sweet,— the great man thus opened his case. 'This is a very serious matter, Miss Lovel.'

'Very serious indeed.'

'You can hardly perhaps conceive how great a load of responsibility lies upon a lawyer's shoulders, when he has to give advice in such a case as this, when perhaps the prosperity of a whole family may turn upon his words.'

'He can only do his best.'

'Ah yes, Miss Lovel. That is easy to say; but how shall he know what is the best?'

'I suppose the truth will prevail at last. It is impossible to think that a young man such as my nephew should be swindled out of a noble fortune by the intrigues of two such women as these. I can't believe it, and I won't believe it. Of course I am only a woman, but I always thought it wrong to offer them even a shilling.'

Sir William smiled and rubbed his head, fixing his eyes on those of the lady. Though he smiled she could see that there was real sadness in his face. 'You don't mean to say you doubt?' she said.

'Indeed I do.'

'You think that a wicked scheme like this can succeed before an English judge?'

'But if the scheme be not wicked? Let me tell you one or two things, Miss Lovel;—or rather my own private opinion on one or two points. I do not believe that these two ladies are swindlers.'

'They are not ladies, and I feel sure that they are swindlers,' said Miss Lovel very firmly, turning her face as she spoke to the attorney.

'I am telling you, of course, merely my own opinion, and I will beg you to believe of me that in forming it I have used all the experience and all the caution which a long course of practice in these matters has taught me. Your nephew is entitled to my best services, and at the present moment I can perhaps do my duty to him most thoroughly by asking you to listen to me.' The lady closed her lips together, and sat silent. 'Whether Mrs. Murray, as we have hitherto called her, was or was not the legal wife of the late Earl, I will not just now express an opinion; but I am sure that she thinks that she was. The marriage was formal and accurate. The Earl was tried for bigamy, and acquitted. The people with whom we have to do across the water, in Sicily, are not respectable. They cannot be induced to come here to give evidence. An English jury will be naturally averse to them.

The question is one simply of facts for a jury, and we cannot go beyond a jury. Had the daughter been a son, it would have been in the House of Lords to decide which young man should be the peer;—but as it is, it is simply a question of property, and of facts as to the ownership of the property. Should we lose the case, your nephew would be—a very poor man.'

'A very poor man, indeed, Sir William.'

'His position would be distressing. I am bound to say that we should go into court to try the case with very great distrust. Mr. Flick quite agrees with me.'

'Quite so, Sir William,' said Mr. Flick.

Miss Lovel again looked at the attorney, closed her lips tighter than ever, but did not say a word.

'In such cases as this prejudices will arise, Miss Lovel. It is natural that you and your family should be prejudiced against these ladies. For myself, I am not aware that anything true can be alleged against them.'

'The girl has disgraced herself with a tailor's son,' almost screamed Miss Lovel.

'You have been told so, but I do not believe it to be true. They were, no doubt, brought up as children together; and Mr. Thwaite has been most kind to both the ladies.' It at once occurred to Miss Lovel that Sir William was a Whig, and that there was in truth but little difference between a Whig and a Radical. To be at heart a gentleman, or at heart a lady, it was, to her thinking, necessary to be a Tory. 'It would be a thousand pities that so noble a property should pass out of a family which, by its very splendour and ancient nobility, is placed in need of ample means.' On hearing this sentiment, which might have become even a Tory, Miss Lovel relaxed somewhat the muscles of her face. 'Were the Earl to marry his cousin——'

'She is not his cousin.'

'Were the Earl to marry the young lady who, it may be, will be proved to be his cousin, the whole difficulty would be cleared away.'

'Marry her!'

'I am told that she is very lovely, and that pains have been taken with her education. Her mother was well born and well bred. If you would get at the truth, Miss Lovel, you must teach yourself to believe that they are not swindlers. They are no more swindlers than I am a swindler. I will go further,—though perhaps you, and the young Earl, and Mr. Flick, may think me unfit to be intrusted any longer with this case, after such a declaration,—I believe, though it is with a doubting belief, that the elder lady is the Countess Lovel, and that her daughter is the legitimate child and the heir of the late Earl.'

Mr. Flick sat with his mouth open as he heard this,—beating his breast almost with despair. . His opinion tallied exactly with Sir William's. Indeed, it was by his opinion, hardly expressed, but perfectly understood, that Sir William had been led. But he had not thought that Sir William would be so bold and candid.

'You believe that Anna Murray is the real heir?' gasped Miss Lovel.

'I do,—with a doubting belief. I am inclined that way,—having to form my opinion on very conflicting evidence.' Mr. Flick was by this time quite sure that Sir William was right, in his opinion,—though perhaps wrong in declaring it,—having been corroborated in his own belief by the reflex of it on a mind more powerful than his own. 'Thinking as I do,' continued Sir William,—'with a natural bias towards my own client,—what will a jury think, who will have no such bias? If they are cousins,—distant cousins,—why should they not marry and be happy, one bringing the title, and the other the wealth? There could be no more rational union, Miss Lovel.'

Then there was a long pause before any one spoke a word. Mr. Flick had been forbidden to speak, and Sir William, having made his proposition, was determined to await the lady's reply. The lady was aghast, and for awhile could neither think nor utter a word. At last she opened her mouth. 'I must speak to my brother about this.'

'Quite right, Miss Lovel.'

'Now I may go, Sir William?'

'Good morning, Miss Lovel.' And Miss Lovel went.

'You have gone farther than I thought you would, Sir William,' said Mr. Flick.

'I hardly went far enough, Mr. Flick. We must go farther yet if we mean to save any part of the property for the young man. What should we gain, even if we succeeded in proving that the Earl was married in early life to the old Sicilian hag that still lives? She would inherit the property then;—not the Earl.'

CHAPTER VI

Yoxham Rectory

MISS LOVEL, wise and strong-minded as she was, did not dare to come to any decision on the proposition made to her without consulting some one. Strong as she was, she found herself at once to be too weak to speak to her nephew on the subject of her late interview with the great lawyer without asking her brother's opinion. The parson had accompanied her up to London, in a state of wrath against Sir William, in that he had not been sent for instead of his sister, and to him she told all that had been said. Her brother was away at his club when she got back to her hotel, and she had some hours in which to think of what had taken place. She could not at once bring herself to believe that all her former beliefs were vain and ill founded.

But if the opinion of the Solicitor-General had not prevailed with her, it prevailed still less when it reached her brother second-hand. She had been shaken, but Mr. Lovel at first was not shaken at all. Sir William was a Whig and a traitor. He had never known a Whig who was not a traitor. Sir William was throwing them over. The Murray people, who were all Whigs, had got hold of him. He, Mr. Lovel, would go at once to Mr. Hardy, and tell Mr. Hardy what he thought. The case should be immediately taken out of the hands of Messrs. Norton and Flick. Did not all the world know that these impostors were impostors? Sir William should be exposed and degraded,—though, in regard to his threatened degradation, Mr. Lovel was almost of opinion that his party would like their Solicitor-General better for having shown himself to be a traitor, and therefore proved himself to be a good Whig. He stormed and flew about the room, using language which hardly became his cloth. If his nephew married the girl, he would never own his nephew again. If that swindle was to prevail, let his nephew be poor and honest. He would give half of all he had towards supporting the peerage, and was sure that his boys would thank him for what he had done. But they should never call that woman cousin; and as for himself, might his tongue be blistered if ever he spoke of either of those women as Countess Lovel. He was inclined to think that the whole case should immediately be taken out of the hands of Norton and Flick, without further notice, and another solicitor employed. But at last he consented to call on Mr. Norton on the following morning.

Mr. Norton was a heavy, honest old man, who attended to simple conveyancing, and sat amidst the tin boxes of his broad-acred clients. He had no alternative but to send for Mr. Flick, and Mr. Flick came. When Mr. Lovel showed his anger, Mr. Flick became somewhat indignant. Mr. Flick knew how to assert himself, and Mr. Lovel was not quite the same man in the lawyer's chambers that he had been in his own parlour at the hotel. Mr. Flick was of opinion that no better counsel was to be had in England than the Solicitor-General, and no opinion more worthy of trust than his. If the Earl chose to put his case into other hands, of course he could do so, but it would behove his lordship to be very careful lest he should prejudice most important interests by showing his own weakness to his opponents. Mr. Flick spoke in the interests of his client,—so he said,—and not in his own. Mr. Flick was clearly of opinion that a compromise should be arranged; and having given that opinion, could say nothing more on the present occasion. On the next day the young Earl saw Mr. Flick, and also saw Sir William, and was then told by his aunt of the proposition which had been made. The parson retired to Yoxham, and Miss Lovel remained in London with her nephew. By the end of the week Miss Lovel was brought round to think that some compromise was expedient. All this took place in May. The cause had been fixed for trial in the following November, the long interval having been allowed because of the difficulty expected in producing the evidence necessary for rebutting the claims of the late Earl's daughter.

By the middle of June all the Lovels were again in London,—the parson, his sister, the parson's wife, and the Earl. 'I never saw the young woman in my life,' said the Earl to his aunt.

'As for that,' said his aunt, 'no doubt you could see her if you thought it wise to do so.'

'I suppose she might be asked to the rectory?' said Mrs. Lovel.

'That would be giving up altogether,' said the rector.

'Sir William said that it would not be against us at all,' said Aunt Julia.

'You would have to call her Lady Anna,' said Mrs. Lovel.

'I couldn't do it,' said the rector. 'It would be much better to give her half.'

'But why should she take the half if the whole belongs to her?' said the young lord. 'And why should I ask even for the half if nothing belongs to me?' At this time the young lord had become almost despondent as to his alleged rights, and now and again had made everybody belonging to him miserable by talking of withdrawing from his claim. He had come to understand that Sir William believed that the daughter was the real heir, and he thought that Sir William must know better than others. He was down-hearted and low in spirits, but not the less determined to be just in all that he did.

'I have made inquiry,' said Aunt Julia, 'and I do believe that the stories which we heard against the girl were untrue.'

'The tailor and his son have been their most intimate friends,' said Mr. Lovel.

'Because they had none others,' said Mrs. Lovel.

It had been settled that by the 24th of June the lord was to say whether he would or would not take Sir William's advice. If he would do so, Sir William was to suggest what step should next be taken as to making the necessary overtures to the two ladies. If he would not, then Sir William was to advise how best the case might be carried on. They were all again at Yoxham that day, and the necessary communication was to be made to Mr. Flick by post. The young man had been alone the whole morning thinking of his condition, and undoubtedly the desire for the money had grown on him strongly. Why should it not have done so? Is there a nobleman in Great Britain who can say that he could lose the fortune which he possesses or the fortune which he expects without an agony that would almost break his heart? Young Lord Lovel sighed for the wealth without which his title would only be to him a terrible burden, and yet he was resolved that he would take no part in anything that was unjust. This girl, he heard, was beautiful and soft and pleasant, and now they told him that the evil things which had been reported against her had been slanders. He was assured that she was neither coarse, nor vulgar, nor unmaidenly. Two or three old men, of equal rank with his own,—men who had been his father's friends and were allied to the Lovels, and had been taken into confidence by Sir William,— told him that the proper way out of the difficulty had been suggested to him. There could be nothing, they said, more fitting than that two cousins so situated should marry. With such an acknowledgment of her rank and birth everybody would visit his wife. There was not a countess or a duchess in London who would not be willing to take her by the hand. His two aunts had gradually given way, and it was clear to him that his uncle would give way,— even his uncle,—if he would but yield himself. It was explained to him that if the girl came to Yoxham, with the privilege of being called Lady

Anna by the inhabitants of the rectory, she would of course do so on the understanding that she should accept her cousin's hand. 'But she might not like me,' said the young Earl to his aunt.

'Not like you!' said Mrs. Lovel, putting her hand up to his brow and pushing away his hair. Was it possible that any girl should not like such a man as that, and he an earl?

'And if I did not like her, Aunt Lovel?'

'Then I would not ask her to be my wife.' He thought that there was an injustice in this, and yet before the day was over he had assented.

'I do not think that I can call her Lady Anna,' said the rector. 'I don't think I can bring my tongue to do it.'

CHAPTER VII

The Solicitor-General perseveres

THERE was considerable difficulty in making the overture to the two ladies,—or rather in making it to the elder lady; for the suggestion, if made to the daughter, must of course come to her from her mother. It had been decided at last that the Lady Anna could not be invited to the rectory till it had been positively settled that she should be the Lady Anna without further opposition; and that all opposition to the claim should be withdrawn, at any rate till it was found that the young people were not inclined to be engaged to each other. 'How can I call her Lady Anna before I have made up my mind to think that she is Lady Anna?' said the parson, almost in tears. As to the rest of the family, it may be said that they had come silently to think that the Countess was the Countess and that the Lady Anna was the Lady Anna; —silently in reference to each other, for not one of them except the young lord had positively owned to such a conviction. Sir William Patterson had been too strong for them. It was true that he was a Whig. It was possible that he was a traitor. But he was a man of might, and his opinion had domineered over theirs. To make things as straight as they could be made it would be well that the young people should be married. What would be the Earldom of Lovel without the wealth which the old mad Earl had amassed?

Sir William and Mr. Flick were strongly in favour of the marriage, and Mr. Hardy at last assented. The worst of it was that something of all this doubt on the part of the Earl and his friends was sure to reach the opposite party. 'They are shaking in their shoes,' Serjeant Bluestone said to his junior counsel, Mr. Mainsail. 'I do believe they are not going to fight at all,' he said to Mr. Goffe, the attorney for the Countess. Mr. Mainsail rubbed his hands. Mr. Goffe shook his head. Mr. Goffe was sure that they would fight. Mr. Mainsail, who had worked like a horse in getting up and arranging all the evidence on behalf of the Countess, and in sifting, as best he might, the Italian documents, was delighted. All this Sir William feared, and he felt that it was quite possible that the Earl's overture might be rejected because the Earl would not be thought to be worth having. 'We must count upon his coronet,' said Sir William to Mr. Flick. 'She could not do better even if the property were undoubtedly her own.'

But how was the first suggestion to be made? Mr. Hardy was anxious that everything should be straightforward,—and Sir William assented, with a certain inward peevishness at Mr. Hardy's stiff-necked propriety. Sir William was anxious to settle the thing comfortably for all parties. Mr. Hardy was determined not only that right should be done, but also that it should be done in a righteous manner. The great question now was whether they could approach the widow and her daughter otherwise than through Serjeant Bluestone. 'The Serjeant is such a blunderbuss,' said the Solicitor-General. But the Serjeant was counsel for these ladies, and it was at last settled that there should be a general conference at Sir William's chambers. A very short note was written by Mr. Flick to Mr. Goffe, stating that the Solicitor-General thought that a meeting might be for the advantage of all parties;— and the meeting was arranged. There were present the two barristers and the one attorney for each side, and many an anxious thought was given to the manner in which the meeting should be conducted. Serjeant Bluestone was fully resolved that he would hold his own against the Solicitor-General, and would speak his mind freely. Mr. Mainsail got up little telling questions. Mr. Goffe and Mr. Flick both felt that it would behove them to hold their peace, unless questioned, but were equally determined to hang fast by their clients. Mr. Hardy in his heart of hearts thought that his learned friend was about to fling away his case. Sir William had quite made up his mind as to his line of action. He seated them all most courteously, giving them place according to their rank,— a great arm-chair for Serjeant Bluestone, from which the Serjeant would hardly be able to use his arms with his accustomed energy,—and then he began at once. 'Gentlemen,' said he, 'it would be a great pity that this property should be wasted.'

'No fear of that, Mr. Solicitor,' said the Serjeant.

'It would be a great pity that this property should be wasted,' repeated Sir William, bowing to the Serjeant, 'and I am disposed to think that the best thing the two young people can do is to marry each other.' Then he paused, and the three gentlemen opposite sat erect, the barristers as speechless as the attorneys. But the Solicitor-General had nothing to add. He had made his proposition, and was desirous of seeing what effect it might have before he spoke another word.

'Then you acknowledge the Countess's marriage, of course,' said the Serjeant.

'Pardon me, Serjeant, we acknowledge nothing. As a matter of course she is the Countess till it be proved that another wife was living when she was married.'

'Quite as a matter of course,' said the Serjeant.

'Quite as a matter of course, if that will make the case stronger,' continued Sir William. 'Her marriage was formal and regular. That she believed her marriage to be a righteous marriage before God, I have never doubted. God forbid that I should have a harsh thought against a poor lady who has suffered so much cruel treatment.'

'Why have things been said then?' asked the Serjeant, beginning to throw about his left arm.

'If I am not mistaken,' said Mr. Mainsail, 'evidence has been prepared to show that the Countess is a party to a contemplated fraud.'

'Then you are mistaken, Mr. Mainsail,' said Sir William. 'I admit at once and clearly that the lady is not suspected of any fraud. Whether she be actually the Countess Lovel or not it may, —I fear it must,—take years to prove, if the law be allowed to take its course.'

'We think that we can dispose of any counter-claim in much less time than that,' said the Serjeant.

'It may be so. I myself think that it would not be so. Our evidence in favour of the lady who is now living some two leagues out of Palermo, is very strong. She is a poor creature, old, ignorant,—fairly well off through the bounty of the late Earl, but always craving for some trifle more,—unwilling to come to this country, —childless, and altogether indifferent to the second marriage, except in so far as might interfere with her hopes of getting some further subsidy from the Lovel family. One is not very anxious on her behalf. One is only anxious,— can only be anxious,—that the vast property at stake should not get into improper hands.'

'And that justice should be done,' said Mr. Hardy.

'And that justice should be done of course, as my friend observes. Here is a young man who is undoubtedly Earl of Lovel, and who claims a property as heir to the late Earl. And here is a young lady, I am told very beautiful and highly educated, who is the daughter of the late Earl, and who claims that property believing herself to be his legitimate heiress. The question between them is most intricate.'

'The onus probandi lies with you, Mr. Solicitor,' said the Serjeant.

'We acknowledge that it does, but the case on that account is none the less intricate. With the view of avoiding litigation and expense, and in the certainty that by such an arrangement the enjoyment of the property will fall to the right owner, we propose that steps shall

be taken to bring these two young people together. The lady, whom for the occasion I am
quite willing to call the Countess, the mother
of the lady whom I hope the young Earl will
make his own Countess, has not been sounded
on this subject.'

'I should hope not,' said the Serjeant.

'My excellent friend takes me up a little short,'
said Sir William, laughing. 'You gentlemen
will probably consult together on the subject,
and whatever may be the advice which you shall
consider it to be your duty to give to the mother,
—and I am sure that you will feel bound to let
her know the proposition that has been made;
I do not hesitate to say that we have a right to
expect that it shall be made known to her,—
I need hardly remark that were the young lady
to accept the young lord's hand we should all
be in a boat together in reference to the mother's
rank, and to the widow's claim upon the personal property left behind him by her late
husband.'

And so the Solicitor-General had made his
proposition, and the conference was broken up
with a promise that Mr. Flick should hear from
Mr. Goffe upon the subject. But the Serjeant
had at once made up his mind against the compromise now proposed. He desired the danger
and the dust and the glory of the battle. He was
true to his clients' interests, no doubt,—intended
to be intensely true; but the personal, doggish
love of fighting prevailed in the man, and he
was clear as to the necessity of going on. 'They
know they are beat,' he said to Mr. Goffe.
'Mr. Solicitor knows as well as I do that he has

not an inch of ground under his feet.' Therefore
Mr. Goffe wrote the following letter to Messrs.
Norton and Flick:—

'Raymond's Buildings, Gray's Inn,
'1st *July*, 183-.

'DEAR SIRS,

'In reference to the interview which took place
at the chambers of the Solicitor-General on
the 27th ult., we are to inform you that we are
not disposed, as acting for our clients, the Countess of Lovel and her daughter the Lady Anna
Lovel, to listen to the proposition then made.
Apart from the very strong feeling we entertain
as to the certainty of our client's success,—
which certainly was not weakened by what we
heard on that occasion,—we are of opinion that
we could not interfere with propriety in suggesting the marriage of two young persons who
have not as yet had any opportunity of becoming
acquainted with each other. Should the Earl of
Lovel seek the hand of his cousin, the Lady Anna
Lovel, and marry her with the consent of the
Countess, we should be delighted at such a family
arrangement; but we do not think that we, as
lawyers,—or, if we may be allowed to say so,
that you as lawyers,—have anything to do with
such a matter.

'We are, dear Sirs,
'Yours very faithfully,
'GOFFE AND GOFFE.

'Messrs. Norton and Flick.'

'Balderdash!' said Sir William, when he had
read the letter. 'We are not going to be done in
that way. It was all very well going to that

Serjeant as he has the case in hand, though a
worse messenger in an affair of love——'

'Not love, as yet, Mr. Solicitor,' said Mr.
Flick.

'I mean it to be love, and I'm not going to
be put off by Serjeant Bluestone. We must
get to the lady by some other means. Do you
write to that tailor down at Keswick, and say
that you want to see him.'

'Will that be regular, Sir William?'

'I'll stand the racket,* Mr. Flick.' Mr. Flick
did write to Thomas Thwaite, and Thomas
Thwaite came up to London and called at
Mr. Flick's chambers.

When Thomas Thwaite received his commission he was much rejoiced. Injustice would be
done him unless so much were owned on his
behalf. But, nevertheless, some feeling of disappointment which he could not analyze crept
across his heart. If once the girl were married
to Earl Lovel there would be an end of his
services and of his son's. He had never really
entertained an idea that his son would marry
the girl. As the reader will perhaps remember,
he had warned his son that he must seek a
sweetheart elsewhere. He had told himself over
and over again that when the Countess came
to her own there must be an end of this intimacy,—that there could be nothing in common
between him, the radical tailor of Keswick, and
a really established Countess. The Countess,
while not yet really established, had already
begged that his son might be instructed not to
call her daughter simply by her Christian name.
Old Thwaite on receiving this intimation of the

difference of their positions, though he had acknowledged its truth, had felt himself bitterly aggrieved, and now the moment had come. Of course the Countess would grasp at such an offer. Of course it would give her all that she had desired, and much more than she expected. In adjusting his feelings on the occasion the tailor thought but little of the girl herself. Why should she not be satisfied? Of the young Earl he had only heard that he was a handsome, modest, gallant lad, who only wanted a fortune to make him one of the most popular of the golden youth of England. Why should not the girl rejoice at the prospect of winning such a husband? To have a husband must necessarily be in her heart, whether she were the Lady Anna Lovel, or plain Anna Murray. And what espousals could be so auspicious as these? Feeling all this, without much of calculation, the tailor said that he would do as he was bidden. 'We have sent for you because we know that you have been so old a friend,' said Mr. Flick, who did not quite approve of the emissary whom he had been instructed by Sir William to employ.

'I will do my best, sir,' said Mr. Thwaite, making his bow. Thomas Thwaite, as he went along the streets alone, determined that he would perform this new duty imposed upon him without any reference to his son.

CHAPTER VIII
Impossible!

'THEY sent for me, Lady Lovel, to bid me
come to your ladyship and ask your ladyship whether you would consent to a marriage
between the two young people.' It was thus
that the tailor repeated for the second time the
message which had been confided to him, showing the gall and also the pride which were at
work about his heart by the repeated titles
which he gave to his old friend.

'They desire that Anna should marry the
young lord!'

'Yes, my lady. That's the meaning of it.'

'And what am I to be?'

'Just the Countess Lovel,—with a third of
the property as your own. I suppose it would
be a third; but you might trust the lawyers to
settle that properly. When once they take your
daughter among them they won't scrimp you
in your honours. They'll all swear that the
marriage was good enough then. They know
that already, and have made this offer because
they know it. Your ladyship needn't fear now
but what all the world will own you as the
Countess Lovel. I don't suppose I'll be troubled
to come up to London any more.'

'Oh, my friend!' The ejaculation she made
feeling the necessity of saying something to soothe
the tailor's pride; but her heart was fixed upon
the fruition of that for which she had spent so
many years in struggling. Was it to come to

her at last? Could it be that now, now at once, people throughout the world would call her the Countess Lovel, and would own her daughter to be the Lady Anna,—till she also should become a countess? Of the young man she had heard nothing but good, and it was impossible that she should have fear in that direction, even had she been timorous by nature. But she was bold and eager, hopeful in spite of all that she had suffered, full of ambition, and not prone to feminine scruples. She had been fighting all her life in order that she and her daughter might be acknowledged to be among the aristocrats of her country. She was so far a loving, devoted mother that in all her battles she thought more of her child than of herself. She would have consented to carry on the battle in poverty to the last gasp of her own breath, could she thereby have insured success for her surviving daughter. But she was not a woman likely to be dismayed at the idea of giving her girl in marriage to an absolute stranger, when that stranger was such a one as the young Earl Lovel. She herself had been a countess, but a wretched, unacknowledged, poverty-stricken countess, for the last half of her eventful life. This marriage would make her daughter a countess, prosperous, accepted by all, and very wealthy. What better end could there be to her long struggles? Of course she would assent.

'I don't know why they should have troubled themselves to send for me,' said the tailor.

'Because you are the best friend that I have in the world. Whom else could I have trusted as I do you? Has the Earl agreed to it?'

'They didn't tell me that, my lady.'

'They would hardly have sent, unless he had agreed. Don't you think so, Mr. Thwaite?'

'I don't know much about such things, my lady.'

'You have told—Daniel?'

'No, my lady.'

'Oh, Mr. Thwaite, do not talk to me in that way. It sounds as though you were deserting me.'

'There'll be no reason for not deserting now. You'll have friends by the score more fit to see you through this than old Thomas Thwaite. And, to own the truth, now that the matter is coming to an end, I am getting weary of it. I'm not so young as I was, and I'd be better left at home to my business.'

'I hope that you may disregard your business now without imprudence, Mr. Thwaite.'

'No, my lady;—a man should always stick to his business. I hope that Daniel will do so better than his father before him,—so that his son may never have to go out to be servant to another man.'

'You are speaking daggers*to me.'

'I have not meant it then. I am rough by nature, I know, and perhaps a little low just at present. There is something sad in the parting of old friends.'

'Old friends needn't be parted, Mr. Thwaite.'

'When your ladyship was good enough to point out to me my boy's improper manner of speech to Lady Anna, I knew how it must be. You were quite right, my lady. There can be no becoming friendship between the future

Lady Lovel and a journeyman tailor. I was wrong from the beginning.'

'Oh, Mr. Thwaite! without such wrong where should we have been?'

'There can be no holding ground of friendship between such as you and such as we. Lords and ladies, earls and countesses, are our enemies, and we are theirs. We may make their robes and take their money, and deal with them as the Jew dealt with the Christians in the play; but we cannot eat with them or drink with them.'

'How often have I eaten and drank at your table, when no other table was spread for me?'

'You were a Jew almost as ourselves then. We cannot now well stand shoulder to shoulder and arm to arm as friends should do.'

'How often has my child lain in your arms when she was a baby, and been quieter there than she would be even in her mother's?'

'That has all gone by. Other arms will be open to receive her.' As the tailor said this he remembered how his boy used to take the little child out to the mountain side, and how the two would ramble away together through the long summer evenings; and he reflected that the memory of those days was no doubt still strong in the heart of his son. Some shadow of the grief which would surely fall upon the young man now fell upon the father, and caused him almost to repent of the work of his life. 'Tailors should consort with tailors,' he said, 'and lords and ladies should consort together.'

Something of the same feeling struck the Countess also. If it were not for the son, the father, after all that he had done for them, might be almost as near and as dear to them as ever. He might have called the Lady Anna by her Christian name, at any rate till she had been carried away as a bride by the Earl. But, though all this was so exquisitely painful, it had been absolutely necessary to check the son. 'Ah, well,' she said; 'it is hardly to be hoped that so many crooked things should be made straight without much pain. If you knew, Mr. Thwaite, how little it is that I expect for myself!'

'It is because I have known it that I am here.'

'It will be well for her,—will it not,—to be the wife of her cousin?'

'If he be a good man. A woman will not always make herself happy by marrying an Earl.'

'How many daggers you can use, Mr. Thwaite! But this young man is good. You yourself have said that you have heard so.'

'I have heard nothing to the contrary, my lady.'

'And what shall I do?'

'Just explain it all to Lady Anna. I think it will be clear then.'

'You believe that she will be so easily pleased?'

'Why should she not be pleased? She'll have some maiden scruples, doubtless. What maid would not? But she'll exult at such an end to all her troubles;—and what maid would not? Let them meet as soon as may be and have it over. When he shall have placed the ring on her finger, your battle will have been won.'

Then the tailor felt that his commission was done and he might take his leave. It had been arranged that in the event of the Countess consenting to the proposed marriage, he should call upon Mr. Flick to explain that it was so. Had she dissented, a short note would have been sufficient. Had such been the case, the Solicitor-General would have instigated the young lord to go and try what he himself could do with the Countess and her daughter. The tailor had suggested to the mother that she should at once make the proposition known to Lady Anna, but the Countess felt that one other word was necessary as her old friend left her. 'Will you go back at once to Keswick, Mr. Thwaite?'

'To-morrow morning, my lady.'

'Perhaps you will not tell your son of this, —yet?'

'No, my lady. I will not tell my son of this, —yet. My son is high-minded and stiff-necked, and of great heart. If he saw aught to object to in this marriage, it might be that he would express himself loudly.' Then the tailor took his leave without even shaking hands with the Countess.

The woman sat alone for the next two hours, thinking of what had passed. There had sprung up in these days a sort of friendship between Mrs. Bluestone and the two Miss Bluestones and the Lady Anna, arising rather from the forlorn condition of the young lady than from any positive choice of affection. Mrs. Bluestone was kind and motherly. The girls were girlish and good. The father was the Jupiter Tonans*of the household,—as was of course proper,—and was worshipped in everything. To the world at large Serjeant Bluestone was a thundering, blundering, sanguine, energetic lawyer, whom nobody disliked very much though he was so big and noisy. But at home Serjeant Bluestone was all the judges of the land rolled into one. But he was a kind-hearted man, and he had sent his wife and girls to call upon the disconsolate Countess. The disconsolate Lady Anna having no other friends, had found the companionship of the Bluestone girls to be pleasant to her, and she was now with them at the Serjeant's house in Bedford Square. Mrs. Bluestone talked of the wrongs and coming rights of the Countess Lovel wherever she went, and the Bluestone girls had all the case at their fingers' ends. To doubt that the Serjeant would succeed, or to doubt that the success of the Countess and her daughter would have had any other source than the Serjeant's eloquence and the Serjeant's zeal, would have been heresy in Bedford Square. The grand idea that young Jack Bluestone, who was up at Brasenose,* should marry the Lady Anna, had occurred only to the mother.

Lady Anna was away with her friends as the Countess sat brooding over the new hopes that had been opened to her. At first, she could not tear her mind away from the position which she herself would occupy as soon as her daughter should have been married and taken away from her. The young Earl would not want his mother-in-law,—a mother-in-law who had spent the best years of her life in the society of a tailor. And the daughter, who would still be young enough to begin a new life in a new sphere, would no longer want her mother to help her. As regarded herself, the Countess was aware

that the life she had led so long, and the condition of agonizing struggling to which she
had been brought, had unfitted her for smiling,
happy, prosperous, aristocratic luxury. There
was but one joy left for her, and that was to be
the joy of success. When that cup should have
been drained, there would be nothing left to her.
She would have her rank, of course,—and money
enough to support it. She no longer feared that
any one would do her material injury. Her
daughter's husband no doubt would see that
she had a fitting home, with all the appanages
and paraphernalia suited to a dowager Countess.
But who would share her home with her, and
where should she find her friends? Even now
the two Miss Bluestones were more to her
daughter than she was. When she should be
established in her new luxurious home, with
servants calling her my lady, with none to
contradict her right, she would no longer be
enabled to sit late into the night discussing
matters with her friend the tailor. As regarded
herself, it would have been better for her, perhaps,
if the fight had been carried on.

But the fight had been, not for herself, but
for her child; and the victory for her girl would
have been won by her own perseverance. Her
whole life had been devoted to establishing the
rights of her daughter, and it should be so
devoted to the end. It had been her great
resolve that the world should acknowledge the
rank of her girl, and now it would be acknowledged. Not only would she become the Countess
Lovel by marriage, but the name which had
been assumed for her amidst the ridicule of

many, and in opposition to the belief of nearly all, would be proved to have been her just and proper title. And then, at last, it would be known by all men that she herself, the ill-used, suffering mother, had gone to the house of that wicked man, not as his mistress, but as his true wife!

Hardly a thought troubled her, then, as to the acquiescence of her daughter. She had no faintest idea that the girl's heart had been touched by the young tailor. She had so lived that she knew but little of lovers and their love, and in her fear regarding Daniel Thwaite she had not conceived danger such as that. It had to her simply been unfitting that there should be close familiarity between the two. She expected that her daughter would be ambitious, as she was ambitious, and would rejoice greatly at such perfect success. She herself had been preaching ambition and practising ambition all her life. It had been the necessity of her career that she should think more of her right to a noble name than of any other good thing under the sun. It was only natural that she should believe that her daughter shared the feeling.

And then Lady Anna came in. 'They wanted me to stay and dine, mamma, but I did not like to think that you should be left alone.'

'I must get used to that, my dear.'

'Why, mamma? Wherever we have been, we have always been together. Mrs. Bluestone was quite unhappy because you would not come. They are so good-natured! I wish you would go there.'

'I am better here, my dear.' Then there was

a pause for a few moments. 'But I am glad that you have come home this evening.'

'Of course, I should come home.'

'I have something special to say to you.'

'To me, mamma! What is it, mamma?'

'I think we will wait till after dinner. The things are here now. Go upstairs and take off your hat, and I will tell you after dinner.'

'Mamma,' Lady Anna said, as soon as the maid had left the room, 'has old Mr. Thwaite been here?'

'Yes, my dear, he was here.'

'I thought so, because you have something to tell me. It is something from him?'

'Not from himself, Anna;—though he was the messenger. Come and sit here, my dear,—close to me. Have you ever thought, Anna, that it would be good for you to be married?'

'No, mamma; why should I?' But that surely was a lie! How often had she thought that it would be good to be married to Daniel Thwaite and to have done with this weary searching after rank! And now what could her mother mean? Thomas Thwaite had been there, but it was impossible that her mother should think that Daniel Thwaite would be a fit husband for her daughter. 'No, mamma;—why should I?'

'It must be thought of, my dearest.'

'Why now?' She could understand perfectly that there was some special cause for her mother's manner of speech.

'After all that we have gone through, we are about to succeed at last. They are willing to own everything, to give us all our rights,—on one condition.'

'What condition, mamma?'

'Come nearer to me, dearest. It would not make you unhappy to think that you were going to be the wife of a man you could love?'

'No;—not if I really loved him.'

'You have heard of your cousin,—the young Earl?'

'Yes mamma;—I have heard of him.'

'They say that he is everything that is good. What should you think of having him for your husband?'

'That would be impossible, mamma.'

'Impossible!—why impossible? What could be more fitting? Your rank is equal to his;—higher even in this, that your father was himself the Earl. In fortune you will be much more than his equal. In age you are exactly suited. Why should it be impossible?'

'Oh, mamma, i is impossible!'

'What makes you say so, Anna?'

'We have never seen each other.'

'Tush! my child. Why should you not see each other?'

'And then we are his enemies.'

'We are no longer enemies, dearest. They have sent to say that if we,—you and I,—will consent to this marriage, then will they consent to it also. It is their wish, and it comes from them. There can be no more proper ending to all this weary law-suit. It is quite right that the title and the name should be supported. It is quite right that the fortune which your father left should, in this way, go to support your father's family. You will be the Countess Lovel; and all will have been conceded to us. There cannot possibly be any fitter way out of our difficulties.' Lady Anna sat looking at her mother in dismay, but could say nothing. 'You need have no fear about the young man. Every one tells me that he is just the man that a mother would welcome as a husband for her daughter. Will you not be glad to see him?' But the Lady Anna would only say that it was impossible. 'Why impossible, my dear;—what do you mean by impossible?'

'Oh, mamma, it is impossible!'

The Countess found that she was obliged to give the subject up for that night, and could only comfort herself by endeavouring to believe that the suddenness of the tidings had confused her child.

CHAPTER IX
It isn't Law

ON the next morning Lady Anna was ill, and would not leave her bed. When her mother spoke to her, she declared that her head ached wretchedly, and she could not be persuaded to dress herself.

'Is it what I said to you last night?' asked the Countess.

'Oh, mamma, that is impossible,' she said.

It seemed to the mother that the mention of the young lord's name had produced a horror in the daughter's mind which nothing could for the present subdue. Before the day was over, however, the girl had acknowledged that she was bound in duty, at any rate, to meet her cousin; and the Countess, forced to satisfy herself with so much of concession, and acting upon that, fixed herself in her purpose to go on with the project. The lawyers on both sides would assist her. It was for the advantage of them all that there should be such a marriage. She determined, therefore, that she would at once see Mr. Goffe, her own attorney, and give him to understand in general terms that the case might be proceeded with on this new matrimonial basis.

But there was a grievous doubt on her mind, —a fear, a spark of suspicion, of which she had unintentionally given notice to Thomas Thwaite when she asked him whether he had as yet spoken of the proposed marriage to his son. He

had understood what was passing in her mind
when she exacted from him a promise that
nothing should as yet be said to Daniel Thwaite
upon the matter. And yet she assured herself
over and over again that her girl could not be
so weak, so vain, so foolish, so wicked as that!
It could not be that, after all the struggles of her
life,—when at last success, perfect success, was
within their grasp, when all had been done and
all well done, when the great reward was then
coming up to their very lips with a full tide,—
it could not be that in the very moment of
victory all should be lost through the base weakness of a young girl! Was it possible that her
daughter,—the daughter of one who had spent
the very marrow of her life in fighting for the
position that was due to her,—should spoil all
by preferring a journeyman tailor to a young
nobleman of high rank, of ancient lineage, and
one, too, who by his marriage with herself
would endow her with wealth sufficient to make
that rank splendid as well as illustrious? But
if it were not so, what had the girl meant by
saying that it was impossible? That the word
should have been used once or twice in maidenly
scruple, the Countess could understand; but it
had been repeated with a vehemence beyond
that which such natural timidity might have
produced. And now the girl professed herself
to be ill in bed, and when the subject was
broached would only weep, and repeat the one
word with which she had expressed her repug-
nance to the match.

Hitherto she had not been like this. She had,
in her own quiet way, shared her mother's

aspirations, and had always sympathised with her mother's sufferings; and she had been dutiful through it all, carrying herself as one who was bound to special obedience by the peculiarity of her parent's position. She had been keenly alive to the wrongs that her mother endured, and had in every respect been a loving child. But now she protested that she would not do the one thing necessary to complete their triumph, and would give no reason for not doing so. As the Countess thought of all this, she swore to herself that she would prefer to divest her bosom of all soft motherly feeling than be vanquished in this matter by her own child. Her daughter should find that she could be stern and rough enough if she were really thwarted. What would her life be worth to her if her child, Lady Anna Lovel, the heiress and only legitimate offspring of the late Earl Lovel, were to marry a—tailor?

And then, again, she told herself that there was no sufficient excuse for such alarm. Her daughter's demeanour had ever been modest. She had never been given to easy friendship, or to that propensity to men's acquaintance which the world calls flirting. It might be that the very absence of such propensity,—the very fact that hitherto she had never been thrust into society among her equals,—had produced that feeling almost of horror which she had expressed. But she had been driven, at any rate, to say that she would meet the young man; and the Countess, acting upon that, called on Mr. Goffe in his chambers, and explained to that gentleman that she proposed to settle the whole question in dispute by giving her daughter to the young Earl in marriage. Mr. Goffe, who had been present at the conference among the lawyers, understood it all in a moment. The overture had been made from the other side to his client.

'Indeed, my lady!' said Mr. Goffe.

'Do you not think it will be an excellent arrangement?'

In his heart of hearts Mr. Goffe thought that it would be an excellent arrangement; but he could not commit himself to such an opinion. Serjeant Bluestone thought that the matter should be fought out, and Mr. Goffe was not prepared to separate himself from his legal adviser. As Serjeant Bluestone had said after the conference, with much argumentative vehemence,—'If we were to agree to this, how would it be if the marriage should not come off? The court can't agree to a marriage. The court must direct to whom the property belongs. They profess that they can prove that our marriage was no marriage. They must do so, or else they must withdraw the allegation. Suppose the Italian woman were to come forward afterwards with her claim as the widow, where then would be my client's position, and her title as dowager countess, and her claim upon her husband's personal estate? I never heard anything more irregular in my life. It is just like Patterson, who always thinks he can make laws according to the light of his own reason.' So Serjeant Bluestone had said to the lawyers who were acting with him; and Mr. Goffe, though he did himself think that this marriage would be the best thing in the world, could not differ from the Serjeant.

No doubt there might even yet be very great difficulties, even though the young Earl and Lady Anna Lovel should agree to be married. Mr. Goffe on that occasion said very little to the Countess, and she left him with a feeling that a certain quantity of cold water had been thrown upon the scheme. But she would not allow herself to be disturbed by that. The marriage could go on without any consent on the part of the lawyers, and the Countess was quite satisfied that, should the marriage be once completed, the money and the titles would all go as she desired. She had already begun to have more faith in the Solicitor-General than in Mr. Goffe or in Serjeant Bluestone.

But Serjeant Bluestone was not a man to bear such treatment and be quiet under it. He heard that very day from Mr. Goffe what had been done, and was loud in the expression of his displeasure. It was the most irregular thing that he had ever known. No other man except Patterson in the whole profession would have done it! The counsel on the other side—probably Patterson himself—had been to his client, and given advice to his client, and had done so after her own counsel had decided that no such advice should be given! He would see the Attorney-General, and ask the Attorney-General what he thought about it. Now, it was supposed in legal circles, just at this period, that the Attorney-General and the Solicitor-General were not the best friends in the world; and the latter was wont to call the former an old fogey, and the former to say of the latter that he might be a very clever philosopher, but certainly no lawyer. And so by degrees the thing got much talked about in the profession; and there was perhaps a balance of opinion that the Solicitor-General had done wrong.

But this was certain,—that no one could be put into possession of the property till the court had decided to whom it belonged. If the Earl withdrew from his claim, the widow would simply be called on to prove her own marriage, —which had in truth been proved more than once already,—and the right of her legitimate child would follow as a matter of course. It was by no means probable that the woman over in Italy would make any claim on her own behalf, —and even, should she do so, she could not find the means of supporting it. 'They must be asses,' said the Solicitor-General, 'not to see that I am fighting their battle for them, and that I am doing so because I can best secure my own client's interests by securing theirs also.' But even he became nervous after a day or two, and was anxious to learn that the marriage scheme was progressing. He told his client, Lord Lovel, that it would be well that the marriage should take place before the court sat in November. 'In that case settlements will, of course, have been made, and we shall simply withdraw. We shall state the fact of this new marriage, and assert ourselves to be convinced that the old marriage was good and valid. But you should lose no time in the wooing, my lord.' At this time the Earl had not seen his cousin, and it had not yet been decided when they should meet.

'It is my duty to explain to you, Lady Lovel, as my client,' said Serjeant Bluestone to the Countess, 'that this arrangement cannot afford a satisfactory mode to you of establishing your own position.'

'It would be so happy for the whole family!'

'As to that I can know nothing, Lady Lovel. If your daughter and the Earl are attached to each other, there can be no reason on earth why they should not be married. But it should be a separate thing. Your position should not be made to depend upon hers.'

'But they will withdraw, Serjeant Bluestone.'

'How do you know that they will withdraw? Supposing at the last moment Lady Anna were to decline the alliance, would they withdraw then? Not a bit of it. The matter would be further delayed, and referred over to next year. You and your daughter would be kept out of your money, and there would still be danger.'

'I should not care for that;—if they were married.'

'And they have set up this Italian countess,—who never was a countess,—any more than I am. Now they have put her up, they are bound to dispose of her. If she came forward afterwards, on her own behalf, where would you all be then?'

'My daughter would, at any rate, be safe.'

The Serjeant did not like it at all. He felt that he was being thrown over, not only by his client the Countess,—as to which he might have been indifferent, knowing that the world at large, the laity as distinguished from the lawyers, the children of the world as all who were not lawyers seemed to him to be, will do and must be expected to do, foolish things continually. They cannot be persuaded to subject themselves to lawyers in all their doings, and, of course, go wrong when they do not do so. The infinite simplicity and silliness of mankind and womankind at large were too well known to the Serjeant to cause him dismay, let them be shown in ever so egregious a fashion. But in this case the fault came from another lawyer, who had tampered with his clients, and who seemed to be himself as ignorant as though he belonged to the outside world. And this man had been made Solicitor-General,—over the heads of half the profession,—simply because he could make a speech in Parliament!

But the Solicitor-General was himself becoming uneasy when at the end of a fortnight he learned that the young people,—as he had come to call them on all occasions,—had not as yet seen each other. He would not like to have it said of him that he had thrown over his client. And there were some who still believed that the Italian marriage had been a real marriage, and the Italian wife alive at the time of the Cumberland marriage,—though the Italian woman now living had never been the countess. Mr. Hardy so believed, and, in his private opinion, thought that the Solicitor-General had been very indiscreet.

'I don't think that we could ever dare to face a jury,' said Sir William to Mr. Hardy when they discussed the matter, about a fortnight after the proposition had been made.

'Why did the Earl always say that the Italian woman was his wife?'

'Because the Earl was a very devil.'

'Mr. Flick does not think so.'

'Yes, he does; but Mr. Flick, like all attorneys with a bad case, does not choose to say quite what he thinks, even to his own counsel. Mr. Flick does not like to throw his client over, nor do I, nor do you. But with such a case we have no right to create increased expenses, and all the agony of prolonged fallacious hope. The girl is her father's heir. Do you suppose I would not stick to my brief if I did not feel sure that it is so?'

'Then let the Earl be told, and let the girl have her rights.'

'Ah! there you have me. It may be that such would be the juster course; but then, Hardy, cannot you understand that though I am sure, I am not quite sure; that though the case is a bad one, it may not be quite bad enough to be thrown up? It is just the case in which a compromise is expedient. If but a quarter, or but an eighth of a probability be with you, take your proportion of the thing at stake. But here is a compromise that gives all to each. Who would wish to rob the girl of her noble name and great inheritance if she be the heiress? Not I, though the Earl be my client. And yet how sad would it be to have to tell that young man that there was nothing for him but to submit to lose all the wealth belonging to the family of which he has been born the head! If we can bring them together there will be nothing to make sore the hearts of any of us.'

Mr. Hardy acknowledged to himself that the Solicitor-General pleaded his own case very well; but yet he felt that it wasn't law.

CHAPTER X

The first Interview

FOR some days after the intimation of her mother's purpose, Lady Anna kept her bed. She begged that she might not see a doctor. She had a headache,—nothing but a headache. But it was quite impossible that she should ever marry Earl Lovel. This she said whenever her mother would revert to that subject,—'I have not seen him, mamma; I do not know him. I am sure it would be impossible.' Then, when at last she was induced to dress herself, she was still unwilling to be forced to undergo the interview to which she had acknowledged that she must be subjected. At last she consented to spend a day in Bedford Square; to dine there, and to be brought home in the evening. The Countess was at this time not very full of trust in the Serjeant, having learned that he was opposed to the marriage scheme, but she was glad that her daughter should be induced to go out, even to the Serjeant's house, as after that visit the girl could have no ground on which to oppose the meeting which was to be arranged. She could hardly plead that she was too ill to see her cousin when she had dined with Mrs. Bluestone.

During this time many plans had been proposed for the meeting. The Solicitor-General, discussing the matter with the young lord, had thought it best that Lady Anna should at once be asked down to Yoxham,—as the

Lady Anna; and the young lord would have been quite satisfied with such an arrangement. He could have gone about his obligatory wooing among his own friends, in the house to which he had been accustomed, with much more ease than in a London lodging. But his uncle, who had corresponded on the subject with Mr. Hardy, still objected. 'We should be giving up everything,' he said, 'if we were once to call her Lady Anna. Where should we be then if they didn't hit it off together? I don't believe, and I never shall believe, that she is really Lady Anna Lovel.' The Solicitor-General, when he heard of this objection, shook his head, finding himself almost provoked to anger. What asses were these people not to understand that he could see further into the matter than they could do, and that their best way out of their difficulty would be frankly to open their arms to the heiress! Should they continue to be pig-headed and prejudiced, everything would soon be gone.

Then he had a scheme for inviting the girl to his own house, and to that scheme he obtained his wife's consent. But here his courage failed him; or, it might be fairer to say, that his prudence prevailed. He was very anxious, intensely eager, so to arrange this great family dispute that all should be benefited,—believing, nay feeling positively certain that all concerned in the matter were honest; but he must not go so far as to do himself an absolute and grievous damage, should it at last turn out that he was wrong in any of his surmises. So that plan was abandoned.

There was nothing left for it but that the young Earl should himself face the difficulty, and be introduced to the girl at the lodging in Wyndham Street. But, as a prelude to this, a meeting was arranged at Mr. Flick's chambers between the Countess and her proposed son-in-law. That the Earl should go to his own attorney's chambers was all in rule. While he was there the Countess came,—which was not in rule, and almost induced the Serjeant to declare, when he heard it, that he would have nothing more to do with the case. 'My lord,' said the Countess, 'I am glad to meet you, and I hope that we may be friends.' The young man was less collected, and stammered out a few words that were intended to be civil.

'It is a pity that you should have conflicting interests,' said the attorney.

'I hope it need not continue to be so,' said the Countess. 'My heart, Lord Lovel, is all in the welfare of our joint family. We will begrudge you nothing if you will not begrudge us the names which are our own, and without which we cannot live honourably before the world.' Then some other few words were muttered, and the Earl promised to come to Wyndham Street at a certain hour. Not a word was then said about the marriage. Even the Countess, with all her resolution and all her courage, did not find herself able in set terms to ask the young man to marry her daughter.

'She is a very handsome woman,' said the lord to the attorney, when the Countess had left them.

'Yes, indeed.'

'And like a lady.'

'Quite like a lady. She herself was of a good family.'

'I suppose she certainly was the late Earl's wife, Mr. Flick?'

'Who can say, my lord? That is just the question. The Solicitor-General thinks that she would prove her right, and I do not know that I have ever found him to be wrong when he has had a steadfast opinion.'

'Why should we not give it up to her at once?'

'I couldn't recommend that, my lord. Why should we give it up? The interests at stake are very great. I couldn't for a moment think of suggesting to you to give it up.'

'I want nothing, Mr. Flick, that does not belong to me.'

'Just so. But then perhaps it does belong to you. We can never be sure. No doubt the safest way will be for you to contract an alliance with this lady. Of course we should give it up then, but the settlements would make the property all right.' The young Earl did not quite like it. He would rather have commenced his wooing after the girl had been established in her own right, and when she would have had no obligation on her to accept him. But he had consented, and it was too late for him now to recede. It had been already arranged that he should call in Wyndham Street at noon on the following day, in order that he might be introduced to his cousin.

On that evening the Countess sat late with her daughter, purposing that on the morrow nothing should be said before the interview calculated to disturb the girl's mind. But as they sat together through the twilight and into the darkness of night, close by the open window, through which the heavily laden air of the metropolis came to them, hot with all the heat of a London July day, very many words were spoken by the Countess. 'It will be for you, to-morrow, to make or to mar all that I have been doing since the day on which you were born.'

'Oh! mamma, that is so terrible a thing to say!'

'But terrible things must be said if they are true. It is so. It is for you to decide whether we shall triumph, or be utterly and for ever crushed.'

'I cannot understand it. Why should we be crushed? He would not wish to marry me if this fortune were not mine. He is not coming, mamma, because he loves me.'

'You say that because you do not understand. Do you suppose that my name will be allowed to me if you should refuse your cousin's suit? If so, you are very much mistaken. The fight will go on, and as we have not money, we shall certainly go to the wall at last. Why should you not love him? There is no one else that you care for.'

'No, mamma,' she said slowly.

'Then, what more can you want?'

'I do not know him, mamma.'

'But you will know him. According to that, no girl would ever get married. Is it not a great thing that you should be asked to assume and to enjoy the rank which has belonged to your mother, but which she has never been able to enjoy?'

'I do not think, mamma, that I care much about rank.'

'Anna!' The mother's mind as she heard this flew off to the young tailor. Had misery so great as this overtaken her after all?

'I mean that I don't care so much about it. It has never done us any good.'

'But if it is a thing that is your own, that you are born to, you must bear it, whether it be in sorrow or in joy; whether it be a blessing or a curse. If it be yours, you cannot fling it away from you. You may disgrace it, but you must still have it. Though you were to throw yourself away upon a chimney-sweeper, you must still be Lady Anna, the daughter of Earl Lovel.'

'I needn't call myself so.'

'Others must call you so. It is your name, and you cannot be rid of it. It is yours of right, as my name has been mine of right; and not to assert it, not to live up to it, not to be proud of it, would argue incredible baseness. "Noblesse oblige." You have heard that motto, and know what it means. And then would you throw away from you in some childish phantasy all that I have been struggling to win for you during my whole life? Have you ever thought of what my life has been, Anna?'

'Yes, mamma.'

'Would you have the heart to disappoint me, now that the victory is won;—now that it may be made our own by your help? And what is it that I am asking you to do? If this man were bad,—if he were such a one as your father, if he were drunken, cruel, ill-conditioned, or even heavy, foolish, or deformed; had you been told stories to set you against him, as that he had been false with other women, I could understand it. In that case we would at any rate find out the truth before we went on. But of this man we hear that he is good, and pleasant; an excellent young man, who has endeared himself to all who know him. Such a one that all the girls of his own standing in the world would give their eyes to win him.'

'Let some girl win him then who cares for him.'

'But he wishes to win you, dearest.'

'Not because he loves me. How can he love me when he never saw me? How can I love him when I never saw him?'

'He wishes to win you because he has heard what you are, and because he knows that by doing so he can set things right which for many years have been wrong.'

'It is because he would get all this money.'

'You would both get it. He desires nothing unfair. Whatever he takes from you, so much he will give. And it is not only for this generation. Is it nothing to you that the chiefs of your own family who shall come after you shall be able to hold their heads up among other British peers? Would you not wish that your own son should come to be Earl Lovel, with wealth sufficient to support the dignity?'

'I don't think it would make him happy, mamma.'

'There is something more in this, Anna, than I can understand. You used not to be so. When we talked of these things in past years you used not to be indifferent.'

'I was not asked then to—to—marry a man I did not care for.'

'There is something else, Anna.

'No, mamma.'

'If there be nothing else you will learn to care for him. You will see him to-morrow, and will be left alone with him. I will sit with you for a time, and then I will leave you. All that I ask of you is to receive him to-morrow without any prejudice against him. You must remember how much depends on you, and that you are not as other girls are.' After that Lady Anna was allowed to go to her bed, and to weep in solitude over the wretchedness of her condition. It was not only that she loved Daniel Thwaite with all her heart,—loved him with a love that had grown with every year of her growth;—but that she feared him also. The man had become her master; and even could she have brought herself to be false, she would have lacked the courage to declare her falsehood to the man to whom she had vowed her love

On the following morning Lady Anna did not come down to breakfast, and the Countess began to fear that she would be unable to induce her girl to rise in time to receive their visitor. But the poor child had resolved to receive the man's visit, and contemplated no such escape as that. At eleven o'clock she slowly dressed herself, and before twelve crept down into the one sitting-room which they occupied. The Countess glanced round at her, anxious to see that she was looking her best. Certain instructions had been given as to her dress, and the garniture of her hair, and the disposal of her ribbons. All these had been fairly well obeyed; but there was a fixed, determined hardness in her face which made her mother fear that the Earl might be dismayed. The mother knew that her child had never looked like that before.

Punctually at twelve the Earl was announced. The Countess received him very pleasantly, and with great composure. She shook hands with him as though they had known each other all their lives, and then introduced him to her daughter with a sweet smile. 'I hope you will acknowledge her as your far-away cousin, my lord. Blood, they say, is thicker than water; and, if so, you two ought to be friends.'

'I am sure I hope we may be,' said the Earl.

'I hope so too,—my lord,' said the girl, as she left her hand quite motionless in his.

'We heard of you down in Cumberland,' said the Countess. 'It is long since I have seen the old place, but I shall never forget it. There is not a bush among the mountains there that I shall not remember,—ay, into the next world, if aught of our memories are left to us.'

'I love the mountains; but the house is very gloomy.'

'Gloomy indeed. If you found it sad, what must it have been to me? I hope that I may tell you some day of all that I suffered there. There are things to tell of which I have never yet spoken to human being. She, poor child, has been too young and too tender to be troubled by such a tale. I sometimes think that no tragedy ever written, no story of horrors ever told, can have exceeded in description the things which

I endured in that one year of my married life.'
Then she went on at length, not telling the
details of that terrible year, but speaking
generally of the hardships of her life. 'I have
never wondered, Lord Lovel, that you and your
nearest relations should have questioned my
position. A bad man had surrounded me with
such art in his wickedness, that it has been
almost beyond my strength to rid myself of his
toils.' All this she had planned beforehand,
having resolved that she would rush into the
midst of things at once, and if possible enlist
his sympathies on her side.

'I hope it may be over now,' he said.

'Yes,' she replied, rising slowly from her seat,
'I hope it may be over now.' The moment had
come in which she had to play the most difficult
stroke of her whole game, and much might
depend on the way in which she played it. She
could not leave them together, walking abruptly
out of the room, without giving some excuse for
so unusual a proceeding. 'Indeed, I hope it
may be over now, both for us and for you, Lord
Lovel. That wicked man, in leaving behind
such cause of quarrel, has injured you almost as
deeply as us. I pray God that you and that
dear girl there may so look into each other's
hearts and trust each other's purposes, that you
may be able to set right the ill which your
predecessor did. If so, the family of Lovel
for centuries to come may be able to bless your
names.' Then with slow steps she left the room.

Lady Anna had spoken one word, and that
was all. It certainly was not for her now to
speak. She sat leaning on the table, with her

eyes fixed upon the ground, not daring to look at the man who had been brought to her as her future husband. A single glance she had taken as he entered the room, and she had seen at once that he was fair and handsome, that he still had that sweet winsome boyishness of face which makes a girl feel that she need not fear a man,—that the man has something of her own weakness, and need not be treated as one who is wise, grand, or heroic. And she saw too in one glance how different he was from Daniel Thwaite, the man to whom she had absolutely given herself;—and she understood at the moment something of the charm of luxurious softness and aristocratic luxury. Daniel Thwaite was swarthy, hard-handed, black-bearded,—with a noble fire in his eyes, but with an innate coarseness about his mouth which betokened roughness as well as strength. Had it been otherwise with her than it was, she might, she thought, have found it easy enough to love this young earl. As it was, there was nothing for her to do but to wait and answer him as best she might.

'Lady Anna,' he said.

'My lord!'

'Will it not be well that we should be friends?'

'Oh,—friends;—yes, my lord.'

'I will tell you all and everything;—that is, about myself. I was brought up to believe that you and your mother were just—impostors.'

'My lord, we are not impostors.'

'No;—I believe it. I am sure you are not. Mistakes have been made, but it has not been of my doing. As a boy, what could I believe but what I was told? I know now that you are and always have been as you have called yourself. If nothing else comes of it, I will at any rate say so much. The estate which your father left is no doubt yours. If I could hinder it, there should be no more law.'

'Thank you, my lord.'

'Your mother says that she has suffered much. I am sure she has suffered. I trust that all that is over now. I have come here to-day more to say that on my own behalf than anything else.' A shadow of a shade of disappointment, the slightest semblance of a cloud, passed across her heart as she heard this. But it was well. She could not have married him, even if he had wished it, and now, as it seemed, that difficulty was over. Her mother and those lawyers had been mistaken, and it was well that he should tell her so at once.

'It is very good of you, my lord.'

'I would not have you think of me that I could come to you hoping that you would promise me your love before I had shown you whether I had loved you or not.'

'No, my lord.' She hardly understood him now,—whether he intended to propose himself as a suitor for her hand or not.

'You, Lady Anna, are your father's heir. I am your cousin, Earl Lovel, as poor a peer as there is in England. They tell me that we should marry because you are rich and I am an earl.'

'So they tell me;—but that will not make it right.'

'I would not have it so, even if I dared to think that you would agree to it.'

'Oh no, my lord; nor would I.'

'But if you could learn to love me——'

'No, my lord;—no.'

'Do not answer me yet, my cousin. If I swore that I loved you,—loved you so soon after seeing you,—and loved you, too, knowing you to be so wealthy an heiress——'

'Ah, do not talk of that.'

'Well;—not of that. But if I said that I loved you, you would not believe me.'

'It would not be true, my lord.'

'But I know that I shall love you. You will let me try? You are very lovely, and they tell me you are sweet-humoured. I can believe well that you are sweet and pleasant. You will let me try to love you, Anna?'

'No, my lord.'

'Must it be so, so soon?'

'Yes, my lord.'

'Why that? Is it because we are strangers to each other? That may be cured;—if not quickly, as I would have it cured, slowly and by degrees; slowly as you can wish, if only I may come where you shall be. You have said that we may be friends.'

'Oh yes,—friends, I hope.'

'Friends at least. We are born cousins.'

'Yes, my lord.'

'Cannot you call me by my name? Cousins, you know, do so. And remember this, you will have and can have no nearer cousin than I am. I am bound at least to be a brother to you.'

'Oh, be my brother!'

'That,—or more than that. I would fain be more than that. But I will be that, at least.

As I came to you, before I saw you, I felt that whenever we knew each other I could not be less to you than that. If I am your friend, I must be your best friend,—as being, though poor, the head of your family. The Lovels should at least love each other; and cousins may love, even though they should not love enough to be man and wife.'

'I will love you so always.'

'Enough to be my wife?'

'Enough to be your dear cousin,—your loving sister.'

'So it shall be,—unless it can be more. I would not ask you for more now. I would not wish you to give more now. But think of me, and ask yourself whether you can dare to give yourself to me altogether.'

'I cannot dare, my lord.'

'You would not call your brother, lord. My name is Frederic. But Anna, dear Anna,'— and then he took her unresisting hand,—'you shall not be asked for more now. But cousins, new-found cousins, who love each other, and will stand by each other for help and aid against the world, may surely kiss,—as would a brother and a sister. You will not grudge me a kiss.' Then she put up her cheek innocently, and he kissed it gently,—hardly with a lover's kiss. 'I will leave you now,' he said, still holding her hand. 'But tell your mother thus:—that she shall no longer be troubled by lawyers at the suit of her cousin Frederic. She is to me the Countess Lovel, and she shall be treated by me with the honour suited to her rank.' And so he left the house without seeing the Countess again.

CHAPTER XI

It is too late

THE Countess had resolved that she would let their visitor depart without saying a word to him. Whatever might be the result of the interview, she was aware that she could not improve it by asking any question from the young lord, or by hearing any account of it from him. The ice had been broken, and it would now be her object to have her daughter invited down to Yoxham as soon as possible. If once the Earl's friends could be brought to be eager for the match on his account, as was she on her daughter's behalf, then probably the thing might be done. For herself, she expected no invitation, no immediate comfort, no tender treatment, no intimate familiar cousinship. She had endured hitherto, and would be contented to endure, so that triumph might come at last. Nor did she question her daughter very closely, anxious as she was to learn the truth.

Could she have heard every word that had been spoken she would have been sure of success. Could Daniel Thwaite have heard every word he would have been sure that the girl was about to be false to him. But the girl herself believed herself to have been true. The man had been so soft with her, so tender, so pleasant, —so loving with his sweet cousinly offers of affection, that she could not turn herself against him. He had been to her eyes beautiful, noble,

—almost divine. She knew of herself that she could not be his wife,—that she was not fit to be his wife,—because she had given her troth to the tailor's son. When her cousin touched her cheek with his lips she remembered that she had submitted to be kissed by one with whom her noble relative could hold no fellow-ship whatever. A feeling of degradation came upon her, as though by contact with this young man she was suddenly awakened to a sense of what her own rank demanded from her. When her mother had spoken to her of what she owed to her family, she had thought only of all the friendship that she and her mother had received from her lover and his father. But when Lord Lovel told her what she was,—how she should ever be regarded by him as a dear cousin,—how her mother should be accounted a countess, and receive from him the respect due to her rank,—then she could understand how unfitting were a union between the Lady Anna Lovel and Daniel Thwaite, the journeyman tailor. Hitherto Daniel's face had been noble in her eyes,—the face of a man who was manly, gener-ous, and strong. But after looking into the eyes of the young Earl, seeing how soft was the down upon his lips, how ruddy the colour of his cheek, how beautiful was his mouth with its pearl-white teeth, how noble the curve of his nostrils, after feeling the softness of his hand, and catching the sweetness of his breath, she came to know what it might have been to be wooed by such a one as he.

But not on that account did she meditate falseness. It was settled firm as fate. The

dominion of the tailor over her spirit had lasted
in truth for years. The sweet, perfumed graces
of the young nobleman had touched her senses
but for a moment. Had she been false-minded
she had not courage to be false. But in truth
she was not false-minded. It was to her, as
that sunny moment passed across her, as to
some hard-toiling youth who, while roaming
listlessly among the houses of the wealthy, hears,
as he lingers on the pavement of a summer night,
the melodies which float upon the air from the
open balconies above him. A vague sense of
unknown sweetness comes upon him, mingled
with an irritating feeling of envy that some
favoured son of Fortune should be able to
stand over the shoulders of that singing syren,
while he can only listen with intrusive ears from
the street below. And so he lingers and is envi-
ous, and for a moment curses his fate,—not
knowing how weary may be the youth who
stands, how false the girl who sings. But he
does not dream that his life is to be altered for
him, because he has chanced to hear the daughter
of a duchess warble through a window. And
so it was with this girl. The youth was very
sweet to her, intensely sweet when he told her
that he would be a brother, perilously sweet
when he bade her not to grudge him one kiss.
But she knew that she was not as he was. That
she had lost the right, could she ever have had
the right, to live his life, to drink of his cup, and
to lie on his breast. So she passed on, as the
young man does in the street, and consoled
herself with the consciousness that strength after
all may be preferable to sweetness.

And she was an honest girl from her heart, and prone to truth, with a strong glimmer of common sense in her character, of which her mother hitherto had been altogether unaware. What right had her mother to think that she could be fit to be this young lord's wife, having brought her up in the companionship of small traders in Cumberland? She never blamed her mother. She knew well that her mother had done all that was possible on her behalf. But for that small trader they would not even have had a roof to shelter them. But still there was the fact, and she understood it. She was as her bringing up had made her, and it was too late now to effect a change. Ah yes;—it was indeed too late. It was all very well that lawyers should look upon her as an instrument, as a piece of goods that might now, from the accident of her ascertained birth, be made of great service to the Lovel family. Let her be the lord's wife, and everything would be right for everybody. It had been very easy to say that! But she had a heart of her own,—a heart to be touched, and won, and given away,—and lost. The man who had been so good to them had sought for his reward, and had got it, and could not now be defrauded. Had she been dishonest she would not have dared to defraud him; had she dared, she would not have been so dishonest.

'Did you like him?' asked the mother, not immediately after the interview, but when the evening came.

'Oh yes,—how should one not like him?'

'How indeed! He is the finest, noblest youth that ever my eyes rested on, and so like the Lovels.'

'Was my father like that?'

'Yes indeed, in the shape of his face, and the tone of his voice, and the movement of his eyes; though the sweetness of the countenance was all gone in the Devil's training to which he had submitted himself. And you too are like him, though darker, and with something of the Murrays' greater breadth of face. But I can remember portraits at Lovel Grange,—every one of them,—and all of them were alike. There never was a Lovel but had that natural grace of appearance. You will gaze at those portraits, dear, oftener even than I have done; and you will be happy where I was,—oh—so miserable!'

'I shall never see them, mamma.'

'Why not?'

'I do not want to see them.'

'You say you like him?'

'Yes; I like him.'

'And why should you not love him well enough to make him your husband?'

'I am not fit to be his wife.'

'You are fit;—none could be fitter; none others so fit. You are as well born as he, and you have the wealth which he wants. You must have it, if, as you tell me, he says that he will cease to claim it as his own. There can be no question of fitness.'

'Money will not make a girl fit, mamma.'

'You have been brought up as a lady,—and are a lady. I swear I do not know what you mean. If he thinks you fit, and you can like him, —as you say you do,—what more can be wanted? Does he not wish it?'

'I do not know. He said he did not, and then,
—I think he said he did.'

'Is that it?'

'No, mamma. It is not that; not that only.
It is too late!'

'Too late! How too late? Anna, you must
tell me what you mean. I insist upon it that
you tell me what you mean. Why is it too late?'
But Lady Anna was not prepared to tell her
meaning. She had certainly not intended to
say anything to her mother of her solemn
promise to Daniel Thwaite. It had been
arranged between him and her that nothing
was to be said of it till this law business should
be all over. He had sworn to her that to him
it made no difference, whether she should be
proclaimed to be the Lady Anna, the undoubted
owner of thousands a year, or Anna Murray,
the illegitimate daughter of the late Earl's mistress, a girl without a penny, and a nobody in
the world's esteem. No doubt they must shape
their life very differently in this event or in
that. How he might demean himself should
this fortune be adjudged to the Earl, as he
thought would be the case when he first made
the girl promise to be his wife, he knew well
enough. He would do as his father had done
before him, and, he did not doubt,—with better
result. What might be his fate should the wealth
of the Lovels become the wealth of his intended
wife, he did not yet quite foreshadow to himself.
How he should face and fight the world when
he came to be accused of having plotted to get
all this wealth for himself he did not know.
He had dreams of distributing the greater part

among the Lovels and the Countess, and taking himself and his wife with one-third of it to some new country in which they would not in derision call his wife the Lady Anna, and in which he would be as good a man as any earl. But let all that be as it might, the girl was to keep her secret till the thing should be settled. Now, in these latter days, it had come to be believed by him, as by nearly everybody else, that the thing was well-nigh settled. The Solicitor-General had thrown up the sponge. So said the bystanders. And now there was beginning to be a rumour that everything was to be set right by a family marriage. The Solicitor-General would not have thrown up the sponge,—so said they who knew him best,—without seeing a reason for doing so. Serjeant Bluestone was still indignant, and Mr. Hardy was silent and moody. But the world at large were beginning to observe that in this, as in all difficult cases, the Solicitor-General tempered the innocence of the dove with the wisdom of the serpent. In the meantime Lady Anna by no means intended to allow the secret to pass her lips. Whether she ever could tell her mother, she doubted; but she certainly would not do so an hour too soon. 'Why is it too late?' demanded the Countess, repeating her question with stern severity of voice.

'I mean that I have not lived all my life as his wife should live.'

'Trash! It is trash. What has there been in your life to disgrace you? We have been poor and we have lived as poor people do live. We have not been disgraced.'

'No, mamma.'

'I will not hear such nonsense. It is a re-proach to me.'

'Oh, mamma, do not say that. I know how good you have been,—how you have thought of me in every thing. Pray do not say that I reproach you!' And she came and knelt at her mother's lap.

'I will not, darling; but do not vex me by saying that you are unfit. There is nothing else, dearest?'

'No, mamma,' she said in a low tone, pausing before she told the falsehood.

'I think it will be arranged that you shall go down to Yoxham. The people there even are beginning to know that we are right, and are willing to acknowledge us. The Earl, whom I cannot but love already for his gracious good-ness, has himself declared that he will not carry on the suit. Mr. Goffe has told me that they are anxious to see you there. Of course you must go,—and will go as Lady Anna Lovel. Mr. Goffe says that some money can now be allowed from the estate, and you shall go as becomes the daughter of Earl Lovel when visit-ing among her cousins. You will see this young man there. If he means to love you and to be true to you, he will be much there. I do not doubt but that you will continue to like him. And remember this, Anna;—that even though your name be acknowledged,—even though all the wealth be adjudged to be your own,—even though some judge on the bench shall say that I am the widowed Countess Lovel, it may be all undone some day,—unless you become this young man's wife. That woman in Italy may be bolstered up at last, if you refuse him. But when you are once the wife of young Lord Lovel, no one then can harm us. There can be no going back after that.' This the Countess said rather to promote the marriage, than from any fear of the consequences which she described. Daniel Thwaite was the enemy that now she dreaded, and not the Italian woman, or the Lovel family.

Lady Anna could only say that she would go to Yoxham, if she were invited there by Mrs. Lovel.

CHAPTER XII

Have they Surrendered?

As all the world heard of what was going on, so did Daniel Thwaite hear it among others. He was a hard-working, conscientious, moody man, given much to silence among his fellow workmen;—one to whom life was serious enough; not a happy man, though he had before him a prospect of prosperity which would make most men happy. But he was essentially a tender-hearted, affectionate man, who could make a sacrifice of himself if he thought it needed for the happiness of one he loved. When he heard of this proposed marriage, he asked himself many questions as to his duty and as to the welfare of the girl. He did love her with all his heart, and he believed thoroughly in her affection for himself. He had, as yet, no sufficient reason to doubt that she would be true to him;—but he knew well that an earl's coronet must be tempting to a girl so circumstanced as was Lady Anna. There were moments in which he thought that it was almost his duty to give her up, and bid her go and live among those of her own rank. But then he did not believe in rank. He utterly disbelieved in it; and in his heart of hearts he felt that he would make a better and a fitter husband to this girl than would an earl, with all an earl's temptation to vice. He was ever thinking of some better world to which he might take her, which had not been contaminated by empty names and an impudent assumption of hereditary, and therefore false, dignity. As regarded the money, it would be hers whether she married him or the Earl. And if she loved him, as she had sworn that she did, why should he be false to her? Or why, as yet, should he think that she would prefer an empty, gilded lordling to the friend who had been her friend as far back as her memory could carry her? If she asked to be released, then indeed he would release her,— but not without explaining to her, with such eloquence as he might be able to use,—what it was she proposed to abandon, and what to take in place of that which she lost. He was a man, silent and under self-control, but self-confident also; and he did believe himself to be a better man than young Earl Lovel.

In making this resolution,—that he would give her back her troth if she asked for it, but not without expressing to her his thoughts as he did so,—he ignored the masterfulness of his own character. There are men who exercise dominion, from the nature of their disposition, and who do so from their youth upwards, without knowing, till advanced life comes upon them, that any power of dominion belongs to them. Men are persuasive, and imperious withal, who are unconscious that they use burning words to others, whose words to them are never even warm. So it was with this man when he spoke to himself in his solitude of his purpose of resigning the titled heiress. To the arguments, the entreaties, or the threats of others he would pay no heed. The Countess might bluster about her rank, and he would heed her not at all.

He cared nothing for the whole tribe of Lovels. If Lady Anna asked for release, she should be released. But not till she had heard his words. How scalding these words might be, how powerful to prevent the girl from really choosing her own fate, he did not know himself.

Though he lived in the same house with her he seldom saw her,—unless when he would knock at the door of an evening, and say a few words to her mother rather than to her. Since Thomas Thwaite had left London for the last time the Countess had become almost cold to the young man. She would not have been so if she could have helped it; but she had begun to fear him, and she could not bring herself to be cordial to him either in word or manner. He perceived it at once, and became, himself, cold and constrained.

Once, and once only, he met Lady Anna alone, after his father's departure, and before her interview with Lord Lovel. Then he met her on the stairs of the house while her mother was absent at the lawyer's chambers.

'Are you here, Daniel, at this hour?' she asked, going back to the sitting-room, whither he followed her.

'I wanted to see you, and I knew that your mother would be out. It is not often that I do a thing in secret, even though it be to see the girl that I love.'

'No, indeed. I do not see you often now.'

'Does that matter much to you, Lady Anna?'

'Lady Anna!'

'I have been instructed, you know, that I am to call you so.'

'Not by me, Daniel.'

'No;—not by you; not as yet. Your mother's manners are much altered to me. Is it not so?'

'How can I tell? Mine are not.'

'It is no question of manners, sweetheart, between you and me. It has not come to that, I hope. Do you wish for any change,—as regards me?'

'Oh, no.'

'As to my love, there can be no change in that. If it suits your mother to be disdainful to me, I can bear it. I always thought that it would come to be so some day.'

There was but little more said then. He asked her no further question;—none at least that it was difficult for her to answer,—and he soon took his leave. He was a passionate rather than a tender lover, and having once held her in his arms, and kissed her lips, and demanded from her a return of his caress, he was patient now to wait till he could claim them as his own. But, two days after the interview between Lord Lovel and his love, he a second time contrived to find her alone.

'I have come again,' he said, 'because I knew your mother is out. I would not trouble you with secret meetings but that just now I have much to say to you. And then, you may be gone from hence before I had even heard that you were going.'

'I am always glad to see you, Daniel.'

'Are you, my sweetheart? Is that true?'

'Indeed, indeed it is.'

'I should be a traitor to doubt you,—and

I do not doubt. I will never doubt you if you tell me that you love me.'

'You know I love you.'

'Tell me, Anna—; or shall I say Lady Anna?'

'Lady Anna,—if you wish to scorn me.'

'Then never will I call you so, till it shall come to pass that I do wish to scorn you. But tell me. Is it true that Earl Lovel was with you the other day?'

'He was here the day before yesterday.'

'And why did he come?'

'Why?'

'Why did he come? you know that as far as I have yet heard he is still your mother's enemy and yours, and is persecuting you to rob you of your name and of your property. Did ne come as a friend?'

'Oh, yes! certainly as a friend.'

'But he still makes his claim.'

'No;—he says that he will make it no longer, that he acknowledges mamma as my father's widow, and me as my father's heir.'

'That is generous,—if that is all.'

'Very generous.'

'And he does this without condition? There is nothing to be given to him to pay him for this surrender?'

'There is nothing to give,' she said, in that low, sweet, melancholy voice which was common to her always when she spoke of herself.

'You do not mean to deceive me, dear, I know; but there is a something to be given; and I am told that he has asked for it, or certainly will ask. And, indeed, I do not think that an earl, noble, but poverty-stricken, would surrender everything without making some counter claim which would lead him by another path to all that he has been seeking. Anna, you know what I mean.'

'Yes, I know.'

'Has he made no such claim?'

'I cannot tell.'

'You cannot tell whether or no he has asked you to be his wife?'

'No; I cannot tell. Do not look at me like that, Daniel. He came here, and mamma left us together, and he was kind to me. Oh! so kind. He said that he would be a cousin to me, and a brother.'

'A brother!'

'That was what he said.'

'And he meant nothing more than that,— simply to be your brother?'

'I think he did mean more. I think he meant that he would try to love me so that he might be my husband.'

'And what said you to that?'

'I told him that it could not be so.'

'And then?'

'Why then again he said that we were cousins; that I had no nearer cousin anywhere, and that he would be good to me and help me, and that the lawsuit should not go on. Oh, Daniel, he was so good!'

'Was that all?'

'He kissed me, saying that cousins might kiss.'

'No, Anna;—cousins such as you and he may not kiss. Do you hear me?'

'Yes, I hear you.'

'If you mean to be true to me, there must be

no more of that. Do you not know that all this
means that he is to win you to be his wife? Did
he not come to you with that object?'

'I think he did, Daniel.'

'I think so too, my dear. Surrender! I'll
tell you what that surrender means. They
perceive at last that they have not a shadow of
justice, or even a shadow of a chance of unjust
success in their claim. That with all their command of money, which is to be spent, however,
out of your property, they can do nothing;
that their false witnesses will not come to aid
them; that they have not another inch of ground
on which to stand. Their great lawyer, Sir
William Patterson, dares not show himself in
court with a case so false and fraudulent. At
last your mother's rights and yours are to be
owned. Then they turn themselves about, and
think in what other way the prize may be won.
It is not likely that such a prize should be surrendered by a noble lord. The young man is
made to understand that he cannot have it all
without a burden, and that he must combine
his wealth with you. That is it, and at once he
comes to you, asking you to be his wife, so that
in that way he may lay his hands on the wealth
of which he has striven to rob you.'

'Daniel, I do not think that he is like that!'

'I tell you he is not only like it,—but that
itself. Is it not clear as noon-day? He comes
here to talk of love who had never seen you
before. Is it thus that men love?'

'But, Daniel, he did not talk so.'

'I wonder that he was so crafty, believing
him as I do to be a fool. He talked of cousinship

and brotherhood, and yet gave you to know that he meant you to be his wife. Was it not so?'

'I think it was so, in very truth.'

'Of course it was so. Do brothers marry their sisters? Were it not for the money, which must be yours, and which he is kind enough to surrender, would he come to you then with his brotherhood, and his cousinship, and his mock love? Tell me that, my lady! Can it be real love,—to which there has been no forerunning acquaintance?'

'I think not, indeed.'

'And must it not be lust of wealth? That may come by hearsay well enough. It is a love which requires no great foreknowledge to burn with real strength. He is a gay looking lad, no doubt.'

'I do not know as to gay, but he is beautiful.'

'Like enough, my girl; with soft hands, and curled hair, and a sweet smell, and a bright colour, and a false heart. I have never seen the lad; but for the false heart I can answer.'

'I do not think that he is false.'

'Not false! and yet he comes to you asking you to be his wife, just at that nick of time in which he finds that you,—the right owner,— are to have the fortune of which he has vainly endeavoured to defraud you! Is it not so?'

'He cannot be wrong to wish to keep up the glory of the family.'

'The glory of the family;—yes, the fame of the late lord, who lived as though he were a fiend let loose from hell to devastate mankind. The glory of the family! And how will he maintain it? At racecourses, in betting-clubs, among loose women, with luscious wines, never doing one stroke of work for man or God, consuming and never producing, either idle altogether or working the work of the devil. That will be the glory of the family. Anna Lovel, you shall give him his choice.' Then he took her hand in his. 'Ask him whether he will have that empty, or take all the wealth of the Lovels. You have my leave.'

'And if he took the empty hand what should I do?' she asked.

'My brave girl, no; though the chance be but one in a thousand against me, I would not run the risk. But I am putting it to yourself, to your reason, to judge of his motives. Can it be that his mind in this matter is not sordid and dishonest? As to you, the choice is open to you.'

'No, Daniel; it is open no longer.'

'The choice is open to you. If you will tell me that your heart is so set upon being the bride of a lord, that truth and honesty and love, and all decent feeling from woman to man can be thrown to the wind, to make way for such an ambition,—I will say not a word against it. You are free.'

'Have I asked for freedom?'

'No, indeed! Had you done so, I should have made all this much shorter.'

'Then why do you harass me by saying it?'

'Because it is my duty. Can I know that he comes here seeking you for his wife; can I hear it said on all sides that this family feud is to be settled by a happy family marriage; can I find that you yourself are willing to love him as a cousin or a brother,—without finding myself compelled to speak? There are two men seeking you as their wife. One can make you a countess; the other simply an honest man's wife, and, so far as that can be low, lower than that title of your own which they will not allow you to put before your name. If I am still your choice, give me your hand.' Of course she gave it him. 'So be it; and now I shall fear nothing.' Then she told him that it was intended that she should go to Yoxham as a visitor; but still he declared that he would fear nothing.

Early on the next morning he called on Mr. Goffe, the attorney, with the object of making some inquiry as to the condition of the lawsuit. Mr. Goffe did not much love the elder tailor, but he specially disliked the younger. He was not able to be altogether uncivil to them, because he knew all that they had done to succour his client; but he avoided them when it was possible, and was chary of giving them information. On this occasion Daniel asked whether it was true that the other side had abandoned their claim.

'Really Mr. Thwaite, I cannot say that they have,' said Mr. Goffe.

'Can you say that they have not?'

'No, nor that either.'

'Had anything of that kind been decided, I suppose you would have known it, Mr. Goffe?'

'Really, sir, I cannot say. There are questions, Mr. Thwaite, which a professional gentleman cannot answer, even to such friends as you and your father have been. When any real settlement is to be made, the Countess Lovel will, as a matter of course, be informed.'

'She should be informed at once,' said Daniel Thwaite sternly: 'and so should they who have been concerned with her in this matter.'

'You, I know, have heavy claims on the Countess.'

'My father has claims, which will never vex her, whether paid or not paid; but it is right that he should know the truth. I do not believe that the Countess herself knows, though she has been led to think that the claim has been surrendered.'

Mr. Goffe was very sorry, but really he had nothing further to tell.

CHAPTER XIII

New Friends

THE introduction to Yoxham followed quickly upon the Earl's visit to Wyndham Street. There was a great consultation at the rectory before a decision could be made as to the manner in which the invitation should be given. The Earl thought that it should be sent to the mother. The rector combated this view very strongly, still hoping that though he might be driven to call the girl Lady Anna, he might postpone the necessity of acknowledging the countess-ship of the mother till the marriage should have been definitely acknowledged. Mrs. Lovel thought that if the girl were Lady Anna, then the mother must be the Countess Lovel, and that it would be as well to be hung for a sheep as a lamb. But the wisdom of Aunt Julia sided with her brother, though she did not share her brother's feelings of animosity to the two women. 'It is understood that the girl is to be invited, and not the mother,' said Miss Lovel; 'and as it is quite possible that the thing should fail,— in which case the lawsuit might possibly go on, —the less we acknowledge the better.' The Earl declared that the lawsuit couldn't go on, —that he would not carry it on. 'My dear Frederic, you are not the only person concerned. The lady in Italy, who still calls herself Countess Lovel, may renew the suit on her own behalf as soon as you have abandoned it. Should she succeed, you would have to make what best compromise you could with her respecting the property. That is the way I understand it.' This exposition of the case by Miss Lovel was so clear that it carried the day, and accordingly a letter was written by Mrs. Lovel, addressed to Lady Anna Lovel, asking her to come and spend a few days at Yoxham. She could bring her maid with her or not as she liked; but she could have the service of Mrs. Lovel's lady's-maid if she chose to come unattended. The letter sounded cold when it was read, but the writer signed herself, 'Yours affectionately, Jane Lovel.' It was addressed to 'The Lady Anna Lovel, to the care of Messrs. Goffe and Goffe, solicitors, Raymond's Buildings, Gray's Inn.'

Lady Anna was allowed to read it first; but she read it in the presence of her mother, to whom she handed it at once, as a matter of course. A black frown came across the Countess's brow, and a look of displeasure, almost of anger, rested on her countenance. 'Is it wrong, mamma?' asked the girl.

'It is a part of the whole;—but, my dear, it shall not signify. Conquerors cannot be conquerors all at once, nor can the vanquished be expected to submit themselves with a grace. But it will come. And though they should ignore me utterly, that will be as nothing. I have not clung to this for years past to win their loves.'

'I will not go, mamma, if they are unkind to you.'

'You must go, my dear. It is only that they are weak enough to think that they can acknowledge you, and yet continue to deny to me my rights. But it matters nothing. Of course you

shall go,—and you shall go as the daughter of
the Countess Lovel.'

That mention of the lady's-maid had been
unfortunate. Mrs. Lovel had simply desired to
make it easy for the young lady to come without
a servant to wait upon her, and had treated her
husband's far-away cousin as elder ladies often
do treat those who are younger when the question of the maid may become a difficulty. But
the Countess, who would hardly herself have
thought of it, now declared that her girl should
go attended as her rank demanded. Lady Anna,
therefore, under her mother's dictation, wrote
the following reply:—

'Wyndham Street, 3rd August, 183–.
'DEAR MRS. LOVEL,

'I shall be happy to accept your kind invitation to Yoxham, but can hardly do so before
the 10th. On that day I will leave London for
York inside the mail-coach. Perhaps you can
be kind enough to have me met where the
coach stops. As you are so good as to say you
can take her in, I will bring my own maid.

'Yours affectionately,
'ANNA LOVEL.'

'But, mamma, I don't want a maid,' said the
girl, who had never been waited on in her life,
and who had more often than not made her
mother's bed and her own till they had come
up to London.

'Nevertheless you shall take one. You will
have to make other changes besides that; and
the sooner that you begin to make them the
easier they will be to you.'

F

Then at once the Countess made a pilgrimage
to Mr. Goffe in search of funds wherewith to
equip her girl properly for her new associations.
She was to go, as Lady Anna Lovel, to stay with
Mrs. Lovel and Miss Lovel and the little Lovels.
And she was to go as one who was to be the
chosen bride of Earl Lovel. Of course she must
be duly caparisoned. Mr. Goffe made difficulties,—as lawyers always do,—but the needful
money was at last forthcoming. Representa-
tions had been made in high legal quarters,—
to the custodians for the moment of the property
which was to go to the established heir of the
late Earl. They had been made conjointly by
Goffe and Goffe, and Norton and Flick, and the
money was forthcoming. Mr. Goffe suggested
that a great deal could not be wanted all at once
for the young lady's dress. The Countess smiled
as she answered, 'You hardly know, Mr. Goffe,
the straits to which we have been reduced. If
I tell you that this dress which I have on is the
only one in which I can fitly appear even in
your chambers, perhaps you will think that I
demean myself.' Mr. Goffe was touched, and
signed a sufficient cheque. They were going to
succeed, and then everything would be easy.
Even if they did not succeed, he could get it
passed in the accounts. And if not that——
well, he had run greater risks than this for clients
whose causes were of much less interest than
this of the Countess and her daughter.

The Countess had mentioned her own gown,
and had spoken strict truth in what she had
said of it;—but not a shilling of Mr. Goffe's
money went to the establishment of a wardrobe

for herself. That her daughter should go down
to Yoxham Rectory in a manner befitting the
daughter of Earl Lovel was at this moment her
chief object. Things were purchased by which
the poor girl, unaccustomed to such finery, was
astounded and almost stupefied. Two needle-
women were taken in at the lodgings in Wyndham Street; parcels from Swan and Edgar's,—
Marshall and Snellgrove* were not then, or at
least had not loomed to the grandeur of an
entire block of houses,—addressed to Lady Anna
Lovel, were frequent at the door, somewhat to
the disgust of the shopmen, who did not like to
send goods to Lady Anna Lovel in Wyndham
Street. But ready money was paid, and the
parcels came home. Lady Anna, poor girl, was
dismayed much by the parcels, but she was at
her wits' end when the lady's-maid came,—a
young lady, herself so sweetly attired that Lady
Anna would have envied her in the old Cumberland days. 'I shall not know what to say to her,
mamma,' said Lady Anna.

'It will all come in two days, if you will only
be equal to the occasion,' said the Countess,
who in providing her child with this expensive
adjunct, had made some calculation that the
more her daughter was made to feel the luxuries
of aristocratic life, the less prone would she be
to adapt herself to the roughnesses of Daniel
Thwaite the tailor.

The Countess put her daughter into the mail-
coach, and gave her much parting advice. 'Hold
up your head when you are with them. That is
all that you have to do. Among them all your
blood will be the best.' This theory of blood

was one of which Lady Anna had never been
able even to realise the meaning. 'And remember this too;—that you are in truth the most
wealthy. It is they that should honour you. Of
course you will be courteous and gentle with
them,—it is your nature; but do not for a moment
allow yourself to be conscious that you are their
inferior.' Lady Anna,—who could think but
little of her birth,—to whom it had been throughout her life a thing plaguesome rather than
profitable,—could remember only what she had
been in Cumberland, and her binding obligation to the tailor's son. She could remember
but that and the unutterable sweetness of the
young man who had once appeared before her,
—to whom she knew that she must be inferior.
'Hold up your head among them, and claim
your own always,' said the Countess.

The rectory carriage was waiting for her at
the inn yard in York, and in it was Miss Lovel.
When the hour had come it was thought better
that the wise woman of the family should go
than any other. For the ladies of Yoxham were
quite as anxious as to the Lady Anna as was she
in respect of them. What sort of a girl was this
that they were to welcome among them as the
Lady Anna,—who had lived all her life with
tailors, and with a mother of whom up to quite
a late date they had thought all manner of evil?
The young lord had reported well of her, saying
that she was not only beautiful, but feminine,
of soft modest manners, and in all respects like a
lady. The Earl, however, was but a young man,
likely to be taken by mere beauty; and it might
be that the girl had been clever enough to hood-

wink him. So much evil had been believed that a report stating that all was good could not be accepted at once as true. Miss Lovel would be sure to find out, even in the space of an hour's drive, and Miss Lovel went to meet her. She did not leave the carriage, but sent the footman to help Lady Anna Lovel from the coach. 'My dear,' said Miss Lovel, 'I am very glad to see you. Oh, you have brought a maid! We didn't think you would. There is a seat behind which she can occupy.'

'Mamma thought it best. I hope it is not wrong, Mrs. Lovel.'

'I ought to have introduced myself. I am Miss Lovel, and the rector of Yoxham is my brother. It does not signify about the maid in the least. We can do very well with her. I suppose she has been with you a long time.'

'No, indeed;—she only came the day before yesterday.' And so Miss Lovel learned the whole story of the lady's-maid.

Lady Anna said very little, but Miss Lovel explained a good many things during the journey. The young lord was not at Yoxham. He was with a friend in Scotland, but would be home about the 20th. The two boys were at home for the holidays, but would go back to school in a fortnight. Minnie Lovel, the daughter, had a governess. The rectory, for a parsonage, was a tolerably large house, and convenient. It had been Lord Lovel's early home, but at present he was not much there. 'He thinks it right to go to Lovel Grange during a part of the autumn. I suppose you have seen Lovel Grange.'

'Never.'

'Oh, indeed. But you lived near it;—did you not?'

'No, not near;—about fifteen miles, I think. I was born there, but have never been there since I was a baby.'

'Oh!—you were born there. Of course you know that it is Lord Lovel's seat now. I do not know that he likes it, though the scenery is magnificent. But a landlord has to live, at least for some period of the year, upon his property. You saw my nephew.'

'Yes; he came to us once.'

'I hope you liked him. We think him very nice. But then he is almost the same as a son here. Do you care about visiting the poor?'

'I have never tried,' said Lady Anna.

'Oh dear!'

'We have been so poor ourselves;—we were just one of them.' Then Miss Lovel perceived that she had made a mistake. But she was generous enough to recognize the unaffected simplicity of the girl, and almost began to think well of her.

'I hope you will come round the parish with us. We shall be very glad. Yoxham is a large parish, with scattered hamlets, and there is plenty to do. The manufactories are creeping up to us, and we have already a large mill at Yoxham Lock. My brother has to keep two curates now. Here we are, my dear, and I hope we shall be able to make you happy.'

Mrs. Lovel did not like the maid, and Mr. Lovel did not like it at all. 'And yet we heard when we were up in town that they literally had not anything to live on,' said the parson. 'I hope that, after all, we may not be making fools of ourselves.' But there was no help for it, and the maid was of course taken in.

The children had been instructed to call their cousin Lady Anna,—unless they heard their mother drop the title, and then they were to drop it also. They were not so young but what they had all heard the indiscreet vigour with which their father had ridiculed the claim to the title, and had been something at a loss to know whence the change had come. 'Perhaps they are as they call themselves,' the rector had said, 'and, if so, heaven forbid that we should not give them their due.' After this the three young ones, discussing the matter among themselves, had made up their minds that Lady Anna was no cousin of theirs,—but 'a humbug.' When, however, they saw her their hearts relented, and the girl became soft, and the boys became civil. 'Papa,' said Minnie Lovel, on the second day, 'I hope she is our cousin.'

'I hope so too, my dear.'

'I think she is. She looks as if she ought to be because she is so pretty.'

'Being pretty, my dear, is not enough. You should love people because they are good.'

'But I would not like all the good people to be my cousins;—would you, papa? Old widow Grimes is a very good old woman; but I don't want to have her for a cousin.'

'My dear, you are talking about what you don't understand.'

But Minnie did in truth understand the matter better than her father. Before three or four days

had passed she knew that their guest was lovable,
—whether cousin or no cousin; and she knew
also that the newcomer was of such nature and
breeding as made her fit to be a cousin. All the
family had as yet called her Lady Anna, but
Minnie thought that the time had come in
which she might break through the law. 'I
think I should like to call you just Anna, if you
will let me,' she said. They two were in the
guest's bedroom, and Minnie was leaning against
her new friend's shoulder.

'Oh, I do so wish you would. I do so hate to
be called Lady.'

'But you are Lady Anna,—arn't you?'

'And you are Miss Mary Lovel, but you
wouldn't like everybody in the house to call
you so. And then there has been so much said
about it all my life, that it makes me quite
unhappy. I do so wish your mamma wouldn't
call me Lady Anna.' Whereupon Minnie very
demurely explained that she could not answer
for her mamma, but that she would always call
her friend Anna,—when papa wasn't by.

But Minnie was better than her promise.
'Mamma,' she said the next day, 'do you know
that she hates to be called Lady Anna?'

'What makes you think so?'

'I am sure of it. She told me so. Everybody
has always been talking about it ever since she
was born, and she says she is so sick of it.'

'But, my dear, people must be called by their
names. If it is her proper name she ought not
to hate it. I can understand that people should
hate an assumed name.'

'I am Miss Mary Lovel, but I should not at all

like it if everybody called me Miss Mary. The
servants call me Miss Mary, but if papa and Aunt
Julia did so, I should think they were scolding
me.'

'But Lady Anna is not papa's daughter.'

'She is his cousin. Isn't she his cousin, mamma?
I don't think people ought to call their cousins
Lady Anna. I have promised that I won't.
Cousin Frederic said that she was his cousin.
What will he call her?'

'I cannot tell, my dear. We shall all know her
better by that time.' Mrs. Lovel, however, followed her daughter's lead, and from that time
the poor girl was Anna to all of them,—except
to the rector. He listened, and thought that he
would try it; but his heart failed him. He would
have preferred that she should be an impostor,
were that still possible. He would so much
have preferred that she should not exist at
all! He did not care for her beauty. He did
not feel the charm of her simplicity. It was one
of the hardships of the world that he should be
forced to have her there in his rectory. The
Lovel wealth was indispensable to the true heir
of the Lovels, and on behalf of his nephew and
his family he had been induced to consent; but
he could not love the interloper. He still dreamed
of coming surprises that would set the matter
right in a manner that would be much preferable
to a marriage. The girl might be innocent,—
as his wife and sister told him; but he was sure
that the mother was an intriguing woman. It
would be such a pity that they should have
entertained the girl if,—after all,—the woman
should at last be but a pseudo-countess!

As others had ceased to call her Lady Anna, he could not continue to do so; but he managed to live on with her without calling her by any name.

In the meantime Cousin Anna went about among the poor with Minnie and Aunt Julia, and won golden opinions. She was soft, feminine, almost humble,—but still with a dash of humour in her, when she was sufficiently at her ease with them to be happy. There was very much in the life which she thoroughly enjoyed. The green fields, and the air which was so pleasant to her after the close heat of the narrow London streets, and the bright parsonage garden, and the pleasant services of the country church,—and doubtless also the luxuries of a rich, well-ordered household. Those calculations of her mother had not been made without a true basis. The softness, the niceness, the ease, the grace of the people around her, won upon her day by day, and hour by hour. The pleasant idleness of the drawing-room, with its books and music, and unstrained chatter of family voices, grew upon her as so many new charms. To come down with bright ribbons and clean unruffled muslin to breakfast, with nothing to do which need ruffle them unbecomingly, and then to dress for dinner with silk and gauds, before ten days were over, had made life beautiful to her. She seemed to live among roses and perfumes. There was no stern hardness in the life, as there had of necessity been in that which she had ever lived with her mother. The caresses of Minnie Lovel soothed and warmed her heart;—and every now and again, when the eyes of Aunt Julia were not upon her, she was tempted to romp with the boys. Oh! that they had really been her brothers!

But in the midst of all there was ever present to her the prospect of some coming wretchedness. The life which she was leading could not be her life. That Earl was coming,—that young Apollo, —and he would again ask her to be his wife. She knew that she could not be his wife. She was there, as she understood well, that she might give all this wealth that was to be hers to the Lovel family; and when she refused to give herself,—as the only way in which that wealth could be conveyed,—they would turn her out from their pleasant home. Then she must go back to the other life, and be the wife of Daniel Thwaite; and soft things must be at an end with her.

CHAPTER XIV

The Earl arrives

AT the end of a fortnight the boys had gone back to school, and Lord Lovel was to reach the rectory in time for dinner that evening. There was a little stir throughout the rectory, as an earl is an earl though he be in his uncle's house, and rank will sway even aunts and cousins. The parson at present was a much richer man than the peer;—but the peer was at the head of all the Lovels, and then it was expected that his poverty would quickly be made to disappear. All that Lovel money which had been invested in bank shares, Indian railways, Russian funds, Devon consols,* and coal mines, was to become his,—if not in one way, then in another. The Earl was to be a topping* man, and the rectory cook was ordered to do her best. The big bedroom had been made ready, and the parson looked at his '99 port and his '16 Margaux.* In those days men drank port, and champagne at country houses was not yet a necessity.* To give the rector of Yoxham his due it must be said of him that he would have done his very best for the head of his family had there been no large fortune within the young lord's grasp. The Lovels had ever been true to the Lovels, with the exception of that late wretched Earl, —the Lady Anna's father.

But if the rector and his wife were alive to the importance of the expected arrival, what must have been the state of Lady Anna! They

had met but once before, and during that meeting
they had been alone together. There had grown
up, she knew not how, during those few minutes,
a heavenly sweetness between them. He had
talked to her with a voice that had been to her
ears as the voice of a god,—it had been so
sweet and full of music! He had caressed her,—
but with a caress so gentle and pure that it had
been to her void of all taint of evil. It had per-
plexed her for a moment,—but had left no sense
of wrong behind it. He had told her that he
loved her,—that he would love her dearly; but
had not scared her in so telling her, though she
knew she could never give him back such love as
that of which he spoke to her. There had been a
charm in it, of which she delighted to dream,—
fancying that she could remember it for ever,
as a green island in her life; but could so best
remember it if she were assured that she should
never see him more. But now she was to see
him again, and the charm must be renewed,—
or else the dream dispelled for ever. Alas! it
must be the latter. She knew that the charm
must be dispelled.

But there was a doubt on her own mind
whether it would not be dispelled without any
effort on her part. It would vanish at once if
he were to greet her as the Lovels had greeted
her on her first coming. She could partly understand that the manner of their meeting in London
had thrust upon him a necessity for flattering
tenderness with which he might well dispense
when he met her among his family. Had he
really loved her,—had he meant to love her,—
he would hardly have been absent so long after

her coming. She had been glad that he had been absent,—so she assured herself,—because there could never be any love between them. Daniel Thwaite had told her that the brotherly love which had been offered was false love,—must be false,—was no love at all. Do brothers marry sisters; and had not this man already told her that he wished to make her his wife? And then there must never be another kiss. Daniel Thwaite had told her that; and he was, not only her lover, but her master also. This was the rule by which she would certainly hold. She would be true to Daniel Thwaite. And yet she looked for the lord's coming, as one looks for the rising of the sun of an early morning,—watching for that which shall make all the day beautiful.

And he came. The rector and his wife, and Aunt Julia and Minnie, all went out into the hall to meet him, and Anna was left alone in the library, where they were wont to congregate before dinner. It was already past seven, and every one was dressed. A quarter of an hour was to be allowed to the lord, and he was to be hurried up at once to his bedroom. She would not see him till he came down ready, and all hurried, to lead his aunt to the dining-room. She heard the scuffle in the hall. There were kisses;—and a big kiss from Minnie to her much-prized Cousin Fred; and a loud welcome from the full-mouthed rector. 'And where is Anna?' —the lord asked. They were the first words he spoke, and she heard them, ah! so plainly. It was the same voice,—sweet, genial, and manly; sweet to her beyond all sweetness that she could conceive.

'You shall see her when you come down from dressing,' said Mrs. Lovel,—in a low voice, but still audible to the solitary girl.

'I will see her before I go up to dress,' said the lord, walking through them, and in through the open door to the library. 'So, here you are. I am so glad to see you! I had sworn to go into Scotland before the time was fixed for your coming,—before I had met you,—and I could not escape. Have you thought ill of me because I have not been here to welcome you sooner?'

'No,—my lord.'

'There are horrible penalties for anybody who calls me lord in this house;—are there not, Aunt Jane? But I see my uncle wants his dinner.'

'I'll take you upstairs, Fred,' said Minnie, who was still holding her cousin's hand.

'I am coming. I will only say that I would sooner see you here than in any house in England.'

Then he went, and during the few minutes that he spent in dressing little or nothing was spoken in the library. The parson in his heart was not pleased by the enthusiasm with which the young man greeted this new cousin; and yet, why should he not be enthusiastic if it was intended that they should be man and wife?

'Now, Lady Anna,' said the rector, as he offered her his arm to lead her out to dinner. It was but a mild corrective to the warmth of his nephew. The lord lingered a moment with his aunt in the library.

'Have you not got beyond that with her yet?' he asked.

'Your uncle is more old fashioned than you

are, Fred. Things did not go so quick when he was young.'

In the evening he came and lounged on a double-seated ottoman behind her, and she soon found herself answering a string of questions. Had she been happy at Yoxham? Did she like the place? What had she been doing? 'Then you know Mrs. Grimes already?' She laughed as she said that she did know Mrs. Grimes. 'The lion of Yoxham is Mrs. Grimes. She is supposed to have all the misfortunes and all the virtues to which humanity is subject. And how do you and Minnie get on? Minnie is my prime minister. The boys, I suppose, teased you out of your life?'

'I did like them so much! I never knew a boy till I saw them, Lord Lovel.'

'They take care to make themselves known, at any rate. But they are nice, good-humoured lads,—taking after their mother. Don't tell their father I said so. Do you think it pretty about here?'

'Beautifully pretty.'

'Just about Yoxham,—because there is so much wood. But this is not the beautiful part of York-shire, you know. I wonder whether we could make an expedition to Wharfedale and Bolton Abbey.* You would say that the Wharfe was pretty. We'll try and plan it. We should have to sleep out one night; but that would make it all the jollier. There isn't a better inn in England than the Devonshire Arms;—and I don't think a pleasanter spot. Aunt Jane,— couldn't we go for one night to Bolton Abbey?'

'It is very far, Frederic.'

'Thirty miles or so;—that ought to be nothing in Yorkshire. We'll manage it. We could get post-horses from York, and the carriage would take us all. My uncle, you must know, is very chary about the carriage horses, thinking that the corn of idleness,*—which is destructive to young men and women,—is very good for cattle. But we'll manage it, and you shall jump over the Stryd.' Then he told her the story how the youth was drowned—and how the monks moaned; and he got away to other legends, to the white doe of Rylston,* and Landseer's picture of the abbey in olden times.* She had heard nothing before of these things,—or indeed of such things, and the hearing them was very sweet to her. The parson, who was still displeased, went to sleep. Minnie had been sent to bed, and Aunt Julia and Aunt Jane every now and again put in a word. It was resolved before the evening was over that the visit should be made to Bolton Abbey. Of course, their nephew ought to have opportunities of making love to the girl he was doomed to marry. 'Good-night, dearest,' he said when she went to bed. She was sure that the last word had been so spoken, and that no ear but her own had heard it. She could not tell him that such word should not be spoken; and yet she felt that the word would be almost as offensive as the kiss to Daniel Thwaite. She must contrive some means of telling him that she could not, would not, must not be his dearest.

She had now received two letters from her mother since she had been at Yoxham, and in each of them there were laid down for her plain instructions as to her conduct. It was now the middle of August, and it was incumbent upon her to allow matters so to arrange themselves, that the marriage might be declared to be a settled thing when the case should come on in November. Mr. Goffe and Mr. Flick had met each other, and everything was now understood by the two parties of lawyers. If the Earl and Lady Anna were then engaged with the mutual consent of all interested,—and so engaged that a day could be fixed for the wedding,—then, when the case was opened in court, would the Solicitor-General declare that it was the intention of Lord Lovel to make no further opposition to the claims of the Countess and her daughter, and it would only remain for Serjeant Bluestone to put in the necessary proofs of the Cumberland marriage and of the baptism of Lady Anna. The Solicitor-General would at the same time state to the court that an alliance had been arranged between these distant cousins, and that in that way everything would be settled. But,—and in this clause of her instructions the Countess was most urgent,—this could not be done unless the marriage were positively settled. Mr. Flick had been very urgent in pointing out to Mr. Goffe that in truth their evidence was very strong to prove that when the Earl married the now so-called Countess, his first wife was still living, though they gave no credit to the woman who now called herself the Countess. But, in either case,—whether the Italian countess were now alive or now dead,—the daughter would be illegitimate, and the second marriage void, if their surmise on this head should prove to be well founded. But the Italian party could of itself do nothing, and the proposed marriage would set everything right. But the evidence must be brought into court and further sifted, unless the marriage were a settled thing by November. All this the Countess explained at great length in her letters, calling upon her daughter to save herself, her mother, and the family.

Lady Anna answered the first epistle,—or rather, wrote another in return to it;—but she said nothing of her noble lover, except that Lord Lovel had not as yet come to Yoxham. She confined herself to simple details of her daily life, and a prayer that her dear mother might be happy. The second letter from the Countess was severe in its tone,—asking why no promise had been made, no assurance given,—no allusion made to the only subject that could now be of interest. She implored her child to tell her that she was disposed to listen to the Earl's suit. This letter was in her pocket when the Earl arrived, and she took it out and read it again after the Earl had whispered in her ear that word so painfully sweet.

She proposed to answer it before breakfast on the following morning. At Yoxham rectory they breakfasted at ten, and she was always up at least before eight. She determined as she laid herself down that she would think of it all night. It might be best, she believed, to tell her mother the whole truth,—that she had already promised everything to Daniel Thwaite, and that she could not go back from her word. Then she began to build castles in the air,—castles which she declared to herself must ever be in the air,— of which Lord Lovel, and not Daniel Thwaite, was the hero, owner, and master. She assured herself that she was not picturing to herself any prospect of a really possible life, but was simply dreaming of an impossible Elysium. How many people would she make happy, were she able to let that young Phœbus know in one half-uttered word,—or with a single silent glance,—that she would in truth be his dearest. It could not be so. She was well aware of that. But surely she might dream of it. All the cares of that careful, careworn mother would then be at an end. How delightful would it be to her to welcome that sorrowful one to her own bright home, and to give joy where joy had never yet been known! How all the lawyers would praise her, and tell her that she had saved a noble family from ruin. She already began to have feelings about the family to which she had been a stranger before she had come among the Lovels. And if it really would make him happy, this Phœbus, how glorious would that be! How fit he was to be made happy! Daniel had said that he was sordid, false, fraudulent, and a fool;—but Daniel did not, could not, understand the nature of the Lovels. And then she herself;—how would it be with her? She had given her heart to Daniel Thwaite, and she had but one heart to give. Had it not been for that, it would have been very sweet to love that young curled darling. There were two sorts of life, and now she had had an insight into each. Daniel had told her that this soft, luxurious life was thoroughly bad. He could not have known when saying so, how much was done for their poor neighbours by such as even these Lovels. It could not be wrong to be soft, and peaceful, and pretty, to enjoy sweet smells, to sit softly, and eat off delicately painted china plates,—as long as no one was defrauded, and many were comforted. Daniel Thwaite, she believed, never went to church. Here at Yoxham there were always morning prayers, and they went to church twice every Sunday. She had found it very pleasant to go to church, and to be led along in the easy path of self-indulgent piety on which they all walked at Yoxham. The church seats at Yoxham were broad, with soft cushions, and the hassocks were well stuffed. Surely, Daniel Thwaite did not know everything. As she thus built her castles in the air,—castles so impossible to be inhabited,—she fell asleep before she had resolved what letter she should write.

But in the morning she did write her letter. It must be written,—and when the family were about the house, she would be too disturbed for so great an effort. It ran as follows:—

'Yoxham, Friday.

'DEAREST MAMMA,

'I am much obliged for your letter, which I got the day before yesterday. Lord Lovel came here yesterday, or perhaps I might have answered it then. Everybody here seems to worship him almost, and he is so good to everybody! We are all to go on a visit to Bolton Abbey, and sleep at an inn somewhere, and I am sure I shall like it very much, for they say it is most beautiful. If you look at the map, it is nearly in a straight line between here and Kendal, but only much nearer to York. The day is not fixed yet, but I believe it will be very soon.

'I shall be so glad if the lawsuit can be got over, for your sake, dearest mamma. I wish they could let you have your title and your share of the money, and let Lord Lovel have the rest, because he is head of the family. That would be fairest, and I can't see why it should not be so. Your share would be quite enough for you and me. I can't say anything about what you speak of. He has said nothing, and I'm sure I hope he won't. I don't think I could do it; and I don't think the lawyers ought to want me to. I think it is very wrong of them to say so. We are strangers, and I feel almost sure that I could never be what he would want. I don't think people ought to marry for money.

'Dearest mamma, pray do not be angry with me. If you are, you will kill me. I am very happy here, and nobody has said anything about my going away. Couldn't you ask Serjeant Blue-stone whether something couldn't be done to divide the money, so that there might be no more law? I am sure he could if he liked, with Mr. Goffe and the other men.

'Dearest mamma, I am,
'Your most affectionate Daughter,
'ANNA LOVEL.'

When the moment came, and the pen was in her hand, she had not the courage to mention the name of Daniel Thwaite. She knew that the fearful story must be told, but at this moment she comforted herself,—or tried to comfort her-self,—by remembering that Daniel himself had enjoined that their engagement must yet for a while be kept secret.

CHAPTER XV

Wharfedale

THE visit to Wharfedale was fixed for Monday and Tuesday, and on the Monday morning they started, after an early breakfast. The party consisted of Aunt Jane, Aunt Julia, Lady Anna, Minnie, and Mr. Cross, one of the rector's curates. The rector would not accompany them, excusing himself to the others generally on the ground that he could not be absent from his parish on those two days. To his wife and sister he explained that he was not able, as yet, to take pleasure in such a party as this with Lady Anna. There was no knowing, he said, what might happen. It was evident that he did not mean to open his heart to Lady Anna, at any rate till the marriage should be settled.

An open carriage, which would take them all was ordered,—with four post horses, and two antiquated postboys, with white hats and blue jackets, and yellow breeches. Minnie and the curate sat on the box,* and there was a servant in the rumble. Rooms at the inn had been ordered, and everything was done in proper lordly manner. The sun shone brightly above their heads, and Anna, having as yet received no further letter from her mother, was determined to be happy. Four horses took them to Bolton Bridge, and then, having eaten lunch and ordered dinner, they started for their ramble in the woods.

The first thing to be seen at Bolton Abbey is,

of course, the Abbey. The Abbey itself, as a ruin,—a ruin not so ruinous but that a part of it is used for a modern church,—is very well; but the glory of Bolton Abbey is in the river which runs round it and in the wooded banks which overhang it. No more luxuriant pasture, no richer foliage, no brighter water, no more picturesque arrangement of the freaks of nature, aided by the art and taste of man, is to be found, perhaps, in England. Lady Anna, who had been used to wilder scenery in her native county, was delighted. Nothing had ever been so beautiful as the Abbey;—nothing so lovely as the running Wharfe! Might they not climb up among those woods on the opposite bank? Lord Lovel declared that, of course they would climb up among the woods,—it was for that purpose they had come. That was the way to the Stryd,— over which he was determined that Lady Anna should be made to jump.

But the river below the Abbey is to be traversed by stepping-stones, which, to the female uninitiated foot, appear to be full of danger. The Wharfe here is no insignificant brook, to be overcome by a long stride and a jump. There is a causeway, of perhaps forty stones, across it, each some eighteen inches distant from the other, which, flat and excellent though they be, are perilous from their number. Mrs. Lovel, who knew the place of old, had begun by declaring that no consideration should induce her to cross the water. Aunt Julia had proposed that they should go along the other bank, on the Abbey side of the river, and thence cross by the bridge half a mile up. But the Earl was resolved that he would

take his cousin over the stepping-stones; and
Minnie and the curate were equally determined.
Minnie, indeed, had crossed the river, and was
back again, while the matter was still being
discussed. Aunt Julia, who was strong-limbed,
as well as strong-minded, at last assented, the
curate having promised all necessary aid. Mrs.
Lovel seated herself at a distance to see the exploit;
and then Lord Lovel started, with Lady Anna,
turning at every stone to give a hand to his
cousin.

'Oh, they are very dreadful!' said Lady Anna,
when about a dozen had been passed.

The black water was flowing fast, fast beneath
her feet; the stones became smaller and smaller
to her imagination, and the apertures between
them broader and broader.

'Don't look at the water, dear,' said the lord,
'but come on quick.'

'I can't come on quick. I shall never get over.
Oh, Frederic!' That morning she had promised
that she would call him Frederic. Even Daniel
could not think it wrong that she should call her
cousin by his Christian name. 'It's no good, I
can't do that one,—it's crooked. Mayn't I go
back again?'

'You can't go back, dear. It is only up to your
knees, if you do go in. But take my hand. There,
—all the others are straight,—you must come on,
or Aunt Julia will catch us. After two or three
times, you'll hop over like a milkmaid. There
are only half-a-dozen more. Here we are. Isn't
that pretty?'

'I thought I never should have got over. I
wouldn't go back for anything. But it is lovely;

and I am so much obliged to you for bringing me here. We can go back another way?'

'Oh, yes;—but now we'll get up the bank. Give me your hand.' Then he took her along the narrow, twisting, steep paths, to the top of the wooded bank, and they were soon beyond the reach of Aunt Julia, Minnie, and the curate.

It was very pleasant, very lovely, and very joyous; but there was still present to her mind some great fear. The man was there with her as an acknowledged lover,—a lover, acknowledged to be so by all but herself; but she could not lawfully have any lover but him who was now slaving at his trade in London. She must tell this gallant lord that he must not be her lover; and, as they went along, she was always meditating how she might best tell him, when the moment for telling him should come. But on that morning, during the entire walk, he said no word to her which seemed quite to justify the telling. He called her by sweet, petting names,—Anna, my girl, pretty coz, and such like. He would hold her hand twice longer than he would have held that of either aunt in helping her over this or that little difficulty,—and would help her when no help was needed. He talked to her, of small things, as though he and she must needs have kindred interests. He spoke to her of his uncle as though, near as his uncle was, the connection were not nigh so close as that between him and her. She understood it with a half understanding,—feeling that in all this he was in truth making love to her, and yet telling herself that he said no more than cousinship might warrant. But the autumn colours were bright, and the river rippled, and the light breeze came down from the mountains, and the last of the wild flowers were still sweet in the woods. After a while she was able to forget her difficulties, to cease to think of Daniel, and to find in her cousin, not a lover, but simply the pleasantest friend that fortune had ever sent her.

And so they came, all alone,—for Aunt Julia, though both limbs and mind were strong, had not been able to keep up with them,—all alone to the Stryd. The Stryd is a narrow gully or passage, which the waters have cut for themselves in the rocks, perhaps five or six feet broad, where the river passes, but narrowed at the top by an overhanging mass which in old days withstood the wearing of the stream, till the softer stone below was cut away, and then was left bridging over a part of the chasm below. There goes a story that a mountain chieftain's son, hunting the stag across the valley when the floods were out, in leaping the stream, from rock to rock, failed to make good his footing, was carried down by the rushing waters, and dashed to pieces among the rocks. Lord Lovel told her the tale, as they sat looking at the now innocent brook, and then bade her follow him as he leaped from edge to edge.

'I couldn't do it;—indeed, I couldn't,' said the shivering girl.

'It is barely a step,' said the Earl, jumping over, and back again. 'Going from this side, you couldn't miss to do it, if you tried.'

'I'm sure I should tumble in. It makes me sick to look at you while you are leaping.'

'You'd jump over twice the distance on dry ground.'

'Then let me jump on dry ground.'

'I've set my heart upon it. Do you think I'd ask you if I wasn't sure?'

'You want to make another legend of me.'

'I want to leave Aunt Julia behind, which we shall certainly do.'

'Oh, but I can't afford to drown myself just that you may run away from Aunt Julia. You can run by yourself, and I will wait for Aunt Julia.'

'That is not exactly my plan. Be a brave girl, now, and stand up, and do as I bid you.'

Then she stood up on the edge of the rock, holding tight by his arm. How pleasant it was to be thus frightened, with such a protector near her to insure her safety! And yet the chasm yawned, and the water ran rapid and was very black. But if he asked her to make the spring, of course she must make it. What would she not have done at his bidding?

'I can almost touch you, you see,' he said, as he stood opposite, with his arm out ready to catch her hand.

'Oh, Frederic, I don't think I can.'

'You can very well, if you will only jump.'

'It is ever so many yards.'

'It is three feet. I'll back Aunt Julia to do it for a promise of ten shillings to the infirmary.'

'I'll give the ten shillings, if you'll only let me off.'

'I won't let you off,—so you might as well come at once.'

Then she stood and shuddered for a moment, looking with beseeching eyes up into his face. Of course she meant to jump. Of course she

would have been disappointed had Aunt Julia
come and interrupted her jumping. Yes,—she
would jump into his arms. She knew that he
would catch her. At that moment her memory
of Daniel Thwaite had become faint as the last
shaded glimmer of twilight. She shut her eyes
for half a moment, then opened them, looked
into his face, and made her spring. As she did
so, she struck her foot against a rising ledge of
the rock, and, though she covered more than
the distance in her leap, she stumbled as she came
to the ground, and fell into his arms. She had
sprained her ankle, in her effort to recover herself.

'Are you hurt?' he asked, holding her close to
his side.

'No;—I think not;—only a little, that is. I
was so awkward.'

'I shall never forgive myself if you are hurt.'

'There is nothing to forgive. I'll sit down for
a moment. It was my own fault because I was
so stupid,—and it does not in the least signify.
I know what it is now; I've sprained my ankle.'

'There is nothing so painful as that.'

'It hurts a little, but it will go off. It wasn't
the jump, but I twisted my foot somehow. If
you look so unhappy, I'll get up and jump back
again.'

'I am unhappy, dearest.'

'Oh, but you mustn't.' The prohibition might
be taken as applying to the epithet of endear-
ment, and thereby her conscience be satisfied.
Then he bent over her, looking anxiously into
her face as she winced with the pain, and he
took her hand and kissed it. 'Oh, no,' she said,

gently struggling to withdraw the hand which he held. 'Here is Aunt Julia. You had better just move.' Not that she would have cared a straw for the eyes of Aunt Julia, had it not been that the image of Daniel Thwaite again rose strong before her mind. Then Aunt Julia, and the curate, and Minnie were standing on the rock within a few paces of them, but on the other side of the stream.

'Is there anything the matter?' asked Miss Lovel.

'She has sprained her ankle in jumping over the Stryd, and she cannot walk. Perhaps Mr. Cross would not mind going back to the inn and getting a carriage. The road is only a quarter of a mile above us, and we could carry her up.'

'How could you be so foolish, Frederic, as to let her jump it?' said the aunt.

'Don't mind about my folly now. The thing is to get a carriage for Anna.' The curate immediately hurried back, jumping over the Stryd as the nearest way to the inn; and Minnie also sprung across the stream so that she might sit down beside her cousin and offer consolation. Aunt Julia was left alone, and after a while was forced to walk back by herself to the bridge.

'Is she much hurt?' asked Minnie.

'I am afraid she is hurt,' said the lord.

'Dear, dear Minnie, it does not signify a bit,' said Anna, lavishing on her younger cousin the caresses which fate forbade her to give to the elder. 'I know I could walk home in a few minutes. I am better now. It is one of those things which go away almost immediately. I'll try and stand, Frederic, if you'll let me.' Then she raised herself, leaning upon him, and declared that she was nearly well,—and then was reseated, still leaning on him.

'Shall we attempt to get her up to the road, Minnie, or wait till Mr. Cross comes to help us?' Lady Anna declared that she did not want any help,—certainly not Mr. Cross's help, and that she could do very well, just with Minnie's arm. They waited there sitting on the rocks for half an hour, saying but little to each other, throwing into the stream the dry bits of stick which the last flood had left upon the stones, and each thinking how pleasant it was to sit there and dream, listening to the running waters. Then Lady Anna hobbled up to the carriage road, helped by a stronger arm than that of her cousin Minnie.

Of course there was some concern and dismay at the inn. Embrocations were used, and doctors were talked of, and heads were shaken, and a couch in the sitting-room was prepared, so that the poor injured one might eat her dinner without being driven to the solitude of her own bedroom.

CHAPTER XVI

For ever

ON the next morning the poor injured one was quite well,—but she was still held to be subject to piteous concern. The two aunts shook their heads when she said that she would walk down to the stepping-stones that morning, before starting for Yoxham; but she was quite sure that the sprain was gone, and the distance was not above half a mile. They were not to start till two o'clock. Would Minnie come down with her, and ramble about among the ruins?

'Minnie, come out on the lawn,' said the lord. 'Don't you come with me and Anna;—you can go where you like about the place by yourself.'

'Why mayn't I come?'

'Never mind, but do as you're bid.'

'I know. You are going to make love to cousin Anna.'

'You are an impertinent little imp.'

'I am so glad, Frederic, because I do like her. I was sure she was a real cousin. Don't you think she is very,—very nice?'

'Pretty well.'

'Is that all?'

'You go away and don't tease,—or else I'll never bring you to the Stryd again.' So it happened that Lord Lovel and Lady Anna went across the meadow together, down to the river, and sauntered along the margin till they came to the stepping-stones. He passed over, and she followed him, almost without a word. Her heart was so full, that she did not think now of the water running at her feet. It had hardly seemed to her to make any difficulty as to the passage. She must follow him whither he would lead her, but her mind misgave her,—that they would not return sweet loving friends as they went out. 'We won't climb,' said he, 'because it might try your ankle too much. But we will go in here by the meadow. I always think this is one of the prettiest views there is,' he said, throwing himself upon the grass.

'It is all prettiest. It is like fairy land. Does the Duke let people come here always?'

'Yes, I fancy so.'

'He must be very good-natured. Do you know the Duke?'

'I never saw him in my life.'

'A duke sounds so awful to me.'

'You'll get used to them some day. Won't you sit down?' Then she glided down to the ground at a little distance from him, and he at once shifted his place so as to be almost close to her. 'Your foot is quite well?'

'Quite well.'

'I thought for a few minutes that there was going to be some dreadful accident, and I was so mad with myself for having made you jump it. If you had broken your leg, how would you have borne it?'

'Like other people, I suppose.'

'Would you have been angry with me?'

'I hope not. I am sure not. You were doing the best you could to give me pleasure. I don't think I should have been angry at all. I don't think we are ever angry with the people we really like.'

'Do you really like me?'

'Yes;—I like you.'

'Is that all?'

'Is not that enough?'

She answered the question as she might have answered it had it been allowed to her, as to any girl that was free, to toy with his love, knowing that she meant to accept it. It was easier so, than in any other way. But her heart within her was sad, and could she have stopped his further speech by any word rough and somewhat rude, she would have done so. In truth, she did not know how to answer him roughly. He deserved from her that all her words should be soft, and sweet and pleasant. She believed him to be good and generous and kind and loving. The hard things which Daniel Thwaite had said of him had all vanished from her mind. To her thinking, it was no sin in him that he should want her wealth,—he, the Earl, to whom by right the wealth of the Lovels should belong. The sin was rather hers,—in that she kept it from him. And then, if she could receive all that he was willing to give, his heart, his name, his house and home, and sweet belongings of natural gifts and personal advantages, how much more would she take than what she gave! She could not speak to him roughly, though,—alas!—the time had come in which she must speak to him truly. It was not fitting that a girl should have two lovers.

'No, dear,—not enough,' he said.

It can hardly be accounted a fault in him that at this time he felt sure of her love. She had been so soft in her ways with him, so gracious, yielding,

and pretty in her manners, so manifestly pleased
by his company, so prone to lean upon him,
that it could hardly be that he should think
otherwise. She had told him, when he spoke to
her more plainly up in London than he had yet
done since they had been together in the country,
that she could never, never be his wife. But
what else could a girl say at a first meeting
with a proposed lover? Would he have wished
that she should at once have given herself up
without one maidenly scruple, one word of
feminine recusancy? If love's course be made to
run too smooth it loses all its poetry, and half its
sweetness. But now they knew each other;—
at least, he thought they did. The scruple might
now be put away. The feminine recusancy had
done its work. For himself,—he felt that he loved
her in very truth. She was not harsh or loud,—
vulgar, or given to coarse manners, as might
have been expected, and as he had been warned
by his friends that he would find her. That she
was very beautiful, all her enemies had acknowledged,—and he was quite assured that her
enemies had been right. She was the Lady Anna
Lovel, and he felt that he could make her his own
without one shade of regret to mar his triumph.
Of the tailor's son,—though he had been warned
of him too,—he made no account whatever.
That had been a slander, which only endeared
the girl to him the more;—a slander against
Lady Anna Lovel which had been an insult to his
family. Among all the ladies he knew, daughters
of peers and high-bred commoners, there were
none,—there was not one less likely so to disgrace
herself than Lady Anna Lovel, his sweet cousin.

'Do not think me too hurried, dear, if I speak to you again so soon, of that of which I spoke once before.' He had turned himself round upon his arm, so as to be very close to her,—so that he would look full into her face, and, if chance favoured him, could take her hand. He paused, as though for an answer; but she did not speak to him a word. 'It is not long yet since we first met.'

'Oh, no;—not long.'

'And I know not what your feelings are. But, in very truth, I can say that I love you dearly. Had nothing else come in the way to bring us together, I am sure that I should have loved you.' She, poor child, believed him as though he were speaking to her the sweetest gospel. And he, too, believed himself. He was easy of heart perhaps, but not deceitful; anxious enough for his position in the world, but not meanly covetous. Had she been distasteful to him as a woman, he would have refused to make himself rich by the means that had been suggested to him. As it was, he desired her as much as her money, and had she given herself to him then would never have remembered,—would never have known that the match had been sordid. 'Do you believe me?' he asked.

'Oh, yes.'

'And shall it be so?'

Her face had been turned away, but now she slowly moved her neck so that she could look at him. Should she be false to all her vows, and try whether happiness might not be gained in that way? The manner of doing it passed through her mind in that moment. She would write to

Daniel, and remind him of his promise to set her
free if she so willed it. She would never see him
again. She would tell him that she had striven
to see things as he would have taught her, and
had failed. She would abuse herself, and ask for
his pardon;—but having thus judged for herself,
she would never go back from such judgment.
It might be done,—if only she could persuade
herself that it were good to do it! But, as she
thought of it, there came upon her a prick of
conscience so sharp, that she could not welcome
the devil by leaving it unheeded. How could she
be forsworn to one who had been so absolutely
good,—whose all had been spent for her and
for her mother,—whose whole life had been one
long struggle of friendship on her behalf,—who
had been the only playfellow of her youth, the
only man she had ever ventured to kiss,—the
man whom she truly loved? He had warned
her against these gauds which were captivating
her spirit, and now, in the moment of her peril,
she would remember his warnings.

'Shall it be so?' Lord Lovel asked again, just
stretching out his hand, so that he could touch
the fold of her garment.

'It cannot be so,' she said.

'Cannot be!'

'It cannot be so, Lord Lovel.'

'It cannot now;—or do you mean the word to
be for ever?'

'For ever!' she replied.

'I know that I have been hurried and sudden,'
he said,—purposely passing by her last assurance;
'and I do feel that you have a right to resent
the seeming assurance of such haste. But in

our case, dearest, the interests of so many are concerned, the doubts and fears, the well-being, and even the future conduct of all our friends are so bound up by the result, that I had hoped you would have pardoned that which would otherwise have been unpardonable.' Oh heavens; —had it not been for Daniel Thwaite, how full of grace, how becoming, how laden with flattering courtesy would have been every word that he had uttered to her! 'But,' he continued, 'if it really be that you cannot love me——'

'Oh, Lord Lovel, pray ask of me no further question.'

'I am bound to ask and to know,—for all our sakes.'

Then she rose quickly to her feet, and with altered gait and changed countenance stood over him. 'I am engaged,' she said, 'to be married— to Mr. Daniel Thwaite.' She had told it all, and felt that she had told her own disgrace. He rose also, but stood mute before her. This was the very thing of which they had all warned him, but as to which he had been so sure that it was not so! She saw it all in his eyes, reading much more there than he could read in hers. She was degraded in his estimation, and felt that evil worse almost than the loss of his love. For the last three weeks she had been a real Lovel among the Lovels. That was all over now. Let this lawsuit go as it might, let them give to her all the money, and make the title which she hated ever so sure, she never again could be the equal friend of her gentle relative, Earl Lovel. Minnie would never again spring into her arms, swearing that she would do as she pleased with her own cousin. She might be Lady Anna, but never Anna again to the two ladies at the rectory. The perfume of his rank had been just scented, to be dashed away from her for ever. 'It is a secret at present,' she said, 'or I should have told you sooner. If it is right that you should repeat it, of course you must.'

'Oh, Anna!'

'It is true.'

'Oh, Anna, for your sake as well as mine this makes me wretched indeed!'

'As for the money, Lord Lovel, if it be mine to give, you shall have it.'

'You think then it is that which I have wanted?'

'It is that which the family wants, and I can understand that it should be wanted. As for myself,—for mamma and me,—you can hardly understand how it has been with us when we were young. You despise Mr. Thwaite,—because he is a tailor.'

'I am sure he is not fit to be the husband of Lady Anna Lovel.'

'When Lady Anna Lovel had no other friend in the world, he sheltered her and gave her a house to live in, and spent his earnings in her defence, and would not yield when all those who might have been her friends strove to wrong her. Where would mamma have been,—and I,—had there been no Mr. Thwaite to comfort us? He was our only friend,—he and his father. They were all we had. In my childhood I had never a kind word from another child,—but only from him. Would it have been right that he should have asked for anything, and that I should have refused it?'

'He should not have asked for this,' said Lord Lovel hoarsely.

'Why not he, as well as you? He is as much a man. If I could believe in your love after two days, Lord Lovel, could I not trust his after twenty years of friendship?'

'You knew that he was beneath you.'

'He was not beneath me. He was above me. We were poor,—while he and his father had money, which we took. He could give, while we received. He was strong while we were weak,— and was strong to comfort us. And then, Lord Lovel, what knew I of rank, living under his father's wing? They told me I was the Lady Anna, and the children scouted*me. My mother was a countess. So she swore, and I at least believed her. But if ever rank and title were a profitless burden, they were to her. Do you think that I had learned then to love my rank?'

'You have learned better now.'

'I have learned,—but whether better I may doubt. There are lessons which are quickly learned; and there are they who say that such are the devil's lessons. I have not been strong enough not to learn. But I must forget again, Lord Lovel. And you must forget also.' He hardly knew how to speak to her now;—whether it would be fit for him even to wish to persuade her to be his, after she had told him that she had given her troth to a tailor. His uneasy thoughts prompted him with ideas which dismayed him. Could he take to his heart one who had been pressed close in so vile a grasp? Could he accept a heart that had once been promised to a tailor's workman? Would not all the world know and say that he had done it solely for the money,—even should he succeed in doing it? And yet to fail in this enterprise,—to abandon all,—to give up so enticing a road to wealth! Then he remembered what he had said,—how he had pledged himself to abandon the lawsuit, —how convinced he had been that this girl was heiress to the Lovel wealth, who now told him that she had engaged herself to marry a tailor.

There was nothing more that either of them could say to the other at the moment, and they went back in silence to the inn.

CHAPTER XVII
The Journey Home

IN absolute silence Lord Lovel and Lady Anna walked back to the inn. He had been dumb-foundered,—nearly so by her first abrupt statement, and then altogether by the arguments with which she had defended herself. She had nothing further to say. She had, indeed, said all, and had marvelled at her own eloquence while she was speaking. Nor was there absent from her a certain pride in that she had done the thing that was right, and had dared to defend herself. She was full of regrets,—almost of remorse; but, nevertheless, she was proud. He knew it all now, and one of her great difficulties had been overcome.

And she was fully resolved that as she had dared to tell him, and to face his anger, his reproaches, his scorn, she would not falter before the scorn and the reproaches, or the anger, of the other Lovels,—of any of the Lovels of Yox-ham. Her mother's reproaches would be dreadful to her; her mother's anger would well-nigh kill her; her mother's scorn would scorch her very soul. But sufficient for the day was the evil thereof. At the present moment she could be strong with the strength she had assumed. So she walked in at the sitting-room window with a bold front, and the Earl followed her. The two aunts were there, and it was plain to them both that something was astray between the lovers. They had said among themselves

that Lady Anna would accept the offer the
moment that it was in form made to her. To
their eyes the manner of their guest had been
the manner of a girl eager to be wooed; but
they had both imagined that their delicately
nurtured and fastidious nephew might too probably be offended by some solecism in conduct,
some falling away from feminine grace, such
as might too readily be shown by one whose
early life had been subjected to rough associates.
Even now it occurred to each of them that it
had been so. The Earl seated himself in a chair,
and took up a book, which they had brought
with them. Lady Anna stood at the open
window, looking across at the broad field and
the river bank beyond; but neither of them
spoke a word. There had certainly been some
quarrel. Then Aunt Julia, in the cause of wisdom, asked a question:—

'Where is Minnie? Did not Minnie go with
you?'

'No,' said the Earl. 'She went in some other
direction at my bidding. Mr. Cross is with her,
I suppose.' It was evident from the tone of his
voice that the displeasure of the head of all the
Lovels was very great.

'We start soon, I suppose?' said Lady Anna.

'After lunch, my dear; it is hardly one yet.'

'I will go up all the same, and see about my
things.'

'Shall I help you, my dear?' asked Mrs. Lovel.

'Oh, no! I would sooner do it alone.' Then
she hurried into her room and burst into a
flood of tears, as soon as the door was closed
behind her.

'Frederic, what ails her?' asked Aunt Julia.

'If anything ails her she must tell you herself,' said the lord.

'Something is amiss. You cannot wonder that we should be anxious, knowing that we know how great is the importance of all this.'

'I cannot help your anxiety just at present, Aunt Julia; but you should always remember that there will be slips between the cup and the lip.'

'Then there has been a slip? I knew it would be so. I always said so, and so did my brother.'

'I wish you would all remember that about such an affair as this, the less said the better.' So saying, the lord walked out through the window and sauntered down to the river side.

'It's all over,' said Aunt Julia.

'I don't see why we should suppose that at present,' said Aunt Jane.

'It's all over. I knew it as soon as I saw her face when she came in. She has said something, or done something, and it's all off. It will be a matter of over twenty thousand pounds a year!'

'He'll be sure to marry somebody with money,' said Aunt Jane. 'What with his title and his being so handsome, he is certain to do well, you know.'

'Nothing like that will come in his way. I heard Mr. Flick say that it was equal to half a million of money. And then it would have been at once. If he goes up to London, and about, just as he is, he'll be head over ears in debt before anybody knows what he is doing. I wonder what it is. He likes pretty girls, and there's no denying that she's handsome.'

'Perhaps she wouldn't have him.'

'That's impossible, Jane. She came down here on purpose to have him. She went out with him this morning to be made love to. They were together three times longer yesterday, and he came home as sweet as sugar to her. I wonder whether she can have wanted to make some condition about the money.'

'What condition?'

'That she and her mother should have it in their own keeping.'

'She doesn't seem to be that sort of a young woman,' said Aunt Jane.

'There's no knowing what that Mr. Goffe, Serjeant Bluestone, and her mother may have put her up to. Frederic wouldn't stand that kind of thing for a minute, and he would be quite right. Better anything than that a man shouldn't be his own master. I think you'd better go up to her, Jane. She'll be more comfortable with you than with me.' Then Aunt Jane, obedient as usual, went up to her young cousin's bedroom.

In the meantime the young lord was standing on the river's brink, thinking what he would do. He had, in truth, very much of which to think, and points of most vital importance as to which he must resolve what should be his action. Must this announcement which he had heard from his cousin dissolve for ever the prospect of his marriage with her; or was it open to him still, as a nobleman, a gentleman, and a man of honour, to make use of all those influences which he might command with the view of getting rid of that impediment of a previous

engagement? Being very ignorant of the world
at large, and altogether ignorant of this man
in particular, he did not doubt that the tailor
might be bought off. Then he was sure that
all who would have access to Lady Anna would
help him in such a cause, and that her own mother
would be the most forward to do so. The girl
would hardly hold to such a purpose if all the
world,—all her own world, were against her.
She certainly would be beaten from it if a bribe
sufficient were offered to the tailor. That this must
be done for the sake of the Lovel family, so that
Lady Anna Lovel might not be known to have
married a tailor, was beyond a doubt; but it was
not so clear to him that he could take to himself
as his Countess her who with her own lips had
told him that she intended to be the bride of a
working artisan. As he thought of this, as his
imagination went to work on all the abominable
circumstances of such a betrothal, he threw from
his hand into the stream with all the vehemence
of passion a little twig which he held. It was too,
too frightful, too disgusting; and then so absolutely unexpected, so unlike her personal demeanour, so contrary to the look of her eyes, to the tone
of her voice, to every motion of her body! She
had been sweet, and gentle, and gracious, till
he had almost come to think that her natural
feminine gifts of ladyship were more even than
her wealth, of better savour than her rank, were
equal even to her beauty, which he had sworn
to himself during the past night to be unsurpassed. And this sweet one had told him,—
this one so soft and gracious,—not that she was
doomed by some hard fate to undergo the

degrading thraldom, but that she herself had willingly given herself to a working tailor from love, and gratitude, and free selection! It was a marvel to him that a thing so delicate should have so little sense of her own delicacy! He did not think that he could condescend to take the tailor's place.

But if not,—if he would not take it, or if, as might still be possible, the tailor's place could not be made vacant for him,—what then? He had pledged his belief in the justice of his cousin's claim; and had told her that, believing his own claim to be unjust, in no case would he prosecute it. Was he now bound by that assurance,—bound to it even to the making of the tailor's fortune; or might he absent himself from any further action in the matter, leaving it entirely in the hands of the lawyers? Might it not be best for her happiness that he should do so? He had been told that even though he should not succeed, there might arise almost interminable delay. The tailor would want his money before he married, and thus she might be rescued from her degradation till she should be old enough to understand it. And yet how could he claim that of which he had said, now a score of times, that he knew that it was not his own? Could he cease to call this girl by the name which all his people had acknowledged as her own, because she had refused to be his wife; and declare his conviction that she was base-born only because she had preferred to his own the addresses of a low-born man, reeking with the sweat of a tailor's board? No, he could not do that. Let her marry but the sweeper of

a crossing, and he must still call her Lady Anna,
—if he called her anything.

Something must be done, however. He had
been told by the lawyers how the matter might
be made to right itself, if he and the young lady
could at once agree to be man and wife; but he
had not been told what would follow, should she
decline to accept his offer. Mr. Flick and the
Solicitor-General must know how to shape their
course before November came round,—and
would no doubt want all the time to shape it
that he could give them. What was he to say
to Mr. Flick and to the Solicitor-General? Was
he at liberty to tell to them the secret which the
girl had told to him? That he was at liberty
to say that she had rejected his offer must be a
matter of course; but might he go beyond that,
and tell them the whole story? It would be
most expedient for many reasons that they should
know it. On her behalf even it might be most
salutary,—with that view of liberating her from
the grasp of her humiliating lover. But she had
told it him, against her own interests, at her
own peril, to her own infinite sorrow,—in order
that she might thus allay hopes in which he
would otherwise have persevered. He knew
enough of the little schemes and by-ways of love,
of the generosity and self-sacrifice of lovers, to
feel that he was bound to confidence. She had
told him that if needs were he might repeat her
tale;—but she had told him at the same time
that her tale was a secret. He could not go with
her secret to a lawyer's chambers, and there
divulge in the course of business that which
had been extracted from her by the necessity to

which she had submitted of setting him free.
He could write to Mr. Flick,—if that at last
was his resolve,—that a marriage was altogether
out of the question, but he could not tell him
why it was so.

He wandered slowly on along the river, having
decided only on this,—only on this as a
certainty,—that he must tell her secret neither
to the lawyers, nor to his own people. Then, as
he walked, a little hand touched his behind, and
when he turned Minnie Lovel took him by the
arm. 'Why are you all alone, Fred?'

'I am meditating how wicked the world is,—
and girls in particular.'

'Where is Cousin Anna?'

'Up at the house, I suppose.'

'Is she wicked?'

'Don't you know that everybody is wicked,
because Eve ate the apple?'

'Adam ate it too.'

'Who bade him?'

'The devil,' said the child whispering.

'But he spoke by a woman's mouth. Why
don't you go in and get ready to go?'

'So I will. Tell me one thing, Fred. May I
be a bridesmaid when you are married?'

'I don't think you can.'

'I have set my heart upon it. Why not?'

'Because you'll be married first.'

'That's nonsense, Fred; and you know it's
nonsense. Isn't Cousin Anna to be your wife?'

'Look here, my darling. I'm awfully fond
of you, and think you the prettiest little girl in
the world. But if you ask impertinent questions
I'll never speak to you again. Do you

understand?' She looked up into his face, and did
understand that he was in earnest, and, leaving
him, walked slowly across the meadow back to
the house alone. 'Tell them not to wait lunch for
me,' he holloaed after her;—and she told her
Aunt Julia that Cousin Frederic was very sulky
down by the river, and that they were not to
wait for him.

When Mrs. Lovel went upstairs into Lady
Anna's room not a word was said about the
occurrence of the morning. The elder lady was
afraid to ask a question, and the younger was
fully determined to tell nothing even had a
question been asked her. Lord Lovel might
say what he pleased. Her secret was with him,
and he could tell it if he chose. She had given
him permission to do so, of which no doubt he
would avail himself. But, on her own account,
she would say nothing; and when questioned
she would merely admit the fact. She would
neither defend her engagement, nor would she
submit to have it censured. If they pleased she
would return to her mother in London at any
shortest possible notice.

The party lunched almost in silence, and when
the horses were ready Lord Lovel came in to
help them into the carriage. When he had
placed the three ladies he desired Minnie to
take the fourth seat, saying that he would sit
with Mr. Cross on the box. Minnie looked at
his face, but there was still the frown there,
and she obeyed him without any remonstrance.
During the whole of the long journey home
there was hardly a word spoken. Lady Anna
knew that she was in disgrace, and was ignorant

how much of her story had been told to the two elder ladies. She sat almost motionless looking out upon the fields, and accepting her position as one that was no longer thought worthy of notice. Of course she must go back to London. She could not continue to live at Yoxham, neither spoken to nor speaking. Minnie went to sleep, and Minnie's mother and aunt now and then addressed a few words to each other. Anna felt sure that to the latest day of her existence she would remember that journey. On their arrival at the Rectory door Mr. Cross helped the ladies out of the carriage, while the lord affected to make himself busy with the shawls and luggage. Then he vanished, and was seen no more till he appeared at dinner.

'What sort of a trip have you had?' asked the rector, addressing himself to the three ladies indifferently.

For a moment nobody answered him, and then Aunt Julia spoke. 'It was very pretty, as it always is at Bolton in summer. We were told that the duke has not been there this year at all. The inn was comfortable, and I think that the young people enjoyed themselves yesterday very much.' The subject was too important, too solemn, too great, to allow of even a word to be said about it without proper consideration.

'Did Frederic like it?'

'I think he did yesterday,' said Mrs. Lovel. 'I think we were all a little tired coming home to-day.'

'Anna sprained her ankle, jumping over the Stryd,' said Minnie.

'Not seriously, I hope.'

'Oh dear no;—nothing at all to signify.' It was the only word which Anna spoke till it was suggested that she should go up to her room. The girl obeyed, as a child might have done, and went upstairs, followed by Mrs. Lovel. 'My dear,' she said, 'we cannot go on like this. What is the matter?'

'You must ask Lord Lovel.'

'Have you quarrelled with him?'

'I have not quarrelled, Mrs. Lovel. If he has quarrelled with me, I cannot help it.'

'You know what we have all wished.'

'It can never be so.'

'Have you said so to Frederic?'

'I have.'

'Have you given him any reason, Anna?'

'I have,' she said after a pause.

'What reason, dear?'

She thought for a moment before she replied. 'I was obliged to tell him the reason, Mrs. Lovel; but I don't think that I need tell anybody else. Of course I must tell mamma.'

'Does your mamma know it?'

'Not yet.'

'And is it a reason that must last for ever?'

'Yes;—for ever. But I do not know why everybody is to be angry with me. Other girls may do as they please. If you are angry with me I had better go back to London at once.'

'I do not know that anybody has been angry with you. We may be disappointed without being angry.' That was all that was said, and then Lady Anna was left to dress for dinner. At dinner Lord Lovel had so far composed himself as to be able to speak to his cousin, and an effort at courtesy was made by them all, —except by the rector. But the evening passed away in a manner very different from any that had gone before it.

CHAPTER XVIII

Too Heavy for Secrets

DURING that night the young lord was still thinking of his future conduct,—of what duty and honour demanded of him, and of the manner in which he might best make duty and honour consort with his interests. In all the emergencies of his short life he had hitherto had some one to advise him,—some elder friend whose counsel he might take even though he would seem to make little use of it when it was offered to him. He had always somewhat disdained Aunt Julia, but nevertheless Aunt Julia had been very useful to him. In latter days, since the late Earl's death, when there came upon him, as the first of his troubles, the necessity of setting aside that madman's will, Mr. Flick had been his chief counsellor; and yet in all his communications with Mr. Flick he had assumed to be his own guide and master. Now it seemed that he must in truth guide himself, but he knew not how to do it. Of one thing he felt certain. He must get away from Yoxham and hurry up to London.

It behoved him to keep his cousin's secret; but would he not be keeping it with a sanctity sufficiently strict if he imparted it to one sworn friend,—a friend who should be bound not to divulge it further without his consent? If so, the Solicitor-General should be his friend. An intimacy had grown up between the great lawyer and his noble client, not social in its nature, but still sufficiently close, as Lord Lovel thought, to admit of such confidence. He had begun to be aware that without assistance of this nature he would not know how to guide himself. Undoubtedly the wealth of the presumed heiress had become dearer to him,—had become at least more important to him,—since he had learned that it must probably be lost. Sir William Patterson was a gentleman as well as a lawyer;—one who had not simply risen to legal rank by diligence and intellect, but a gentleman born and bred, who had been at a public school, and had lived all his days with people of the right sort. Sir William was his legal adviser, and he would commit Lady Anna's secret to the keeping of Sir William.

There was a coach which started in those days from York at noon, reaching London early on the following day. He would go up by this coach, and would thus avoid the necessity of much further association with his family before he had decided what should be his conduct. But he must see his cousin before he went. He therefore sent a note to her before she had left her room on the following morning:—

'DEAR ANNA,

'I purpose starting for London in an hour or so, and wish to say one word to you before I go. Will you meet me at nine in the drawing-room? Do not mention my going to my uncle or aunts, as it will be better that I should tell them myself.

'Yours, L.'

At ten minutes before nine Lady Anna was

in the drawing-room waiting for him, and at ten minutes past nine he joined her.

'I beg your pardon for keeping you waiting.' She gave him her hand, and said that it did not signify in the least. She was always early. 'I find that I must go up to London at once,' he said. To this she made no answer, though he seemed to expect some reply. 'In the first place, I could not remain here in comfort after what you told me yesterday.'

'I shall be sorry to drive you away. It is your home; and as I must go soon, had I not better go at once?'

'No;—that is, I think not. I shall go at any rate. I have told none of them what you told me yesterday.'

'I am glad of that, Lord Lovel.'

'It is for you to tell it,—if it must be told.'

'I did tell your Aunt Jane,—that you and I never can be as—you said you wished.'

'I did wish it most heartily. You did not tell it—all.'

'No;—not all.'

'You astounded me so, that I could hardly speak to you as I should have spoken. I did not mean to be uncourteous.'

'I did not think you uncourteous, Lord Lovel. I am sure you would not be uncourteous to me.'

'But you astounded me. It is not that I think much of myself, or of my rank as belonging to me. I know that I have but little to be proud of. I am very poor,—and not clever like some young men who have not large fortunes, but who can become statesmen and all that. But I do think much of my order; I think much of being a gentleman,—and much of ladies being ladies. Do you understand me?'

'Oh, yes;—I understand you.'

'If you are Lady Anna Lovel——'

'I am Lady Anna Lovel.'

'I believe you are with all my heart. You speak like it, and look like it. You are fit for any position. Everything is in your favour. I do believe it. But if so——'

'Well, Lord Lovel;—if so?'

'Surely you would not choose to—to—to degrade your rank. That is the truth. If I be your cousin, and the head of your family, I have a right to speak as such. What you told me would be degradation.'

She thought a moment, and then she replied to him,—'It would be no disgrace.'

He too found himself compelled to think before he could speak again. 'Do you think that you could like your associates if you were to be married to Mr. Thwaite?'

'I do not know who they would be. He would be my companion, and I like him. I love him dearly. There! you need not tell me, Lord Lovel. I know it all. He is not like you;—and I, when I had become his wife, should not be like your Aunt Jane. I should never see people of that sort any more, I suppose. We should not live here in England at all,—so that I should escape the scorn of all my cousins. I know what I am doing, and why I am doing it; —and I do not think you ought to tempt me.'

She knew at least that she was open to temptation. He could perceive that, and was thankful for it. 'I do not wish to tempt you, but I would save you from unhappiness if I could. Such a marriage would be unnatural. I have not seen Mr. Thwaite.'

'Then, my lord, you have not seen a most excellent man, who, next to my mother, is my best friend.'

'But he cannot be a gentleman.'

'I do not know;—but I do know that I can be his wife. Is that all, Lord Lovel?'

'Not quite all. I fear that this weary lawsuit will come back upon us in some shape. I cannot say whether I have the power to stop it if I would. I must in part be guided by others.'

'I cannot do anything. If I could, I would not even ask for the money for myself.'

'No, Lady Anna. You and I cannot decide it. I must again see my lawyer. I do not mean the attorney,—but Sir William Patterson, the Solicitor-General. May I tell him what you told me yesterday?'

'I cannot hinder you.'

'But you can give me your permission. If he will promise me that it shall go no farther, —then may I tell him? I shall hardly know what to do unless he knows all that I know.'

'Everybody will know soon.'

'Nobody shall know from me,—but only he. Will you say that I may tell him?'

'Oh, yes.'

'I am much indebted to you even for that. I cannot tell you now how much I hoped when I got up yesterday morning at Bolton Bridge that I should have to be indebted to you for making me the happiest man in England. You must forgive me if I say that I still hope at heart that this infatuation may be made to cease. And now, good-bye, Lady Anna.'

'Good-bye, Lord Lovel.'

She at once went to her room, and sent down her maid to say that she would not appear at prayers or at breakfast. She would not see him again before he went. How probable it was that her eyes had rested on his form for the last time! How beautiful he was, how full of grace, how like a god! How pleasant she had found it to be near him; how full of ineffable sweetness had been everything that he had touched, all things of which he had spoken to her! He had almost overcome her, as though she had eaten of the lotus. And she knew not whether the charm was of God or devil. But she did know that she had struggled against it, —because of her word, and because she owed a debt which falsehood and ingratitude would ill repay. Lord Lovel had called her Lady Anna now. Ah, yes; how good he was! When it became significant to her that he should recognise her rank, he did so at once. He had only dropped the title when, having been recognised, it had become a stumbling-block to her. Now he was gone from her, and, if it was possible, she would cease even to dream of him.

'I suppose, Frederic, that the marriage is not to be?' the rector said to him as he got into the dog-cart at the rectory door.

'I cannot tell. I do not know. I think not. But, uncle, would you oblige me by not speaking of it just at present? You will know all very soon.'

The rector stood on the gravel, watching the

dog-cart as it disappeared, with his hands in the pockets of his clerical trousers, and with heavy signs of displeasure on his face. It was very well to be uncle to an earl, and out of his wealth to do what he could to assist, and, if possible, to dispel his noble nephew's poverty. But surely something was due to him! It was not for his pleasure that this girl,—whom he was forced to call Lady Anna, though he could never believe her to be so, whom his wife and sister called Cousin Anna, though he still thought that she was not, and could not be, cousin to anybody,—it was not for anything that he could get, that he was entertaining her as an honoured guest at his rectory. And now his nephew was gone, and the girl was left behind. And he was not to be told whether there was to be a marriage or not! 'I cannot tell. I do not know. I think not.' And then he was curtly requested to ask no more questions. What was he to do with the girl? While the young Earl and the lawyers were still pondering the question of her legitimacy, the girl, whether a Lady Anna and a cousin,—or a mere nobody, who was trying to rob the family,—was to be left on his hands! Why,—oh, why had he allowed himself to be talked out of his own opinion? Why had he ever permitted her to be invited to his rectory? Ah, how the title stuck in his throat as he asked her to take the customary glass of wine with him at dinner-time that evening!

On reaching London, towards the end of August, Lord Lovel found that the Solicitor-General was out of town. Sir William had gone down to Somersetshire with the intention of saying some comforting words to his constituents. Mr. Flick knew nothing of his movements; but his clerk was found, and his clerk did not expect him back in London till October. But, in answer to Lord Lovel's letter, Sir William undertook to come up for one day. Sir William was a man who quite recognised the importance of the case he had in hand.

'Engaged to the tailor,—is she?' he said; not, however, with any look of surprise.

'But, Sir William,—you will not repeat this, even to Mr. Flick, or to Mr. Hardy. I have promised Lady Anna that it shall not go beyond you.'

'If she sticks to her bargain, it cannot be kept secret very long;—nor would she wish it. It's just what we might have expected, you know.'

'You wouldn't say so if you knew her.'

'H—m. I'm older than you, Lord Lovel. You see, she had nobody else near her. A girl must cotton to somebody, and who was there? We ought not to be angry with her.'

'But it shocks me so.'

'Well, yes. As far as I can learn, his father and he have stood by them very closely;—and did so, too, when there seemed to be but little hope. But they might be paid for all they did at a less rate than that. If she sticks to him nobody can beat him out of it. What I mean is, that it was all fair game. He ran his chance, and did it in a manly fashion.' The Earl did not quite understand Sir William, who seemed to take almost a favourable view of these monstrous betrothals. 'What I mean is, that nobody can touch him, or find fault with him. He has not carried her away, and got up a marriage before she was of age. He hasn't kept her from going out among her friends. He hasn't— wronged her, I suppose?'

'I think he has wronged her frightfully.'

'Ah,—well. We mean different things. I am obliged to look at it as the world will look at it.'

'Think of the disgrace of such a marriage;— to a tailor.'

'Whose father had advanced her mother some five or six thousand pounds to help her to win back her position. That's about the truth of it. We must look at it all round, you know.'

'You think, then, that nothing should be done?'

'I think that everything should be done that can be done. We have the mother on our side. Very probably we may have old Thwaite on our side. From what you say, it is quite possible that at this very moment the girl herself may be on our side. Let her remain at Yoxham as long as you can get her to stay, and let everything be done to flatter and amuse her. Go down again yourself, and play the lover as well as I do not doubt you know how to do it.' It was clear then that the great legal pundit did not think that an Earl should be ashamed to carry on his suit to a lady who had confessed her attachment to a journeyman tailor. 'It will be a trouble to us all, of course, because we must change our plan when the case comes on in November.'

'But you still think that she is the heiress?'

'So strongly, that I feel all but sure of it. We shouldn't, in truth, have had a leg to stand on, and we couldn't fight it. I may as well tell you at once, my lord, that we couldn't do it with any chance of success. And what should we have gained had we done so? Nothing! Unless we could prove that the real wife were dead, we should have been fighting for that Italian woman, whom I most thoroughly believe to be an impostor.'

'Then there is nothing to be done?'

'Very little in that way. But if the young lady be determined to marry the tailor, I think we should simply give notice that we withdraw our opposition to the English ladies, and state that we had so informed the woman who asserts her own claim and calls herself a Countess in Sicily; and we should let the Italian woman know that we had done so. In such case, for aught anybody can say here, she might come forward with her own case. She would find men here who would take it up on speculation readily enough. There would be a variety of complications, and no doubt very great delay. In such an event we should question very closely the nature of the property; as, for aught I have seen as yet, a portion of it might revert to you as real estate. It is very various,—and it is not always easy to declare at once what is real and what personal. Hitherto you have appeared as contesting the right of the English widow to her rank, and not necessarily as a claimant of the estate. The Italian widow, if a widow, would be the heir, and not your lordship. For that, among other reasons, the marriage would be most expedient. If the Italian Countess were to succeed in proving that the Earl had a wife

living when he married Miss Murray,—which
I feel sure he had not,—then we should come
forward again with our endeavours to show
that that first wife had died since,—as the Earl
himself undoubtedly declared more than once.
It would be a long time before the tailor got his
money with his wife. The feeling of the court
would be against him.'

'Could we buy the tailor, Sir William?'

The Solicitor-General nursed his leg before
he answered.

'Mr. Flick could answer that question better
than I can do. In fact, Mr. Flick should know
it all. The matter is too heavy for secrets, Lord
Lovel.'

CHAPTER XIX

Lady Anna returns to London

AFTER the Earl was gone Lady Anna had but a bad time of it at Yoxham. She herself could not so far regain her composure as to live on as though no disruption had taken place. She knew that she was in disgrace, and the feeling was dreadful to her. The two ladies were civil, and tried to make the house pleasant, but they were not cordial as they had been hitherto. For one happy halcyon week,—for a day or two before the Earl had come, and for those bright days during which he had been with them,—she had found herself to be really admitted into the inner circle as one of the family. Mrs. Lovel had been altogether gracious with her. Minnie had been her darling little friend. Aunt Julia had been so far won as to be quite alive to the necessity of winning. The rector himself had never quite given way,—had never been so sure of his footing as to feel himself safe in abandoning all power of receding; but the effect of this had been to put the rector himself, rather than his guest, into the back ground. The servants had believed in her, and even Mrs. Grimes had spoken in her praise,—expressing an opinion that she was almost good enough for the young Earl. All Yoxham had known that the two young people were to be married, and all Yoxham had been satisfied. But now everything was wrong. The Earl had fled, and all Yoxham knew that everything was wrong. It was impossible that her position should be as it had been.

There were consultations behind her back as to what should be done, of which,—though she heard no word of them,—she was aware. She went out daily in the carriage with Mrs. Lovel, but Aunt Julia did not go with them. Aunt Julia on these occasions remained at home discussing the momentous affair with her brother. What should be done? There was a great dinner-party, specially convened to do honour to the Earl's return, and not among them a single guest who had not heard that there was to be a marriage. The guests came to see, not only the Earl, but the Earl's bride. When they arrived the Earl had flown. Mrs. Lovel expressed her deep sorrow that business of great importance had made it necessary that the Earl should go to London. Lady Anna was, of course, introduced to the strangers; but it was evident to the merest tyro in such matters, that she was not introduced as would have been a bride expectant. They had heard how charming she was, how all the Lovels had accepted her, how deeply was the Earl in love; and, lo, she sat in the house silent and almost unregarded. Of course, the story of the lawsuit, with such variations as rumour might give it, was known to them all. A twelvemonth ago,—nay, at a period less remote than that,—the two female claimants in Cumberland had always been spoken of in those parts as wretched, wicked, vulgar impostors. Then came the reaction. Lady Anna was the heiress, and Lady Anna was to be the Countess. It had flown about the country during the last ten days that there was no one like the Lady Anna. Now they came to see her, and another reaction had set in. She was the Lady Anna they must suppose. All the Lovels, even the rector, so called her. Mrs. Lovel introduced her as Lady Anna Lovel, and the rector,—hating himself as he did so,— led her out to dinner though there was a baronet's wife in the room,—the wife of a baronet who dated back from James I.* She was the Lady Anna, and therefore the heiress;—but it was clear to them all that there was to be no marriage.

'Then poor Lord Lovel will absolutely not have enough to starve upon,' said the baronet's wife to the baronet, as soon as the carriage door had been shut upon them.

What were they to do with her? The dinner party had taken place on a Wednesday,—the day after the Earl's departure; and on the Thursday Aunt Julia wrote to her nephew thus:—

'Yoxham Rectory, 3rd September.

'MY DEAR FREDERIC,

'My brother wishes me to write to you and say that we are all here very uneasy about Lady Anna. We have only heard from her that the match which was contemplated is not to take place. Whether that be so from unwillingness on her part or yours we have never yet been told;—but both to your Aunt Jane and myself she speaks of it as though the decision were irrevocable. What had we better do? Of course, it is our most anxious desire,—as it is our pleasure and our duty,—to arrange everything according to your wishes and welfare. Nothing can be of so much importance to any of us in this world as your position in it. If it is your wish that Lady Anna should remain here, of course she shall remain. But if, in truth, there is no longer any prospect of a marriage, will not her longer sojourn beneath your uncle's roof be a trouble to all of us,—and especially to her?

'Your Aunt Jane thinks that it may be only a lover's quarrel. For myself, I feel sure that you would not have left us as you did, had it not been more than that. I think that you owe it to your uncle to write to me,—or to him, if you like it better,—and to give us some clue to the state of things.

'I must not conceal from you the fact that my brother has never felt convinced, as you do, that Lady Anna's mother was, in truth, the Countess Lovel. At your request, and in compliance with the advice of the Solicitor-General, he has been willing to receive her here; and, as she has been here, he has given her the rank which she claims. He took her out to dinner yesterday before Lady Fitz-warren,—which will never be forgiven should it turn out ultimately that the first wife was alive when the Earl married Anna's mother. Of course, while here she must be treated as Lady Anna Lovel; but my brother does not wish to be forced so to do, if it be intended that any further doubt should be raised. In such case he desires to be free to hold his former opinion. Therefore pray write to us, and tell us what you wish to have done. I can assure you that we are at present very uncomfortable.

   'Believe me to be,
      My dear Frederic,
         'Your most affectionate aunt,
            'JULIA LOVEL.'

The Earl received this before his interview with Sir William, but left it unanswered till after he had seen that gentleman. Then he wrote as follows:—

     'Carlton Club, 5th September, 183–.
'MY DEAR AUNT JULIA,
   'Will you tell my uncle that I think you had better get Lady Anna to stay at the rectory as long as possible. I'll let you know all about it very soon. Best love to Aunt Jane.
     'I am,
        'Your affectionate nephew,
           'LOVEL.'

This very short epistle was most unsatisfactory to the rector, but it was felt by them all that nothing could be done. With such an injunction before them, they could not give the girl a hint that they wished her to go. What uncle or what aunt, with such a nephew as Lord Lovel, so noble and so poor, could turn out an heiress with twenty thousand a year, as long as there was the slightest chance of a marriage? Not a doubt would have rankled in their minds had they been quite sure that she was the heiress. But, as it was, the Earl ought to have said more than he did say.

'I cannot keep myself from feeling sometimes

that Frederic does take liberties with me,' the rector said to his sister. But he submitted. It was a part of the religion of the family,— and no little part,—that they should cling to their head and chief. What would the world have been to them if they could not talk with comfortable ease and grace of their nephew Frederic?

During this time Anna spoke more than once to Mrs. Lovel as to her going. 'I have been a long time here,' she said, 'and I'm sure that I am in Mr. Lovel's way.'

'Not in the least, my dear. If you are happy, pray stay with us.'

This was before the arrival of the brief epistle, —when they were waiting to know whether they were to dismiss their guest from Yoxham, or to retain her.

'As for being happy, nobody can be happy, I think, till all this is settled. I will write to mamma, and tell her that I had better return to her. Mamma is all alone.'

'I don't know that I can advise, my dear; but as far as we are concerned, we shall be very glad if you can stay.'

The brief epistle had not then arrived, and they were, in truth, anxious that she should go; —but one cannot tell one's visitor to depart from one's house without a downright rupture. Not even the rector himself dared to make such rupture, without express sanction from the Earl.

Then Lady Anna, feeling that she must ask advice, wrote to her mother. The Countess had answered her last letter with great severity,—

that letter in which the daughter had declared that people ought not to be asked to marry for money. The Countess, whose whole life had made her stern and unbending, said very hard things to her child; had told her that she was ungrateful and disobedient, unmindful of her family, neglectful of her duty, and willing to sacrifice the prosperity and happiness of all belonging to her, for some girlish feeling of mere romance. The Countess was sure that her daughter would never forgive herself in after years, if she now allowed to pass by this golden opportunity of remedying all the evil that her father had done. 'You are simply asked to do that which every well-bred girl in England would be delighted to do,' wrote the Countess.

'Ah! she does not know,' said Lady Anna.

But there had come upon her now a fear heavier and more awful than that which she entertained for her mother. Earl Lovel knew her secret, and Earl Lovel was to tell it to the Solicitor-General. She hardly doubted that it might as well be told to all the judges on the bench at once. Would it not be better that she should be married to Daniel Thwaite out of hand, and so be freed from the burden of any secret? The young lord had been thoroughly ashamed of her when she told it. Those aunts at Yoxham would hardly speak to her if they knew it. That lady before whom she had been made to walk out to dinner, would disdain to sit in the same room with her if she knew it. It must be known,—must be known to them all. But she need not remain there, beneath their

eyes, while they learned it. Her mother must
know it, and it would be better that she should
tell her mother. She would tell her mother,—
and request that she might have permission
to return at once to the lodgings in Wyndham
Street. So she wrote the following letter,—in
which, as the reader will perceive, she could
not even yet bring herself to tell her secret:—

'Yoxham Rectory, Monday.

'MY DEAR MAMMA,

'I want you to let me come home, because I
think I have been here long enough. Lord
Lovel has gone away, and though you are so
very angry, it is better I should tell you that
we are not any longer friends. Dear, dear,
dearest mamma; I am so very unhappy that
you should not be pleased with me. I would
die to-morrow if I could make you happy. But
it is all over now, and he would not do it even
if I could say that it should be so. He has gone
away, and is in London, and would tell you so
himself if you would ask him. He despises me,
as I always knew he would,—and so he has
gone away. I don't think anything of myself,
because I knew it must be so; but I am so very
unhappy because you will be unhappy.

'I don't think they want to have me here any
longer, and of course there is no reason why
they should. They were very nice to me before
all this happened, and they never say anything
ill-natured to me now. But it is very different,
and there cannot be any good in remaining.
You are all alone, and I think you would be
glad to see your poor Anna, even though you

are so angry with her. Pray let me come home.
I could start very well on Friday, and I think I
will do so, unless I hear from you to the contrary.
I can take my place by the coach, and go away
at twelve o'clock from York, and be at that
place in London on Saturday at eleven. I must
take my place on Thursday. I have plenty of
money, as I have not spent any since I have
been here. Of course Sarah will come with me.
She is not nearly so nice since she knew that
Lord Lovel was to go away.

'Dear mamma, I do love you so much.
'Your most affectionate daughter,
'ANNA.'

It was not wilfully that the poor girl gave her
mother no opportunity of answering her before
she had taken her place by the coach. On
Thursday morning the place had to be taken,
and on Thursday evening she got her mother's
letter. By the same post came the Earl's letter
to his aunt, desiring that Lady Anna might,
if possible, be kept at Yoxham. The places
were taken, and it was impossible. 'I don't see
why you should go,' said Aunt Julia, who clearly
perceived that her nephew had been instigated
to pursue the marriage scheme since he had
been in town. Lady Anna urged that the money
had been paid for two places by the coach.
'My brother could arrange that, I do not doubt,'
said Aunt Julia. But the Countess now expected
her daughter, and Lady Anna stuck to her
resolve. Her mother's letter had not been pro-
pitious to the movement. If the places were
taken, of course she must come. So said the

Countess. It was not simply that the money should not be lost, but that the people at Yoxham must not be allowed to think that her daughter was over anxious to stay. 'Does your mamma want to have you back?' asked Aunt Julia. Lady Anna would not say that her mother wanted her back, but simply pleaded again that the places had been taken.

When the morning came for her departure, the carriage was ordered to take her into York, and the question arose as to who should go with her. It was incumbent on the rector, who held an honorary stall in the cathedral, to be with the dean and his brother prebendaries on that day, and the use of his own carriage would be convenient to him.

'I think I'll have the gig,' said the rector.

'My dear Charles,' pleaded his sister, 'surely that will be foolish. She can't hurt you.'

'I don't know that,' said the rector. 'I think she has hurt me very much already. I shouldn't know how to talk to her.'

'You may be sure that Frederic means to go on with it,' said Mrs. Lovel.

'It would have been better for Frederic if he had never seen her,' said the rector; 'and I'm sure it would have been better for me.'

But he consented at last, and he himself handed Lady Anna into the carriage. Mrs. Lovel accompanied them, but Aunt Julia made her farewells in the rectory drawing-room. She managed to get the girl to herself for a moment or two, and thus she spoke to her. 'I need not tell you that, for yourself, my dear, I like you very much.'

'Oh, thank you, Miss Lovel.'

'I have heartily wished that you might be our Frederic's wife.'

'It can never be,' said Lady Anna.

'I won't give up all hope. I don't pretend to understand what there is amiss between you and Frederic, but I won't give it up. If it is to be so, I hope that you and I may be loving friends till I die. Give me a kiss, my dear.' Lady Anna, whose eyes were suffused with tears, threw herself into the arms of the elder lady and embraced her.

Mrs. Lovel also kissed her, and bade God bless her as she parted from her at the coach door; but the rector was less demonstrative. 'I hope you will have a pleasant journey,' he said, taking off his clerical hat.

'Let it go as it may,' said Mrs. Lovel, as she walked into the close with her husband, 'you may take my word, she's a good girl.'

'I'm afraid she's sly,' said the rector.

'She's no more sly than I am,' said Mrs. Lovel, who herself was by no means sly.

CHAPTER XX

Lady Anna's Reception

THE Countess went into the City to meet her daughter at the Saracen's Head, whither the York coach used to run, and received her almost in silence. 'Oh, mamma, dear mamma,' said Lady Anna, 'I am so glad to be back with you again.' Sarah, the lady's-maid, was there, useless, officious, and long-eared. The Countess said almost nothing; she submitted to be kissed, and she asked after the luggage. At that time she had heard the whole story about Daniel Thwaite.

The Solicitor-General had disregarded altogether his client's injunctions as to secrecy. He had felt that in a matter of so great importance it behoved him to look to his client's interests, rather than his client's instructions. This promise of a marriage with the tailor's son must be annihilated. On behalf of the whole Lovel family it was his duty, as he thought, to see that this should be effected, if possible,—and as quickly as possible. This was his duty, not only as a lawyer employed in a particular case, but as a man who would be bound to prevent any great evil which he saw looming in the future. In his view of the case the marriage of Lady Anna Lovel, with a colossal fortune, to Daniel Thwaite the tailor, would be a grievous injury to the social world of his country,—and it was one of those evils which may probably be intercepted by due and discreet precautions. No

doubt the tailor wanted money. The man was
entitled to some considerable reward for all that
he had done and all that he had suffered in
the cause. But Sir William could not himself
propose the reward. He could not chaffer* for
terms with the tailor. He could not be seen in
that matter. But having heard the secret
from the Earl, he thought that he could
get the work done. So he sent for Mr. Flick,
the attorney, and told Mr. Flick all that
he knew. 'Gone and engaged herself to the
tailor!' said Mr. Flick, holding up both his
hands. Then Sir William took Lady Anna's
part. After all, such an engagement was not,—
as he thought,—unnatural. It had been made
while she was very young, when she knew no
other man of her own age in life, when she was
greatly indebted to this man, when she had had
no opportunity of measuring a young tailor
against a young lord. She had done it probably
in gratitude;—so said Sir William;—and now
clung to it from good faith rather than affection.
Neither was he severe upon the tailor. He was
a man especially given to make excuses for poor
weak, erring, unlearned mortals, ignorant of
the law,—unless when a witness attempted to
be impervious;—and now he made excuses for
Daniel Thwaite. The man might have done so
much worse than he was doing. There seemed
already to be a noble reliance on himself in his
conduct. Lord Lovel thought that there had
been no correspondence while the young lady
had been at Yoxham. There might have been,
but had not been, a clandestine marriage.
Other reasons he gave why Daniel Thwaite

should not be regarded as altogether villanous. But, nevertheless, the tailor must not be allowed to carry off the prize. The prize was too great for him. What must be done? Sir William condescended to ask Mr. Flick what he thought ought to be done. 'No doubt we should be very much guided by you, Mr. Solicitor,' said Mr. Flick.

'One thing is, I think, plain, Mr. Flick. You must see the Countess and tell her, or get Mr. Goffe to do so. It is clear that she has been kept in the dark between them. At present they are all living together in the same house. She had better leave the place and go elsewhere. They should be kept apart, and the girl, if necessary, should be carried abroad.'

'I take it there is a difficulty about money, Mr. Solicitor.'

'There ought to be none,—and I will take it upon myself to say that there need be none. It is a case in which the court will willingly allow money out of the income of the property. The thing is so large that there should be no grudging of money for needful purposes. Seeing what *primâ facie* claims these ladies have, they are bound to allow them to live decently, in accordance with their alleged rank, till the case is settled. No doubt she is the heiress.'

'You feel quite sure, Sir William?'

'I do;—though, as I have said before, it is a case of feeling sure, and not being sure. Had that Italian woman been really the widow, somebody would have brought her case forward more loudly.'

'But if the other Italian woman who died was the wife?'

'You would have found it out when you were there. Somebody from the country would have come to us with evidence, knowing how much we could afford to pay for it. Mind you, the matter has been tried before, in another shape. The old Earl was indicted for bigamy and acquitted. We are bound to regard that young woman as Lady Anna Lovel, and we are bound to regard her and her mother conjointly as co-heiresses, in different degrees, to all the personal property which the old Earl left behind him. We can't with safety take any other view. There will still be difficulties in their way;— and very serious difficulties, were she to marry this tailor; but, between you and me, he would eventually get the money. Perhaps, Mr. Flick, you had better see him. You would know how to get at his views without compromising anybody. But, in the first place, let the Countess know everything. After what has been done, you won't have any difficulty in meeting Mr. Goffe.'

Mr. Flick had no difficulty in seeing Mr. Goffe,—though he felt that there would be very much difficulty in seeing Mr. Daniel Thwaite. He did tell Mr. Goffe the story of the wicked tailor,—by no means making those excuses which the Solicitor-General had made for the man's presumptuous covetousness. 'I knew the trouble we should have with that man,' said Mr. Goffe, who had always disliked the Thwaites. Then Mr. Flick went on to say that Mr. Goffe had better tell the Countess,—and Mr. Goffe on this point agreed with his adversary. Two or three days after that, but subsequently to

the date of the last letter which the mother had
written to her daughter, Lady Lovel was told
that Lady Anna was engaged to marry Mr.
Daniel Thwaite.

She had suspected how it might be; her heart
had for the last month been heavy with the
dread of this great calamity; she had made her
plans with the view of keeping the two apart;
she had asked her daughter questions founded
on this very fear:—and yet she could not for a
while be brought to believe it. How did Mr.
Goffe know? Mr. Goffe had heard it from Mr.
Flick, who had heard it from Sir William Patterson; to whom the tale had been told by Lord
Lovel. 'And who told Lord Lovel?' said the
Countess flashing up in anger.

'No doubt Lady Anna did so,' said the attorney. But in spite of her indignation she could
retain her doubts. The attorney, however, was
certain. 'There could be no hope but that it
was so.' She still pretended not to believe it,
though fully intending to take all due precautions in the matter. Since Mr. Goffe thought
that it would be prudent, she would remove to
other lodgings. She would think of that plan
of going abroad. She would be on her guard,
she said. But she would not admit it to be
possible that Lady Anna Lovel, the daughter of
Earl Lovel, her daughter, should have so far
disgraced herself.

But she did believe it. Her heart had in
truth told her that it was true at the first word
the lawyer had spoken to her. How blind she
must have been not to have known it! How
grossly stupid not to have understood those

asseverations from the girl, that the marriage
with her cousin was impossible! Her child had
not only deceived her, but had possessed cunning
enough to maintain her deception. It must
have been going on for at least the last twelvemonth, and she, the while, had been kept in
the dark by the manœuvres of a simple girl!
And then she thought of the depth of the degradation which was prepared for her. Had she
passed twenty years of unintermittent combat
for this,—that when all had been done, when
at last success was won, when the rank and
wealth of her child had been made positively
secure before the world, when she was about
to see the unquestioned coronet of a Countess
placed upon her child's brow—all should be
destroyed through a passion so mean as this!
Would it not have been better to have died in
poverty and obscurity,—while there were yet
doubts,—before any assured disgrace had rested
on her? But, oh! to have proved that she was a
Countess, and her child the heiress of an Earl, in
order that the Lady Anna Lovel might become
the wife of Daniel Thwaite, the tailor!

She made many resolutions; but the first was
this, that she would never smile upon the girl
again till this baseness should have been abandoned. She loved her girl as only mothers do
love. More devoted than the pelican, she would
have given her heart's blood,—had given all her
life,—not only to nurture, but to aggrandize
her child. The establishment of her own position, her own honour, her own name, was to her
but the incidental result of her daughter's embla-
zonment in the world. The child which she had

borne to Earl Lovel, and which the father had stigmatised as a bastard, should by her means be known as the Lady Anna, the heiress of that father's wealth,—the wealthiest, the fairest, the most noble of England's daughters. Then there had come the sweet idea that this high-born heiress of the Lovels, should herself become Countess Lovel, and the mother had risen higher in her delighted pride. It had all been for her child! Had she not loved as a mother, and with all a mother's tenderness? And for what?

She would love still, but she would never again be tender till her daughter should have repudiated her base,—her monstrous engagement. She bound up all her faculties to harshness, and a stern resolution. Her daughter had been deceitful, and she would now be ruthless. There might be suffering, but had not she suffered? There might be sorrow, but had not she sorrowed? There might be a contest, but had not she ever been contesting? Sooner than that the tailor should reap the fruit of her labours,—labours which had been commenced when she first gave herself in marriage to that dark, dreadful man,—sooner than that her child should make ignoble the blood which it had cost her so much to ennoble, she would do deeds which should make even the wickedness of her husband child's play in the world's esteem. It was in this mood of mind that she went to meet her daughter at the Saracen's Head.

She had taken fresh lodgings very suddenly, —in Keppel Street, near Russell Square, a long

way from Wyndham Street. She had asked
Mr. Goffe to recommend her a place, and
he had sent her to an old lady with whom
he himself had lodged in his bachelor's days.
Keppel Street cannot be called fashionable, and
Russell Square is not much affected by the
nobility. Nevertheless the house was superior
in all qualifications to that which she was now
leaving, and the rent was considerably higher.
But the affairs of the Countess in regard to
money were in the ascendant; and Mr. Goffe
did not scruple to take for her a 'genteel' suite
of drawing-rooms,—two rooms with folding-
doors, that is,—with the bedrooms above, first-
class lodging-house attendance, and a garret
for the lady's-maid. 'And then it will be quite
close to Mrs. Bluestone,' said Mr. Goffe, who
knew of that intimacy.

The drive in a glass coach home from the
coach-yard to Keppel Street was horrible to
Lady Anna. Not a word was spoken, as Sarah,
the lady's-maid, sat with them in the carriage.
Once or twice the poor girl tried to get hold
of her mother's hand, in order that she might
entice something of a caress. But the Countess
would admit of no such softness, and at last
withdrew her hand roughly. 'Oh mamma!'
said Lady Anna, unable to suppress her dismay.
But the Countess said never a word. Sarah, the
lady's-maid, began to think that there must be
a second lover. 'Is this Wyndham Street?' said
Lady Anna when the coach stopped.

'No, my dear;—this is not Wyndham Street.
I have taken another abode. This is where we
are to live. If you will get out I will follow you,

and Sarah will look to the luggage.' Then the
daughter entered the house, and met the old
woman curtseying to her. She at once felt that
she had been removed from contact with Daniel
Thwaite, and was sure that her mother knew
her story. 'That is your room,' said her mother.
'You had better get your things off. Are you
tired?'

'Oh! so tired!' and Lady Anna burst into
tears.

'What will you have?'

'Oh, nothing! I think I will go to bed,
mamma. Why are you unkind to me? Do tell
me. Anything is better than that you should
be unkind.'

'Anna,—have not you been unkind to me?'

'Never, mamma;—never. I have never meant
to be unkind. I love you better than all the
world. I have never been unkind. But, you;—
Oh, mamma, if you look at me like that, I shall
die.'

'Is it true that you have promised that you
would be the wife of Mr. Daniel Thwaite?'

'Mamma!'

'Is it true? I will be open with you. Mr.
Goffe tells me that you have refused Lord Lovel,
telling him that you must do so because you
were engaged to Mr. Daniel Thwaite. Is that
true?'

'Yes, mamma;—it is true.'

'And you have given your word to that man?'

'I have, mamma.'

'And yet you told me that there was no one
else when I spoke to you of Lord Lovel? You
lied to me?' The girl sat confounded, astounded,

without power of utterance. She had travelled
from York to London, inside one of those awful
vehicles of which we used to be so proud when
we talked of our stage coaches. She was
thoroughly weary and worn out. She had not
breakfasted that morning, and was sick and ill
at ease, not only in heart, but in body also. Of
course it was so. Her mother knew that it was
so. But this was no time for fond compassion.
It would be better, far better that she should
die than that she should not be compelled to
abandon this grovelling abasement. 'Then you
lied to me?' repeated the Countess still standing
over her.

'Oh, mamma, you mean to kill me.'

'I would sooner die here, at your feet, this
moment, and know that you must follow me
within an hour, than see you married to such
a one as that. You shall never marry him.
Though I went into court myself and swore
that I was that lord's mistress,—that I knew it
when I went to him,—that you were born a
brat beyond the law, that I had lived a life of
perjury, I would prevent such greater disgrace
as this. It shall never be. I will take you away
where he shall never hear of you. As to the
money, it shall go to the winds, so that he shall
never touch it. Do you think that it is you that
he cares for? He has heard of all this wealth,—
and you are but the bait upon his hook to catch
it.'

'You do not know him, mamma.'

'Will you tell me of him, that I do not know
him; impudent slut! Did I not know him before
you were born? Have I not known him all

through? Will you give me your word of honour
that you will never see him again?' Lady Anna
tried to think, but her mind would not act for
her. Everything was turning round, and she
became giddy and threw herself on the bed.
'Answer me, Anna. Will you give me your
word of honour that you will never see him
again?'

She might still have said yes. She felt that
enough of speech was left to her for so small an
effort,—and she knew that if she did so the
agony of the moment would pass away from
her. With that one word spoken her mother
would be kind to her, and would wait upon her;
would bring her tea, and would sit by her bedside, and caress her. But she too was a Lovel,
and she was, moreover, the daughter of her who
once had been Josephine Murray.

'I cannot say that, mamma,' she said, 'because
I have promised.'

Her mother dashed from the room, and she
was left alone upon the bed.

CHAPTER XXI

Daniel and the Lawyer

IT has been said that the Countess, when she
sent her daughter down to Yoxham, laid her
plans with the conviction that the associations
to which the girl would be subjected among the
Lovels would fill her heart and mind with a
new-born craving for the kind of life which she
would find in the rector's family;—and she had
been right. Daniel Thwaite also had known
that it would be so. He had been quite alive
to the fact that he and his conversation would
be abased, and that his power, both of pleasing
and of governing, would be lessened, by this
new contact. But, had he been able to hinder
her going, he would not have done so. None of
those who were now interested in his conduct
knew aught of the character of this man. Sir
William Patterson had given him credit for
some honesty, but even he had not perceived,—
had had no opportunity of perceiving,—the
staunch uprightness which was as it were a
backbone to the man in all his doings. He was
ambitious, discontented, sullen, and tyrannical.
He hated the domination of others, but was
prone to domineer himself. He suspected evil
of all above him in rank, and the millennium
to which he looked forward was to be produced
by the gradual extirpation of all social distinctions. Gentlemen, so called, were to him as
savages, which had to be cleared away in order
that that perfection might come at last which

the course of nature was to produce in obedience
to the ordinances of the Creator. But he was a
man who reverenced all laws,—and a law, if
recognised as a law, was a law to him whether
enforced by a penalty, or simply exigent of
obedience from his conscience. This girl had
been thrown in his way, and he had first pitied
and then loved her from his childhood. She had
been injured by the fiendish malice of her own
father,—and that father had been an Earl. He
had been strong in fighting for the rights of the
mother,—not because it had been the mother's
right to be a Countess,—but in opposition to
the Earl. At first,—indeed throughout all these
years of conflict, except the last year,—there had
been a question, not of money, but of right.
The wife was entitled to due support,—to
what measure of support Daniel had never
known or inquired; but the daughter had been
entitled to nothing. The Earl, had he made his
will before he was mad,—or, more probably,
had he not destroyed, when mad, the will which
he had before made,—might and would have
left the girl without a shilling. In those days,
when Daniel's love was slowly growing, when
he wandered about with the child among the
rocks, when the growing girl had first learned
to swear to him that he should always be her
friend of friends, when the love of the boy had
first become the passion of the man, there
had been no thought of money in it. Money!
Had he not been well aware from his earliest
understanding of the need of money for all noble
purposes, that the earnings of his father, which
should have made the world to him a world of

promise, were being lavished in the service of
these forlorn women? He had never complained.
They were welcome to it all. That young girl
was all the world to him; and it was right that
all should be spent; as though she had been a
sister, as though she had already been his wife.
There had been no plot then by which he was
to become rich on the Earl's wealth. Then had
come the will, and the young Earl's claims,
and the general belief of men in all quarters
that the young Earl was to win everything.
What was left of the tailor's savings was still
being spent on behalf of the Countess. The
first fee that ever found its way into the pocket
of Serjeant Bluestone had come from the diminished hoard of old Thomas Thwaite. Then the
will had been set aside; and gradually the cause
of the Countess had grown to be in the ascendant. Was he to drop his love, to confess himself
unworthy, and to slink away out of her sight,
because the girl would become an heiress? Was
he even to conceive so badly of her as to think
that she would drop her love because she was
an heiress? There was no such humility about
him,—nor such absence of self-esteem. But, as
regarded her, he told himself at once that she
should have the chance of being base and noble,
—all base, and all noble as far as title and social
standing could make her so,—if such were her
desire. He had come to her and offered her her
freedom;—had done so, indeed, with such hot
language of indignant protest against the gilded
gingerbread of her interested suitor, as would
have frightened her from the acceptance of his
offer had she been minded to accept it;—but

his words had been hot, not from a premeditated
purpose to thwart his own seeming liberality,
but because his nature was hot and his temper
imperious. This lordling was ready to wed his
bride,—the girl he had known and succoured
throughout their joint lives,—simply because
she was rich and the lordling was a pauper.
From the bottom of his heart he despised the
lordling. He had said to himself a score of
times that he could be well content to see the
lord take the money, waste it among thieves and
prostitutes, and again become a pauper, while
he had the girl to sit with him at his board, and
share with him the earnings of his honest labour.
Of course he had spoken out. But the girl
should be at liberty to do as she pleased.

He wrote no line to her before she went, or
while she was at Yoxham, nor did he speak a
word concerning her during her absence. But
as he sat at his work, or walked to and fro
between his home and the shop, or lay sleepless
in bed, all his thoughts were of her. Twice or
thrice a week he would knock at the door of
the Countess's room, and say a word or two,
as was rendered natural by their long previous
intercourse. But there had been no real intercourse between them. The Countess told him
nothing of her plans; nor did he ever speak to
her of his. Each suspected the other; and each
was grimly civil. Once or twice the Countess
expressed a hope that the money advanced by
Thomas Thwaite might soon be repaid to him
with much interest. Daniel would always treat
the subject with a noble indifference. His
father, he said, had never felt an hour's regret

at having parted with his money. Should it, perchance, come back to him, he would take it no doubt, with thanks.

Then he heard one evening, as he returned from his work, that the Countess was about to remove herself on the morrow to another home. The woman of the house, who told him, did not know where the Countess had fixed her future abode. He passed on up to his bedroom, washed his hands, and immediately went down to his fellow-lodger. After the first ordinary greeting, which was cold and almost unkind, he at once asked his question. 'They tell me that you go from this to-morrow, Lady Lovel.' She paused a moment, and then bowed her head. 'Where is it that you are going to live?' She paused again, and paused long, for she had to think what answer she would make him. 'Do you object to let me know?' he asked.

'Mr. Thwaite, I must object.'

Then at that moment there came upon him the memory of all that he and his father had done, and not the thought of that which he intended to do. This was the gratitude of a Countess! 'In that case of course I shall not ask again. I had hoped that we were friends.'

'Of course we are friends. Your father has been the best friend I ever had. I shall write to your father and let him know. I am bound to let your father know all that I do. But at present my case is in the hands of my lawyers, and they have advised that I should tell no one in London where I live.'

'Then good evening, Lady Lovel. I beg your pardon for having intruded.' He left the room without another word, throwing off the dust from his feet as he went with violent indignation. He and she must now be enemies. She had told him that she would separate herself from him,— and they must be separated. Could he have expected better things from a declared Countess? But how would it be with Lady Anna? She also had a title. She also would have wealth. She might become a Countess if she wished it. Let him only know by one sign from her that she did wish it, and he would take himself off at once to the farther side of the globe, and live in a world contaminated by no noble lords and titled ladies. As it happened, the Countess might as well have given him the address, as the woman at the lodgings informed him on the next morning that the Countess had removed herself to No. — Keppel Street.

He did not doubt that Lady Anna was about to return to London. That quick removal would not otherwise have been made. But what mattered it to him whether she were at Yoxham or in Keppel Street? He could do nothing. There would come a time,—but it had not come as yet,—when he must go to the girl boldly, let her be guarded as she might, and demand her hand. But the demand must be made to herself and herself only. When that time came there should be no question of money. Whether she were the undisturbed owner of hundreds of thousands, or a rejected claimant to her father's name, the demand should be made in the same tone and with the same assurance. He knew well the whole history of her life. She had been twenty years old last

May, and it was now September. When the next spring should come round she would be her own mistress, free to take herself from her mother's hands, and free to give herself to whom she would. He did not say that nothing should be done during those eight months; but, according to his lights, he could not make his demand with full force till she was a woman, as free from all legal control, as was he as a man.

The chances were much against him. He knew what were the allurements of luxury. There were moments in which he told himself that of course she would fall into the nets that were spread for her. But then again there would grow within his bosom a belief in truth and honesty which would buoy him up. How grand would be his victory, how great the triumph of a human soul's nobility, if, after all these dangers, if after all the enticements of wealth and rank, the girl should come to him, and lying on his bosom, should tell him that she had never wavered from him through it all! Of this, at any rate, he assured himself,—that he would not go prying, with clandestine manœuvres, about that house in Keppel Street. The Countess might have told him where she intended to live without increasing her danger.

While things were in this state with him he received a letter from Messrs. Norton and Flick, the attorneys, asking him to call on Mr. Flick at their chambers in Lincoln's Inn. The Solicitor-General had suggested to the attorney that he should see the man, and Mr. Flick had found himself bound to obey; but in truth he hardly knew what to say to Daniel Thwaite. It must

be his object of course to buy off the tailor; but
such arrangements are difficult, and require
great caution. And then Mr. Flick was employed
by Earl Lovel, and this man was the friend of
the Earl's opponents in the case. Mr. Flick did
feel that the Solicitor-General was moving into
great irregularities in this cause. The cause
itself was no doubt peculiar,—unlike any other
cause with which Mr. Flick had become acquainted in his experience; there was no saying at the
present moment who had opposed interests, and
who combined interests in the case; but still
etiquette is etiquette, and Mr. Flick was aware
that such a house as that of Messrs. Norton and
Flick should not be irregular. Nevertheless he
sent for Daniel Thwaite.

After having explained who he was, which
Daniel knew very well, without being told,
Mr. Flick began his work. 'You are aware,
Mr. Thwaite, that the friends on both sides are
endeavouring to arrange this question amicably
without any further litigation.'

'I am aware that the friends of Lord Lovel,
finding that they have no ground to stand on
at law, are endeavouring to gain their object
by other means.'

'No, Mr. Thwaite. I cannot admit that for a
moment. That would be altogether an erroneous
view of the proceeding.'

'Is Lady Anna Lovel the legitimate daughter
of the late Earl?'

'That is what we do not know. That is what
nobody knows. You are not a lawyer, Mr.
Thwaite, or you would be aware that there is
nothing more difficult to decide than questions

of legitimacy. It has sometimes taken all the
Courts a century to decide whether a marriage
is a marriage or not. You have heard of the
great MacFarlane case. To find out who was
the MacFarlane they had to go back a hundred
and twenty years, and at last decide on the
memory of a man whose grandmother had told
him that she had seen a woman wearing a
wedding-ring. The case cost over forty thousand
pounds, and took nineteen years. As far as I
can see this is more complicated even than that.
We should in all probability have to depend
on the proceedings of the courts in Sicily, and
you and I would never live to see the end of it.'

'You would live on it, Mr. Flick, which is
more than I could do.'

'Mr. Thwaite, that I think is a very improper
observation; but, however——. My object is to
explain to you that all these difficulties may be
got over by a very proper and natural alliance
between Earl Lovel and the lady who is at
present called by courtesy Lady Anna Lovel.'

'By the Crown's courtesy, Mr. Flick,' said the
tailor, who understood the nature of the titles
which he hated.

'We allow the name, I grant you, at present;
and are anxious to promote the marriage. We
are all most anxious to bring to a close this
ruinous litigation. Now, I am told that the
young lady feels herself hampered by some
childish promise that has been made——to you.'

Daniel Thwaite had expected no such announcement as this. He did not conceive that
the girl would tell the story of her engagement,
and was unprepared at the moment for any

reply. But he was not a man to remain unready long. 'Do you call it childish?' he said.

'I do certainly.'

'Then what would her engagement be if now made with the Earl? The engagement with me, as an engagement, is not yet twelve months old, and has been repeated within the last month. She is an infant, Mr. Flick, according to your language, and therefore, perhaps, a child in the eye of the law. If Lord Lovel wishes to marry her, why doesn't he do so? He is not hindered, I suppose, by her being a child.'

'Any marriage with you, you know, would in fact be impossible.'

'A marriage with me, Mr. Flick, would be quite as possible as one with the Lord Lovel. When the lady is of age, no clergyman in England dare refuse to marry us, if the rules prescribed by law have been obeyed.'

'Well, well, Mr. Thwaite; I do not want to argue with you about the law and about possibilities. The marriage would not be fitting, and you know that it would not be fitting.'

'It would be most unfitting,—unless the lady wished it as well as I. Just as much may be said of her marriage with Earl Lovel. To which of us has she given her promise? which of us has she known and loved? which of us has won her by long friendship and steady regard? and which of us, Mr. Flick, is attracted to the marriage by the lately assured wealth of the young woman? I never understood that Lord Lovel was my rival when Lady Anna was regarded as the base-born child of the deceased madman.'

'I suppose, Mr. Thwaite, you are not indifferent to her money?'

'Then you suppose wrongly,—as lawyers mostly do when they take upon themselves to attribute motives.'

'You are not civil, Mr. Thwaite.'

'You did not send for me here, sir, in order that there should be civilities between us. But I will at least be true. In regard to Lady Anna's money, should it become mine by reason of her marriage with me, I will guard it for her sake, and for that of the children she may bear, with all my power. I will assert her right to it as a man should do. But my purpose in seeking her hand will neither be strengthened nor weakened by her money. I believe that it is hers. Nay,—I know that the law will give it to her. On her behalf, as being betrothed to her, I defy Lord Lovel and all other claimants. But her money and her hand are two things apart, and I will never be governed as to the one by any regard as to the other. Perhaps, Mr. Flick, I have said enough,—and so, good morning.' Then he went away.

The lawyer had never dared to suggest the compromise which had been his object in sending for the man. He had not dared to ask the tailor how much ready money he would take down to abandon the lady, and thus to relieve them all from that difficulty. No doubt he exercised a wise discretion, as, had he done so, Daniel Thwaite might have become even more uncivil than before.

CHAPTER XXII

There is a Gulf fixed

'Do you think that you could be happier as the wife of such a one as Daniel Thwaite, a creature infinitely beneath you, separated as you would be from all your kith and kin, from all whose blood you share, from me and from your family, than you would be as the bearer of a proud name, the daughter and the wife of an Earl Lovel,—the mother of the earl to come? I will not speak now of duty, or of fitness, or of the happiness of others which must depend upon you. It is natural that a girl should look to her own joys in marriage. Do you think that your joy can consist in calling that man your husband?'

It was thus that the Countess spoke to her daughter, who was then lying worn out and ill on her bed in Keppel Street. For three days she had been subject to such addresses as this, and during those three days no word of tenderness had been spoken to her. The Countess had been obdurate in her hardness,—still believing that she might thus break her daughter's spirit, and force her to abandon her engagement. But as yet she had not succeeded. The girl had been meek and, in all other things, submissive. She had not defended her conduct. She had not attempted to say that she had done well in promising to be the tailor's bride. She had shown herself willing by her silence to have her engagement regarded as a great calamity, as

a dreadful evil that had come upon the whole
Lovel family. She had not boldness to speak to
her mother as she had spoken on the subject
to the Earl. She threw herself entirely upon
her promise, and spoke of her coming destiny
as though it had been made irrevocable by her
own word. 'I have promised him, mamma, and
have sworn that it should be so.' That was the
answer which she now made from her bed;—
the answer which she had made a dozen times
during the last three days.

'Is everybody belonging to you to be ruined
because you once spoke a foolish word?'

'Mamma, it was often spoken,—very often,
and he does not wish that anybody should be
ruined. He told me that Lord Lovel might have
the money.'

'Foolish, ungrateful girl! It is not for Lord
Lovel that I am pleading to you. It is for the
name, and for your own honour. Do you not
constantly pray to God to keep you in that
state of life to which it has pleased Him to
call you;—and are you not departing from it
wilfully and sinfully by such an act as this?'
But still Lady Anna continued to say that she
was bound by the obligation which was upon
her.

On the following day the Countess was frightened, believing that the girl was really ill. In
truth she was ill,—so that the doctor who visited
her declared that she must be treated with great
care. She was harassed in spirit,—so the doctor
said,—and must be taken away, so that she
might be amused. The Countess was frightened,
but still was resolute. She not only loved her

daughter,—but loved no other human being
on the face of the earth. Her daughter was all
that she had to bind her to the world around
her. But she declared to herself again and again
that it would be better that her daughter should
die than live and be married to the tailor. It
was a case in which persecution even to the
very gate of the grave would be wise and
warrantable,—if by such persecution this odious,
monstrous marriage might be avoided. And
she did believe that persecution would avail at
last. If she were only steady in her resolve, the
girl would never dare to demand the right to
leave her mother's house and walk off to the
church to be married to Daniel Thwaite, without the countenance of a single friend. The
girl's strength was not of that nature. But were
she, the Countess, to yield an inch, then this
evil might come upon them. She had heard
that young people can always beat their parents
if they be sufficiently obdurate. Parents are
soft-hearted to their children, and are prone
to yield. And so would she have been soft-
hearted, if the interests concerned had been
less important, if the deviation from duty had
been less startling, or the union proposed less
monstrous and disgraceful. But in this case it
behoved her to be obdurate,—even though it
should be to the very gates of the grave. 'I
swear to you,' she said, 'that the day of your
marriage to Daniel Thwaite shall be the day
of my death.'

In her straits she went to Serjeant Bluestone
for advice. Now, the Serjeant had hitherto been
opposed to all compromise, feeling certain that

everything might be gained without the sacrifice of a single right. He had not a word to say against a marriage between the two cousins, but let the cousin who was the heiress be first placed in possession of her rights. Let her be empowered, when she consented to become Lady Lovel, to demand such a settlement of the property as would be made on her behalf if she were the undisputed owner of the property. Let her marry the lord if she would, but not do so in order that she might obtain the partial enjoyment of that which was all her own. And then, so the Serjeant had argued, the widowed Countess would never be held to have established absolutely her own right to her name, should any compromise be known to have been effected. People might call her Countess Lovel; but, behind her back, they would say that she was no countess. The Serjeant had been very hot about it, especially disliking the interference of Sir William. But now, when he heard this new story, his heat gave way. Anything must be done that could be done;—everything must be done to prevent such a termination to the career of the two ladies as would come from a marriage with the tailor.

But he was somewhat dismayed when he came to understand the condition of affairs in Keppel Street. 'How can I not be severe?' said the Countess, when he remonstrated with her. 'If I were tender with her she would think that I was yielding. Is not everything at stake,—everything for which my life has been devoted?' The Serjeant called his wife into council, and then suggested that Lady Anna should spend a week or two in Bedford Square. He assured the Countess that she might be quite sure that Daniel Thwaite should find no entrance within his doors.

'But if Lord Lovel would do us the honour to visit us, we should be most happy to see him,' said the Serjeant.

Lady Anna was removed to Bedford Square, and there became subject to treatment that was milder, but not less persistent. Mrs. Bluestone lectured her daily, treating her with the utmost respect, paying to her rank a deference which was not indeed natural to the good lady, but which was assumed, so that Lady Anna might the better comprehend the difference between her own position and that of the tailor. The girls were told nothing of the tailor,—lest the disgrace of so unnatural a partiality might shock their young minds; but they were instructed that there was danger, and that they were always, in speaking to their guest, to take it for granted that she was to become Countess Lovel. Her maid, Sarah, went with her to the Serjeant's, and was taken into a half-confidence. Lady Anna was never to be left a moment alone. She was to be a prisoner with gilded chains,—for whom a splendid, a glorious future was in prospect, if only she would accept it.

'I really think that she likes the lord the best,' said Mrs. Bluestone to her husband.

'Then why the mischief won't she have him?' This was in October, and that November term was fast approaching in which the cause was set down for trial.

'I almost think she would if he'd come and ask her again. Of course, I have never mentioned the other man; but when I speak to her of Earl Lovel, she always answers me as though she were almost in love with him. I was inquiring yesterday what sort of a man he was, and she said he was quite perfect. "It is a thousand pities," she said, "that he should not have this money. He ought to have it, as he is the Earl."'

'Why doesn't she give it to him?'

'I asked her that; but she shook her head and said that it could never be. I think that man has made her swear some sort of awful oath, and has frightened her.'

'No doubt he has made her swear an oath, but we all know how the gods regard the perjuries of lovers,' said the Serjeant. 'We must get the young lord here when he comes back to town.'

'Is he handsome?' asked Alice Bluestone, the younger daughter, who had become Lady Anna's special friend in the family. Of course they were talking of Lord Lovel.

'Everybody says he is.'

'But what do you say?'

'I don't think it matters much about a man being handsome,—but he is beautiful. Not dark, like all the other Lovels; nor yet what you call fair. I don't think that fair men ever look manly.'

'Oh no,' said Alice, who was contemplating an engagement with a black-haired young barrister.

'Lord Lovel is brown,—with blue eyes; but it is the shape of his face that is so perfect,—an oval, you know, that is not too long. But it isn't that makes him look as he does. He looks as though everybody in the world ought to do exactly what he tells them.'

'And why don't you, dear, do exactly what he tells you?'

'Ah,—that is another question. I should do many things if he told me. He is the head of our family. I think he ought to have all this money, and be a rich great man, as the Earl Lovel should be.'

'And yet you won't be his wife?'

'Would you,—if you had promised another man?'

'Have you promised another man?'

'Yes;—I have.'

'Who is he, Lady Anna?'

'They have not told you, then?'

'No;—nobody has told me. I know they all want you to marry Lord Lovel,—and I know he wants it. I know he is quite in love with you.'

'Ah;—I do not think that. But if he were, it could make no difference. If you had once given your word to another man, would you go back because a lord asked you?'

'I don't think I would ever give my word without asking mamma.'

'If he had been good to you, and you had loved him always, and he had been your best friend,—what would you do then?'

'Who is he, Lady Anna?'

'Do not call me Lady Anna, or I shall not like you. I will tell you, but you must not say that I told you. Only I thought everybody knew. I told Lord Lovel, and he, I think, has told all the world. It is Mr. Daniel Thwaite.'

'Mr. Daniel Thwaite!' said Alice, who had heard enough of the case to know who the Thwaites were. 'He is a tailor!'

'Yes,' said Lady Anna proudly; 'he is a tailor.'

'Surely that cannot be good,' said Alice, who, having long since felt what it was to be the daughter of a serjeant, had made up her mind that she would marry nothing lower than a barrister.

'It is what you call bad, I dare say.'

'I don't think a tailor can be a gentleman.'

'I don't know. Perhaps I wasn't a lady when I promised him. But I did promise. You can never know what he and his father did for us. I think we should have died only for them. You don't know how we lived;—in a little cottage, with hardly any money, with nobody to come near us but they. Everybody else thought that we were vile and wicked. It is true. But they always were good to us. Would not you have loved him?'

'I should have loved him in a kind of way.'

'When one takes so much, one must give in return what one has to give,' said Lady Anna.

'Do you love him still?'

'Of course I love him.'

'And you wish to be his wife?'

'Sometimes I think I don't. It is not that I am ashamed for myself. What would it have signified if I had gone away with him straight from Cumberland, before I had ever seen my cousins? Supposing that mamma hadn't been the Countess——'

'But she is.'

'So they say now;—but if they had said that she was not, nobody would have thought it wrong then for me to marry Mr. Thwaite.'

'Don't you think it wrong yourself?'

'It would be best for me to say that I would never marry any one at all. He would be very angry with me.'

'Lord Lovel?'

'Oh no;—not Lord Lovel. Daniel would be very angry, because he really loves me. But it would not be so bad to him as though I became Lord Lovel's wife. I will tell you the truth, dear. I am ashamed to marry Mr. Thwaite,— not for myself, but because I am Lord Lovel's cousin and mamma's daughter. And I should be ashamed to marry Lord Lovel.'

'Why, dear?'

'Because I should be false and ungrateful! I should be afraid to stand before him if he looked at me. You do not know how he can look. He, too, can command. He, too, is noble. They believe it is the money he wants, and when they call him a tailor, they think that he must be mean. He is not mean. He is clever, and can talk about things better than my cousin. He can work hard and give away all that he earns. And so could his father. They gave all they had to us, and have never asked it again. I kissed him once,—and then he said I had paid all my mother's debt.' Alice Bluestone shrank within herself when she was told by this daughter of a countess of such a deed. It was horrid to her mind that a tailor should be kissed by a Lady Anna Lovel. But she herself had perhaps been as generous to the black-browed young barrister, and had thought no harm. 'They think I do not understand,—but I do. They all want this money, and then they accuse him, and say he does it that he may become rich. He would give up all the money,—just for me. How would you feel if it were like that with you?'

'I think that a girl who is a lady, should never marry a man who is not a gentleman. You know the story of the rich man who could not get to Abraham's bosom because there was a gulf fixed. That is how it should be;—just as there is with royal people as to marrying royalty. Otherwise everything would get mingled, and there would soon be no difference. If there are to be differences, there should be differences. That is the meaning of being a gentleman,—or a lady.' So spoke the young female Conservative with wisdom beyond her years;—nor did she speak quite in vain.

'I believe what I had better do would be to die,' said Lady Anna. 'Everything would come right then.'

Some day or two after this Serjeant Bluestone sent a message up to Lady Anna, on his return home from the courts, with a request that she would have the great kindness to come down to him in his study. The Serjeant had treated her with more than all the deference due to her rank since she had been in his house, striving to teach her what it was to be the daughter of an Earl and probable owner of twenty thousand a year. The Serjeant, to give him his due, cared as little as most men for the peerage. He vailed his bonnet to no one but a judge,—and

not always that with much ceremonious obser-
vance. But now his conduct was a part of his
duty to a client whom he was determined to
see established in her rights. He would have
handed her her cup of tea on his knees every
morning, if by doing so he could have made
clear to her eyes how deep would be her degradation were she to marry the tailor. The message was now brought to her by Mrs. Bluestone,
who almost apologized for asking her to trouble
herself to walk downstairs to the back parlour.
'My dear Lady Anna,' said the Serjeant, 'may
I ask you to sit down for a moment or two while
I speak to you? I have just left your mother.'

'How is dear mamma?' The Serjeant assured
her that the Countess was well in health. At
this time Lady Anna had not visited her mother
since she had left Keppel Street, and had been
told that Lady Lovel had refused to see her till
she had pledged herself never to marry Daniel
Thwaite. 'I do so wish I might go to mamma!'

'With all my heart I wish you could, Lady
Anna. Nothing makes such heart-burning sor-
row as a family quarrel. But what can I say?
You know what your mother thinks?'

'Couldn't you manage that she should let me
go there just once?'

'I hope that we can manage it;—but I want
you to listen to me first. Lord Lovel is back in
London.' She pressed her lips together and
fastened one hand firmly on the other. If the
assurance that was required from her was ever
to be exacted, it should not be exacted by Serjeant Bluestone. 'I have seen his lordship to-
day,' continued the Serjeant, 'and he has done

me the honour to promise that he will dine here to-morrow.'

'Lord Lovel?'

'Yes;—your cousin, Earl Lovel. There is no reason, I suppose, why you should not meet him? He has not offended you?'

'Oh no.—But I have offended him.'

'I think not, Lady Anna. He does not speak of you as though there were offence.'

'When we parted he would hardly look at me, because I told him——. You know what I told him.'

'A gentleman is not necessarily offended because a lady does not accept his first offer. Many gentlemen would be offended if that were so;—and very many happy marriages would never have a chance of being made. At any rate he is coming, and I thought that perhaps you would excuse me if I endeavoured to explain how very much may depend on the manner in which you may receive him. You must feel that things are not going on quite happily now.'

'I am so unhappy, Serjeant Bluestone!'

'Yes, indeed. It must be so. You are likely to be placed,—I think I may say you certainly will be placed,—in such a position that the whole prosperity of a noble and ancient family must depend on what you may do. With one word you can make once more bright a fair name that has long been beneath a cloud. Here in England the welfare of the State depends on the conduct of our aristocracy!' Oh, Serjeant Bluestone, Serjeant Bluestone! how could you so far belie your opinion as to give expression to a sentiment utterly opposed to your own

convictions! But what is there that a counsel
will not do for a client? 'If they whom Fate and
Fortune have exalted, forget what the country
has a right to demand from them, farewell,
alas, to the glory of old England!' He had
found this kind of thing very effective with
twelve men, and surely it might prevail with
one poor girl. 'It is not for me, Lady Anna, to
dictate to you the choice of a husband. But it
has become my duty to point out to you the
importance of your own choice, and to explain
to you, if it may be possible, that you are not
like other young ladies. You have in your hands
the marring or the making of the whole family
of Lovel. As for that suggestion of a marriage
to which you were induced to give ear by feelings
of gratitude, it would, if carried out, spread
desolation in the bosom of every relative to
whom you are bound by the close ties of noble
blood.' He finished his speech, and Lady Anna
retired without a word.

CHAPTER XXIII
Bedford Square

THE Earl, without asking any question on the subject, had found that the Solicitor-General thought nothing of that objection which had weighed so heavily on his own mind, as to carrying on his suit with a girl who had been wooed successfully by a tailor. His own spirit rebelled for a while against such condescension. When Lady Anna had first told him that she had pledged her word to a lover low in the scale of men, the thing had seemed to him to be over. What struggle might be made to prevent the accomplishment of so base a marriage must be effected for the sake of the family, and not on his own special behoof. Not even for twenty thousand a year, not even for Lady Anna Lovel, not for all the Lovels, would he take to his bosom as his bride, the girl who had leaned with loving fondness on the shoulders of Daniel Thwaite. But when he found that others did not feel it as he felt it, he turned the matter over again in his mind,—and by degrees relented. There had doubtless been much in the whole affair which had placed it outside the pale of things which are subject to the ordinary judgment of men. Lady Anna's position in the world had been very singular. A debt of gratitude was due by her to the tailor, which had seemed to exact from her some great payment. As she had said herself, she had given the only thing which she had to give. Now there would be

much to give. The man doubtless deserved
his reward and should have it, but that reward
must not be the hand of the heiress of the Lovels.
He, the Earl, would once again claim that as
his own.

He had hurried out of town after seeing Sir
William, but had not returned to Yoxham. He
went again to Scotland, and wrote no further
letter to the rectory after those three lines which
the reader has seen. Then he heard from Mr.
Flick that Lady Anna was staying with the
Serjeant in Bedford Square, and he returned
to London at the lawyer's instance. It was so
expedient that if possible something should be
settled before November!

The only guests asked to meet the Earl at
Serjeant Bluestone's, were Sir William and
Lady Patterson, and the black-browed young
barrister. The whole proceeding was very irregular,—as Mr. Flick, who knew what was going
on, said more than once to his old partner,
Mr. Norton. That the Solicitor-General should
dine with the Serjeant might be all very
well,—though, as schoolboys say, they had
never known each other at home before. But
that they should meet in this way the then two
opposing clients,—the two claimants to the vast
property as to which a cause was to come on
for trial in a few weeks,—did bewilder Mr. Flick.
'I suppose the Solicitor-General sees his way,
but he may be in a mess yet,' said Mr. Flick.
Mr. Norton only scratched his head. It was no
work of his.

Sir William, who arrived before the Earl, was
introduced for the first time to the young lady.

'Lady Anna,' he said, 'for some months past I have heard much of you. And now I have great pleasure in meeting you.' She smiled, and strove to look pleased, but she had not a word to say to him. 'You know I ought to be your enemy,' he continued laughing, 'but I hope that is well nigh over. I should not like to have to fight so fair a foe.' Then the young lord arrived, and the lawyers of course gave way to the lover.

Lady Anna, from the moment in which she was told that he was to come, had thought of nothing but the manner of their greeting. It was not that she was uneasy as to her own fashion of receiving him. She could smile and be silent, and give him her hand or leave it ungiven, as he might demand. But in what manner would he accost her? She had felt sure that he had despised her from the moment in which she had told him of her engagement. Of course he had despised her. Those fine sentiments about ladies and gentlemen, and the gulf which had been fixed, had occurred to her before she heard them from the mouth of Miss Alice Bluestone. She understood, as well as did her young friend, what was the difference between her cousin the Earl, and her lover the tailor. Of course it would be sweet to be able to love such a one as her cousin. They all talked to her as though she was simply obstinate and a fool, not perceiving, as she did herself, that the untowardness of her fortune had prescribed this destiny for her. Good as Daniel Thwaite might be,—as she knew that he was,—she felt herself to be degraded in having promised to be his wife.

The lessons they had taught her had not been
in vain. And she had been specially degraded
in the eyes of him who was to her imagination
the brightest of human beings. They told her
that she might still be his wife if only she would
consent to hold out her hand when he should
ask for it. She did not believe it. Were it true,
it could make no difference,—but she did not
believe it. He had scorned her when she
told him the tale at Bolton Abbey. He had
scorned her when he hurried away from Yoxham. Now he was coming to the Serjeant's
house, with the express intention of meeting
her again. Why should he come? Alas, alas!
She was sure that he would never speak to her
again in that bright sunny manner, with those
dulcet honey words, which he had used when
first they saw each other in Wyndham Street.

Nor was he less uneasy as to this meeting. He
had not intended to scorn her when he parted
from her, but he had intended that she should
understand that there was an end of his suit.
He had loved her dearly, but there are obstacles
to which love must yield. Had she already
married this tailor, how would it have been
with him then? That which had appeared to him
to be most fit for him to do, had suddenly become
altogether unfit,—and he had told himself at
the moment that he must take back his love to
himself as best he might. He could not sue
for that which had once been given to a tailor.
But now all that was changed, and he did
intend to sue again. She was very beautiful—
to his thinking the very pink of feminine grace,
and replete with charms;—soft in voice, soft in

manner, with just enough of spirit to give her
character. What a happy chance it had been,
what marvellous fortune, that he should have
been able to love this girl whom it was so necessary that he should marry;—what a happy
chance, had it not been for this wretched tailor!
But now, in spite of the tailor, he would try his
fate with her once again. He had not intended
to scorn her when he left her, but he knew that
his manner to her must have told her that his
suit was over. How should he renew it again
in the presence of Serjeant and Mrs. Bluestone
and of Sir William and Lady Patterson?

He was first introduced to the wives of the two
lawyers while Lady Anna was sitting silent on
the corner of a sofa. Mrs. Bluestone, foreseeing
how it would be, had endeavoured with much
prudence to establish her young friend at some
distance from the other guests, in order that the
Earl might have the power of saying some word;
but the young barrister had taken this opportunity of making himself agreeable, and stood
opposite to her talking nothings about the empti-
ness of London, and the glories of the season
when it should come. Lady Anna did not hear
a word that the young barrister said. Lady
Anna's ear was straining itself to hear what
Lord Lovel might say, and her eye, though
not quite turned towards him, was watching his
every motion. Of course he must speak to her.
'Lady Anna is on the sofa,' said Mrs. Bluestone.
Of course he knew that she was there. He had
seen her dear face the moment that he entered
the room. He walked up to her and gave her
his hand, and smiled upon her.

She had made up her little speech. 'I hope they are quite well at Yoxham,' she said, in that low, soft, silver voice which he had told himself would so well befit the future Countess Lovel.

'Oh yes;—I believe so. I am a truant there, for I do not answer Aunt Julia's letters as punctually as I ought to do. I shall be down there for the hunting I suppose next month.' Then dinner was announced; and as it was necessary that the Earl should take down Mrs. Bluestone and the Serjeant Lady Anna,—so that the young barrister absolutely went down to dinner with the wife of the Solicitor-General,—the conversation was brought to an end. Nor was it possible that they should be made to sit next each other at dinner. And then, when at last the late evening came and they were all together in the drawing-room, other things intervened and the half hour so passed that hardly a word was spoken between them. But there was just one word as he went away. 'I shall call and see you,' he said.

'I don't think he means it,' the Serjeant said to his wife that evening, almost in anger.

'Why not, my dear?'

'He did not speak to her.'

'People can't speak at dinner-parties when there is anything particular to say. If he didn't mean it, he wouldn't have come. And if you'll all have a little patience she'll mean it too. I can't forgive her mother for being so hard to her. She's one of the sweetest creatures I ever came across.'

A little patience, and here was November

coming! The Earl who had now been dining in his house, meeting his own client there, must again become the Serjeant's enemy in November, unless this matter were settled. The Serjeant at present could see no other way of proceeding. The Earl might no doubt retire from the suit, but a jury must then decide whether the Italian woman had any just claim. And against the claim of the Italian woman the Earl would again come forward. The Serjeant as he thought of it, was almost sorry that he had asked the Earl and the Solicitor-General to his house.

On the very next morning—early in the day —the Earl was announced in Bedford Square. The Serjeant was of course away at his chambers. Lady Anna was in her room and Mrs. Bluestone was sitting with her daughter. 'I have come to see my cousin,' said the Earl boldly.

'I am so glad that you have come, Lord Lovel.'

'Thank you,—well; yes. I know you will not mind my saying so outright. Though the papers say that we are enemies, we have many things in common between us.'

'I will send her to you. My dear, we will go into the dining-room. You will find lunch ready when you come down, Lord Lovel.' Then she left him, and he stood looking for a while at the books that were laid about the table.

It seemed to him to be an age, but at last the door was opened and his cousin crept into the room. When he had parted from her at Yoxham he had called her Lady Anna; but he was determined that she should at any rate be again his cousin. 'I could hardly speak to you yesterday,' he said, while he held her hand.

'No;—Lord Lovel.'

'People never can, I think, at small parties like that. Dear Anna, you surprised me so much by what you told me on the banks of the Wharfe!' She did not know how to answer him even a word. 'I know that I was unkind to you.'

'I did not think so, my lord.'

'I will tell you just the plain truth. Even though it may be bitter, the truth will be best between us, dearest. When first I heard what you said, I believed that all must be over between you and me.'

'Oh, yes,' she said.

'But I have thought about it since, and I will not have it so. I have not come to reproach you.'

'You may if you will.'

'I have no right to do so, and would not if I had. I can understand your feelings of deep gratitude and can respect them.'

'But I love him, my lord,' said Lady Anna, holding her head on high and speaking with much dignity. She could hardly herself understand the feeling which induced her so to address him. When she was alone thinking of him and of her other lover, her heart was inclined to regret in that she had not known her cousin in her early days—as she had known Daniel Thwaite. She could tell herself, though she could not tell any other human being, that when she had thought that she was giving her heart to the young tailor, she had not quite known what it was to have a heart to give. The young lord was as a god to her; whereas Daniel was but a man—to whom she owed so deep a debt of gratitude that she must sacrifice herself, if needs be, on his behalf. And yet when the Earl spoke to her of her gratitude to this man,—praising it, and professing that he also understood those very feelings which had governed her conduct,—she blazed up almost in wrath, and swore that she loved the tailor.

The Earl's task was certainly difficult. It was his first impulse to rush away again, as he had rushed away before. To rush away and leave the country, and let the lawyers settle it all as they would. Could it be possible that such a girl as this should love a journeyman tailor, and should be proud of her love! He turned from her and walked to the door and back again, during which time she had almost repented of her audacity.

'It is right that you should love him—as a friend,' he said.

'But I have sworn to be his wife.'

'And must you keep your oath?' As she did not answer him he pressed on with his suit. 'If he loves you I am sure he cannot wish to hurt you, and you know that such a marriage as that would be very hurtful. Can it be right that you should descend from your position to pay a debt of gratitude, and that you should do it at the expense of all those who belong to you? Would you break your mother's heart, and mine, and bring disgrace upon your family merely because he was good to you?'

'He was good to my mother as well as me.'

'Will it not break her heart? Has she not told you so? But perhaps you do not believe in my love.'

'I do not know,' she said.

'Ah, dearest, you may believe. To my eyes you are the sweetest of all God's creatures. Perhaps you think I say so only for the money's sake.'

'No, my lord, I do not think that.'

'Of course much is due to him.'

'He wants nothing but that I should be his wife. He has said so, and he is never false. I can trust him at any rate, even though I should betray him. But I will not betray him. I will go away with him and they shall not hear of me, and nobody will remember that I was my father's daughter.'

'You are doubting even now, dear.'

'But I ought not to doubt. If I doubt it is because I am weak.'

'Then still be weak. Surely such weakness will be good when it will please all those who must be dearest to you.'

'It will not please him, Lord Lovel.'

'Will you do this, dearest;—will you take one week to consider and then write to me? You cannot refuse me that, knowing that the happiness and the honour and the welfare of every Lovel depends upon your answer.'

She felt that she could not refuse, and she gave him the promise. On that day week she would write to him, and tell him then to what resolve she should have brought herself. He came up close to her, meaning to kiss her if she would let him; but she stood aloof, and merely touched his hand. She would obey her betrothed,—at any rate till she should have made up her mind that she would be untrue to him. Lord Lovel could not press his wish, and left the house unmindful of Mrs. Bluestone's luncheon.

CHAPTER XXIV

The Dog in the Manger

DURING all this time Daniel Thwaite had been living alone, working day after day and hour after hour among the men in Wigmore Street, trusted by his employer, disliked by those over whom he was set in some sort of authority, and befriended by none. He had too heavy a weight on his spirits to be light of heart, even had his nature been given to lightness. How could he even hope that the girl would resist all the temptation that would be thrown in her way, all the arguments that would be used to her, the natural entreaties that would be showered upon her from all her friends? Nor did he so think of himself, as to believe that his own personal gifts would bind her to him when opposed by those other personal gifts which he knew belonged to the lord. Measuring himself by his own standard, regarding that man to be most manly who could be most useful in the world, he did think himself to be infinitely superior to the Earl. He was the working bee, whereas the Earl was the drone. And he was one who used to the best of his abilities the mental faculties which had been given to him; whereas the Earl,—so he believed,—was himself hardly conscious of having had mental faculties bestowed upon him. The Earl was, to his thinking, as were all earls, an excrescence upon society, which had been produced by the evil habits and tendencies of mankind; a thing to be got rid of before any near approach could be made to that social perfection in the future coming of which he fully believed. But, though useless, the Earl was beautiful to the eye. Though purposeless, as regarded any true purpose of speech, his voice was of silver and sweet to the ears. His hands, which could never help him to a morsel of bread, were soft to the touch. He was sweet with perfumes and idleness, and never reeked of the sweat of labour. Was it possible that such a girl as Anna Lovel should resist the popinjay, backed as he would be by her own instincts and by the prayers of every one of her race? And then from time to time another thought would strike him. Using his judgment as best he might on her behalf, ought he to wish that she should do so? The idleness of an earl might be bad, and equally bad the idleness of a countess. To be the busy wife of a busy man, to be the mother of many children who should be all taught to be busy on behalf of mankind, was, to his thinking, the highest lot of woman. But there was a question with him whether the accidents of her birth and fortune had not removed her from the possibility of such joy as that. How would it be with her, and him too, if, in after life, she should rebuke him because he had not allowed her to be the wife of a nobleman? And how would it be with him if hereafter men said of him that he held her to an oath extracted from her in her childhood because of her wealth? He had been able to answer Mr. Flick on that head, but he had more difficulty in answering himself.

He had written to his father after the Countess had left the house in which he lodged, and his father had answered him. The old man was not much given to the writing of letters. 'About Lady Lovel and her daughter,' said he, 'I won't take no more trouble, nor shouldn't you. She and you is different, and must be.' And that was all he said. Yes;—he and Lady Anna were different, and must remain so. Of a morning, when he went fresh to his work, he would resolve that he would send her word that she was entirely free from him, and would bid her do according to the nature of the Lovels. But in the evening, as he would wander back, slowly, all alone, tired of his work, tired of the black solitude of the life he was leading, longing for some softness to break the harsh monotony of his labour, he would remember all her prettinesses, and would, above all, remember the pretty oaths with which she had sworn that she, Anna Lovel, loved him, Daniel Thwaite, with all the woman's love which a woman could give. He would remember the warm kiss which had seemed to make fresh for hours his dry lips, and would try to believe that the bliss of which he had thought so much might still be his own. Had she abandoned him, had she assented to a marriage with the Earl, he would assuredly have heard of it. He also knew well the day fixed for the trial, and understood the importance which would be attached to an early marriage, should that be possible,—or at least to a public declaration of an engagement. At any rate she had not as yet been false to him.

One day he received at his place of work the following note:—

'DEAR MR. THWAITE,

'I wish to speak to you on most important business. Could you call on me to-morrow at eight o'clock in the evening,—here?

'Yours very faithfully and always grateful,
'J. LOVEL.'

And then the Countess had added her address in Keppel Street;—the very address which, about a month back, she had refused to give him. Of course he went to the Countess,— fully believing that Lady Anna would also be at the house, though believing also that he would not be allowed to see her. But at this time Lady Anna was still staying with Mrs. Bluestone in Bedford Square.

It was no doubt natural that every advantage should be taken of the strong position which Lord Lovel held. When he had extracted a promise from Lady Anna that she would write to him at the end of a week, he told Sir William, Sir William told his wife, Lady Patterson told Mrs. Bluestone, and Mrs. Bluestone told the Countess. They were all now in league against the tailor. If they could only get a promise from the girl before the cause came on,—any- thing that they could even call a promise,— then the thing might be easy. United together they would not be afraid of what the Italian woman might do. And this undertaking to write to Lord Lovel was almost as good as a promise. When a girl once hesitates with a lover, she has as good as surrendered. To say even that she will think of it, is to accept the man. Then Mrs. Bluestone and the Countess, putting their heads together, determined that an appeal should be made to the tailor. Had Sir William or the Serjeant been consulted, either would have been probably strong against the measure. But the ladies acted on their own judgment, and Daniel Thwaite presented himself in Keppel Street. 'It is very kind of you to come,' said the Countess.

'There is no great kindness in that,' said Daniel, thinking perhaps of those twenty years of service which had been given by him and by his father.

'I know you think that I have been ungrateful for all that you have done for me.' He did think so, and was silent. 'But you would hardly wish me to repay you for helping me in my struggle by giving up all for which I have struggled.'

'I have asked for nothing, Lady Lovel.'

'Have you not?'

'I have asked you for nothing.'

'But my daughter is all that I have in the world. Have you asked nothing of her?'

'Yes, Lady Lovel. I have asked much from her, and she has given me all that I have asked. But I have asked nothing, and now claim nothing, as payment for service done. If Lady Anna thinks she is in my debt after such fashion as that, I will soon make her free.'

'She does think so, Mr. Thwaite.'

'Let her tell me so with her own lips.'

'You will not think that I am lying to you.'

'And yet men do lie, and women too, without

remorse, when the stakes are high. I will believe no one but herself in this. Let her come down and stand before me and look me in the face and tell me that it is so,—and I promise you that there shall be no further difficulty. I will not even ask to be alone with her. I will speak but a dozen words to her, and you shall hear them.'

'She is not here, Mr. Thwaite. She is not living in this house.'

'Where is she then?'

'She is staying with friends.'

'With the Lovels,—in Yorkshire?'

'I do not think that good can be done by my telling you where she is.'

'Do you mean me to understand that she is engaged to the Earl?'

'I tell you this,—that she acknowledges herself to be bound to you, but bound to you simply by gratitude. It seems that there was a promise.'

'Oh yes,—there was a promise, Lady Lovel; a promise as firmly spoken as when you told the late lord that you would be his wife.'

'I know that there was a promise,—though I, her mother, living with her at the time, had no dream of such wickedness. There was a promise, and by that she feels herself to be in some measure bound.'

'She should do so,—if words can ever mean anything.'

'I say she does,—but it is only by a feeling of gratitude. What;—is it probable that she should wish to mate so much below her degree, if she were now left to her own choice? Does it seem natural to you? She loves the young Earl,—as why should she not? She has been thrown into his company on purpose that she might learn to love him,—when no one knew of this horrid promise which had been exacted from her before she had seen any in the world from whom to choose.'

'She has seen two now, him and me, and she can choose as she pleases. Let us both agree to take her at her word, and let us both be present when that word is spoken. If she goes to him and offers him her hand in my presence, I would not take it then though she were a princess, in lieu of being Lady Anna Lovel. Will he treat me as fairly? Will he be as bold to abide by her choice?'

'You can never marry her, Mr. Thwaite.'

'Why can I never marry her? Would not my ring be as binding on her finger as his? Would not the parson's word make me and her one flesh and one bone as irretrievably as though I were ten times an earl? I am a man and she a woman. What law of God, or of man,—what law of nature can prevent us from being man and wife? I say that I can marry her,—and with her consent, I will.'

'Never! You shall never live to call yourself the husband of my daughter. I have striven and suffered,—as never woman strove and suffered before, to give to my child the name and the rank which belong to her. I did not do so that she might throw them away on such a one as you. If you will deal honestly by us——'

'I have dealt by you more than honestly.'

'If you will at once free her from this thraldom in which you hold her, and allow her to act in accordance with the dictates of her own heart——'

'That she shall do.'

'If you will not hinder us in building up again the honour of the family, which was nigh ruined by the iniquities of my husband, we will bless you.'

'I want but one blessing, Lady Lovel.'

'And in regard to her money——'

'I do not expect you to believe me, Countess; but her money counts as nothing with me. If it becomes hers and she becomes my wife, as her husband I will protect it for her. But there shall be no dealing between you and me in regard to money.'

'There is money due to your father, Mr. Thwaite.'

'If so, that can be paid when you come by your own. It was not lent for the sake of a reward.'

'And you will not liberate that poor girl from her thraldom.'

'She can liberate herself if she will. I have told you what I will do. Let her tell me to my face what she wishes.'

'That she shall never do, Mr. Thwaite;—no, by heavens. It is not necessary that she should have your consent to make such an alliance as her friends think proper for her. You have entangled her by a promise, foolish on her part, and very wicked on yours, and you may work us much trouble. You may delay the settlement of all this question,—perhaps for years; and half ruin the estate by prolonged lawsuits; you may make it impossible for me to pay your father what I owe him till he, and I also, shall be no more; but you cannot, and shall not, have access to my daughter.'

Daniel Thwaite, as he returned home, tried to think it all over dispassionately. Was it as the Countess had represented? Was he acting the part of the dog in the manger, robbing others of happiness without the power of achieving his own? He loved the girl, and was he making her miserable by his love? He was almost inclined to think that the Countess had spoken truth in this respect.

CHAPTER XXV

Daniel Thwaite's Letter

ON the day following that on which Daniel Thwaite had visited Lady Lovel in Keppel Street, the Countess received from him a packet containing a short note to herself, and the following letter addressed to Lady Anna. The enclosure was open, and in the letter addressed to the Countess the tailor simply asked her to read and to send on to her daughter that which he had written, adding that if she would do so he would promise to abide by any answer which might come to him in Lady Anna's own handwriting. Daniel Thwaite, when he made this offer, felt that he was giving up everything. Even though the words might be written by the girl, they would be dictated by the girl's mother, or by those lawyers who were now leagued together to force her into a marriage with the Earl. But it was right, he thought,—and upon the whole best for all parties,—that he should give up everything. He could not bring himself to say so to the Countess or to any of those lawyers, when he was sent for and told that because of the lowliness of his position a marriage between him and the highly born heiress was impossible. On such occasions he revolted from the authority of those who endeavoured to extinguish him. But, when alone, he could see at any rate as clearly as they did, the difficulties which lay in his way. He also knew that there was a great gulf fixed, as Miss Alice Bluestone

had said,—though he differed from the young
lady as to the side of the gulf on which lay
heaven, and on which heaven's opposite. The
letter to Lady Anna was as follows:—

'MY DEAREST,

'This letter, if it reaches you at all, will be
given to you by your mother, who will have
read it. It is sent to her open that she may see
what I say to you. She sent for me and I went
to her this evening, and she told me that it was
impossible that I should ever be your husband.
I was so bold as to tell her ladyship that there
could be no impossibility. When you are of age
you can walk out from your mother's house and
marry me, as can I you; and no one can hinder
us. There is nothing in the law, either of God
or man, that can prevent you from becoming
my wife,—if it be your wish to be so. But your
mother also said that it was not your wish, and
she went on to say that were you not bound to
me by ties of gratitude you would willingly
marry your cousin, Lord Lovel. Then I offered
to meet you in the presence of your mother,—
and in the presence, too, of Lord Lovel,—and to
ask you then before all of us to which of us two
your heart was given. And I promised that if
in my presence you would stretch out your right
hand to the Earl neither you nor your mother
should be troubled further by Daniel Thwaite.
But her ladyship swore to me, with an oath,
that I should never be allowed to see you
again.

'I therefore write to you, and bid you think
much of what I say to you before you answer

me. You know well that I love you. You do not suspect that I am trying to win you because you are rich. You will remember that I loved you when no one thought that you would be rich. I do love you in my heart of hearts. I think of you in my dreams and fancy then that all the world has become bright to me, because we are walking together, hand-in-hand, where none can come between to separate us. But I would not wish you to be my wife, just because you have promised. If you do not love me,—above all, if you love this other man,—say so, and I will have done with it. Your mother says that you are bound to me by gratitude. I do not wish you to be my wife unless you are bound to me by love. Tell me, then, how it is;—but, as you value my happiness and your own, tell me the truth.

'I will not say that I shall think well of you, if you have been carried away by this young man's nobility. I would have you give me a fair chance. Ask yourself what has brought him as a lover to your feet. How it came to pass that I was your lover you cannot but remember. But, for you, it is your first duty not to marry a man unless you love him. If you go to him because he can make you a countess you will be vile indeed. If you go to him because you find that he is in truth dearer to you than I am, because you prefer his arm to mine, because he has wound himself into your heart of hearts,—I shall think your heart indeed hardly worth the having; but according to your lights you will be doing right. In that case you shall have no further word from me to trouble you.

'But I desire that I may have an answer to this in your own handwriting.

'Your own sincere lover,
DANIEL THWAITE.'

In composing and copying and recopying this letter the tailor sat up half the night, and then very early in the morning he himself carried it to Keppel Street, thus adding nearly three miles to his usual walk to Wigmore Street. The servant at the lodging-house was not up, and could hardly be made to rise by the modest appeals which Daniel made to the bell; but at last the delivery was effected, and the forlorn lover hurried back to his work.

The Countess as she sat at breakfast read the letter over and over again, and could not bring herself to decide whether it was right that it should be given to her daughter. She had not yet seen Lady Anna since she had sent the poor offender away from the house in anger, and had more than once repeated her assurance through Mrs. Bluestone that she would not do so till a promise had been given that the tailor should be repudiated. Should she make this letter an excuse for going to the house in Bedford Square, and of seeing her child, towards whom her very bowels were yearning? At this time, though she was a countess, with the prospect of great wealth, her condition was not enviable. From morning to night she was alone, unless when she would sit for an hour in Mr. Goffe's office, or on the rarer occasions of a visit to the chambers of Serjeant Bluestone. She had no acquaintances in London whatever. She knew that she

was unfitted for London society even if it should
be open to her. She had spent her life in struggling with poverty and powerful enemies,—
almost alone,—taking comfort in her happiest
moments in the strength and goodness of her
old friend Thomas Thwaite. She now found
that those old days had been happier than these
later days. Her girl had been with her and had
been,—or had at any rate seemed to be,—true
to her. She had something then to hope, something to expect, some happiness of glory to which
she could look forward. But now she was
beginning to learn,—nay had already learned,
that there was nothing for her to expect. Her
rank was allowed to her. She no longer suffered
from want of money. Her cause was about to
triumph,—as the lawyers on both sides had
seemed to say. But in what respect could the
triumph be sweet to her? Even should her girl
become the Countess Lovel, she would not be
the less isolated. None of the Lovels wanted
her society. She had banished her daughter
to Bedford Square, and the only effect of the
banishment was that her daughter was less miserable in Bedford Square than she would have
been with her mother in Keppel Street.

She did not dare to act without advice, and
therefore she took the letter to Mr. Goffe. Had
it not been for a few words towards the end of
the letter she would have sent it to her daughter
at once. But the man had said that her girl
would be vile indeed if she married the Earl
for the sake of becoming a countess, and the
widow of the late Earl did not like to put such
doctrine into the hands of Lady Anna. If she

delivered the letter of course she would endeavour to dictate the answer;—but her girl could be stubborn as her mother; and how would it be with them if quite another letter should be written than that which the Countess would have dictated?

Mr. Goffe read the letter and said that he would like to consider it for a day. The letter was left with Mr. Goffe, and Mr. Goffe consulted the Serjeant. The Serjeant took the letter home to Mrs. Bluestone, and then another consultation was held. It found its way to the very house in which the girl was living for whom it was intended, but was not at last allowed to reach her hand. 'It's a fine manly letter,' said the Serjeant.

'Then the less proper to give it to her,' said Mrs. Bluestone, whose heart was all softness towards Lady Anna, but as hard as a millstone towards the tailor.

'If she does like this young lord the best, why shouldn't she tell the man the truth?' said the Serjeant.

'Of course she likes the young lord the best,—as is natural.'

'Then in God's name let her say so, and put an end to all this trouble.'

'You see, my dear, it isn't always easy to understand a girl's mind in such matters. I haven't a doubt which she likes best. She is not at all the girl to have a vitiated taste about young men. But you see this other man came first, and had the advantage of being her only friend at the time. She has felt very grateful to him, and as yet she is only beginning to learn the

difference between gratitude and love. I don't
at all agree with her mother as to being severe
with her. I can't bear severity to young people,
who ought to be made happy. But I am quite
sure that this tailor should be kept away from
her altogether. She must not see him or his
handwriting. What would she say to herself if
she got that letter? "If he is generous, I can be
generous too;" and if she ever wrote him a
letter, pledging herself to him, all would be over.
As it is, she has promised to write to Lord Lovel.
We will hold her to that; and then, when she
has given a sort of a promise to the Earl, we will
take care that the tailor shall know it. It will be
best for all parties. What we have got to do is
to save her from this man, who has been both
her best friend and her worst enemy.' Mrs.
Bluestone was an excellent woman, and in this
emergency was endeavouring to do her duty at
considerable trouble to herself and with no hope
of any reward. The future Countess when she
should become a Countess would be nothing
to her. She was a good woman;—but she did
not care what evil she inflicted on the tailor,
in her endeavours to befriend the daughter of
the Countess.

The tailor's letter, unseen and undreamt of
by Lady Anna, was sent back through the
Serjeant and Mr. Goffe to Lady Lovel, with
strong advice from Mr. Goffe that Lady Anna
should not be allowed to see it. 'I don't hesitate
to tell you, Lady Lovel, that I have consulted
the Serjeant, and that we are both of opinion
that no intercourse whatever should be permitted between Lady Anna Lovel and Mr.

Daniel Thwaite.' The unfortunate letter was therefore sent back to the writer with the following note;—'The Countess Lovel presents her compliments to Mr. Daniel Thwaite, and thinks it best to return the enclosed. The Countess is of opinion that no intercourse whatever should take place between her daughter and Mr. Daniel Thwaite.'

Then Daniel swore an oath to himself that the intercourse between them should not thus be made to cease. He had acted as he thought not only fairly but very honourably. Nay;— he was by no means sure that that which had been intended for fairness and honour might not have been sheer simplicity. He had purposely abstained from any clandestine communication with the girl he loved, even though she was one to whom he had had access all his life, with whom he had been allowed to grow up together;—who had eaten of his bread and drank of his cup. Now her new friends,—and his own old friend the Countess,—would keep no measures with him. There was to be no intercourse whatever! But, by the God of Heaven, there should be intercourse!

CHAPTER XXVI

The Keswick Poet

INFINITE difficulties were now complicating themselves on the head of poor Daniel Thwaite. The packet which the Countess addressed to him did not reach him in London, but was forwarded after him down to Cumberland, whither he had hurried on receipt of news from Keswick that his father was like to die. The old man had fallen in a fit, and when the message was sent it was not thought likely that he would ever see his son again. Daniel went down to the north as quickly as his means would allow him, going by steamer to Whitehaven, and thence by coach to Keswick. His entire wages were but thirty-five shillings a week, and on that he could not afford to travel by the mail*to Keswick. But he did reach home in time to see his father alive, and to stand by the bedside when the old man died.

Though there was not time for many words between them, and though the apathy of coming death had already clouded the mind of Thomas Thwaite, so that he, for the most part, disregarded,—as dying men do disregard,—those things which had been fullest of interest to him; still something was said about the Countess and Lady Anna. 'Just don't mind them any further, Dan,' said the father.

'Indeed that will be best,' said Daniel.

'Yes, in truth. What can they be to the likes o' you? Give me a drop of brandy, Dan.' The

drop of brandy was more to him now than the
Countess; but though he thought but little of
this last word, his son thought much of it. What
could such as the Countess and her titled
daughter be to him, Daniel Thwaite, the broken
tailor? For, in truth, his father was dying, a
broken man. There was as much owed by him
in Keswick as all the remaining property would
pay; and as for the business, it had come to
that, that the business was not worth preserving.

The old tailor died and was buried, and all
Keswick knew that he had left nothing behind
him, except the debt that was due to him by the
Countess, as to which, opinion in the world of
Keswick varied very much. There were those
who said that the two Thwaites, father and son,
had known very well on which side their bread
was buttered, and that Daniel Thwaite would
now, at his father's death, become the owner of
bonds to a vast amount on the Lovel property.
It was generally understood in Keswick that
the Earl's claim was to be abandoned, that the
rights of the Countess and her daughter were
to be acknowledged, and that the Earl and his
cousin were to become man and wife. If so, the
bonds would be paid, and Daniel Thwaite would
become a rich man. Such was the creed of those
who believed in the debt. But there were others
who did not believe in the existence of any such
bonds, and who ridiculed the idea of advances
of money having been made. The old tailor
had, no doubt, relieved the immediate wants
of the Countess by giving her shelter and food,
and had wasted his substance in making jour-
neys, and neglecting his business; but that was

supposed to be all. For such services on behalf of the father, it was not probable that much money would be paid to the son; and the less so, as it was known in Keswick that Daniel Thwaite had quarrelled with the Countess. As this latter opinion preponderated, Daniel did not find that he was treated with any marked respect in his native town.

The old man did leave a will;—a very simple document, by which everything that he had was left to his son. And there was this paragraph in it; 'I expect that the Countess Lovel will repay to my son Daniel all moneys that I have advanced on her behalf.' As for bonds,—or any single bond,—Daniel could find none. There was an account of certain small items due by the Countess, of long date, and there was her ladyship's receipt for a sum of £500, which had apparently been lent at the time of the trial for bigamy. Beyond this he could find no record of any details whatever, and it seemed to him that his claim was reduced to something less than £600. Nevertheless, he had understood from his father that the whole of the old man's savings had been spent on behalf of the two ladies, and he believed that some time since he had heard a sum named exceeding £6,000. In his difficulty he asked a local attorney, and the attorney advised him to throw himself on the generosity of the Countess. He paid the attorney some small fee, and made up his mind at once that he would not take the lawyer's advice. He would not throw himself on the generosity of the Countess.

There was then still living in that neighbourhood a great man, a poet, who had nearly

carried to its close a life of great honour and of
many afflictions. He was one who, in these,
his latter days, eschewed all society, and cared
to see no faces but those of the surviving few
whom he had loved in early life. And as those
few survivors lived far away, and as he was but
little given to move from home, his life was
that of a recluse. Of the inhabitants of the place
around him, who for the most part had congre-
gated there since he had come among them, he
saw but little, and his neighbours said that he
was sullen and melancholic. But, according to
their degrees, he had been a friend to Thomas
Thwaite, and now, in his emergency, the son
called upon the poet. Indifferent visitors, who
might be and often were intruders, were but
seldom admitted at that modest gate; but Daniel
Thwaite was at once shown into the presence
of the man of letters. They had not seen each
other since Daniel was a youth, and neither
would have known the other. The poet was
hardly yet an old man, but he had all the charac-
teristics of age. His shoulders were bent, and
his eyes were deep set in his head, and his lips
were thin and fast closed. But the beautiful
oval of his face was still there, in spite of the
ravages of years, of labours, and of sorrow; and
the special brightness of his eye had not yet
been dimmed. 'I have been sorry, Mr. Thwaite,
to hear of your father's death,' said the poet.
'I knew him well, but it was some years since,
and I valued him as a man of singular probity
and spirit.' Then Daniel craved permission to
tell his story;—and he told it all from beginning
to end,—how his father and he had worked

for the Countess and her girl, how their time
and then their money had been spent for her;
how he had learned to love the girl, and how,
as he believed, the girl had loved him. And
he told with absolute truth the whole story,
as far as he knew it, of what had been done in
London during the last nine months. He exaggerated nothing, and did not scruple to speak
openly of his own hopes. He showed his letter
to the Countess, and her note to him, and while
doing so hid none of his own feelings. Did the
poet think that there was any reason why, in
such circumstances, a tailor should not marry
the daughter of a Countess? And then he gave,
as far as he knew it, the history of the money
that had been advanced, and produced a copy
of his father's will. 'And now, sir, what would
you have me do?'

'When you first spoke to the girl of love,
should you not have spoken to the mother also,
Mr. Thwaite?'

'Would you, sir, have done so?'

'I will not say that;—but I think that I ought.
Her girl was all that she had.'

'It may be that I was wrong. But if the girl
loves me now——'

'I would not hurt your feelings for the world,
Mr. Thwaite.'

'Do not spare them, sir. I did not come to
you that soft things might be said to me.'

'I do not think it of your father's son. Seeing
what is your own degree in life and what is
theirs, that they are noble and of an old nobility,
among the few hot-house plants of the nation,
and that you are one of the people,—a blade of

corn out of the open field, if I may say so,—
born to eat your bread in the sweat of your brow,
can you think that such a marriage would be
other than distressing to them?'

'Is the hot-house plant stronger or better, or
of higher use, than the ear of corn?'

'Have I said that it was, my friend? I will
not say that either is higher in God's sight than
the other, or better, or of a nobler use. But they
are different; and though the differences may
verge together without evil when the limits are
near, I do not believe in graftings so violent as
this.'

'You mean, sir, that one so low as a tailor
should not seek to marry so infinitely above himself as with the daughter of an Earl.'

'Yes, Mr. Thwaite, that is what I mean;
though I hope that in coming to me you knew
me well enough to be sure that I would not
willingly offend you.'

'There is no offence;—there can be no offence.
I am a tailor, and am in no sort ashamed of my
trade. But I did not think, sir, that you believed
in lords so absolutely as that.'

'I believe but in one Lord,' said the poet.
'In Him who, in His wisdom and for His own
purposes, made men of different degrees.'

'Has it been His doing, sir,—or the devil's?'

'Nay, I will not discuss with you a question
such as that. I will not at any rate discuss it
now.'

'I have read, sir, in your earlier books——'

'Do not quote my books to me, either early
or late. You ask me for advice, and I give it
according to my ability. The time may come

too, Mr. Thwaite,'—and this he said laughing, —'when you also will be less hot in your abhorrence of a nobility than you are now.'

'Never!'

'Ah;—'tis so that young men always make assurances to themselves of their own present wisdom.'

'You think then that I should give her up entirely?'

'I would leave her to herself, and to her mother,—and to this young lord, if he be her lover.'

'But if she loves me! Oh, sir, she did love me once. If she loves me, should I leave her to think, as time goes on, that I have forgotten her? What chance can she have if I do not interfere to let her know that I am true to her?'

'She will have the chance of becoming Lady Lovel, and of loving her husband.'

'Then, sir, you do not believe in vows of love?'

'How am I to answer that?' said the poet. 'Surely I do believe in vows of love. I have written much of love, and have ever meant to write the truth, as I knew it, or thought that I knew it. But the love of which we poets sing is not the love of the outer world. It is more ecstatic, but far less serviceable. It is the picture of that which exists, but grand with imaginary attributes, as are the portraits of ladies painted by artists who have thought rather of their art than of their models. We tell of a constancy in love which is hardly compatible with the usages of this as yet imperfect world. Look abroad, and see whether girls do not love twice, and young men thrice. They come together, and rub their feathers like birds, and fancy that each ·has found in the other an eternity of weal or woe. Then come the causes of their parting. Their fathers perhaps are Capulets and Montagues, but their children, God be thanked, are not Romeos and Juliets. Or money does not serve, or distance intervenes, or simply a new face has the poor merit of novelty. The constancy of which the poets sing is the unreal,—I may almost say the unnecessary, —constancy of a Juliet. The constancy on which our nature should pride itself is that of an Imogen. You read Shakespeare, I hope, Mr. Thwaite.'

'I know the plays you quote, sir. Imogen was a king's daughter, and married a simple gentleman.'

'I would not say that early vows should mean nothing,' continued the poet, unwilling to take notice of the point made against him. 'I like to hear that a girl has been true to her first kiss. But this girl will have the warrant of all the world to justify a second choice. And can you think that because your company was pleasant to her here among your native mountains, when she knew none but you, that she will be indifferent to the charms of such a one as you tell me this Lord Lovel is? She will have regrets,— remorse even; she will sorrow, because she knows that you have been good to her. But she will yield, and her life will be happier with him,— unless he be a bad man, which I do not know,— than it would be with you. Would there be no regrets, think you, no remorse, when she found that as your wife she had separated herself from all that she had been taught to regard as delightful in this world? Would she be happy in quarrelling with her mother and her new-found relatives? You think little of noble blood, and perhaps I think as little of it in matters relating to myself. But she is noble, and she will think of it. As for your money, Mr. Thwaite, I should make it a matter of mere business with the Countess, as though there was no question relating to her daughter. She probably has an account of the money, and doubtless will pay you when she has means at her disposal.'

Daniel left his Mentor without another word on his own behalf, expressing thanks for the counsel that had been given to him, and assuring the poet that he would endeavour to profit by it. Then he walked away, over the very paths on which he had been accustomed to stray with Anna Lovel, and endeavoured to digest the words that he had heard. He could not bring himself to see their truth. That he should not force the girl to marry him, if she loved another better than she loved him, simply by the strength of her own obligation to him, he could understand. But that it was natural that she should transfer to another the affection that she had once bestowed upon him, because that other was a lord, he would not allow. Not only his heart but all his intellect rebelled against such a decision. A transfer so violent would, he thought, show that she was incapable of loving. And yet this doctrine had come to him from one who, as he himself had said, had written much of love.

But, though he argued after this fashion with himself, the words of the old poet had had their efficacy. Whether the fault might be with the girl, or with himself, or with the untoward circumstances of the case, he determined to teach himself that he had lost her. He would never love another woman. Though the Earl's daughter could not be true to him, he, the suitor, would be true to the Earl's daughter. There might no longer be Romeos among the noble Capulets and the noble Montagues,—whom indeed he believed to be dead to faith; but the salt of truth had not therefore perished from the world. He would get what he could from this wretched wreck of his father's property,—obtain payment if it might be possible of that poor £500 for which he held the receipt,—and then go to some distant land in which the wisest of counsellors would not counsel him that he was unfit because of his trade to mate himself with noble blood.

When he had proved his father's will he sent a copy of it up to the Countess with the following letter;—

'Keswick, November 4, 183—.

'MY LADY,

'I do not know whether your ladyship will yet have heard of my father's death. He died here on the 24th of last month. He was taken with apoplexy on the 15th, and never recovered from the fit. I think you will be sorry for him.

'I find myself bound to send your ladyship a copy of his will. Your ladyship perhaps may have some account of what money has passed between you and him. I have none except a receipt for £500 given to you by him many

years ago. There is also a bill against your
ladyship for £71 18s. 9d. It may be that no
more is due than this, but you will know. I
shall be happy to hear from your ladyship on
the subject, and am,

'Yours respectfully,
'DANIEL THWAITE.'

But he still was resolved that before he departed for the far western land he would obtain
from Anna Lovel herself an expression of her
determination to renounce him.

CHAPTER XXVII
Lady Anna's Letter

IN the meantime the week had gone round, and Lady Anna's letter to the Earl had not yet been written. An army was arrayed against the girl to induce her to write such a letter as might make it almost impossible for her afterwards to deny that she was engaged to the lord, but the army had not as yet succeeded. The Countess had not seen her daughter,—had been persistent in her refusal to let her daughter come to her till she had at any rate repudiated her other suitor; but she had written a strongly worded but short letter, urging it as a great duty that Lady Anna Lovel was bound to support her family and to defend her rank. Mrs. Bluestone, from day to day, with soft loving words taught the same lesson. Alice Bluestone in their daily conversations spoke of the tailor, or rather of this promise to the tailor, with a horror which at any rate was not affected. The Serjeant, almost with tears in his eyes, implored her to put an end to the lawsuit. Even the Solicitor-General sent her tender messages,—expressing his great hope that she might enable them to have this matter adjusted early in November. All the details of the case as it now stood had been explained to her over and over again. If, when the day fixed for the trial should come round, it could be said that she and the young Earl were engaged to each other, the Earl would altogether abandon his claim,—and no further statement would be made. The fact of the marriage in Cumberland would then be proved, —the circumstances of the trial for bigamy would be given in evidence,—and all the persons concerned would be together anxious that the demands of the two ladies should be admitted in full. It was the opinion of the united lawyers that were this done, the rank of the Countess would be allowed, and that the property left behind him by the old lord would be at once given up to those who would inherit it under the order of things as thus established. The Countess would receive that to which she would be entitled as widow, the daughter would be the heir-at-law to the bulk of the personal property, and the Earl would merely claim any real estate, if,—as was very doubtful,—any real estate had been left in question. In this case the disposition of the property would be just what they would all desire, and the question of rank would be settled for ever. But if the young lady should not have then agreed to this very pleasant compromise, the Earl indeed would make no further endeavours to invalidate the Cumberland marriage, and would retire from the suit. But it would then be stated that there was a claimant in Sicily,—or at least evidence in Italy, which if sifted might possibly bar the claim of the Countess. The Solicitor-General did not hesitate to say that he believed the living woman to be a weak impostor, who had been first used by the Earl and had then put forward a falsehood to get an income out of the property; but he was by no means convinced that the other foreign woman, whom the

Earl had undoubtedly made his first wife, might not have been alive when the second marriage was contracted. If it were so, the Countess would be no Countess, Anna Lovel would simply be Anna Murray, penniless, baseborn, and a fit wife for the tailor, should the tailor think fit to take her. 'If it be so,' said Lady Anna through her tears, 'let it be so; and he will take me.'

It may have been that the army was too strong for its own purpose,—too much of an army to gain a victory on that field,—that a weaker combination of forces would have prevailed when all this array failed. No one had a word to say for the tailor; no one admitted that he had been a generous friend; no feeling was expressed for him. It seemed to be taken for granted that he, from the beginning, had laid his plans for obtaining possession of an enormous income in the event of the Countess being proved to be a Countess. There was no admission that he had done aught for love. Now, in all these matters, Lady Anna was sure of but one thing alone, and that was of the tailor's truth. Had they acknowledged that he was good and noble, they might perhaps have persuaded her,—as the poet had almost persuaded her lover,—that the fitness of things demanded that they should be separated.

But she had promised that she would write the letter by the end of the week, and when the end of a fortnight had come she knew that it must be written. She had declared over and over again to Mrs. Bluestone that she must go away from Bedford Square. She could not live there always, she said. She knew that she was in

the way of everybody. Why should she not go
back to her own mother? 'Does mamma mean to
say that I am never to live with her any more?'
Mrs. Bluestone promised that if she would write
her letter and tell her cousin that she would try
to love him, she should go back to her mother at
once. 'But I cannot live here always,' persisted
Lady Anna. Mrs. Bluestone would not admit
that there was any reason why her visitor should
not continue to live in Bedford Square as long
as the arrangement suited Lady Lovel.

Various letters were written for her. The
Countess wrote one which was an unqualified
acceptance of the Earl's offer, and which was
very short. Alice Bluestone wrote one which
was full of poetry. Mrs. Bluestone wrote a third,
in which a great many ambiguous words were
used,—in which there was no definite promise,
and no poetry. But had this letter been sent it
would have been almost impossible for the girl
afterwards to extricate herself from its obligations. The Serjeant, perhaps, had lent a word
or two, for the letter was undoubtedly very
clever. In this letter Lady Anna was made to
say that she would always have the greatest
pleasure in receiving her cousin's visits, and that
she trusted that she might be able to co-operate
with her cousins in bringing the lawsuit to a
close;—that she certainly would not marry any
one without her mother's consent, but that she
did not find herself able at the present to say
more than that. 'It won't stop the Solicitor-
General, you know,' the Serjeant had remarked,
as he read it. 'Bother the Solicitor-General!'
Mrs. Bluestone had answered, and had then

gone on to show that it would lead to that which
would stop the learned gentleman. The Serjeant had added a word or two, and great
persuasion was used to induce Lady Anna to
use this epistle.

But she would have none of it. 'Oh, I couldn't,
Mrs. Bluestone;—he would know that I hadn't
written all that.'

'You have promised to write, and you are
bound to keep your promise,' said Mrs. Bluestone.

'I believe I am bound to keep all my promises,'
said Lady Anna, thinking of those which she had
made to Daniel Thwaite.

But at last she sat down and did write a letter
for herself, specially premising that no one should
see it. When she had made her promise, she
certainly had not intended to write that which
should be shown to all the world. Mrs. Bluestone had begged that at any rate the Countess
might see it. 'If mamma will let me go to her,
of course I will show it her,' said Lady Anna.
At last it was thought best to allow her to write
her own letter and to send it unseen. After
many struggles and with many tears she wrote
her letter as follows:—

'Bedford Square, Tuesday.
'MY DEAR COUSIN,

'I am sorry that I have been so long in doing
what I said I would do. I don't think I ought to
have promised, for I find it very difficult to say
anything, and I think that it is wrong that I
should write at all. It is not my fault that there
should be a lawsuit. I do not want to take

anything away from anybody, or to get anything for myself. I think papa was very wicked when he said that mamma was not his wife, and of course I wish it may all go as she wishes. But I don't think anybody ought to ask me to do what I feel to be wrong.

'Mr. Daniel Thwaite is not at all such a person as they say. He and his father have been mamma's best friends, and I shall never forget that. Old Mr. Thwaite is dead, and I am very sorry to hear it. If you had known them as we did, you would understand what I feel. Of course he is not your friend; but he is my friend, and I dare say that makes me unfit to be friends with you. You are a nobleman and he is a tradesman; but when we knew him first he was quite as good as we, and I believe we owe him a great deal of money, which mamma can't pay him. I have heard mamma say before she was angry with him, that she would have been in the workhouse, but for them, and that Mr. Daniel Thwaite might now be very well off, and not a working tailor at all, as Mrs. Bluestone calls him, if they hadn't given all they had to help us. I cannot bear after that to hear them speak of him as they do.

'Of course I should like to do what mamma wants; but how would you feel if you had promised somebody else? I do so wish that all this might be stopped altogether. My dear mamma will not allow me to see her; and though everybody is very kind, I feel that I ought not to be here with Mrs. Bluestone. Mamma talked of going abroad somewhere. I wish she would, and take me away. I should see nobody then, and there would be no trouble. But I suppose she hasn't got enough money. This is a very poor letter, but I do not know what else I can say.

> 'Believe me to be,
>> 'My dear cousin,
>>> 'Yours affectionately,
>>>> 'ANNA LOVEL.'

Then came, in a postscript, the one thing that she had to say,—'I think that I ought to be allowed to see Mr. Daniel Thwaite.'

Lord Lovel, after receiving this letter, called in Bedford Square and saw Mrs. Bluestone,—but he did not show the letter. His cousin was out with the girls and he did not wait to see her. He merely said that he had received a letter which had not given him much comfort. 'But I shall answer it,' he said,—and the reader who has seen the one letter shall see also the other.

> 'Brown's Hotel,* Albemarle Street,
>> 4th November, 183—.

'DEAREST ANNA,

'I have received your letter and am obliged to you for it, though there is so little in it to flatter or to satisfy me. I will begin by assuring you that, as far as I am concerned, I do not wish to keep you from seeing Mr. Daniel Thwaite. I believe in my heart of hearts that if you were now to see him often you would feel aware that a union between you and him could not make either of you happy. You do not even say that you think it would do so.

'You defend him, as though I had accused him. I grant all that you say in his favour. I do not doubt that his father behaved to you and to your mother with true friendship. But that will not make him fit to be the husband of Anna Lovel. You do not even say that you think that he would be fit. I fancy I understand it all, and I love you better for the pride with which you cling to so firm a friend.

'But, dearest, it is different when we talk of marriage. I imagine that you hardly dare now to think of becoming his wife. I doubt whether you say even to yourself that you love him with that kind of love. Do not suppose me vain enough to believe that therefore you must love me. It is not that. But if you would once tell yourself that he is unfit to be your husband, then you might come to love me, and would not be the less willing to do so, because all your friends wish it. It must be something to you that you should be able to put an end to all this trouble.

'Yours, dearest Anna,
'Most affectionately,
'L.

'I called in Bedford Square this morning, but you were not at home!'

'But I do dare,' she said to herself, when she had read the letter. 'Why should I not dare? And I do say to myself that I love him. Why should I not love him now, when I was not ashamed to love him before?' She was being persecuted; and as the step of the wayfarer brings out the sweet scent of the herb which he crushes with his heel, so did persecution with her extract from her heart that strength of character which had hitherto been latent. Had they left her at Yoxham, and said never a word to her about the tailor; had the rector and the two aunts showered soft courtesies on her head, —they might have vanquished her. But now the spirit of opposition was stronger within her than ever.

CHAPTER XXVIII

Lovel v. Murray and Another

Monday, the 9th of November, was the day down for the trial of the case which had assumed the name of 'Lovel versus Murray and Another.' This denomination had been adopted many months ago, when it had been held to be practicable by the Lovel party to prove that the lady who was now always called the Countess, was not entitled to bear the name of Lovel, but was simply Josephine Murray, and her daughter simply Anna Murray. Had there been another wife alive when the mother was married that name and that name only could have been hers, whether she had been the victim of the old Earl's fraud,—or had herself been a party to it. The reader will have understood that as the case went on the opinions of those who acted for the young Earl, and more especially the opinion of the young Earl himself, had been changed. Prompted to do so by various motives, they, who had undertaken to prove that the Countess was no Countess, had freely accorded to her her title, and had themselves entertained her daughter with all due acknowledgment of rank and birth. Nevertheless the name of the case remained and had become common in people's mouths. The very persons who would always speak of the Countess Lovel spoke also very familiarly of the coming trial in 'Lovel v. Murray,' and now the 9th of November had come round and the case of 'Lovel v. Murray and Another' was to be tried. The nature of the case was this. The two ladies, mother and daughter, had claimed the personal property of the late lord as his widow and daughter. Against that claim Earl Lovel made his claim, as heir-at-law,*alleging that there was no widow, and no legitimate child. The case had become infinitely complicated by the alleged existence of the first wife,—in which case she as widow would have inherited. But still the case went on as Lovel v. Murray,—the Lovel so named being the Earl, and not the alleged Italian widow.

Such being the question presumably at issue, it became the duty of the Solicitor-General to open the pleadings. In the ordinary course of proceeding it would have been his task to begin by explaining the state of the family, and by assuming that he could prove the former marriage and the existence of the former wife at the time of the latter marriage. His evidence would have been subject to cross-examination, and then another counter-statement would have been made on behalf of the Countess, and her witnesses would have been brought forward. When all this had been done the judge would have charged the jury, and with the jury would have rested the decision. This would have taken many days, and all the joys and sorrows, all the mingled hopes and anxieties of a long trial had been expected. Bets had been freely made, odds being given at first on behalf of Lord Lovel, and afterwards odds on behalf of the Countess. Interest had been made to get places in the court, and the clubs had resounded now with this fact and now with that which had just been

brought home from Sicily as certain. Then had
come suddenly upon the world the tidings that
there would absolutely be no trial, that the
great case of 'Lovel v. Murray and Another'
was to be set at rest for ever by the marriage
of 'Lovel' with 'Another,' and by the acceptance
by 'Lovel' of 'Murray' as his mother-in-law.
But the quidnuncs*would not accept this solution. No doubt Lord Lovel might marry the
second party in the defence, and it was admitted
on all hands that he probably would do so;—
but that would not stop the case. If there were
an Italian widow living, that widow was the
heir to the property. Another Lovel would
take the place of Lord Lovel,—and the cause
of Lovel v. Murray must still be continued.
The first marriage could not be annulled simply
by the fact that it would suit the young Earl
that it should be annulled. Then, while this
dispute was in progress, it was told at all the
clubs that there was to be no marriage,—that
the girl had got herself engaged to a tailor, and
that the tailor's mastery over her was so strong
that she did not dare to shake him off. Dreadful things were told about the tailor and poor
Lady Anna. There had been a secret marriage;
there was going to be a child;—the latter fact
was known as a certain fact to a great many men
at the clubs;—the tailor had made everything
safe in twenty different ways. He was powerful
over the girl equally by love, by fear, and by
written bond. The Countess had repelled her
daughter from her house by turning her out
into the street by night, and had threatened
both murder and suicide. Half the fortune had

been offered to the tailor, in vain. The romance of the story had increased greatly during the last few days preceding the trial,—but it was admitted by all that the trial as a trial would be nothing. There would probably be simply an adjournment.

It would be hard to say how the story of the tailor leaked out, and became at last public and notorious. It had been agreed among all the lawyers that it should be kept secret,—but it may perhaps have been from someone attached to them that it was first told abroad. No doubt all Norton and Flick knew it, and all Goffe and Goffe. Mr. Mainsail and his clerk, Mr. Hardy and his clerk, Serjeant Bluestone and his clerk, all knew it; but they had all promised secrecy. The clerk of the Solicitor-General was of course beyond suspicion. The two Miss Bluestones had known the story, but they had solemnly undertaken to be silent as the grave. Mrs. Bluestone was a lady with most intimately confidential friends,—but she was sworn to secrecy. It might have come from Sarah, the lady's-maid, whom the Countess had unfortunately attached to her daughter when the first gleam of prosperity had come upon them.

Among the last who heard the story of the tailor,—the last of any who professed the slightest interest in the events of the Lovel family,— were the Lovels of Yoxham. The Earl had told them nothing. In answer to his aunt's letters, and then in answer to a very urgent appeal from his uncle, the young nobleman had sent only the most curt and most ambiguous replies. When there was really something to tell he would tell everything, but at present he could only say that he

hoped that everything would be well. That had
been the extent of the information given by the
Earl to his relations, and the rector had waxed
wrathful. Nor was his wrath lessened, or the
sorrow of the two aunts mitigated, when the truth
reached them by the mouth of that very Lady
Fitzwarren who had been made to walk out of
the room after—Anna Murray, as Lady Fitzwarren persisted in calling the 'young person'
after she had heard the story of the tailor. She
told the story at Yoxham parsonage to the two
aunts, and brought with her a printed paragraph
from a newspaper to prove the truth of it. As it
is necessary that we should now hurry into the
court to hear what the Solicitor-General had to
say about the case, we cannot stop to sympathize
with the grief of the Lovels at Yoxham. We
may, however, pause for a moment to tell the
burden of the poor rector's song for that evening.
'I knew how it would be from the beginning.
I told you so. I was sure of it. But nobody
would believe me.'

The Court of Queen's Bench at Westminster
was crowded on the 9th of November. The
case was to be heard before the Lord Chief
Justice, and it was known that at any rate Sir
William Patterson would have something to
tell. If nothing else came of it, the telling of
that story would be worth the hearing. All the
preliminaries of the trial went on, as though
every one believed that it was to be carried
through to the bitter end,—as though evidence
were to be adduced and rebutted, and further
contradicted by other evidence, which would
again be rebutted with that pleasing animosity

between rival lawyers, which is so gratifying
to the outside world, and apparently to themselves also. The jurors were sworn in,—a special
jury,—and long was the time taken, and many
the threats made by the Chief Justice, before
twelve gentlemen would consent to go into the
box. Crowds were round the doors of the court,
of which every individual man would have paid
largely for standing-room to hear the trial; but
when they were wanted for use, men would not
come forward to accept a seat, with all that
honour which belongs to a special juryman.
And yet it was supposed that at last there would
be no question to submit to a jury.

About noon the Solicitor began his statement.
He was full of smiles and nods and pleasant
talk, gestures indicative of a man who had a
piece of work before him in which he could
take delight. It is always satisfactory to see the
assurance of a cock crowing in his own farm-
yard, and to admire his easy familiarity with
things that are awful to a stranger bird. If you,
O reader, or I were bound to stand up in that
court, dressed in wig and gown, and to tell a
story that would take six hours in the telling,
the one or the other of us knowing it to be his
special duty so to tell it that judge, and counsellors, and jury, should all catch clearly every
point that was to be made,—how ill would that
story be told, how would those points escape
the memory of the teller, and never come near
the intellect of the hearers! And how would the
knowledge that it would be so, confuse your
tongue or mine,—and make exquisitely miserable that moment of rising before the audience!

But our Solicitor-General rose to his legs a
happy man, with all that grace of motion, that
easy slowness, that unassumed confidence which
belongs to the ordinary doings of our familiar
life. Surely he must have known that he looked
well in his wig and gown, as with low voice and
bent neck, with only half-suppressed laughter,
he whispered into the ears of the gentleman
who sat next to him some pleasant joke that
had just occurred to him. He could do that,
though the eyes of all the court were upon him;
so great was the man! And then he began with
a sweet low voice, almost modest in its tones.
For a few moments it might have been thought
that some young woman was addressing the
court, so gentle, so dulcet were the tones.

'My lord, it is my intention on this occasion
to do that which an advocate can seldom do,—
to make a clean breast of it, to tell the court
and the jury all that I know of this case, all that
I think of it, and all that I believe,—and in
short to state a case as much in the interest of
my opponents as of my clients. The story with
which I must occupy the time of the court, I
fear, for the whole remainder of the day, with
reference to the Lovel family, is replete with
marvels and romance. I shall tell you of great
crimes and of singular virtues, of sorrows that
have been endured and conquered, and of
hopes that have been nearly realised; but the
noble client on whose behalf I am here called
upon to address you, is not in any manner the
hero of this story. His heroism will be shown to
consist in this,—unless I mar the story in telling
it,—that he is only anxious to establish the

truth, whether that truth be for him or against
him. We have now to deal with an ancient and
noble family, of which my client, the present
Earl Lovel, is at this time the head and chief.
On the question now before us depends the
possession of immense wealth. Should this trial
be carried to its natural conclusion it will be
for you to decide whether this wealth belongs
to him as the heir-at-law of the late Earl, or
whether there was left some nearer heir when
that Earl died, whose rightful claim would bar
that of my client. But there is more to be tried
than this,—and on that more depends the right
of two ladies to bear the name of Lovel. Such
right, or the absence of such right, would in
this country of itself be sufficient to justify, nay,
to render absolutely necessary, some trial before
a jury in any case of well-founded doubt. Our
titles of honour bear so high a value among us,
are so justly regarded as the outward emblem
of splendour and noble conduct, are recognised
so universally as passports to all society, that
we are naturally prone to watch their assumption with a caution most exact and scrupulous.
When the demand for such honour is made on
behalf of a man it generally includes the claim
to some parliamentary privilege, the right to
which has to be decided not by a jury, but by
the body to which that privilege belongs. The
claim to a peerage must be tried before the
House of Lords,—if made by a woman as by a
man, because the son of the heiress would be a
peer of Parliament. In the case with which we
are now concerned no such right is in question.
The lady who claims to be the Countess Lovel,

and her daughter who claims to be Lady Anna Lovel, make no demand which renders necessary other decision than that of a jury. It is as though any female commoner in the land claimed to have been the wife of an alleged husband. But not the less is the claim made to a great and a noble name; and as a grave doubt has been thrown upon the justice of the demand made by these ladies, it has become the duty of my client as the head of the Lovels, as being himself, without any doubt, the Earl Lovel of the day, to investigate the claim made, and to see that no false pretenders are allowed to wear the highly prized honours of his family. Independently of the great property which is at stake, the nature of which it will be my duty to explain to you, the question at issue whether the elder lady be or be not Countess Lovel, and whether the younger lady be or be not Lady Anna Lovel, has demanded the investigation which could not adequately have been made without this judicial array. I will now state frankly to you our belief that these two ladies are fully entitled to the names which they claim to bear; and I will add to that statement a stronger assurance of my own personal conviction and that of my client that they themselves are fully assured of the truth and justice of their demand. I think it right also to let you know that since these inquiries were first commenced, since the day for this trial was fixed, the younger of these ladies has been residing with the uncle of my client, under the same roof with my client, as an honoured and most welcome guest, and there, in the face of the whole country, has received that appellation of nobility from all the assembled members of my client's family, to dispute which I apparently now stand before you on that client's behalf.' The rector of Yoxham, who was in court, shook his head vehemently when the statement was made that Lady Anna had been his welcome guest; but nobody was then regarding the rector of Yoxham, and he shook his head in vain.

'You will at once ask why, if this be so, should the trial be continued. "As all is thus conceded," you will say, "that these two ladies claim, whom in your indictment you have misnamed Murray, why not, in God's name, give them their privileges, and the wealth which should appertain to them, and release them from the persecution of judicial proceedings?" In the first place I must answer that neither my belief, nor that of my friends who are acting with me, nor even that of my noble client himself, is sufficient to justify us in abstaining from seeking a decision which shall be final as against further claimants. If the young Earl should die, then would there be another Earl, and that other Earl might also say, with grounds as just as those on which we have acted, that the lady, whom I shall henceforward call the Countess Lovel, is no Countess. We think that she is,— but it will be for you to decide whether she is or is not, after hearing the evidence which will, no doubt, be adduced of her marriage,—and any evidence to the contrary which other parties may bring before you. We shall adduce no evidence to the contrary, nor do I think it probable that we shall ask a single question to

shake that with which my learned friend opposite is no doubt prepared. In fact, there is no
reason why my learned friend and I should not
sit together, having our briefs and our evidence
in common. And then, as the singular facts of
this story become clear to you,—as I trust that
I may be able to make them clear,—you will
learn that there are other interests at stake
beyond those of my client and of the two ladies
who appear here as his opponents. Two statements have been made tending to invalidate
the rights of Countess Lovel,—both having ori-
ginated with one who appears to have been
the basest and blackest human being with whose
iniquities my experience as a lawyer has made
me conversant. I speak of the late Earl. It
was asserted by him, almost from the date of
his marriage with the lady who is now his widow,
—falsely stated, as I myself do not doubt,—
that when he married her he had a former wife
living. But it is, I understand, capable of absolute proof that he also stated that this former
wife died soon after that second marriage,—
which in such event would have been but a
mock marriage. Were such the truth,—should
you come to the belief that the late Earl spoke
truth in so saying,—the whole property at issue
would become the undisputed possession of my
client. The late Earl died intestate, the will
which he did leave having been already set
aside by my client as having been made when
the Earl was mad. The real wife, according
to this story, would be dead. The second wife,
according to this story, would be no wife,—
and no widow. The daughter, according to this

story, would be no daughter in the eye of the law,—would, at any rate, be no heiress. The Earl would be the undisputed heir to the personal property, as he is to the real property and to the title. But we disbelieve this story utterly, —we intend to offer no evidence to show that the first wife,—for there was such a wife,— was living when the second marriage was contracted. We have no such evidence, and believe that none such can be found. Then that recreant nobleman, in whose breast there was no touch of nobility, in whose heart was no spark of mercy, made a second statement,— to this effect—that his first wife had not died at all. His reason for this it is hardly for us to seek. He may have done so, as affording a reason why he should not go through a second marriage ceremony with the lady whom he had so ill used. But that he did make this statement is certain,—and it is also certain that he allowed an income to a certain woman as though to a wife, that he allowed her to be called the Countess, though he was then living with another Italian woman; and it is also certain that this woman is still living,—or at least that she was living some week or two ago. We believe her to have been an elder sister of her who was the first wife, and whose death occurred before the second marriage. Should it be proved that this living woman was the legitimate wife of the late Earl, not only would the right be barred of those two English ladies to whom all our sympathies are now given, but no portion of the property in dispute would go either to them or to my client. I am told that before his lordship.

the Chief Justice, shall have left the case in your hands, an application will be made to the court on behalf of that living lady. I do not know how that may be, but I am so informed. If such application be made,—if there be any attempt to prove that she should inherit as widow,—then will my client again contest the case. We believe that the Countess Lovel, the English Countess, is the widow, and that Lady Anna Lovel is Lady Anna Lovel, and is the heiress. Against them we will not struggle. As was our bounden duty, we have sent not once only, but twice and thrice, to Italy and to Sicily in search of evidence which, if true, would prove that the English Countess was no Countess. We have failed, and have no evidence which we think it right to ask a jury to believe. We think that a mass of falsehood has been heaped together among various persons in a remote part of a foreign country, with the view of obtaining money, all of which was grounded on the previous falsehoods of the late Earl. We will not use these falsehoods with the object of disputing a right in the justice of which we have ourselves the strongest confidence. We withdraw from any such attempt.

'But as yet I have only given you the preliminaries of my story.' He had, in truth, told his story. He had, at least, told all of it that it will import that the reader should hear. He, indeed, —unfortunate one,—will have heard the most of that story twice or thrice before. But the audience in the Court of Queen's Bench still listened with breathless attention, while, under this new head of his story, he told every detail again with much greater length than he had done in the prelude which has been here given. He stated the facts of the Cumberland marriage, apologizing to his learned friend the Serjeant for taking, as he said, the very words out of his learned friend's mouth. He expatiated with an eloquence that was as vehement as it was touching on the demoniacal schemes of that wicked Earl, to whom, during the whole of his fiendish life, women had been a prey. He repudiated, with a scorn that was almost terrible in its wrath, the idea that Josephine Murray had gone to the Earl's house with the name of wife, knowing that she was, in fact, but a mistress. She herself was in court, thickly veiled, under the care of one of the Goffes, having been summoned there as a necessary witness, and could not control her emotion as she listened to the words of warm eulogy with which the adverse counsel told the history of her life. It seemed to her then that justice was at last being done to her. Then the Solicitor-General reverted again to the two Italian women,—the Sicilian sisters, as he called them,—and at much length gave his reasons for discrediting the evidence which he himself had sought, that he might use it with the object of establishing the claim of his client. And lastly, he described the nature of the possessions which had been amassed by the late Earl, who, black with covetousness as he was with every other sin, had so manipulated his property that almost the whole of it had become personal, and was thus inheritable by a female heiress. He knew, he said, that he was somewhat irregular in alluding to facts,—or to fiction, if any one

should call it fiction,—which he did not intend
to prove, or to attempt to prove; but there was
something, he said, beyond the common in the
aspect which this case had taken, something in
itself so irregular, that he thought he might
perhaps be held to be excused in what he had
done. 'For the sake of the whole Lovel family,
for the sake of these two most interesting ladies,
who have been subjected, during a long period
of years, to most undeserved calamities, we are
anxious to establish the truth. I have told you
what we believe to be the truth, and as that in
no single detail militates against the case as it will
be put forward by my learned friends opposite,
we have no evidence to offer. We are content to
accept the marriage of the widowed Countess as
a marriage in every respect legal and binding.'
So saying the Solicitor-General sat down.

It was then past five o'clock, and the court,
as a matter of course, was adjourned, but it was
adjourned by consent to the Wednesday, instead
of to the following day, in order that there
might be due consideration given to the nature
of the proceedings that must follow. As the
thing stood at present it seemed that there
need be no further plea of 'Lovel v. Murray
and Another.' It had been granted that Murray
was not Murray, but Lovel; yet it was thought
that something further would be done.

It had all been very pretty; but yet there
had been a feeling of disappointment throughout the audience. Not a word had been said
as to that part of the whole case which was
supposed to be the most romantic. Not a word
had been said about the tailor.

CHAPTER XXIX

Daniel Thwaite Alone

THERE were two persons in the court who heard the statement of the Solicitor-General with equal interest,—and perhaps with equal disapprobation,—whose motives and ideas on the subject were exactly opposite. These two were the Rev. Mr. Lovel, the uncle of the plaintiff, and Daniel Thwaite, the tailor, whose whole life had been passed in furthering the cause of the defendants. The parson, from the moment in which he had heard that the young lady whom he had entertained in his house had engaged herself to marry the tailor, had reverted to his old suspicions,—suspicions which, indeed, he had never altogether laid aside. It had been very grievous to him to prefer a doubtful Lady Anna to a most indubitable Lady Fitzwarren. He liked the old-established things,—things which had always been unsuspected, which were not only respectable but firm-rooted. For twenty years he had been certain that the Countess was a false countess; and he, too, had lamented with deep inward lamentation over the loss of the wealth which ought to have gone to support the family earldom. It was monstrous to him that the property of one Earl Lovel should not appertain to the next Earl. He would on the moment have had the laws with reference to the succession of personal property altered, with retrospective action, so that so great an iniquity should be impossible.

When the case against the so-called Countess was, as it were, abandoned by the Solicitor-General, and the great interests at stake thrown up, he would have put the conduct of the matter into other hands. Then had come upon him the bitterness of having to entertain in his own house the now almost undisputed,—though by him still suspected,—heiress, on behalf of his nephew, of a nephew who did not treat him well. And now the heiress had shown what she really was by declaring her intention of marrying a tailor! When that became known, he did hope that the Solicitor-General would change his purpose and fight the cause.

The ladies of the family, the two aunts, had affected to disbelieve the paragraph which Lady Fitzwarren had shown them with so much triumph. The rector had declared that it was just the kind of thing that he had expected. Aunt Julia, speaking freely, had said it was just the kind of thing which she, knowing the girl, could not believe. Then the rector had come up to town to hear the trial, and on the day preceding it had asked his nephew as to the truth of the rumour which had reached him. 'It is true,' said the young lord, knitting his brow, 'but it had better not be talked about.'

'Why not talked about? All the world knows it. It has been in the newspapers.'

'Any one wishing to oblige me will not mention it,' said the Earl. This was too bad. It could not be possible,—for the honour of all the Lovels it could not surely be possible,—that Lord Lovel was still seeking the hand of a young woman who had confessed that she was

engaged to marry a journeyman tailor! And
yet to him, the uncle,—to him who had not
long since been in loco parentis to the lord,—
the lord would vouchsafe no further reply than
that above given! The rector almost made himself believe that, great as might be the sorrow
caused by such disruption, it would become his
duty to quarrel with the Head of his family!

He listened with most attentive ears to every
word spoken by the Solicitor-General, and
quarrelled with almost every word. Would not
any one have imagined that this advocate had
been paid to plead the cause, not of the Earl,
but of the Countess? As regarded the interests
of the Earl, everything was surrendered. Appeal
was made for the sympathies of all the court,—
and, through the newspapers, for the sympathies
of all England,—not on behalf of the Earl who
was being defrauded of his rights, but on behalf
of the young woman who had disgraced the
name which she pretended to call her own,—
and whose only refuge from that disgrace must
be in the fact that to that name she had no
righteous claim! Even when this apostate barrister came to a recapitulation of the property
at stake, and explained the cause of its being
vested, not in land as is now the case with the
bulk of the possessions of noble lords,—but in
shares and funds and ventures of commercial
speculation here and there, after the fashion
of tradesmen,—he said not a word to stir up in
the minds of the jury a feeling of the injury
which had been done to the present Earl. 'Only
that I am told that he has a wife of his own I
should think that he meant to marry one of the

women himself,' said the indignant rector in the letter which he wrote to his sister Julia.

And the tailor was as indignant as the rector. He was summoned as a witness and was therefore bound to attend,—at the loss of his day's work. When he reached the court, which he did long before the judge had taken his seat, he found it to be almost impossible to effect an entrance. He gave his name to some officer about the place, but learned that his name was altogether unknown. He showed his subpœna and was told that he must wait till he was called. 'Where must I wait?' asked the angry radical. 'Anywhere,' said the man in authority; ·'but you can't force your way in here.' Then he remembered that no one had as yet paid so dearly for this struggle, no one had suffered so much, no one had been so instrumental in bringing the truth to light, as he, and this was the way in which he was treated! Had there been any justice in those concerned a seat would have been provided for him in the court, even though his attendance had not been required. There were hundreds there, brought thither by simple curiosity, to whom priority of entrance into the court had been accorded by favour, because they were wealthy, or because they were men of rank, or because they had friends high in office. All his wealth had been expended in this case; it was he who had been the most constant friend of this Countess; but for him and his father there might probably have been no question of a trial at this day. And yet he was allowed to beg for admittance, and to be shoved out of court because he had no friends.

'The court is a public court, and is open to the public,' he said, as he thrust his shoulders forward with a resolution that he would effect an entrance. Then he was taken in hand by two constables and pushed back through the doorway,—to the great detriment of the apple-woman who sat there in those days.

But by pluck and resolution he succeeded in making good some inch of standing-room within the court before the Solicitor-General began his statement, and he was able to hear every word that was said. That statement was not more pleasing to him than to the rector of Yoxham. His first quarrel was with the assertion that titles of nobility are in England the outward emblem of noble conduct. No words that might have been uttered could have been more directly antagonistic to his feelings and political creed. It had been the accident of his life that he should have been concerned with ladies who were noble by marriage and birth, and that it had become a duty to him to help to claim on their behalf empty names which were in themselves odious to him. It had been the woman's right to be acknowledged as the wife of the man who had disowned her, and the girl's right to be known as his legitimate daughter. Therefore had he been concerned. But he had declared to himself, from his first crude conception of an opinion on the subject, that it would be hard to touch pitch and not be defiled. The lords of whom he heard were, or were believed by him to be, bloated with luxury, were both rich and idle, were gamblers, debauchers of other men's wives, deniers of all rights of citizenship, drones who

were positively authorised to eat the honey
collected by the working bees. With his half-
knowledge, his ill-gotten and ill-digested information, with his reading which had all been on
one side, he had been unable as yet to catch
a glimpse of the fact that from the ranks of the
nobility are taken the greater proportion of the
hard-working servants of the State. His eyes saw
merely the power, the privileges, the titles, the
ribbons, and the money;—and he hated a lord.
When therefore the Solicitor-General spoke of
the recognised virtue of titles in England, the
tailor uttered words of scorn to his stranger
neighbour. 'And yet this man calls himself a
Liberal, and voted for the Reform Bill,'*he said.
'In course he did,' replied the stranger; 'that
was the way of his party.' 'There isn't an
honest man among them all,' said the tailor to
himself. This was at the beginning of the
speech, and he listened on through five long
hours, not losing a word of the argument, not
missing a single point made in favour of the
Countess and her daughter. It became clear
to him at any rate that the daughter would
inherit the money. When the Solicitor-General
came to speak of the nature of the evidence
collected in Italy, Daniel Thwaite was unconsciously carried away into a firm conviction that
all those concerned in the matter in Italy were
swindlers. The girl was no doubt the heiress.
The feeling of all the court was with her,—as
he could well perceive. But in all that speech
not one single word was said of the friend who
had been true to the girl and to her mother
through all their struggles and adversity. The

name of Thomas Thwaite was not once mentioned. It might have been expedient for them to ignore him, Daniel, the son; but surely had there been any honour among them, any feeling of common honesty towards folk so low in the scale of humanity as tailors, some word would have been spoken to tell of the friendship of the old man who had gone to his grave almost a pauper because of his truth and constancy. But no;—there was not a word!

And he listened, with anxious ears, to learn whether anything would be said as to that proposed 'alliance,'—he had always heard it called an alliance with a grim smile,—between the two noble cousins. Heaven and earth had been moved to promote 'the alliance.' But the Solicitor-General said not a word on the subject, —any more than he did of that other disreputable social arrangement, which would have been no more than a marriage. All the audience might suppose from anything that was said there that the young lady was fancy free and had never yet dreamed of a husband. Nevertheless there was hardly one there who had not heard something of the story of the Earl's suit,— and something also of the tailor's success.

When the court broke up, Daniel Thwaite had reached standing-room, which brought him near to the seat that was occupied by Serjeant Bluestone. He lingered as long as he could, and saw all the barristers concerned standing with their heads together laughing, chatting, and well pleased, as though the day had been for them a day of pleasure. 'I fancy the speculation is too bad for any one to take it up,' he heard the Serjeant say, among whose various gifts was not that of being able to moderate his voice. 'I dare say not,' said Daniel to himself as he left the court; 'and yet we took it up when the risk was greater, and when there was nothing to be gained.' He had as yet received no explicit answer to the note which he had written to the Countess when he had sent her the copy of his father's will. He had, indeed, received a notice from Mr. Goffe that the matter would receive immediate attention, and that the Countess hoped to be able to settle the claim in a very short time. But that he thought was not such a letter as should have been sent to him on an occasion so full of interest to him! But they were all hard and unjust and bad. The Countess was bad because she was a Countess,—the lawyers because they were lawyers,—the whole Lovel family because they were Lovels. At this moment poor Daniel Thwaite was very bitter against all mankind. He would, he thought, go at once to the Western world of which he was always dreaming, if he could only get that sum of £500 which was manifestly due to him.

But as he wandered away after the court was up, getting some wretched solitary meal at a cheap eating-house on his road, he endeavoured to fix his thoughts on the question of the girl's affection to himself. Taking all that had been said in that courtly lawyer's speech this morning as the groundwork of his present judgment, what should he judge to be her condition at the moment? He had heard on all sides that it was intended that she should marry the young Earl, and it had been said in his hearing that such would be declared before the judge. No such declaration had been made. Not a word had been uttered to signify that such an 'alliance' was contemplated. Efforts had been made with him to induce him to withdraw his claim to the girl's hand. The Countess had urged him, and the lawyers had urged him. Most assuredly they would not have done so,—would have in no wise troubled themselves with him at all,— had they been able to prevail with Lady Anna. And why had they not so prevailed? The girl, doubtless, had been subjected to every temptation. She was kept secure from his interference. Hitherto he had not even made an effort to see her since she had left the house in which he himself lived. She had nothing to fear from him. She had been sojourning among those Lovels, who would doubtless have made the way to deceit and luxury easy for her. He could not doubt but that she had been solicited to enter into this alliance. Could he be justified in flattering himself that she had hitherto resisted temptation because in her heart of hearts she was true to her first love? He was true. He was conscious of his own constancy. He was sure of himself that he was bound to her by his love, and not by the hope of any worldly advantage. And why should he think that she was weaker, vainer, less noble than himself? Had he not evidence to show him that she was strong enough to resist a temptation to which he had never been subjected? He had read of women who were above the gilt and glitter of the world. When he was disposed to think that she would be false, no terms of reproach seemed to him too severe to heap upon her name; and yet, when he found that he had no ground on which to accuse her, even in his own thoughts, of treachery to himself, he could hardly bring himself to think it possible that she should not be treacherous. She had sworn to him, as he had sworn to her, and was he not bound to believe her oath?

Then he remembered what the poet had said to him. The poet had advised him to desist altogether, and had told him that it would certainly be best for the girl that he should do so. The poet had not based his advice on the ground that the girl would prove false, but that it would be good for the girl to be allowed to be false,—good for the girl that she should be encouraged to be false, in order that she might become an earl's wife! But he thought that it would be bad for any woman to be an earl's wife; and so thinking, how could he abandon his love in order that he might hand her over to a fashion of life which he himself despised? The poet must be wrong. He would cling to his love till he should know that his love was false to him. Should he ever learn that, then his love should be troubled with him no further.

But something must be done. Even, on her behalf, if she were true to him, something must be done. Was it not pusillanimous in him to make no attempt to see his love and to tell her that he at any rate was true to her? These people, who were now his enemies, the lawyers and the Lovels, with the Countess at the head of them, had used him like a dog, had repudiated him without remorse, had not a word even to say of the services which his father had rendered. Was he bound by honour or duty to stand on any terms with them? Could there be anything due to them from him? Did it not behove him as a man to find his way into the girl's presence and to assist her with his courage? He did not fear them. What cause had he to fear them? In all that had been between them his actions to them had been kind and good, whereas they were treating him with the basest ingratitude.

But how should he see Lady Anna? As he thought of all this he wandered up from Westminster, where he had eaten his dinner, to Russell Square and into Keppel Street, hesitating whether he would at once knock at the door and ask to see Lady Anna Lovel. Lady Anna was still staying with Mrs. Bluestone; but Daniel Thwaite had not believed the Countess when she told him that her daughter was not living with her. He doubted, however, and did not knock at the door.

CHAPTER XXX

Justice is to be done

IT must not be thought that the Countess was unmoved when she received Daniel Thwaite's letter from Keswick enclosing the copy of his father's will. She was all alone, and she sat long in her solitude, thinking of the friend who was gone and who had been always true to her. She herself would have done for old Thomas Thwaite any service which a woman could render to a man, so strongly did she feel all that the man had done for her. As she had once said, no menial office performed by her on behalf of the old tailor would have been degrading to her. She had eaten his bread, and she never for a moment forgot the obligation. The slow tears stood in her eyes as she thought of the long long hours which she had passed in his company, while, almost desponding herself, she had received courage from his persistency. And her feeling for the son would have been the same, had not the future position of her daughter and the standing of the house of Lovel been at stake. It was not in her nature to be ungrateful; but neither was it in her nature to postpone the whole object of her existence to her gratitude. Even though she should appear to the world as a monster of ingratitude, she must treat the surviving Thwaite as her bitterest enemy as long as he maintained his pretensions to her daughter's hand. She could have no friendly communication with him. She herself would hold no com-

munication with him at all, if she might possibly
avoid it, lest she should be drawn into some
renewed relation of friendship with him. He
was her enemy,—her enemy in such fierce degree that she was always plotting the means of
ridding herself altogether of his presence and
influence. To her thinking the man had turned
upon her most treacherously, and was using, for
his own purposes and his own aggrandizement,
that familiarity with her affairs which he had
acquired by reason of his father's generosity.
She believed but little in his love; but whether
he loved the girl or merely sought her money,
was all one to her. Her whole life had been
passed in an effort to prove her daughter to be
a lady of rank, and she would rather sacrifice
her life in the basest manner than live to see
all her efforts annulled by a low marriage. Love,
indeed, and romance! What was the love of one
individual, what was the romance of a childish
girl, to the honour and well-being of an ancient
and noble family? It was her ambition to see
her girl become the Countess Lovel, and no
feeling of gratitude should stand in her way.
She would rather slay that low-born artisan with
her own hand than know that he had the right
to claim her as his mother-in-law. Nevertheless,
the slow tears crept down her cheeks as she
thought of former days, and of the little parlour
behind the tailor's shop at Keswick, in which
the two children had been wont to play.

But the money must be paid; or, at least, the
debt must be acknowledged. As soon as she had
somewhat recovered herself she opened the old
desk which had for years been the receptacle

of all her papers, and taking out sundry scribbled documents, went to work at a sum in addition. It cannot be said of her that she was a good accountant, but she had been so far careful as to have kept entries of all the monies she had received from Thomas Thwaite. She had once carried in her head a correct idea of the entire sum she owed him; but now she set down the items with dates, and made the account fair on a sheet of note paper. So much money she certainly did owe to Daniel Thwaite, and so much she would certainly pay if ever the means of paying it should be hers. Then she went off with her account to Mr. Goffe.

Mr. Goffe did not think that the matter pressed. The payment of large sums which have been long due never is pressing in the eyes of lawyers. Men are always supposed to have a hundred pounds in their waistcoat pockets; but arrangements have to be made for the settling of thousands. 'You had better let me write him a line and tell him that it shall be looked to as soon as the question as to the property is decided,' said Mr. Goffe. But this did not suit the views of the Countess. She spoke out very openly as to all she owed to the father, and as to her eternal enmity to the son. It behoved her to pay the debt, if only that she might be able to treat the man altogether as an enemy. She had understood that, even pending the trial, a portion of the income would be allowed by the courts for her use and for the expenses of the trial. It was assented that this money should be paid. Could steps be taken by which it might be settled at once? Mr. Goffe, taking the memorandum, said that he would see what could be done, and then wrote his short note to Daniel Thwaite. When he had computed the interest which must undoubtedly be paid on the borrowed money he found that a sum of about £9,000 was due to the tailor. 'Nine thousand pounds!' said one Mr. Goffe to another. 'That will be better to him than marrying the daughter of an earl.' Could Daniel have heard the words he would have taken the lawyer by the throat and have endeavoured to teach him what love is.

Then the trial came on. Before the day fixed had come round, but only just before it, Mr. Goffe showed the account to Serjeant Bluestone. 'God bless my soul!' said the Serjeant. 'There should be some vouchers for such an amount as that.' Mr. Goffe declared that there were no vouchers, except for a very trifling part of it; but still thought that the amount should be allowed. The Countess was quite willing to make oath, if need be, that the money had been supplied to her. Then the further consideration of the question was for the moment postponed, and the trial came on.

On the Tuesday, which had been left a vacant day as regarded the trial, there was a meeting, —like all other proceedings in this cause, very irregular in its nature,—at the chambers of the Solicitor-General, at which Serjeant Bluestone attended with Messrs. Hardy, Mainsail, Flick, and Goffe; and at this meeting, among other matters of business, mention was made of the debt due by the Countess to Daniel Thwaite. Of this debt the Solicitor-General had not as yet heard,—

though he had heard of the devoted friendship of the old tailor. That support had been afforded to some extent,—that for a period the shelter of old Thwaite's roof had been lent to the Countess, —that the man had been generous and trusting, he did know. He had learned, of course, that thence had sprung that early familiarity which had enabled the younger Thwaite to make his engagement with Lady Anna. That something should be paid when the ladies came by their own he was aware. But the ladies were not his clients, and into the circumstances he had not inquired. Now he was astounded and almost scandalized by the amount of the debt.

'Do you mean to say that he advanced £9,000 in hard cash?' said the Solicitor-General.

'That includes interest at five per cent., Sir William, and also a small sum for bills paid by Thomas Thwaite on her behalf. She has had in actual cash about £7,000.'

'And where has it gone?'

'A good deal of it through my hands,' said Mr. Goffe boldly. 'During two or three years she had no income at all, and during the last twenty years she has been at law for her rights. He advanced all the money when that trial for bigamy took place.'

'God bless my soul!' said Mr. Serjeant Bluestone.

'Did he leave a will?' asked the Solicitor-General.

'Oh, yes; a will which has been proved, and of which I have a copy. There was nothing else to leave but this debt, and that is left to the son.'

'It should certainly be paid without delay,' said Mr. Hardy. Mr. Mainsail questioned whether they could get the money. Mr. Goffe doubted whether it could be had before the whole affair was settled. Mr. Flick was sure that on due representation the amount would be advanced at once. The income of the property was already accumulating in the hands of the court, and there was an anxiety that all just demands,—demands which might be considered to be justly made on the family property,—should be paid without delay. 'I think there would hardly be a question,' said Mr. Hardy.

'Seven thousand pounds advanced by these two small tradesmen to the Countess Lovel,' said the Solicitor-General, 'and that done at a time when no relation of her own or of her husband would lend her a penny! I wish I had known that when I went into court yesterday.'

'It would hardly have done any good,' said the Serjeant.

'It would have enabled one at any rate to give credit where credit is due. And this son is the man who claims to be affianced to the Lady Anna?'

'The same man, Sir William,' said Mr. Goffe.

'One is almost inclined to think that he deserves her.'

'I can't agree with you there at all,' said the Serjeant angrily.

'One at any rate is not astonished that the young lady should think so,' continued the Solicitor-General. 'Upon my word, I don't know how we are to expect that she should throw her early lover overboard after such evidence of devotion.'

'The marriage would be too incongruous,' said Mr. Hardy.

'Quite horrible,' said the Serjeant.

'It distresses one to think of it,' said Mr. Goffe.

'It would be much better that she should not be Lady Anna at all, if she is to do that,' said Mr. Mainsail.

'Very much better,' said Mr. Flick, shaking his head, and remembering that he was employed by Lord Lovel and not by the Countess, —a fact of which it seemed to him that the Solicitor-General altogether forgot the importance.

'Gentlemen, you have no romance among you,' said Sir William. 'Have not generosity and valour always prevailed over wealth and rank with ladies in story?'

'I do not remember any valorous tailors who have succeeded with ladies of high degree,' said Mr. Hardy.

'Did not the lady of the Strachy marry the yeoman of the wardrobe?'* asked the Solicitor-General.

'I don't know that we care much about romance here,' said the Serjeant. 'The marriage would be so abominable, that it is not to be thought of.'

'The tailor should at any rate get his money,' said the Solicitor-General, 'and I will undertake to say that if the case be as represented by Mr. Goffe——'

'It certainly is,' said the attorney.

'Then there will be no difficulty in raising the funds for paying it. If he is not to have his wife, at any rate let him have his money. I think, Mr. Flick, that intimation should be made to him that Earl Lovel will join the Countess in immediate application to the court for means to settle his claim. Circumstanced as we are at present, there can be no doubt that such application will have the desired result. It should, of course, be intimated that Serjeant Bluestone and myself are both of opinion that the money should be allowed for the purpose.'

As the immediate result of this conversation, Daniel Thwaite received on the following morning letters both from Mr. Goffe and Mr. Flick. The former intimated to him that a sum of nine thousand odd pounds was held to be due to him by the Countess, and that immediate steps would be taken for its payment. That from Mr. Flick, which was much shorter than the letter from his brother attorney, merely stated that as a very large sum of money appeared to be due by the Countess Lovel to the estate of the late Thomas Thwaite, for sums advanced to the Countess during the last twenty years, the present Earl Lovel had been advised to join the Countess in application to the courts, that the amount due might be paid out of the income of the property left by the late Earl; and that that application would be made '*immediately*.' Mr. Goffe in his letter, went on to make certain suggestions, and to give much advice. As this very large debt, of which no proof was extant, was freely admitted by the Countess, and as steps were being at once taken to ensure payment of the whole sum named to Daniel Thwaite, as his father's heir, it was hoped that Daniel

Thwaite would at once abandon his preposterous claim to the hand of Lady Anna Lovel. Then Mr. Goffe put forward in glowing colours the iniquity of which Daniel Thwaite would be guilty should he continue his fruitless endeavours to postpone the re-establishment of a noble family which was thus showing its united benevolence by paying to him the money which it owed him.

CHAPTER XXXI

The Verdict

ON the Wednesday the court reassembled in all its judicial glory. There was the same crowd, the same Lord Chief Justice, the same jury, and the same array of friendly lawyers. There had been a rumour that a third retinue of lawyers would appear on behalf of what was now generally called the Italian interest, and certain words which had fallen from the Solicitor-General on Monday had assured the world at large that the Italian interest would be represented. It was known that the Italian case had been confined to a firm of enterprising solicitors, named Mowbray and Mopus, perhaps more feared than respected, which was supposed to do a great amount of speculative business. But no one from the house of Messrs. Mowbray and Mopus was in court on the Wednesday morning; and no energetic barrister was ever enriched by a fee from them on behalf of the Italian widow. The speculation had been found to be too deep, the expenditure which would be required in advance too great, and the prospect of remuneration too remote even for Mowbray and Mopus. It appeared afterwards that application had been made by those gentlemen for an assurance that expenses incurred on behalf of the Italian Countess should be paid out of the estate; but this had been refused. No guarantee to this effect could be given, at any rate till it should be seen whether the Italian lady had any show of justice on her

side. It was now the general belief that if there
was any truth at all in the Italian claim, it
rested on the survivorship, at the time of the
Cumberland marriage, of a wife who had long
since died. As the proof of this would have given
no penny to any one in Italy,—would simply
have shown that the Earl was the heir,—Messrs.
Mowbray and Mopus retired, and there was an
end, for ever and a day, of the Italian interest.

Though there was the same throng in the court
as on the Monday, there did not seem to be the
same hubbub on the opening of the day's proceedings. The barristers were less busy with
their papers, the attorneys sat quite at their
ease, and the Chief Justice with an assistant
judge, who was his bench-fellow, appeared for
some minutes to be quite passive. Then the
Solicitor-General arose and said that, with permission, he would occupy the court for only a
few minutes. He had stated on Monday his
belief that an application would be made to the
court on behalf of other interests than those
which had been represented when the court
first met. It appeared that he had been wrong
in that surmise. Of course he had no knowledge
on the subject, but it did not appear that any
learned gentleman was prepared to address the
court for any third party. As he, on behalf of
his client, had receded from the case, his Lordship would probably say what, in his Lordship's
opinion, should now be the proceeding of the
court. The Earl Lovel abandoned his plea, and
perhaps the court would, in those circumstances,
decide that its jurisdiction in the matter was over.
Then the Lord Chief Justice, with his assistant

judge, retired for a while, and all the assembled crowd appeared to be at liberty to discuss the matter just as everybody pleased.

It was undoubtedly the opinion of the bar at large, and at that moment of the world in general, that the Solicitor-General had done badly for his client. The sum of money which was at stake was, they said, too large to be played with. As the advocate of the Earl, Sir William ought to have kept himself aloof from the Countess and her daughter. In lieu of regarding his client, he had taken upon himself to set things right in general, according to his idea of right. No doubt he was a clever man, and knew how to address a jury, but he was always thinking of himself, and bolstering up something of his own, instead of thinking of his case and bolstering up his client. And this conception of his character in general, and of his practice in this particular, became the stronger, as it was gradually believed that the living Italian Countess was certainly an impostor. There would have been little good in fighting against the English Countess on her behalf;—but if they could have only proved that the other Italian woman, who was now dead, had been the real Countess when the Cumberland marriage was made, then what a grand thing it would have been for the Lovel family! Of those who held this opinion, the rector of Yoxham was the strongest, and the most envenomed against the Solicitor-General. During the whole of that Tuesday he went about declaring that the interests of the Lovel family had been sacrificed by their own counsel, and late in the afternoon he managed to get hold of Mr. Hardy. Could nothing be done? Mr. Hardy was of opinion that nothing could be done now; but in the course of the evening he did, at the rector's instance, manage to see Sir William, and to ask the question, 'Could nothing be done?'

'Nothing more than we propose to do.'

'Then the case is over,' said Mr. Hardy. 'I am assured that no one will stir on behalf of that Italian lady.'

'If any one did stir it would be loss of time and money. My dear Hardy, I understand as well as any one what people are saying, and I know what must be the feeling of many of the Lovels. But I can only do my duty by my client to the best of my judgment. In the first place, you must remember that he has himself acknowledged the Countess.'

'By our advice,' said Mr. Hardy.

'You mean by mine. Exactly so;—but with such conviction on his own part that he positively refuses to be a party to any suit which shall be based on the assumption that she is not Countess Lovel. Let an advocate be ever so obdurate, he can hardly carry on a case in opposition to his client's instructions. We are acting for Lord Lovel, and not for the Lovel family. And I feel assured of this, that were we to attempt to set up the plea that the other woman was alive when the marriage took place in Cumberland, you, yourself, would be ashamed of the evidence which it would become your duty to endeavour to foist upon the jury. We should certainly be beaten, and, in the ultimate settlement of the property, we should have to do with enemies instead of friends. The man was tried for bigamy and acquitted. Would any jury get over that unless you had evidence to offer to them that was plain as a pikestaff, and absolutely incontrovertible?'

'Do you still think the girl will marry the Earl?'

'No; I do not. She seems to have a will of her own, and that will is bent the other way. But I do think that a settlement may be made of the property which shall be very much in the Earl's favour.' When on the following morning the Solicitor-General made his second speech, which did not occupy above a quarter of an hour, it became manifest that he did not intend to alter his course of proceeding, and while the judges were absent it was said by everybody in the court that the Countess and Lady Anna had gained their suit.

'I consider it to be a most disgraceful course of proceeding on the part of Sir William Patterson,' said the rector to a middle-aged legal functionary, who was managing clerk to Norton and Flick.

'We all think, sir, that there was more fight in it,' said the legal functionary.

'There was plenty of fight in it. I don't believe that any jury in England would willingly have taken such an amount of property from the head of the Lovel family. For the last twenty years,—ever since I first heard of the pretended English marriage,—everybody has known that she was no more a Countess than I am. I can't understand it; upon my word I can't. I have not had much to do with law, but I've always

been brought up to think that an English
barrister would be true to his client. I believe
a case can be tried again if it can be shown that
the lawyers have mismanaged it.' The unfortunate rector, when he made this suggestion, no
doubt forgot that the client in this case was in
full agreement with the wicked advocate.

The judges were absent for about half an
hour, and on their return the Chief Justice
declared that his learned brother,—the Serjeant
namely,—had better proceed with the case on
behalf of his clients. He went on to explain that
as the right to the property in dispute, and
indeed the immediate possession of that property,
would be ruled by the decision of the jury, it
was imperative that they should hear what
the learned counsel for the so-called Countess
and her daughter had to say, and what evidence they had to offer, as to the validity of her
marriage. It was not to be supposed that he
intended to throw any doubt on that marriage,
but such would be the safer course. No doubt,
in the ordinary course of succession, a widow
and a daughter would inherit and divide among
them in certain fixed proportions the personal
property of a deceased but intestate husband
and father, without the intervention of any jury
to declare their rights. But in this case suspicion
had been thrown and adverse statements had
been made; and as his learned brother was, as a
matter of course, provided with evidence to prove
that which the plaintiff had come into the court
with the professed intention of disproving, the
case had better go on. Then he wrapped his
robes around him and threw himself back in

the attitude of a listener. Serjeant Bluestone, already on his legs, declared himself prepared and willing to proceed. No doubt the course as now directed was the proper course to be pursued. The Solicitor-General, rising gracefully and bowing to the court, gave his consent with complaisant patronage. 'Your Lordship, no doubt, is right.' His words were whispered, and very probably not heard; but the smile as coming from a Solicitor-General,—from such a Solicitor-General as Sir William Patterson,—was sufficient to put any judge at his ease.

Then Serjeant Bluestone made his statement, and the case was proceeded with after the fashion of such trials. It will not concern us to follow the further proceedings of the court with any close attention. The Solicitor-General went away to some other business, and much of the interest seemed to drop. The marriage in Cumberland was proved; the trial for bigamy, with the acquittal of the Earl, was proved; the two opposed statements of the Earl, as to the death of the first wife, and afterwards as to the fact that she was living, were proved. Serjeant Bluestone and Mr. Mainsail were very busy for two days, having everything before them. Mr. Hardy, on behalf of the young lord, kept his seat, but he said not a word—not even asking a question of one of Serjeant Bluestone's witnesses. Twice the foreman of the jury interposed, expressing an opinion, on behalf of himself and his brethren, that the case need not be proceeded with further; but the judge ruled that it was for the interest of the Countess,—he ceased to style her the so-called Countess,—that her advocates should be

allowed to complete their case. In the afternoon
of the second day they did complete it, with
great triumph and a fine flourish of forensic
oratory as to the cruel persecution which their
client had endured. The Solicitor-General came
back into court in time to hear the judge's
charge, which was very short. The jury were
told that they had no alternative but to find a
verdict for the defendants. It was explained to
them that this was a plea to show that a certain
marriage which had taken place in Cumberland
in 181–, was no real or valid marriage. Not only
was that plea withdrawn, but evidence had been
adduced proving that that marriage was valid.
Such a marriage was, as a matter of course,
primâ facie valid, let what statements might be
made to the contrary by those concerned or not
concerned. In such case the burden of proof
would rest entirely with the makers of such
statement. No such proof had been here attempted, and the marriage must be declared
a valid marriage. The jury had nothing to do
with the disposition of the property, and it
would be sufficient for them simply to find a
verdict for the defendants. The jury did as they
were bid; but, going somewhat beyond this,
declared that they found the two defendants to
be properly named the Countess Lovel, and
Lady Anna Lovel. So ended the case of 'Lovel
v. Murray and Another.'

The Countess, who had been in the court all
day, was taken home to Keppel Street by the
Serjeant in a glass coach that had been hired to
be in waiting for her. 'And now, Lady Lovel,'
said Serjeant Bluestone, as he took his seat

opposite to her, 'I can congratulate your ladyship on the full restitution of your rights.' She
only shook her head. 'The battle has been
fought and won at last, and I will make free to
say that I have never seen more admirable
persistency than you have shown since first that
bad man astounded your ears by his iniquity.'

'It has been all to no purpose,' she said.

'To no purpose, Lady Lovel! I may as well
tell you that it is expected that His Majesty will
send to congratulate you on the restitution of
your rights.'

Again she shook her head. 'Ah, Serjeant
Bluestone;—that will be but of little service.'

'No further objection can now be made to the
surrender of the whole property. There are
some mining shares as to which there may be a
question whether they are real or personal, but
they amount to but little. A third of the remainder, which will, I imagine, exceed——'

'If it were ten times as much, Serjeant Bluestone, there would be no comfort in it. If it were
ten times that, it would not at all help to heal
my sorrow. I have sometimes thought that
when one is marked for trouble, no case can
come.'

'I don't think more of money than another
man,' began the Serjeant.

'You do not understand.'

'Nor yet of titles,—though I feel for them,
when they are worthily worn, the highest
respect,' as he so spoke the Serjeant lifted his
hat from his brow. 'But, upon my word, to have
won such a case as this justifies triumph.'

'I have won nothing,—nothing,—nothing!'

'You mean about Lady Anna?'

'Serjeant Bluestone, when first I was told that
I was not that man's wife, I swore to myself
that I would die sooner than accept any lower
name; but when I found that I was a mother,
then I swore that I would live till my child
should bear the name that of right belonged
to her.'

'She does bear it now.'

'What name does she propose to bear? I would
sooner be poor, in beggary,—still fighting, even
without means to fight, for an empty title,—
still suffering, still conscious that all around me
regarded me as an impostor, than conquer only
to know that she, for whom all this has been
done, has degraded her name and my own. If
she does this thing, or, if she has a mind so low,
a spirit so mean, as to think of doing it, would it
not be better for all the world that she should be
the bastard child of a rich man's kept mistress,
than the acknowledged daughter of an earl,
with a countesss for her mother, and a princely
fortune to support her rank? If she marries this
man, I shall heartily wish that Lord Lovel had
won the case. I care nothing for myself now.
I have lost all that. The king's message will not
comfort me at all. If she do this thing I shall
only feel the evil we have done in taking the
money from the Earl. I would sooner see her
dead at my feet than know that she was that
man's wife;—ay, though I had stabbed her
with my own hand!'

The Serjeant for the nonce could say nothing
more to her. She had worked herself into such
a passion that she would listen to no words but

her own, and think of nothing but the wrong that was still being done to her. He put her down at the hall door in Keppel Street, saying, as he lifted his hat again, that Mrs. Bluestone should come and call upon her.

CHAPTER XXXII

Will you Promise?

THE news of the verdict was communicated the same evening to Lady Anna,—as to whose name there could now no longer be any dispute. 'I congratulate you, Lady Anna,' said the Serjeant, holding her hand, 'that everything as far as this trial is concerned has gone just as we could wish.'

'We owe it all to you,' said the girl.

'Not at all. My work has been very easy. In fact I have some feeling of regret that I have not been placed in a position that would enable me to earn my wages. The case was too good,— so that a poor aspiring lawyer has not been able to add to his reputation. But as far as you are concerned, my dear, everything has gone as you should wish. You are now a very wealthy heiress and the great duty devolves upon you of disposing of your wealth in a fitting manner.' Lady Anna understood well what was meant, and was silent. Even when she was alone her success did not make her triumphant. She could anticipate that the efforts of all her friends to make her false to her word would be redoubled. Unless she could see Daniel Thwaite, it would be impossible that she should not be conquered.

The Serjeant told his wife the promise which he had made on her behalf, and she, of course, undertook to go to Keppel Street on the following morning. 'You had better bring her here,' said the Serjeant. Mrs. Bluestone remarked that that might be sooner said than done. 'She'll be glad of an excuse to come,' answered the Serjeant. 'On such an occasion as this, of course they must see each other. Something must be arranged about the property. In a month or two, when she is of age, she will have the undisputed right to do what she pleases with about three hundred thousand pounds. It is a most remarkable position for a young girl who has never yet had the command of a penny, and who professes that she is engaged to marry a working tailor. Of course her mother must see her.'

Mrs. Bluestone did call in Keppel Street, and sat with the Countess a long time, undergoing a perfect hailstorm of passion. For a long time Lady Lovel declared that she would never see her daughter again till the girl had given a solemn promise that she would not marry Daniel Thwaite. 'Love her! Of course I love her. She is all that I have in the world. But of what good is my love to me, if she disgraces me? She has disgraced me already. When she could bring herself to tell her cousin that she was engaged to this man, we were already disgraced. When she once allowed the man to speak to her in that strain, without withering him with her scorn, she disgraced us both. For what have I done it all, if this is to be the end of it?' But at last she assented and promised that she would come. No;—it would not be necessary to send a carriage for her. The habits of her own life need not be at all altered because she was now a Countess beyond dispute, and also wealthy. She would be content to live as she had ever lived. It had gone on too long for her to desire personal

comfort,—luxury for herself, or even social rank.
The only pleasure that she had anticipated, the
only triumph that she desired, was to be found
in the splendour of her child. She would walk
to Bedford Square, and then walk back to her
lodgings in Keppel Street. She wanted no
carriage.

Early on the following day there was heard
the knock at the door which Lady Anna had
been taught to expect. The coming visit had been
discussed in all its bearings, and it had been
settled that Mrs. Bluestone should be with the
daughter when the mother arrived. It was
thought that in this way the first severity of
the Countess would be mitigated, and that the
chance of some agreement between them might
be increased. Both the Serjeant and Mrs. Bluestone now conceived that the young lady had a
stronger will of her own than might have been
expected from her looks, her language, and her
manners. She had not as yet yielded an inch,
though she would not argue the matter at all
when she was told that it was her positive duty
to abandon the tailor. She would sit quite silent;
and if silence does give consent, she consented
to this doctrine. Mrs. Bluestone, with a diligence which was equalled only by her good
humour, insisted on the misery which must
come upon her young friend should she quarrel
with the Countess, and with all the Lovels,—
on the unfitness of the tailor, and the impossibility that such a marriage should make a
lady happy,—on the sacred duty which Lady
Anna's rank imposed upon her to support her
order, and on the general blessedness of a well-

preserved and exclusive aristocracy. 'I don't mean to say that nobly born people are a bit better than commoners,' said Mrs. Bluestone. 'Neither I nor my children have a drop of noble blood in our veins. It is not that. But God Almighty has chosen that there should be different ranks to carry out His purposes, and we have His word to tell us that we should all do our duties in that state of life to which it has pleased Him to call us.' The excellent lady was somewhat among the clouds in her theology, and apt to mingle the different sources of religious instruction from which she was wont to draw lessons for her own and her children's guidance; but she meant to say that the proper state of life for an earl's daughter could not include an attachment to a tailor; and Lady Anna took it as it was meant. The nobly born young lady did not in heart deny the truth of the lesson;— but she had learned another lesson, and did not know how to make the two compatible. That other lesson taught her to believe that she ought to be true to her word;—that she specially ought to be true to one who had ever been specially true to her. And latterly there had grown upon her a feeling less favourable to the Earl than that which he had inspired when she first saw him and which he had increased when they were together at Yoxham. It is hard to say why the Earl had ceased to charm her, or by what acts or words he had lowered himself in her eyes. He was as handsome as ever, as much like a young Apollo, as gracious in his manner, and as gentle in his gait. And he had been constant to her. Perhaps it was that she had expected

that one so god-like should have ceased to adore
a woman who had degraded herself to the level
of a tailor, and that, so conceiving, she had
begun to think that his motives might be merely
human, and perhaps sordid. He ought to have
abstained and seen her no more after she had
owned her own degradation. But she said
nothing of all this to Mrs. Bluestone. She made
no answer to the sermons preached to her.
She certainly said no word tending to make
that lady think that the sermons had been of
any avail. 'She looks as soft as butter,' Mrs.
Bluestone said that morning to her husband;
'but she is obstinate as a pig all the time.'

'I suppose her father was the same way before
her,' said the Serjeant, 'and God knows her
mother is obstinate enough.'

When the Countess was shown into the room
Lady Anna was trembling with fear and emotion.
Lady Lovel, during the last few weeks, since her
daughter had seen her, had changed the nature
of her dress. Hitherto, for years past, she had
worn a brown stuff gown, hardly ever varying
even the shade of the sombre colour,—so that
her daughter had perhaps never seen her otherwise clad. No woman that ever breathed was
less subject to personal vanity than had been the
so-called Countess who lived in the little cottage
outside Keswick. Her own dress had been as
nothing to her, and in the days of her close
familiarity with old Thomas Thwaite she had
rebuked her friend when he had besought her
to attire herself in silk. 'We'll go into Keswick
and get Anna a new ribbon,' she would say,
'and that will be grandeur enough for her and

me too.' In this brown dress she had come up
to London, and so she had been clothed when
her daughter last saw her. But now she wore
a new, full, black silk dress, which, plain as it
was, befitted her rank and gave an increased
authority to her commanding figure. Lady
Anna trembled all the more, and her heart
sank still lower within her, because her mother
no longer wore the old brown gown. When the
Countess entered the room she took no immediate notice of Mrs. Bluestone, but went up to her
child and kissed her. 'I am comforted, Anna,
in seeing you once again,' she said.

'Dear, dearest mamma!'

'You have heard, I suppose, that the trial has
been decided in your favour?'

'In yours, mamma.'

'We have explained it all to her, Lady Lovel,
as well as we could. The Serjeant yesterday
evening gave us a little history of what occurred.
It seems to have been quite a triumph.'

'It may become a triumph,' said the Countess;
—'a triumph so complete and glorious that I
shall desire nothing further in this world. It has
been my work to win the prize; it is for her to
wear it,—if she will do so.'

'I hope you will both live to enjoy it
many years,' said Mrs. Bluestone. 'You will
have much to say to each other, and I will
leave you now. We shall have lunch, Lady
Lovel, at half-past one, and I hope that you
will join us.'

Then they were alone together. Lady Anna
had not moved from her chair since she had
embraced her mother, but the Countess had

stood during the whole time that Mrs. Bluestone
had been in the room. When the room door
was closed they both remained silent for a few
moments, and then the girl rushed across the
room and threw herself on her knees at her
mother's feet. 'Oh, mamma, mamma, tell me
that you love me. Oh, mamma, why have you
not let me come to you? Oh, mamma, we never
were parted before.'

'My child never before was wilfully disobedient to me.'

'Oh, mamma;—tell me that you love me.'

'Love you! Yes, I love you. You do not
doubt that, Anna. How could it be possible
that you should doubt it after twenty years of a
mother's care? You know I love you.'

'I know that I love you, mamma, and that
it kills me to be sent away from you. You will
take me home with you now;—will you not?'

'Home! You shall make your own home, and
I will take you whither you will. I will be a
servant to minister to every whim; all the world
shall be a Paradise to you; you shall have every
joy that wealth, and love, and sweet friends can
procure for you,—if you will obey me in one
thing.' Lady Anna, still crouching upon the
ground, hid her face in her mother's dress, but
she was silent. 'It is not much that I ask after a
life spent in winning for you all that has now
been won. I only demand of you that you shall
not disgrace yourself.'

'Oh, mamma, I am not disgraced.'

'Say that you will marry Lord Lovel, and all
that shall be forgotten. It shall at any rate be
forgiven, or remembered only as the folly of a

child. Will you say that you will become Lord Lovel's wife?'

'Oh, mamma!'

'Answer me, Anna;—will you say that you will receive Lord Lovel as your accepted lover? Get up, girl, and look me in the face. Of what use is it to grovel there, while your spirit is in rebellion? Will you do this? Will you save us all from destruction, misery, and disgrace? Will you remember who you are;—what blood you have in your veins;—what name it is that you bear? Stand up, and look me in the face, if you dare.'

Lady Anna did stand up, and did look her mother in the face. 'Mamma,' she said, 'we should understand each other better if we were living together as we ought to do.'

'I will never live with you till you have promised obedience. Will you, at any rate, pledge to me your word that you will never become the wife of Daniel Thwaite?' Then she paused, and stood looking at the girl, perhaps for a minute. Lady Anna stood before her, with her eyes turned upon the ground. 'Answer me the question that I have asked you. Will you promise me that you will never become the wife of Daniel Thwaite?'

'I have promised him that I would.'

'What is that to me? Is your duty to him higher than your duty to me? Can you be bound by any promise to so great a crime as that would be? I will ask you the question once more, and I will be governed by your answer. If you will promise to discard this man, you shall return home with me, and shall then choose everything for yourself. We will go abroad and travel if you wish it, and all things shall be prepared to give you pleasure. You shall have at once the full enjoyment of all that has been won for you; and as for your cousin,—you shall not for a while be troubled even by his name. It is the dear wish of my heart that you should be the wife of Earl Lovel;—but I have one wish dearer even than that,—one to which that shall be altogether postponed. If you will save yourself, and me, and all your family from the terrible disgrace with which you have threatened us,—I will not again mention your cousin's name to you till it shall please you to hear it. Anna, you knelt to me, just now. Shall I kneel to you?'

'No, mamma, no;—I should die.'

'Then, my love, give me the promise that I have asked.'

'Mamma, he has been so good to us!'

'And we will be good to him,—good to him in his degree. Of what avail to me will have been his goodness, if he is to rob me of the very treasure which his goodness helped to save? Is he to have all, because he gave some aid? Is he to take from me my heart's blood, because he bound up my arm when it was bruised? Because he helped me some steps on earth, is he to imprison me afterwards in hell? Good! No, he is not good in wishing so to destroy us. He is bad, greedy, covetous, self-seeking, a very dog, and by the living God he shall die like a dog unless you will free me from his fangs. You have not answered me. Will you tell me that you will discard him as a suitor for your hand? If you will say so, he shall receive tenfold reward for his——goodness. Answer me, Anna;—I claim an answer from you.'

'Mamma!'

'Speak, if you have anything to say. And remember the commandment, Honour thy——' But she broke down, when she too remembered it, and bore in mind that the precept would have called upon her daughter to honour the memory of the deceased Earl. 'But if you cannot do it for love, you will never do it for duty.'

'Mamma, I am sure of one thing.'

'Of what are you sure?'

'That I ought to be allowed to see him before I give him up.'

'You shall never be allowed to see him.'

'Listen to me, mamma, for a moment. When he asked me to—love him, we were equals.'

'I deny it. You were never equals.'

'We lived as such,—except in this, that they had money for our wants, and we had none to repay them.'

'Money can have nothing to do with it.'

'Only that we took it. And then he was everything to us. It seemed as though it would be impossible to refuse anything that he asked. It was impossible to me. As to being noble, I am sure that he was noble. You always used to say that nobody else ever was so good as those two. Did you not say so, mamma?'

'If I praise my horse or my dog, do I say that they are of the same nature as myself?'

'But he is a man; quite as much a man as,—— as any man could be.'

'You mean that you will not do as I bid you.'

'Let me see him, mamma. Let me see him but once. If I might see him, perhaps I might do as you wish——about him. I cannot say anything more unless I may see him.'

The Countess still stormed and still threatened but she could not move her daughter. She also found that the child had inherited particles of the nature of her parents. But it was necessary that some arrangement should be made as to the future life, both of Lady Anna and of herself. She might bury herself where she would, in the most desolate corner of the earth, but she could not leave Lady Anna in Bedford Square. In a few months Lady Anna might choose any residence she pleased for herself, and there could be no doubt whose house she would share, if she were not still kept in subjection. The two parted then in deep grief,—the mother almost cursing her child in her anger, and Lady Anna overwhelmed with tears. 'Will you not kiss me, mamma, before you go?'

'No, I will not kiss you again till you have shown me that you are my child.'

But before she left the house, the Countess was closeted for a while with Mrs. Bluestone, and, in spite of all that she had said, it was agreed between them that it would be better to permit an interview between the girl and Daniel Thwaite. 'Let him say what he will,' argued Mrs. Bluestone, 'she will not be more headstrong than she is now. You will still be able to take her away with you to some foreign country.'

'But he will treat her as though he were her lover,' said the Countess, unable to conceal the

infinite disgust with which the idea overwhelmed her.

'What does it matter, Lady Lovel? We have
got to get a promise from her, somehow. Since
she was much with him, she has seen people of
another sort, and she will feel the difference.
It may be that she wants to ask him to release
her. At any rate she speaks as though she might
be released by what he would say to her. Unless
she thought it might be so herself, she would not
make a conditional promise. I would let them
meet.'

'But where?'

'In Keppel Street.'

'In my presence?'

'No, not that; but you will, of course, be in
the house,—so that she cannot leave it with
him. Let her come to you. It will be an excuse
for her doing so, and then she can remain. If
she does not give the promise, take her abroad,
and teach her to forget it by degrees.' So it was
arranged, and on that evening Mrs. Bluestone
told Lady Anna that she was to be allowed to
meet Daniel Thwaite.

CHAPTER XXXIII

Daniel Thwaite receives his Money

THERE was of course much commotion among all circles of society in London as soon as it was known to have been decided that the Countess Lovel was the Countess Lovel, and that Lady Anna was the heiress of the late Earl. Bets were paid,—and bets no doubt were left unpaid,—to a great amount. Men at the clubs talked more about the Lovels than they had done even during the month preceding the trial. The Countess became on a sudden very popular. Exaggerated stories were told of the romance of her past life,—though it would have been well nigh impossible to exaggerate her sufferings. Her patience, her long endurance and persistency were extolled by all. The wealth that would accrue to her and to her daughter was of course doubled. Had anybody seen her? Did anybody know her? Even the Murrays began to be proud of her, and old Lady Jemima Magtaggart, who had been a Murray before she married General Mag, as he was called, went at once and called upon the Countess in Keppel Street. Being the first that did so, before the Countess had suspected any invasion, she was admitted,—and came away declaring that sorrow must have driven the Countess mad. The Countess, no doubt, did not receive her distant relative with any gentle courtesy. She had sworn to herself often, that come what come might, she would never cross the threshold of a

Murray. Old Lord Swanage, who had married some very distant Lovel, wrote to her a letter full of very proper feeling. It had been, he said, quite impossible for him to know the truth before the truth had come to light, and therefore he made no apology for not having before this made overtures of friendship to his connection. He now begged to express his great delight that she who had so well deserved success had been successful, and to offer her his hand in friendship, should she be inclined to accept it. The Countess answered him in a strain which certainly showed that she was not mad. It was not her policy to quarrel with any Lovel, and her letter was very courteous. She was greatly obliged to him for his kindness, and had felt as strongly as he could do that she could have no claim on her husband's relations till she should succeed in establishing her rights. She accepted his hand in the spirit in which it had been offered, and hoped that his Lordship might yet become a friend of her daughter. For herself,—she feared that all that she had suffered had made her unfit for much social intercourse. Her strength, she said, had been sufficient to carry her thus far, but was now failing her.

Then, too, there came to her that great glory of which the lawyer had given her a hint. She received a letter from the private secretary of His Majesty the King, telling her that His Majesty had heard her story with great interest, and now congratulated her heartily on the re-establishment of her rank and position. She wrote a very curt note, begging that her thanks might be given to His Majesty,—and then she burned the private secretary's letter. No congratulations were anything to her till she should see her daughter freed from the debasement of her engagement to the tailor.

Speculation was rife as to the kind of life which the Countess would lead. That she would have wealth sufficient to blaze forth in London with all the glories of Countess-ship, there was no doubt. Her own share of the estate was put down as worth at least ten thousand a year for her life, and this she would enjoy without deductions, and with no other expenditure than that needed for herself. Her age was ascertained to a day, and it was known that she was as yet only forty-five. Was it not probable that some happy man might share her wealth with her? What an excellent thing it would be for old Lundy,—the Marquis of Lundy,—who had run through every shilling of his property! Before a week was over, the suggestion had been made to old Lundy. 'They say she is mad, but she can't be mad enough for that,' said the Marquis.

The rector hurried home full of indignation, but he had a word or two with his nephew before he started. 'What do you mean to do now, Frederic?' asked the rector with a very grave demeanour.

'Do? I don't know that I shall do anything.'

'You give up the girl, then?'

'My dear uncle; that is a sort of question that I don't think a man ever likes to be asked.'

'But I suppose I may ask how you intend to live?'

'I trust, Uncle Charles, that I shall not, at any rate, be a burden to my relatives.'

'Oh; very well; very well. Of course I have nothing more to say. I think it right, all the same, to express my opinion that you have been grossly misused by Sir William Patterson. Of course what I say will have no weight with you; but that is my opinion.'

'I do not agree with you, Uncle Charles.'

'Very well; I have nothing more to say. It is right that I should let you know that I do not believe that this woman was ever Lord Lovel's wife. I never did believe it, and I never will believe it. All that about marrying the girl has been a take in from beginning to end;—all planned to induce you to do just what you have done. No word in courtesy should ever have been spoken to either of them.'

'I am as sure that she is the Countess as I am that I am the Earl.'

'Very well. It costs me nothing, but it costs you thirty thousand a year. Do you mean to come down to Yoxham this winter?'

'No.'

'Are the horses to be kept there?' Now hitherto the rich rector had kept the poor lord's hunters without charging his nephew aught for their expense. He was a man so constituted that it would have been a misery to him that the head of his family should not have horses to ride. But now he could not but remember all that he had done, all that he was doing, and the return that was made to him. Nevertheless he could have bit the tongue out of his mouth for asking the question as soon as the words were spoken.

'I will have them sold immediately,' said the

Earl. 'They shall come up to Tattersal's before the week is over.'

'I didn't mean that.'

'I am glad that you thought of it, Uncle Charles. They shall be taken away at once.'

'They are quite welcome to remain at Yoxham.'

'They shall be removed,—and sold,' said the Earl. 'Remember me to my aunts. Good bye.' Then the rector went down to Yoxham an angry and a miserable man.

There were very many who still agreed with the rector in thinking that the Earl's case had been mismanaged. There was surely enough of ground for a prolonged fight to have enabled the Lovel party to have driven their opponents to a compromise. There was a feeling that the Solicitor-General had been carried away by some romantic idea of abstract right, and had acted in direct opposition to all the usages of forensic advocacy as established in England. What was it to him whether the Countess were or were not a real Countess? It had been his duty to get what he could for the Earl, his client. There had been much to get, and with patience no doubt something might have been got. But he had gotten nothing. Many thought that he had altogether cut his own throat, and that he would have to take the first 'puny' judgeship vacant. 'He is a great man,—a very great man indeed,' said the Attorney-General, in answer to someone who was abusing Sir William. 'There is not one of us can hold a candle to him. But, then, as I have always said, he ought to have been a poet!'

In discussing the Solicitor-General's conduct

men thought more of Lady Anna than her mother. The truth about Lady Anna and her engagement was generally known in a misty, hazy, half-truthful manner. That she was engaged to marry Daniel Thwaite, who was now becoming famous and the cause of a greatly increased business in Wigmore Street, was certain. It was certain also that the Earl had desired to marry her. But as to the condition in which the matter stood at present there was a very divided opinion. Not a few were positive that a written engagement had been given to the Earl that he should have the heiress before the Solicitor-General had made his speech,— but according to these, the tailor's hold over the young lady was so strong, that she now refused to abide by her own compact. She was in the tailor's hands and the tailor could do what he liked with her. It was known that Lady Anna was in Bedford Square, and not a few walked before the Serjeant's house in the hopes of seeing her. The romance at any rate was not over, and possibly there might even yet be a compromise. If the Earl could get even five thousand a year out of the property, it was thought that the Solicitor-General might hold his own and in due time become at any rate a Chief Baron.*

In the mean time Daniel Thwaite remained in moody silence among the workmen in Wigmore Street, unseen of any of those who rushed there for new liveries in order that they might catch a glimpse of the successful hero,—till one morning, about five days after the trial was over, when he received a letter from Messrs. Goffe and Goffe. Messrs. Goffe and Goffe had the pleasure of informing him that an accurate account of all money transactions between Countess Lovel and his father had been kept by the Countess;—that the Countess on behalf of herself and Lady Anna Lovel acknowledged a debt due to the estate of the late Mr. Thomas Thwaite, amounting to £9,109 3s. 4d., and that a cheque to that amount should be at once handed to him,—Daniel Thwaite the son,—if he would call at the chambers of Messrs. Goffe and Goffe, with a certified copy of the probate of the will of Thomas Thwaite the father.

Nine thousand pounds,—and that to be paid to him immediately,—on that very day if he chose to call for it! The copy of the probate of the will he had in his pocket at that moment. But he worked out his day's work without going near Goffe and Goffe. And yet he thought much of his money; and once, when one of his employers spoke to him somewhat roughly, he remembered that he was probably a better man than his master. What should he now do with himself and his money,—how bestow himself,—how use it so that he might be of service to the world? He would go no doubt to some country in which there were no earls and no countesses;—but he could go nowhere till he should know what might be his fate with the Earl's daughter, who at present was his destiny. His mind was absolutely divided. In one hour he would say to himself that the poet was certainly right;—and in the next he was sure that the poet must have been wrong. As regarded money, nine thousand pounds were as good to him as any sum that could be named. He could do with that all that he required that money should do for him. Could he at this time have had his own way absolutely, he would have left all the remainder of the wealth behind him, to be shared as they pleased to share it between the Earl and the Countess, and he would have gone at once, taking with him the girl whom he loved. He would have revelled in the pride of thinking that all of them should say that he had wanted and won the girl only,—and not the wealth of the Lovels; that he had taken only what was his own, and that his wife would be dependent on him, not he on her. But this was not possible. It was now months since he had heard the girl's voice, or had received any assurance from her that she was still true to him. But, in lieu of this, he had the assurance that she was in possession of enormous wealth, and that she was the recognised cousin of lords and ladies by the dozen.

When the evening came he saw one of his employers and told the man that he wished that his place might be filled. Why was he going? Did he expect to better himself? When was he going? Was he in earnest? Daniel told the truth at once as far as the payment of the money was concerned. He was to receive on the following day a sum of money which had been due to his father, and, when that should have been paid him, it would not suit him to work longer for weekly wages. The tailor grumbled, but there was nothing else to be said. Thwaite might leave them to-morrow if he wished. Thwaite took him at his word and never returned to the shop in Wigmore Street after that night.

On reaching his lodgings he found another

letter,—from Serjeant Bluestone. The Countess
had so far given way to accede to the proposition
that there should be a meeting between her
daughter and the tailor, and then there had
arisen the question as to the manner in which
this meeting should be arranged. The Countess
would not write herself, nor would she allow her
daughter to do so. It was desirable, she thought,
that as few people should know of the meeting
as possible, and at last, most unwillingly, the
Serjeant undertook the task of arranging it.
He wrote therefore as follows:—

'Mr. Serjeant Bluestone presents his compliments to Mr. Daniel Thwaite. Mr. Thwaite
has no doubt heard of the result of the trial by
which the Countess Lovel and her daughter
have succeeded in obtaining the recognition
of their rank. It is in contemplation with the
Countess and Lady Anna Lovel to go abroad,
but Lady Anna is desirous before she goes of
seeing the son of the man who was her mother's
staunch friend during many years of suffering.
Lady Anna will be at home, at No. — Keppel
Street, at eleven o'clock on Monday, 23rd
instant, if Mr. Thwaite can make it convenient
to call then and there.

    'Bedford Square,
        17th November, 18—.

'If Mr. Daniel Thwaite could call on the
Serjeant before that date, either in the morning
at his house, or on Saturday at his chambers,
———, Inner Temple, it might perhaps be
serviceable.'

The postscript had not been added without much consideration. What would the tailor think of this invitation? Would he not be disposed to take it as encouragement in his pernicious suit? Would he not go to Keppel Street with a determination to insist upon the girl's promise? The Serjeant thought that it would be best to let the thing take its chance. But the Serjeant's wife, and the Serjeant's daughters, and the Countess, too, had all agreed that something if possible should be said to disabuse him of this idea. He was to have nine thousand pounds paid to him. Surely that might be sufficient. But if he was greedy and wanted more money, more money should be given to him. Only he must be made to understand that the marriage was out of the question. So the Serjeant again gave way, and proposed the interview. Daniel sent back his compliments to the Serjeant and begged to say he would do as he was bid. He would call at the Serjeant's chambers on the Saturday, and in Keppel Street on the following Monday, at the hours named.

On the next morning,—the first morning of his freedom from the servitude of Wigmore Street,—he went to Messrs. Goffe and Goffe. He got up late and breakfasted late, in order that he might feel what it is to be an idle man. 'I might now be as idle as the young Earl,' he said to himself; 'but were I to attempt it, what should I do with myself? How should I make the hours pass by?' He felt that he was lauding himself as the idea passed through his mind, and struggled to quench his own pride. 'And yet,' said he in his thoughts, 'is it not fit that I should know myself to be better than he is? If I have no self-confidence how can I be bold to persevere? The man that works is to him that is idle, as light is to darkness.'

He was admitted at once to Mr. Goffe's private room, and was received with a smiling welcome, and an outstretched hand. 'I am delighted, Mr. Thwaite, to be able to settle your claim on Lady Lovel with so little delay. I hope you are satisfied with her ladyship's statement of the account.'

'Much more than satisfied with the amount. It appeared to me that I had no legal claim for more than a few hundred pounds.'

'We knew better than that, Mr. Thwaite. We should have seen that no great injury was done. But luckily the Countess has been careful, and has put down each sum advanced, item by item. Full interest has been allowed at five per cent., as is proper. The Countess is an excellent woman of business.'

'No doubt, Mr. Goffe. I could have wished that she would have condescended to honour me with a line;—but that is a matter of feeling.'

'Oh, Mr. Thwaite; there are reasons;—you must know that there are reasons.'

'There may be good reasons or bad reasons.'

'And there may be good judgment in such matters and bad judgment. But, however,——. You will like to have this money by a cheque, no doubt. There it is, £9,109 3s. 4d. It is not often that we write one cheque for a bigger sum than that, Mr. Thwaite. Shall I cross it on your bankers? No bankers! With such a sum as that let me recommend you to open an account at once.' And Mr. Goffe absolutely walked down to Fleet Street with Daniel Thwaite the tailor, and introduced him at his own bank. The business was soon transacted, and Daniel Thwaite went away westward, a capitalist, with a cheque book in his pocket. What was he to do with himself? He walked east again before the day was over, and made inquiries at various offices as to vessels sailing for Boston, New York, Baltimore, and Quebec. Or how would it be with him if he should be minded to go east instead of go west? So he supplied himself also with information as to the vessels for Sydney. And what should he do when he got to the new country? He did not mean to be a tailor. He was astonished to find how little he had as yet realised in his mind the details of the exodus which he had proposed to himself.

CHAPTER XXXIV

'*I will take your Word for Nothing*'

ON the Saturday, Daniel was at the Serjeant's chambers early in the morning,—long before the hour at which the Serjeant himself was wont to attend. No time had in fact been named, and the tailor had chosen to suppose that as he had been desired to be early in Bedford Square, so had it also been intended that he should be early in the Temple. For two hours he walked about the passages and the courts, thinking ill of the lawyer for being so late at his business, and endeavouring to determine what he would do with himself. He had not a friend in the world, unless Lady Anna were a friend;—hardly an acquaintance. And yet, remembering what his father had done, what he himself had helped to do, he thought that he ought to have had many friends. Those very persons who were now his bitterest enemies, the Countess and all they who had supported her, should have been bound to him by close ties. Yet he knew that it was impossible that they should not hate him. He could understand their feelings with reference to their own rank, though to him that rank was contemptible. Of course he was alone. Of course he would fail. He was almost prepared to acknowledge as much to the Serjeant. He had heard of a certain vessel that would start in three days for the rising colony called New South Wales, and he almost wished that he had taken his passage in her.

At ten o'clock he had been desired to call at eleven, and as the clock struck eleven he knocked at the Serjeant's door. 'Serjeant Bluestone is not here yet,' said the clerk, who was disposed to be annoyed by the man's pertinacity.

'He told me to come early in the morning, and this is not early.'

'He is not here yet, sir.'

'You told me to come at eleven, and it is past eleven.'

'It is one minute past, and you can sit down and wait for him if you please.' Daniel refused to wait, and was again about to depart in his wrath, when the Serjeant appeared upon the stairs. He introduced himself, and expressed regret that he should have found his visitor there before him. Daniel muttering something, followed the lawyer into his room, and then the door was closed. He stood till he was invited to sit, and was determined to make himself disagreeable. This man was one of his enemies, —was one who no doubt thought little of him because he was a tailor, who suspected his motives, and was anxious to rob him of his bride. The Serjeant retired for a moment to an inner room, while the tailor girded up his loins and prepared himself for battle.

'Mr. Thwaite,' said the Serjeant, as he re-entered the room, 'you probably know that I have been counsel for Lady Lovel and her daughter in the late trial.' Daniel assented by a nod of his head. 'My connection with the Countess would naturally have been closed. We have gained our cause, and there would be an end of it. But as things have turned out it has been

otherwise. Lady Anna Lovel has been staying
with Mrs. Bluestone.'

'In Bedford Square?'

'Yes, at my house.'

'I did not know. The Countess told me she
was not in Keppel Street, but refused to inform
me where she was staying. I should not have
interfered with her ladyship's plans, had she
been less secret with me.'

'Surely it was unnecessary that she should
tell you.'

'Quite unnecessary;—but hardly unnatural
after all that has occurred. As the Countess is
with you only a friend of late date, you are
probably unaware of the former friendship
which existed between us. There was a time
in which I certainly did not think that Lady
Lovel would ever decline to speak to me about
her daughter. But all this is nothing to you,
Serjeant Bluestone.'

'It is something to me, Mr. Thwaite, as her
friend. Is there no reason why she should have
treated you thus? Ask your own conscience.'

'My conscience is clear in the matter.'

'I have sent for you here, Mr. Thwaite, to
ask you whether you cannot yourself understand
that this which you have proposed to do must
make you an enemy to the Countess, and annul
and set aside all that kindness which you have
shown her? I put it to your own reason. Do
you think it possible that the Countess should be
otherwise than outraged at the proposition you
have made to her?'

'I have made no proposition to her ladyship.'

'Have you made none to her daughter?'

'Certainly I have. I have asked her to be my wife.'

'Come, Mr. Thwaite, do not palter with me.'

'Palter with you! Who dares to say that I palter? I have never paltered. Paltering is—— lying, as I take it. Let the Countess be my enemy. I have not said that she should not be so. She might have answered my letter, I think, when the old man died. In our rank of life we should have done so. It may be different with lords and titled ladies. Let it pass, however. I did not mean to make any complaint. I came here because you sent for me.'

'Yes;—I did send for you,' said the Serjeant, wishing with all his heart that he had never been persuaded to take a step which imposed upon him so great a difficulty. 'I did send for you. Lady Anna Lovel has expressed a wish to see you, before she leaves London.'

'I will wait upon Lady Anna Lovel.'

'I need hardly tell you that her wish has been opposed by her friends.'

'No doubt it was.'

'But she said with so much earnestness that she cannot consider herself to be absolved from the promise which she made to you when she was a child——'

'She was no child when she made it.'

'It does not signify. She cannot be absolved from the promise which I suppose she did make——'

'She certainly made it, Serjeant Bluestone.'

'Will you allow me to continue my statement? It will not occupy you long. She assures her mother that she cannot consider herself to be absolved from the promise without your sanction. She has been living in my house for some weeks, and I do not myself doubt in the least that were she thus freed an alliance would soon be arranged between her and her cousin.'

'I have heard of that——alliance.'

'It would be in every respect a most satisfactory and happy marriage. The young Earl has behaved with great consideration and forbearance in abstaining from pushing his claims.'

'In abstaining from asking for that which he did not believe to be his own.'

'You had better hear me to the end, Mr. Thwaite. All the friends of the two young people desire it. The Earl himself is warmly attached to his cousin.'

'So am I,—and have been for many years.'

'We all believe that she loves him.'

'Let her say so to me, Serjeant Bluestone, and there shall be an end of it all. It seems to me that Lord Lovel and I have different ideas about a woman. I would not take the hand of a girl who told me that she loved another man, even though she was as dear to me, as,——as Lady Anna is dear to me now. And as for what she might have in her hand, it would go for naught with me, though I might have to face beggary without her. It seems to me that Lord Lovel is less particular in this matter.'

'I do not see that you and I have anything to do with that,' replied the Serjeant, hardly knowing what to say.

'I have nothing to do with Lord Lovel, certainly,—nor has he with me. As to his cousin, —it is for her to choose.'

'We think,—I am only telling you what we think;—but we think, Mr. Thwaite, that the young lady's affections are fixed on her cousin. It is natural that they should be so; and watching her as closely as we can, we believe such to be the case. I will be quite on the square with you, Mr. Thwaite.'

'With me and with everybody else, I hope, Serjeant Bluestone.'

'I hope so,' said the Serjeant, laughing; 'but at any rate I will be so with you now. We have been unable to get from Lady Anna any certain reply,—any assurance of her own wishes. She has told her mother that she cannot accept Lord Lovel's addresses till she has seen you.' The Serjeant in this was not quite on the square, as Lady Anna had never said so. 'We believe that she considers it necessary, to her conscience, to be made free by your permission, before she can follow her own inclinations and accede to those of all her friends.'

'She shall have my permission in a moment, —if she will ask for it.'

'Could you not be more generous even than that?'

'How more generous, Serjeant Bluestone?'

'Offer it to her unasked. You have already said that you would not accept her hand if you did not believe that you had her heart also,— and the sentiment did you honour. Think of her condition, and be generous to her.'

'Generous to her! You mean generous to Lady Lovel,—generous to Lord Lovel,—generous to all the Lovels except her. It seems to me that all the generosity is to be on one side.'

'By no means. We can be generous too.'

'If that be generosity, I will be generous. I will offer her that permission. I will not wait till she asks for it. I will beg her to tell me if it be true that she loves her cousin, and if she can say that it is true, she shall want no permission from me to be free. She shall be free.'

'It is not a question, you see, between yourself and Lord Lovel. It is quite out of the question that she should in any event become your wife. Even had she power to do it——'

'She has the power.'

'Practically she has no such power, Mr. Thwaite. A young person such as Lady Anna Lovel is and must be under the control of her natural guardian. She is so altogether. Her mother could not,—and would not,—constrain her to any marriage; but has quite sufficient power over her to prevent any marriage. Lady Anna has never for a moment supposed that she could become your wife since she learned what were the feelings of her mother and her family.' The Serjeant certainly did not keep his promise of being 'on the square.' 'But your generosity is necessary to enable Lady Lovel to bring to a happy termination all those sufferings with which her life has been afflicted.'

'I do not owe much to the Countess; but if it be generous to do as I have said I would do,— I will be generous. I will tell her daughter, without any question asked from her, that she is free to marry her cousin if she wishes.'

So far the Serjeant, though he had not been altogether as truthful as he had promised, had been discreet. He had said nothing to set the tailor vehemently against the Lovel interest, and had succeeded in obtaining a useful pledge. But, in his next attempt, he was less wise. 'I think, you know, Mr. Thwaite, that the Countess also has been generous.'

'As how?'

'You have received £9,000 already, I believe.'

'I have received what I presume to be my own. If I have had more it shall be refunded.'

'No;—no; by no means. Taking a liberal view of the matter, as the Countess was bound to do in honour, she was, I think, right in paying you what she has paid.'

'I want nothing from her in what you call honour. I want nothing liberal. If the money be not mine in common honesty she shall have it back again. I want nothing but my own.'

'I think you are a little high flown, Mr. Thwaite.'

'I dare say I may be,—to the thinking of a lawyer.'

'The Countess, who is in truth your friend,—and will always be your friend if you will only be amenable to reason,—has been delighted to think that you are now in possession of a sum of money which will place you above want.'

'The Countess is very kind.'

'And I can say more than that. She and all her friends are aware how much is due to your father's son. If you will only aid us in our present project, if you will enable Lady Anna to become the wife of her cousin the Earl, much more shall be done than the mere payment of the debt which was due to you. It has been proposed to settle on you for life an annuity of four hundred pounds a year. To this the Countess, Earl Lovel, and Lady Anna will all agree.'

'Has the consent of Lady Anna been asked?' demanded the tailor, in a voice which was low, but which the Serjeant felt at the moment to be dangerous.

'You may take my word that it shall be forthcoming,' said the Serjeant.

'I will take your word for nothing, Serjeant Bluestone. I do not think that among you all, you would dare to make such a proposition to Lady Anna Lovel, and I wonder that you should dare to make it to me. What have you seen in me to lead you to suppose that I would sell myself for a bribe? And how can you have been so unwise as to offer it after I have told you that she shall be free,—if she chooses to be free? But it is all one. You deal in subterfuges till you think it impossible that a man should be honest. You mine underground, till your eyes see nothing in the open daylight. You walk crookedly, till a straight path is an abomination to you. Four hundred a year is nothing to me for such a purpose as this,—would have been nothing to me even though no penny had been paid to me of the money which is my own. I can easily understand what it is that makes the Earl so devoted a lover. His devotion began when he had been told that the money was hers, and not his,—and that in no other way could he get it. Mine began when no one believed that she would ever have a shilling for her fortune,— when all who bore her name and her mother's ridiculed their claim. Mine was growing when my father asked me whether I grudged that he

should spend all that he had in their behalf.
Mine came from giving. His springs from the
desire to get. Make the four hundred, four
thousand;—make it eight thousand, Serjeant
Bluestone, and offer it to him. I also will agree.
With him you may succeed. Good morning,
Serjeant Bluestone. On Monday next I will not
be worse than my word,—even though you have
offered me a bribe.'

The Serjeant let the tailor go without a word
further,—not, indeed, having a word to say. He
had been insulted in his own chambers,—told
that his word was worthless, and his honesty
questionable. But he had been so told, that at
the moment he had been unable to stop the
speaker. He had sat, and smiled, and stroked
his chin, and looked at the tailor as though he
had been endeavouring to comfort himself with
the idea that the man addressing him was merely
an ignorant, half-mad, enthusiastic tailor, from
whom decent conduct could not be expected. He
was still smiling when Daniel Thwaite closed
the door, and he almost laughed as he asked his
clerk whether that energetic gentleman had
taken himself down-stairs. 'Oh, yes, sir; he
glared at me when I opened the door, and rushed
down four steps at a time.' But, on the whole,
the Serjeant was contented with the interview.
It would, no doubt, have been better had he
said nothing of the four hundred a year. But in
offering of bribes there is always that danger.
One can never be sure who will swallow his
douceur* at an easy gulp, so as hardly to betray
an effort, and who will refuse even to open his
lips. And then the latter man has the briber so

much at advantage. When the luscious morsel has been refused, it is so easy to be indignant, so pleasant to be enthusiastically virtuous! The bribe had been refused, and so far the Serjeant had failed;—but the desired promise had been made, and the Serjeant felt certain that it would be kept. He did not doubt but that Daniel Thwaite would himself offer the girl her freedom. But there was something in the man, though he was a tailor. He had an eye and a voice, and it might be that freedom offered, as he could offer it, would not be accepted.

Daniel, as he went into the court from the lawyer's presence, was less satisfied than the lawyer. He had told the lawyer that his word was worth nothing, and yet he had believed much that the lawyer had said to him. The lawyer had told him that the girl loved her cousin, and only wanted his permission to be free that she might give her hand and her heart together to the young lord. Was it not natural that she should wish to do so? Within each hour, almost within each minute, he regarded the matter in lights that were perfectly antagonistic to each other. It was natural that she should wish to be a Countess, and that she should love a young lord who was gentle and beautiful;—and she should have his permission accorded freely. But then, again, it was most unnatural, bestial, and almost monstrous, that a girl should change her love for a man, going from one to another, simply because the latter man was gilt with gold, and decked with jewels, and sweet with perfume from a hairdresser's. The poet must have been wrong there. If love be anything but a dream, surely it must adhere to the person, and not be liable to change at every offered vantage of name or birth, of rank or wealth.

But she should have the offer. She should certainly have the offer.

CHAPTER XXXV

The Serjeant and Mrs. Bluestone at Home

LADY ANNA was not told till the Saturday that she was to meet her lover, the tailor, on the following Monday. She was living at this time, as it were, in chains, though the chains were gilded. It was possible that she might be off at any moment with Daniel Thwaite,—and now the more possible because he had money at his command. If this should occur, then would the game which the Countess and her friends were playing, be altogether lost. Then would the checkmate have been absolute. The reader will have known that such a step had never been contemplated by the man, and will also have perceived that it would have been altogether opposed to the girl's character; but it is hoped that the reader has looked more closely into the man's motives and the girl's character than even her mother was able to do. The Countess had thought that she had known her daughter. She had been mistaken, and now there was hardly anything of which she could not suspect her girl to be capable. Lady Anna was watched, therefore, during every minute of the four and twenty hours. A policeman was told off to protect the house at night from rope ladders or any other less cumbrous ingenuity. The servants were set on guard. Sarah, the lady's maid, followed her mistress almost like a ghost when the poor young lady went to her bedroom. Mrs. Bluestone, or one of the girls, was always with her, either indoors or out of doors. Out of doors, indeed, she never went without more guards than one. A carriage had been hired,—a luxury with which Mrs. Bluestone had hitherto dispensed,—and the carriage was always there when Lady Anna suggested that she should like to leave the house. She was warmly invited to go shopping, and made to understand that in the way of ordinary shopping she could buy what she pleased. But her life was inexpressibly miserable. 'What does mamma mean to do?' she said to Mrs. Bluestone on the Saturday morning.

'In what way, my dear?'

'Where does she mean to go? She won't live always in Keppel Street?'

'No,—I do not think that she will live always in Keppel Street. It depends a good deal upon you, I think.'

'I will go wherever she pleases to take me. The lawsuit is over now, and I don't know why we should stay here. I am sure you can't like it.'

To tell the truth, Mrs. Bluestone did not like it at all. Circumstances had made her a gaoler, but by nature she was very ill constituted for that office. The harshness of it was detestable to her, and then there was no reason whatever why she should sacrifice her domestic comfort for the Lovels. The thing had grown upon them, till the Lovels had become an incubus to her. Personally, she liked Lady Anna, but she was unable to treat Lady Anna as she would treat any other girl that she liked. She had told the Serjeant more than once that she could not endure it much longer. And the Serjeant did

not like it better than did his wife. It was all
a labour of love, and a most unpleasant labour.
'The Countess must take her away,' the Serjeant
had said. And now the Serjeant had been told
by the tailor, in his own chambers, that his
word was worth nothing!

'To tell you the truth, Lady Anna, we none
of us like it,—not because we do not like you,
but because the whole thing is disagreeable.
You are creating very great misery, my dear,
because you are obstinate.'

'Because I won't marry my cousin?'

'No, my dear; not because you won't marry
your cousin. I have never advised you to marry
your cousin, unless you could love him. I don't
think girls should ever be told to marry this
man or that. But it is very proper that they
should be told not to marry this man or that.
You are making everybody about you miserable,
because you will not give up a most improper
engagement, made with a man who is in every
respect beneath you.'

'I wish I were dead,' said Lady Anna.

'It is very easy to say that, my dear; but what
you ought to wish is, to do your duty.'

'I do wish to do my duty, Mrs. Bluestone.'

'It can't be dutiful to stand out against your
mother in this way. You are breaking your
mother's heart. And if you were to do this
thing, you would soon find that you had broken
your own. It is downright obstinacy. I don't
like to be harsh, but as you are here, in my
charge, I am bound to tell you the truth.'

'I wish mamma would let me go away,' said
Lady Anna, bursting into tears.

'She will let you go at once, if you will only make the promise that she asks of you.' In saying this, Mrs. Bluestone was hardly more upon the square than her husband had been, for she knew very well, at the moment, that Lady Anna was to go to Keppel Street early on the Monday morning, and she had quite made up her mind that her guest should not come back to Bedford Square. She had now been moved to the special severity which she had shown by certain annoyances of her own to which she had been subjected by the presence of Lady Anna in her house. She could neither entertain her friends nor go out to be entertained by them, and had told the Serjeant more than once that a great mistake had been made in having the girl there at all. But judgment had operated with her as well as feeling. It was necessary that Lady Anna should be made to understand before she saw the tailor that she could not be happy, could not be comfortable, could not be other than very wretched, —till she had altogether dismissed her low-born lover.

'I did not think you would be so unkind to me,' sobbed Lady Anna through her tears.

'I do not mean to be unkind, but you must be told the truth. Every minute that you spend in thinking of that man is a disgrace to you.'

'Then I shall be disgraced all my life,' said Lady Anna, bursting out of the room.

On that day the Serjeant dined at his club, but came home about nine o'clock. It had all been planned so that the information might be given in the most solemn manner possible. The two girls were sitting up in the drawing-room with the guest who, since the conversation in the morning, had only seen Mrs. Bluestone during dinner. First there was the knock at the door, and then, after a quarter of an hour, which was spent up-stairs in perfect silence, there came a message. Would Lady Anna have the kindness to go to the Serjeant in the dining-room? In silence she left the room, and in silence descended the broad staircase. The Serjeant and Mrs. Bluestone were sitting on one side of the fireplace, the Serjeant in his own peculiar arm-chair, and the lady close to the fender, while a seat opposite them had been placed for Lady Anna. The room was gloomy with dark red curtains and dark flock paper. On the table there burned two candles, and no more. The Serjeant got up and motioned Lady Anna to a chair. As soon as she had seated herself, he began his speech. 'My dear young lady, you must be no doubt aware that you are at present causing a great deal of trouble to your best friends.'

'I don't want to cause anybody trouble,' said Lady Anna, thinking that the Serjeant in speaking of her best friends alluded to himself and his wife. 'I only want to go away.'

'I am coming to that directly, my dear. I cannot suppose that you do not understand the extent of the sorrow that you have inflicted on your parent, by,—by the declaration which you made to Lord Lovel in regard to Mr. Daniel Thwaite.' There is nothing, perhaps, in the way of exhortation and scolding which the ordinary daughter,—or son,—dislikes so much as to be told of her, or his, 'parent.' 'My dear fellow, your father will be annoyed,' is taken in good part. 'What will mamma say?' is seldom received amiss. But when young people have their 'parents' thrown at them, they feel themselves to be aggrieved, and become at once antagonistic. Lady Anna became strongly antagonistic. If her mother, who had always been to her her 'own, own mamma,' was going to be her parent, there must be an end of all hope of happiness. She said nothing, but compressed her lips together. She would not allow herself to be led an inch any way by a man who talked to her of her parent. 'The very idea of such a marriage as this man had suggested to you under the guise of friendship was dreadful to her. It could be no more than an idea;—but that you should have entertained it was dreadful. She has since asked you again and again to repudiate the idea, and hitherto you have refused to obey.'

'I can never know what mamma really wants till I go and live with her again.'

'I am coming to that, Lady Anna. The Countess has informed Mrs. Bluestone that you refused to give the desired promise unless you should be allowed to see Mr. Daniel Thwaite, intimating, I presume, that his permission would be necessary to free you from your imaginary bond to him.'

'It would be necessary.'

'Very well. The Countess naturally felt an abhorrence at allowing you again to be in the presence of one so much beneath you,—who had ventured to address you as he has done. It was a most natural feeling. But it has occurred to

Mrs. Bluestone and myself, that as you entertain this idea of an obligation, you should be
allowed to extricate yourself from it after your
own fashion. You are to meet Mr. Thwaite,—
on Monday,—at eleven o'clock,—in Keppel
Street.'

'And I am not to come back again?'

When one executes the office of gaoler without
fee or reward, giving up to one's prisoner one's
best bedroom, and having a company dinner,
more or less, cooked for one's prisoner every day,
one does not like to be told too plainly of the
anticipated joys of enfranchisement. Mrs. Bluestone, who had done her best for the mother and
the girl, and had done it all from pure motherly
sympathy, was a little hurt. 'I am sure, Lady
Anna, we shall not wish you to return,' she said.

'Oh, Mrs. Bluestone, you don't understand
me. I don't think you know how unhappy I
am because of mamma.'

Mrs. Bluestone relented at once. 'If you will
only do as your mamma wishes, everything will
be made happy for you.'

'Mr. Thwaite will be in Keppel Street at
eleven o'clock on Monday,' continued the Serjeant, 'and an opportunity will then be given
you of obtaining from him a release from that
unfortunate promise which I believe you once
made him. I may tell you that he has expressed himself willing to give you that release.
The debt due to him, or rather to his late father,
has now been paid by the estate, and I think
that you will find that he will make no difficulty.
After that anything that he may require shall
be done to forward his views.'

'Am I to take my things?' she asked.

'Sarah shall pack them up, and they shall be sent after you if it be decided that you are to stay with Lady Lovel.' They then went to bed.

In all this neither the Serjeant nor his wife had been 'on the square.' Neither of them had spoken truly to the girl. Mrs. Bluestone had let the Countess know that with all her desire to assist her ladyship, and her ladyship's daughter, she could not receive Lady Anna back in Bedford Square. As for that sending of her things upon certain conditions,—it was a simple falsehood. The things would certainly be sent. And the Serjeant, without uttering an actual lie, had endeavoured to make the girl think that the tailor was in pursuit of money,—and of money only, though he must have known that it was not so. The Serjeant no doubt hated a lie,—as most of us do hate lies; and had a strong conviction that the devil is the father of them. But then the lies which he hated, and as to the parentage of which he was quite certain, were lies told to him. Who yet ever met a man who did not in his heart of hearts despise an attempt made by others to deceive—himself? They whom we have found to be gentler in their judgment towards attempts made in another direction have been more than one or two. The object which the Serjeant had in view was so good that it seemed to him to warrant some slight deviation from parallelogrammatic squareness;—though he held it as one of his first rules of life that the end cannot justify the means.

CHAPTER XXXVI

It is still True

ON Sunday they all went to church, and not a word was said about the tailor. Alice Bluestone was tender and valedictory; Mrs. Bluestone was courteous and careful; the Serjeant was solemn and civil. Before the day was over Lady Anna was quite sure that it was not intended that she should come back to Bedford Square. Words were said by the two girls, and by Sarah the waiting-maid, which made it certain that the packing up was to be a real packing up. No hindrance was offered to her when she busied herself about her own dresses and folded up her stock of gloves and ribbons. On Monday morning after breakfast, Mrs. Bluestone nearly broke down. 'I am sure, my dear,' she said, 'we have liked you very much, and if there has been anything uncomfortable it has been from unfortunate circumstances.' The Serjeant bade God bless her when he walked off half an hour before the carriage came to take her, and she knew that she was to sit no longer as a guest at the Serjeant's table. She kissed the girls, was kissed by Mrs. Bluestone, got into the carriage with the maid, and in her heart said good-bye to Bedford Square for ever.

It was but three minutes' drive from the Serjeant's house to that in which her mother lived, and in that moment of time, she was hardly able to realise the fact that within half an hour she would be once more in the presence of

Daniel Thwaite. She did not at present at all understand why this thing was to be done. When last she had seen her mother, the Countess had solemnly declared, had almost sworn, that they two should never see each other again. And now the meeting was so close at hand that the man must already be near her. She put up her face to the carriage window as though she almost expected to see him on the pavement. And how would the meeting be arranged? Would her mother be present? She took it for granted that her mother would be present. She certainly anticipated no pleasure from the meeting,— though she would be glad, very glad, to see Daniel Thwaite once again. Before she had time to answer herself a question the carriage had stopped, and she could see her mother at the drawing-room window. She trembled as she went upstairs, and hardly could speak when she found herself in her mother's presence. If her mother had worn the old brown gown it would have been better, but there she was, arrayed in black silk,—in silk that was new and stiff and broad and solemn,—a parent rather than a mother, and every inch a Countess. 'I am so glad to be with you again, mamma.'

'I shall not be less glad to have you with me, Anna,—if you will behave yourself with propriety.'

'Give me a kiss, mamma.' Then the Countess bent her head and allowed her daughter's lips to touch her cheeks. In old days,—days that were not so very old,—she would kiss her child as though such embraces were the only food that nourished her.

'Come upstairs, and I will show you your room.' Then the daughter followed the mother in solemn silence. 'You have heard that Mr. Daniel Thwaite is coming here, to see you, at your own request. It will not be many minutes before he is here. Take off your bonnet.' Again Lady Anna did as she was bid. 'It would have been better,—very much better,—that you should have done as you were desired without subjecting me to this indignity. But as you have taken into your head an idea that you cannot be absolved from an impossible engagement without his permission, I have submitted. Do not let it be long, and let me hear then that all this nonsense is over. He has got what he desires, as a very large sum of money has been paid to him.' Then there came a knock at the door from Sarah, who just showed her face to say that Mr. Thwaite was in the room below. 'Now go down. In ten minutes I shall expect to see you here again;—or, after that, I shall come down to you.' Lady Anna took her mother by the hand, looking up with beseeching eyes into her mother's face. 'Go, my dear, and let this be done as quickly as possible. I believe that you have too great a sense of propriety to let him do more than speak to you. Remember,—you are the daughter of an earl; and remember also all that I have done to establish your right for you.'

'Mamma, I do not know what to do. I am afraid.'

'Shall I go with you, Anna?'

'No, mamma;—it will be better without you. You do not know how good he is.'

'If he will abandon this madness he shall be my friend of friends.'

'Oh, mamma, I am afraid. But I had better go.' Then, trembling, she left the room and slowly descended the stairs. She had certainly spoken the truth in saying that she was afraid. Up to this moment she had not positively made up her mind whether she would or would not yield to the entreaties of her friends. She had decided upon nothing,—leaving in fact the arbitrament of her faith in the hands of the man who had now come to see her. Throughout all that had been said and done her sympathies had been with him, and had become the stronger the more her friends had reviled him. She knew that they had spoken evil of him, not because he was evil,—but with the unholy view of making her believe what was false. She had seen through all this, and had been aroused by it to a degree of firmness of which her mother had not imagined her to be capable. Had they confined themselves to the argument of present fitness, admitting the truth and honesty of the man,—and admitting also that his love for her and hers for him had been the natural growth of the familiar friendship of their childhood and youth, their chance of moulding her to their purposes would have been better. As it was they had never argued with her on the subject without putting forward some statement which she found herself bound to combat. She was told continually that she had degraded herself; and she could understand that another Lady Anna might degrade herself most thoroughly by listening to the suit of a tailor. But she had not disgraced herself. Of that she was sure, though she could not well explain to them her reasons when they accused her. Circumstances, and her mother's mode of living, had thrown her into intimacy with this man. For all practical purposes of life he had been her equal,—and being so had become her dearest friend. To take his hand, to lean on his arm, to ask his assistance, to go to him in her troubles, to listen to his words and to believe them, to think of him as one who might always be trusted, had become a second nature to her. Of course she loved him. And now the martyrdom through which she had passed in Bedford Square had changed,—unconsciously as regarded her own thoughts,—but still had changed her feelings in regard to her cousin. He was not to her now the bright and shining thing, the godlike Phœbus, which he had been in Wyndham Street and at Yoxham. In all their lectures to her about her title and grandeur they had succeeded in inculcating an idea of the solemnity of rank, but had robbed it in her eyes of all its grace. She had only been the more tormented because the fact of her being Lady Anna Lovel had been fully established. The feeling in her bosom which was most hostile to the tailor's claim upon her was her pity for her mother.

She entered the room very gently, and found him standing by the table, with his hands clasped together. 'Sweetheart!' he said, as soon as he saw her, calling her by a name which he used to use when they were out in the fields together in Cumberland.

'Daniel!' Then he came to her and took her

hand. 'If you have anything to say, Daniel, you must be very quick, because mamma will come in ten minutes.'

'Have you anything to say, sweetheart?' She had much to say if she only knew how to say it; but she was silent. 'Do you love me, Anna?' Still she was silent. 'If you have ceased to love me, pray tell me so,—in all honesty.' But yet she was silent. 'If you are true to me,—as I am to you, with all my heart,—will you not tell me so?'

'Yes,' she murmured.

He heard her, though no other could have done so.

> '*A lover's ears will hear the lowest sound*
> *When the suspicious head of theft is stopped.*'*

'If so,' said he, again taking her hand, 'this story they have told me is untrue.'

'What story, Daniel?' But she withdrew her hand quickly as she asked him.

'Nay;—it is mine; it shall be mine if you love me, dear. I will tell you what story. They have said that you love your cousin, Earl Lovel.'

'No;' said she scornfully, 'I have never said so. It is not true.'

'You cannot love us both.' His eye was fixed upon hers, that eye to which in past years she had been accustomed to look for guidance, sometimes in joy and sometimes in fear, and which she had always obeyed. 'Is not that true?'

'Oh yes;—that is true of course.'

'You have never told him that you loved him.'

'Oh, never.'

'But you have told me so,—more than once; eh, sweetheart?'

'Yes.'

'And it was true?'

She paused a moment, and then gave him the same answer, 'Yes.'

'And it is still true?'

She repeated the word a third time. 'Yes.' But she again so spoke that none but a lover's ear could have heard it.

'If it be so, nothing but the hand of God shall separate us. You know that they sent for me to come here.' She nodded her head. 'Do you know why? In order that I might abandon my claim to your hand. I will never give it up. But I made them a promise, and I will keep it. I told them that if you preferred Lord Lovel to me, I would at once make you free of your promise, —that I would offer you such freedom, if it would be freedom. I do offer it to you;—or rather, Anna, I would have offered it, had you not already answered the question. How can I offer it now?' Then he paused, and stood regarding her with fixed eyes. 'But there,—there; take back your word if you will. If you think that it is better to be the wife of a lord, because he is a lord, though you do not love him, than to lie upon the breast of the man you do love,— you are free from me.' Now was the moment in which she must obey her mother, and satisfy her friends, and support her rank, and decide that she would be one of the noble ladies of England if such decision were to be made at all. She looked up into his face, and thought that after all it was handsomer than that of the young Earl. He stood thus with dilated nostrils, and fire in his eyes, and his lips just parted, and his

head erect,—a very man. Had she been so
minded she would not have dared to take his
offer. They surely had not known the man
when they allowed him to have his interview.
He repeated his words. 'You are free if you will
say so;—but you must answer me.'

'I did answer you, Daniel.'

'My noble girl! And now, my heart's only
treasure, I may speak out and tell you what I
think. It cannot be good that a woman should
purchase rank and wealth by giving herself to
a man she does not love. It must be bad,—
monstrously bad. I never believed it when they
told it me of you. And yet when I did not hear
of you or see you for months——'

'It was not my fault.'

'No, sweetheart;—and I tried to find comfort
by so saying to myself. "If she really loves me,
she will be true," I said. And yet who was I
that I should think that you would suffer so
much for me? But I will repay you,—if the
truth and service of a life may repay such a debt
as that. At any rate hear this from me;—I will
never doubt again.' And as he spoke he was
moving towards her, thinking to take her in his
arms, when the door was opened and Countess
Lovel was within the room. The tailor was the
first to speak. 'Lady Lovel, I have asked your
daughter, and I find that it is her wish to adhere
to the engagement which she made with me in
Cumberland. I need hardly say that it is my
wish also.'

'Anna! Is this true?'

'Mamma; mamma! Oh, mamma!'

'If it be so I will never speak word to you more.'

'You will; you will! Do not look at me like that. You will speak to me!'

'You shall never again be child of mine.' But in saying this she had forgotten herself, and now she remembered her proper cue. 'I do not believe a word of it. The man has come here and has insulted and frightened you. He knows, —he must know,—that such a marriage is impossible. It can never take place. It shall never take place. Mr. Thwaite, as you are a living man, you shall never live to marry my daughter.'

'My lady, in this matter of marriage your daughter must no doubt decide for herself. Even now, by all the laws of God,—and I believe of man too,—she is beyond your control either to give her in marriage or to withhold her. In a few months she will be as much her own mistress as you now are yours.'

'Sir, I am not asking you about my child. You are insolent.'

'I came here, Lady Lovel, because I was sent for.'

'And now you had better leave us. You made a promise which you have broken.'

'By heavens, no. I made a promise and I have kept it. I said that I would offer her her freedom, and I have done so. I told her, and I tell her again now, that if she will say that she prefers her cousin to me, I will retire.' The Countess looked at him and also recognised the strength of his face, almost feeling that the man had grown in personal dignity since he had received the money that was due to him. 'She does not prefer the Earl. She has given her heart to me; and I hold it;—and will hold it.

Look up, dear, and tell your mother whether what I say be true.'

'It is true,' said Lady Anna.

'Then may the blight of hell rest upon you both!' said the Countess, rushing to the door. But she returned. 'Mr. Thwaite,' she said, 'I will trouble you at once to leave the house, and never more return to it.'

'I will leave it certainly. Good-bye, my own love.' He attempted again to take the girl by the hand, but the Countess, with violence, rushed at them and separated them. 'If you but touch him, I will strike you,' she said to her daughter. 'As for you, it is her money that you want. If it be necessary, you shall have, not hers, but mine. Now go.'

'That is a slander, Lady Lovel. I want no one's money. I want the girl I love, —whose heart I have won; and I will have her. Good morning, Lady Lovel. Dear, dear Anna, for this time good-bye. Do not let any one make you think that I can ever be untrue to you.' The girl only looked at him. Then he left the room; and the mother and the daughter were alone together. The Countesss stood erect, looking at her child, while Lady Anna, standing also, kept her eyes fixed upon the ground. 'Am I to believe it all,—as that man says?' asked the Countess.

'Yes, mamma.'

'Do you mean to say that you have renewed your engagement to that low-born wretch?'

'Mamma,—he is not a wretch.'

'Do you contradict me? After all, is it come to this?'

'Mamma,—you, you——cursed me.'

'And you will be cursed. Do you think that you will do such wickedness as this, that you can destroy all that I have done for you, that you make yourself the cause of ruin to a whole family, and that you will not be punished for it? You say that you love me.'

'You know that I love you, mamma.'

'And yet you do not scruple to drive me mad.'

'Mamma, it was you who brought us together.'

'Ungrateful child! Where else could I take you then?'

'But I was there,—and of course I loved him. I could not cease to love him because,—because they say that I am a grand lady.'

'Listen to me, Anna. You shall never marry him; never. With my own hands I will kill him first;—or you.' The girl stood looking into her mother's face, and trembling. 'Do you understand that?'

'You do not mean it, mamma.'

'By the God above me, I do! Do you think that I will stop at anything now;—after having done so much? Do you think that I will live to see my daughter the wife of a foul, sweltering tailor? No, by heavens! He tells you that when you are twenty-one, you will not be subject to my control. I warn you to look to it. I will not lose my control, unless when I see you married to some husband fitting your condition in life. For the present you will live in your own room, as I will live in mine. I will hold no intercourse whatever with you, till I have constrained you to obey me.'

CHAPTER XXXVII

Let her Die

AFTER the scene which was described in the last chapter there was a very sad time indeed in Keppel Street. The Countess had been advised by the Serjeant and Mrs. Bluestone to take her daughter immediately abroad, in the event of the interview with Daniel Thwaite being unsatisfactory. It was believed by all concerned, by the Bluestones, and the Goffes, by Sir William Patterson who had been told of the coming interview, and by the Countess herself, that this would not be the case. They had all thought that Lady Anna would come out from that meeting disengaged and free to marry whom she would,—and they thought also that within a very few weeks of her emancipation she would accept her cousin's hand. The Solicitor-General had communicated with the Earl, who was still in town, and the Earl again believed he might win the heiress. But should the girl prove obstinate;—'take her away at once,—very far away; – to Rome, or some such place as that.' Such had been Mrs. Bluestone's advice, and in those days Rome was much more distant than it is now. 'And don't let anybody know where you are going,' added the Serjeant,—'except Mr. Goffe.' The Countess had assented;—but when the moment came, there were reasons against her sudden departure. Mr. Goffe told her that she must wait at any rate for another fortnight. The presence of herself and her daughter was necessary in London for the signing of deeds and for the completion of the now merely formal proofs of identity. And money was again scarce. A great deal of money had been spent lately, and unless money was borrowed without security and at a great cost,—to which Mr. Goffe was averse,—the sum needed could hardly be provided at once. Mr. Goffe recommended that no day earlier than the 20th December should be fixed for their departure.

It was now the end of November; and it became a question how the intermediate time should be passed. The Countess was resolved that she would hold no pleasant intercourse at all with her daughter. She would not even tell the girl of her purpose of going abroad. From hour to hour she assured herself with still increasing obduracy that nothing but severity could avail anything. The girl must be cowed and frightened into absolute submission,—even though at the expense of her health. Even though it was to be effected by the absolute crushing of her spirits,—this must be done. Though at the cost of her life, it must be done. This woman had lived for the last twenty years with but one object before her eyes,—an object sometimes seeming to be near, more often distant and not unfrequently altogether beyond her reach, but which had so grown upon her imagination as to become the heaven to which her very soul aspired. To be and to be known to be among the highly born, the so-called noble, the titled from old dates,—to be of those who were purely aristocratic, had been all the world to her. As a child,—the child of well-born but poor

parents, she had received the idea. In following
it out she had thrown all thoughts of love to the
wind and had married a reprobate earl. Then
had come her punishment,—or, as she had conceived it, her most unmerited misfortunes. For
many years of her life her high courage and
persistent demeanour had almost atoned for the
vice of her youth. The love of rank was strong
in her bosom as ever, but it was fostered for her
child rather than for herself. Through long,
tedious, friendless, poverty-stricken years she had
endured all, still assuring herself that the day
would come when the world should call the
sweet plant that grew by her side by its proper
name. The little children hooted after her
daughter, calling her girl in derision The Lady
Anna,—when Lady Anna had been more poorly
clad and blessed with less of the comforts of
home than any of them. Years would roll by,
and they should live to know that the Lady
Anna,—the sport of their infantine cruelty,—
was Lady Anna indeed. And as the girl became
a woman the dream was becoming a reality.
The rank, the title, the general acknowledgment and the wealth would all be there. Then
came the first great decisive triumph. Overtures of love and friendship were made from the
other side. Would Lady Anna consent to become the Countess Lovel, all animosities might
be buried, and everything be made pleasant,
prosperous, noble, and triumphant!

It is easy to fill with air a half-inflated bladder.
It is already so buoyant with its own lightness,
that it yields itself with ease to receive the generous air. The imagination of the woman flew

higher than ever it had flown when the proposition came home to her in all its bearings. Of
course it had been in her mind that her daughter
should marry well;—but there had been natural
fears. Her child had not been educated, had not
lived, had not been surrounded in her young
days, as are those girls from whom the curled
darlings are wont to choose their wives. She
would too probably be rough in manner, ungentle
in speech, ungifted in accomplishments, as com-
pared with those who from their very cradles
are encompassed by the blessings of wealth and
high social standing. But when she looked at
her child's beauty, she would hope. And then
her child was soft, sweet-humoured, winning in
all her little ways, pretty even in the poor duds
which were supplied to her mainly by the generosity of the tailor. And so she would hope,
and sometimes despair;—and then hope again.
But she had never hoped for anything so good
as this. Such a marriage would not only put
her daughter as high as a Lovel ought to be,
but would make it known in a remarkable
manner to all coming ages that she, she herself,
she the despised and slandered one,—who had
been treated almost as woman had never been
treated before,—was in very truth the Countess
Lovel by whose income the family had been
restored to its old splendour.

And so the longing grew upon her. Then,
almost for the first time, did she begin to feel
that it was necessary for the purposes of her life
that the girl whom she loved so thoroughly,
should be a creature in her hands, to be dealt
with as she pleased. She would have had her

daughter accede to the proposed marriage even before she had seen Lord Lovel, and was petulant when her daughter would not be as clay in the sculptor's hand. But still the girl's refusal had been as the refusal of a girl. She should not have been as other girls. She should have known better. She should have understood what the peculiarity of her position demanded. But it had not been so with her. She had not soared as she should have done, above the love-laden dreams of common maidens. And so the visit to Yoxham was permitted. Then came the great blow,—struck as it were by a third hand, and that the hand of an attorney. The Countess Lovel learned through Mr. Goffe,—who had heard the tale from other lawyers,—that her daughter Lady Anna Lovel had, with her own mouth, told her noble lover that she was betrothed to a tailor! She felt at the moment that she could have died,—cursing this child for her black ingratitude.

But there might still be hope. The trial was going on,—or the work which was progressing towards the trial, and she was surrounded by those who could advise her. Doubtless what had happened was a great misfortune. But there was room for hope;—room for most assured hope. The Earl was not disposed to abandon the match, though he had, of course, been greatly annoyed,—nay, disgusted and degraded by the girl's communication. But he had consented to see the matter in the proper light. The young tailor had got an influence over the girl when she was a child, was doubtless in pursuit of money, and must be paid. The folly of a child

might be forgiven, and the Earl would per-
servere. No one would know what had occurred,
and the thing would be forgotten as a freak of
childhood. The Countess had succumbed to
the policy of all this;—but she was not deceived
by the benevolent falsehood. Lady Anna had
been over twenty when she had been receiving
lover's vows from this man, reeking from his
tailor's board. And her girl, her daughter, had
deceived her. That the girl had deceived her,
saying there was no other lover, was much;
but it was much more and worse and more
damnable that there had been thorough deception as to the girl's own appreciation of her
rank. The sympathy tendered through so many
years must have been always pretended sympathy. With these feelings hot within her
bosom, she could not bring herself to speak one
kindly word to Lady Anna after the return
from Yoxham. The girl was asked to abandon
her odious lover with stern severity. It was
demanded of her that she should do so with
cruel threats. She would never quite yield,
though she had then no strength of purpose
sufficient to enable her to declare that she would
not yield. We know how she was banished to
Bedford Square, and transferred from the ruthless persistency of her mother, to the less stern
but not less fixed manœuvres of Mrs. Bluestone.
At that moment of her existence she was herself
in doubt. In Wyndham Street and at Yoxham
she had almost more than doubted. The softness
of the new Elysium had well nigh unnerved her.
When that young man had caught her from
stone to stone as she passed over the ford at

Bolton, she was almost ready to give herself to him. But then had come upon her the sense of sickness, that faint, overdone flavour of sugared sweetness, which arises when sweet things become too luscious to the eater. She had struggled to be honest and strong, and had just not fallen into the pot of treacle.

But, notwithstanding all this, they who saw her and knew the story, were still sure that the lord must at last win the day. There was not one who believed that such a girl could be true to such a troth as she had made. Even the Solicitor-General, when he told the tale which the amorous steward had remembered to his own encouragement, did not think but what the girl and the girl's fortune would fall into the hands of his client. Human nature demanded that it should be so. That it should be as he wished it, was so absolutely consonant with all nature as he had known it, that he had preferred trusting to this result, in his client's behalf, to leaving the case in a jury's hands. At this moment he was sure he was right in his judgment. And indeed he was right;—for no jury could have done anything for his client.

It went on till at last the wise men decided that the girl only wanted to be relieved by her old lover, that she might take a new lover with his permission. The girl was no doubt peculiar; but as far as the wise ones could learn from her manner,—for with words she would say nothing, —that was her state of mind. So the interview was planned,—to the infinite disgust of the Countess, who, however, believed that it might avail; and we know what was the result. Lady

Anna, who long had doubted,—who had at last
almost begun to doubt whether Daniel Thwaite
was true to her,—had renewed her pledges, strengthened her former promises, and was now more
firmly betrothed than ever to him whom the
Countess hated as a very fiend upon earth. But
there certainly should be no marriage! Though
she pistolled the man at the altar, there should
be no marriage.

And then there came upon her the infinite
disgust arising from the necessity of having to
tell her sorrows to others,—who could not sympathize with her, though their wishes were as
hers. It was hard upon her that no step could
be taken in reference to her daughter without
the knowledge of Mr. Goffe and Serjeant Bluestone,—and the consequent knowledge of Mr.
Flick and the Solicitor-General. It was necessary, too, that Lord Lovel should know all.
His conduct in many things must depend on the
reception which might probably be accorded
to a renewal of his suit. Of course he must be
told. He had already been told that the tailor
was to be admitted to see his love, in order that
she might be absolved by the tailor from her
first vow. It had not been pleasant,—but he had
acceded. Mr. Flick had taken upon himself to
say that he was sure that everything would be
made pleasant. The Earl had frowned, and had
been very short with Mr. Flick. These confi-
dences with lawyers about his lovesuit, and his
love's tone with her low-born lover, had not
been pleasant to Lord Lovel. But he had
endured it,—and now he must be told of the
result. Oh, heavens;—what a hell of misery

was this girl making for her high-born relatives!
But the story of the tailor's visit to Keppel
Street did not reach the unhappy ones at Yox-
ham till months had passed away.

Mr. Goffe was very injudicious in postponing
the departure of the two ladies—as the Solicitor-
General told Mr. Flick afterwards very plainly,
when he heard of what had been done. 'Money;
she might have had any money. I would have
advanced it. You would have advanced it!'
'Oh certainly,' said Mr. Flick, not, however,
at all relishing the idea of advancing money to
his client's adversary. 'I never heard of such
folly,' continued Sir William. 'That comes of
trusting people who should not be trusted.' But
it was too late then. Lady Anna was lying ill in
bed, in fever; and three doctors doubted whether
she would ever get up again. 'Would it not be
better that she should die?' said her mother to
herself, standing over her and looking at her.
It would,—so thought the mother then,—be
better that she should die than get up to become
the wife of Daniel Thwaite. But how much
better that she should live and become the
Countess Lovel! She still loved her child, as
only a mother can love her only child,—as only
a mother can love who has no hope of joy in
the world, but what is founded on her child. But
the other passion had become so strong in her
bosom that it almost conquered her mother's
yearnings. Was she to fight for long years that
she might be beaten at last when the prize was
so near her,—when the cup was almost at her
lips? Were the girl now to be taken to her grave,
there would be an end at any rate of the fear

which now most heavily oppressed her. But the three doctors were called in, one after another; and Lady Anna was tended as though her life was as precious as that of any other daughter.

These new tidings caused new perturbation among the lawyers. 'They say that Clerke and Holland have given her over,' said Mr. Flick to Sir William.

'I am sorry to hear it,' said Mr. Solicitor; 'but girls do live sometimes in spite of the doctors.'

'Yes; very true, Sir William; very true. But if it should go in that way it might not perhaps be amiss for our client.'

'God forbid that he should prosper by his cousin's death, Mr. Flick. But the Countess would be the heir.'

'The Countess is devoted to the Earl. We ought to do something, Sir William. I don't think that we could claim above eight or ten thousand at most as real property. He put his money everywhere, did that old man. There are shares in iron mines in the Alleghanies, worth ever so much.'

'They are no good to us,' said the Solicitor-General, alluding to his client's interests.

'Not worth a halfpenny to us, though they are paying twenty per cent. on the paid-up capital. He seems to have determined that the real heir should get nothing, even if there were no will. A wicked old man!'

'Very wicked, Mr. Flick.'

'A horrible old man! But we really ought to do something, Mr. Solicitor. If the girl won't marry him there should be some compromise, after all that we have done.'

'How can the girl marry any one, Mr. Flick, —if she's going to die?'

A few days after this, Sir William called in Keppel Street and saw the Countess, not with any idea of promoting a compromise,—for the doing which this would not have been the time, nor would he have been the fitting medium, —but in order that he might ask after Lady Anna's health. The whole matter was in truth now going very much against the Earl. Money had been allowed to the Countess and her daughter; and in truth all the money was now their own, to do with it as they listed, though there might be some delay before each was put into absolute possession of her own proportion; but no money had been allowed, or could be allowed, to the Earl. And, that the fact was so, was now becoming known to all men. Hitherto credit had at any rate been easy with the young lord. When the old Earl died, and when the will was set aside, it was thought that he would be the heir. When the lawsuit first came up, it was believed everywhere that some generous compromise would be the worst that could befall him. After that the marriage had been almost a certainty, and then it was known that he had something of his own, so that tradesmen need not fear that their bills would be paid. It can hardly be said that he had been extravagant; but a lord must live, and an earl can hardly live and maintain a house in the country on a thousand a year, even though he has an uncle to keep his hunters for him. Some prudent men in London were already beginning to ask for their money, and the young Earl was in trouble.

As Mr. Flick had said, it was quite time that something should be done. Sir William still depended upon the panacea of a marriage if only the girl would live. The marriage might be delayed; but, if the cards were played prudently, might still make everything comfortable. Such girls do not marry tailors, and will always prefer lords to tradesmen!

'I hope that you do not think that my calling is intrusive,' he said. The Countess, dressed all in black, with that funereal frown upon her brow which she always now wore, with deep sunk eyes, and care legible in every feature of her handsome face, received him with a courtesy that was as full of woe as it was graceful. She was very glad to make his acquaintance. There was no intrusion. He would forgive her, she thought, if he perceived that circumstances had almost overwhelmed her with sorrow. 'I have come to ask after your daughter,' said he.

'She has been very ill, Sir William.'

'Is she better now?'

'I hardly know; I cannot say. They seemed to think this morning that the fever was less violent.'

'Then she will recover, Lady Lovel.'

'They do not say so. But indeed I did not ask them. It is all in God's hands. I sometimes think that it would be better that she should die and there be an end of it.'

This was the first time that these two had been in each other's company, and the lawyer could not altogether repress the feeling of horror with which he heard the mother speak in such a way of her only child. 'Oh, Lady Lovel, do not say that!'

'But I do say it. Why should I not say it to you, who know all? Of what good will her life be to herself, or to any one else, if she pollute herself and her family by this marriage? It would be better that she should be dead,— much better that she should be dead. She is all that I have, Sir William. It is for her sake that I have been struggling from the first moment in which I knew that I was to be a mother. The whole care of my life has been to prove her to be her father's daughter in the eye of the law. I doubt whether you can know what it is to pursue one object, and only one, through your whole life, with never-ending solicitude,— and to do it all on behalf of another. If you did, you would understand my feeling now. It would be better for her that she should die than become the wife of such a one as Daniel Thwaite.'

'Lady Lovel, not only as a mother, but as a Christian, you should get the better of that feeling.'

'Of course I should. No doubt every clergyman in England would tell me the same thing. It is easy to say all that, sir. Wait till you are tried. Wait till all your ambition is to be betrayed, every hope rolled in the dust, till all the honours you have won are to be soiled and degraded, till you are made a mark for general scorn and public pity,—and then tell me how you love the child by whom such evils are brought upon you!'

'I trust that I may never be so tried, Lady Lovel.'

'I hope not; but think of all that before you preach to me. But I do love her; and it is

because I love her that I would fain see her
removed from the reproaches which her own
madness will bring upon her. Let her die;—if it
be God's will. I can follow her without one wish
for a prolonged life. Then will a noble family
again be established, and her sorrowful tale will
be told among the Lovels with a tear and without a curse.'

CHAPTER XXXVIII
Lady Anna's Bedside

ALL December went by, and the neighbours in the houses round spent each his merry Christmas; and the snow and frost of January passed over them, and February had come and nearly gone, before the doctors dared to say that Lady Anna Lovel's life was not still in danger. During this long period the world had known all about her illness,—as it did know, or pretended to know, the whole history of her life. The world had been informed that she was dying, and had, upon the whole, been really very sorry for her. She had interested the world, and the world had heard much of her youth and beauty,—of the romance too of her story, of her fidelity to the tailor, and of her persecutions. During these months of her illness the world was disposed to think that the tailor was a fine fellow, and that he ought to be taken by the hand. He had money now, and it was thought that it would be a good thing to bring him into some club. There was a very strong feeling at the Beaufort that if he were properly proposed and seconded he would be elected,—not because he was going to marry an heiress, but because he was losing the heiress whom he was to have married. If the girl died, then Lord Lovel himself might bring him forward at the Beaufort. Of all this Daniel himself knew nothing; but he heard, as all the world heard, that Lady Anna was on her deathbed.

When the news first reached him,—after a fashion that seemed to him to be hardly worthy of credit,—he called at the house in Keppel Street and asked the question. Yes; Lady Anna was very ill; but as it happened, Sarah the lady's-maid opened the door, and Sarah remembered the tailor. She had seen him when he was admitted to her young mistress, and knew enough of the story to be aware that he should be snubbed. Her first answer was given before she had bethought herself; then she snubbed him, and told no one but the Countess of his visit. After that Daniel went to one of the doctors, and waited at his door with patience till he could be seen. The unhappy man told his story plainly. He was Daniel Thwaite, late a tailor, the man from Keswick, to whom Lady Anna Lovel was engaged. In charity and loving kindness, would the doctor tell him of the state of his beloved one? The doctor took him by the hand and asked him in, and did tell him. His beloved one was then on the very point of death. Whereupon Daniel wrote to the Countess in humble strains, himself taking the letter, and waiting without in the street for any answer that might be vouchsafed. If it was, as he was told, that his beloved was dying, might he be allowed to stand once at her bedside and kiss her hand? In about an hour an answer was brought to him at the area gate. It consisted of his own letter, opened, and returned to him without a word. He went away too sad to curse, but he declared to himself that such cruelty in a woman's bosom could exist only in the bosom of a Countess.

But as others heard early in February that Lady Anna was like to recover, so did Daniel Thwaite. Indeed, his authority was better than that which reached the clubs, for the doctor still stood his friend. Could the doctor take a message from him to Lady Anna;—but one word? No;—the doctor could take no message. That he would not do. But he did not object to give to the lover a bulletin of the health of his sweetheart. In this way Daniel knew sooner than most others when the change took place in the condition of his beloved one.

Lady Anna would be of age in May, and the plan of her betrothed was as follows. He would do nothing till that time, and then he would call upon her to allow their banns to be published in Bloomsbury Church after the manner of the Church of England. He himself had taken lodgings in Great Russell Street, thinking that his object might be aided by living in the same parish. If, as was probable, he would not be allowed to approach Lady Anna either in person or by letter, then he would have recourse to the law, and would allege that the young lady was unduly kept a prisoner in custody. He was told that such complaint would be as idle wind, coming from him,—that no allegation of that kind could obtain any redress unless it came from the young lady herself; but he flattered himself that he could so make it that the young lady would at any rate obtain thereby the privilege of speaking for herself. Let some one ask her what were her wishes and he would be prepared to abide by her expression of them.

In the meantime Lord Lovel also had been

anxious;—but his anxiety had been met in a very different fashion. For many days the Countess saw him daily, so that there grew up between them a close intimacy. When it was believed that the girl would die,—believed with that sad assurance which made those who were concerned speak of her death almost as a certainty, the Countess, sitting alone with the young Earl, had told him that all would be his if the girl left them. He had muttered something as to there being no reason for that. 'Who else should have it?' said the Countess. 'Where should it go? Your people, Lovel, have not understood me. It is for the family that I have been fighting, fighting, fighting,—and never ceasing. Though you have been my adversary, —it has been all for the Lovels. If she goes,— it shall be yours at once. There is no one knows how little I care for wealth myself.' Then the girl had become better, and the Countess again began her plots, and her plans, and her strategy. She would take the girl abroad in May, in April if it might be possible. They would go,—not to Rome then, but to the South of France, and as the weather became too warm for them, on to Switzerland and the Tyrol. Would he, Lord Lovel, follow them? Would he follow them and be constant in his suit, even though the frantic girl should still talk of her tailor lover? If he would do so, as far as money was concerned, all should be in common with them. For what was the money wanted but that the Lovels might be great and noble and splendid? He said that he would do so. He also loved the girl,—thought at least during the tenderness created by her illness that he loved her with all his heart. He sat hour after hour with the Countess in Keppel Street,—sometimes seeing the girl as she lay unconscious, or feigning that she was so; till at last he was daily at her bedside. 'You had better not talk to him, Anna,' her mother would say, 'but of course he is anxious to see you.' Then the Earl would kiss her hand, and in her mother's presence she had not the courage,—perhaps she had not the strength,—to withdraw it. In these days the Countess was not cruelly stern as she had been. Bedside nursing hardly admits of such cruelty of manner. But she never spoke to her child with little tender endearing words, never embraced her,—but was to her a careful nurse rather than a loving mother.

Then by degrees the girl got better, and was able to talk. 'Mamma,' she said one day, 'won't you sit by me?'

'No, my dear; you should not be encouraged to talk.'

'Sit by me, and let me hold your hand.' For a moment the Countess gave way, and sat by her daughter, allowing her hand to remain pressed beneath the bedclothes;—but she rose abruptly, remembering her grievance, remembering that it would be better that her child should die, should die broken-hearted by unrelenting cruelty, than be encouraged to think it possible that she should do as she desired. So she rose abruptly and left the bedside without a word.

'Mamma,' said Lady Anna; 'will Lord Lovel be here to-day?'

'I suppose he will be here.'

'Will you let me speak to him for a minute?'

'Surely you may speak to him.'

'I am strong now, mamma, and I think that I shall be well again some day. I have so often wished that I might die.'

'You had better not talk about it, my dear.'

'But I should like to speak to him, mamma, without you.'

'What to say,—Anna?'

'I hardly know;—but I should like to speak to him. I have something to say about money.'

'Cannot I say it?'

'No, mamma. I must say it myself,—if you will let me.' The Countess looked at her girl with suspicion, but she gave the permission demanded. Of course it would be right that this lover should see his love. The Countess was almost minded to require from Lady Anna an assurance that no allusion should be made to Daniel Thwaite; but the man's name had not been mentioned between them since the beginning of the illness, and she was loth to mention it now. Nor would it have been possible to prevent for long such an interview as that now proposed.

'He shall come in if he pleases,' said the Countess; 'but I hope you will remember who you are and to whom you are speaking.'

'I will remember both, mamma,' said Lady Anna. The Countess looked down on her daughter's face, and could not help thinking that her child was different from what she had been. There had been almost defiance in the words spoken, though they had been spoken with the voice of an invalid.

At three o'clock that afternoon, according to his custom, Lord Lovel came, and was at once told that he was to be spoken to by his cousin. 'She says it is about money,' said the Countess.

'About money?'

'Yes;—and if she confines herself to that, do as she bids you. If she is ever to be your wife it will be all right; and if not,—then it will be better in your hands than in hers. In three months' time she can do as she pleases with it all.' He was then taken into Lady Anna's room. 'Here is your cousin,' said the Countess. 'You must not talk long or I shall interrupt you. If you wish to speak to him about the property,—as the head of your family,—that will be very right; but confine yourself to that for the present.' Then the Countess left them and closed the door.

'It is not only about money, Lord Lovel.'

'You might call me Frederic now,' said he tenderly.

'No;—not now. If I am ever well again and we are then friends I will do so. They tell me that there is ever so much money,—hundreds of thousands of pounds. I forget how much.'

'Do not trouble yourself about that.'

'But I do trouble myself very much about it, —and I know that it ought to be yours. There is one thing I want to tell you, which you must believe. If I am ever any man's wife, I shall be the wife of Daniel Thwaite.' That dark frown came upon his face which she had seen once before. 'Pray believe that it is so,' she continued. 'Mamma does not believe it,—will not believe it; but it is so. I love him with all my heart. I think of him every minute. It is very very cruel that I may not hear from him or send one word to tell him how I am. There! My hand is on the Bible, and I swear to you that if I am ever the wife of any man, I will be his wife.'

He looked down at her and saw that she was wan and thin and weak, and he did not dare to preach to her the old family sermon as to his rank and station. 'But, Anna, why do you tell me this now?' he said.

'That you may believe it and not trouble yourself with me any more. You must believe it when I tell you so in this manner. I may perhaps never live to rise from my bed. If I get well, I shall send to him, or go. I will not be hindered. He is true to me, and I will be true to him. You may tell mamma if you think proper. She would not believe me, but perhaps she may believe you. But, Lord Lovel, it is not fit that he should have all this money. He does not want it, and he would not take it. Till I am married I may do what I please with it;—and it shall be yours.'

'That cannot be.'

'Yes, it can. I know that I can make it yours if I please. They tell me that—that you are not rich, as Lord Lovel should be, because all this has been taken from you. That was the reason why you came to me.'

'By heaven, Anna, I love you most truly.'

'It could not have been so when you had not seen me. Will you take a message from me to Daniel Thwaite?'

He thought awhile before he answered it. 'No, I cannot do that.'

'Then I must find another messenger. Mr. Goffe will do it perhaps. He shall tell me how much he wants to keep, and the rest shall be yours. That is all. If you tell mamma, ask her not to be hard to me.' He stood over her and took her hand, but knew not how to speak a word to her. He attempted to kiss her hand; but she raised herself on her elbow, and shook her head and drew it from him. 'It belongs to Daniel Thwaite,' she said. Then he left her and did not speak another word.

'What has she said?' asked the Countess, with an attempt at smiling.

'I do not know that I should tell you.'

'Surely, Lovel, you are bound to tell me.'

'She has offered me all her property,—or most of it.'

'She is right,' said the Countess.

'But she has sworn to me, on the Bible, that she will never be my wife.'

'Tush!—it means nothing.'

'Ah yes;—it means much. It means all. She never loved me,—not for an instant. That other man has been before me, and she is too firm to be moved.'

'Did she say so?'

He was silent for a moment and then replied, 'Yes; she did say so.'

'Then let her die!' said the Countess.

'Lady Lovel!'

'Let her die. It will be better. Oh, God! that I should be brought to this. And what will you do, my lord? Do you mean to say that you will abandon her?'

'I cannot ask her to be my wife again.'

'What;—because she has said this in her sickness,—when she is half delirious,—while she is dreaming of the words that man spoke to her? Have you no more strength than that? Are you so poor a creature?'

'I think I have been a poor creature to ask her a second time at all.'

'No; not so. Your duty and mine are the same,—as should be hers. We must forget ourselves while we save the family. Do not I bear all? Have not I borne everything—contumely, solitude, ill words, poverty, and now this girl's unkindness? But even yet I will not give it up. Take the property,—as it is offered.'

'I could not touch it.'

'If not for you, then for your children. Take it all, so that we may be the stronger. But do not abandon us now, if you are a man.'

He would not stay to hear her further exhortations, but hurried away from the house full of doubt and unhappiness.

CHAPTER XXXIX

Lady Anna's Offer

EARLY in March Lady Anna was convalescent, but had not left the house in Keppel Street, and the confusion and dismay of the Countess were greater than ever. Lady Anna had declared that she would not leave England for the present. She was reminded that at any rate till the 10th of May she was subject to her mother's control. But by this time her mother's harshness to her had produced some corresponding hardness in her. 'Yes, mamma;—but I will not go abroad. Things must be settled, and I am not well enough to go yet.' The Countess asserted that everything could be arranged abroad, that papers could be sent after them, that Mr. Goffe could come out to them, and with much show of authority persisted. She would do anything by which she might be able to remove Lady Anna from the influence of Daniel Thwaite at the time at which the girl would cease to be subject to her. But in truth the girl had ceased to be subject to her. 'No, mamma, I will not go. If you will ask Serjeant Bluestone, or Sir William Patterson, I am sure they will say that I ought not to be made to go.' There were some terrible scenes in which the mother was driven almost to desperation. Lady Anna repeated to the Countess all that she had said to Lord Lovel, —and swore to her mother with the Bible in hand that if ever she became the wife of any man she would be the wife of Daniel Thwaite.

Then the Countess with great violence knocked the book out of her daughter's grasp, and it was thrown to the other side of the room. 'If this is to go on,' said the Countess, 'one of us must die.'

'Mamma, I have done nothing to make you so unkind to me. You have not spoken one word of kindness to me since I came from Yoxham.'

'If this goes on I shall never speak a word of kindness to you again,' said the mother.

But in the midst of all this there was one point on which they agreed,—on which they came sufficiently near together for action, though there was still a wide difference between them. Some large proportion of the property at stake was to be made over to Lord Lovel on the day that gave the girl the legal power of transferring her own possessions. The Countess began by presuming that the whole of Lady Anna's wealth was to be transferred,—not from any lack of reverence for the great amount which was in question, but feeling that for all good purposes it would be safer in the hands of the Earl than in those of her own child. If it could be arranged that the tailor could get nothing with his bride, then it might still be possible that the tailor might refuse the match. At any rate a quarrel might be fostered and the evil might be staved off. But to this Lady Anna would not assent. If she might act in this business in concert with Mr. Thwaite she would be able, she thought, to do better by her cousin than she proposed. But as she was not allowed to learn what were Mr. Thwaite's wishes, she would halve her property with her cousin. As much as this she was willing to do,—and was determined to do, acting on her own judgment. More she would not do,—unless she could see Mr. Thwaite. As it stood, her proposition was one which would, if carried out, bestow something like £10,000 a year upon the Earl. Then Mr. Goffe was sent for, and Lady Anna was allowed to communicate her suggestion to the lawyer. 'That should require a great deal of thought,' said Mr. Goffe with solemnity. Lady Anna declared that she had been thinking of it all the time she had been ill. 'But it should not be done in a hurry,' said Mr. Goffe. Then Lady Anna remarked that in the meantime, her cousin, the Earl, the head of her family, would have nothing to support his title. Mr. Goffe took his leave, promising to consult his partner, and to see Mr. Flick.

Mr. Goffe did consult his partner and did see Mr. Flick, and then Serjeant Bluestone was asked his advice,—and the Solicitor-General. The Serjeant had become somewhat tired of the Lovels, and did not care to give any strong advice either in one direction or in the other. The young lady, he said, might of course do what she liked with her own when it was her own; but he thought that she should not be hurried. He pointed it out as a fact that the Earl had not the slightest claim upon any portion of the estate,—not more than he would have had if this money had come to Lady Anna from her mother's instead of from her father's relatives. He was still of opinion that the two cousins might ultimately become man and wife if matters were left tranquil and the girl were taken abroad for a year or two. Lady Anna, however, would be of age in a few weeks, and must of course do as she liked with her own.

But they all felt that everything would at last be ruled by what the Solicitor-General might say. The Solicitor-General was going out of town for a week or ten days,—having the management of a great case at the Spring Assizes. He would think over Lady Anna's proposition, and say what he had to say when he returned. Lord Lovel, however, had been his client, and he had said from first to last that more was to be done for his client by amicable arrangement than by hostile opposition. If the Earl could get £10,000 a year by amicable arrangement, the Solicitor-General would be shown to have been right in the eyes of all men, and it was probable,—as both Mr. Goffe and Mr. Flick felt,—that he would not repudiate a settlement of the family affairs by which he would be proved to have been a discreet counsellor.

In the meantime it behoved Lord Lovel himself to have an opinion. Mr. Flick of course had told him of the offer,—which had in truth been made directly to himself by his cousin. At this time his affairs were not in a happy condition. A young earl, handsome and well esteemed, may generally marry an heiress,—if not one heiress then another. Though he be himself a poor man, his rank and position will stand in lieu of wealth. And so would it have been with this young earl,—who was very handsome and excellently well esteemed,—had it not been that all the world knew that it was his especial business to marry one especial heiress.. He could hardly go about looking for other honey, having, as he had, one particular hive devoted by public opinion to himself. After a year or two he might have looked elsewhere,—but what was he to do in the meantime? He was well nigh penniless, and in debt. So he wrote a letter to his uncle, the parson.

It may be remembered that when the uncle and nephew last parted in London there was not much love between them. From that day to this they had not seen each other, nor had there been any communication between them. The horses had been taken away and sold. The rector had spoken to the ladies of his household more than once with great bitterness of the young man's ingratitude; and they more than once had spoken to the rector, with a woman's piteous tenderness, of the young lord's poverty. But it was all sorrow and distress. For in truth the rector could not be happy while he was on bad terms with the head of his family. Then the young lord wrote as though there had been nothing amiss between them. It had in truth all passed away from his mind. This very liberal offer had been made to him. It amounted to wealth in lieu of poverty,—to what would be comfortable wealth even for an earl. Ten thousand a year was offered to him by his cousin. Might he accept it? The rector took the letter in good part, and begged his nephew to come at once to Yoxham. Whereupon the nephew went to Yoxham.

'What does Sir William say?' asked the rector, who, in spite of his disapproval of all that Sir

William had done, felt that the Solicitor-General was the man whose influence in the matter would really prevail.

'He has said nothing as yet. He is out of town.'

'Ten thousand a year! Who was it made the offer?'

'She made it herself.'

'Lady Anna?'

'Yes;—Lady Anna. It is a noble offer.'

'Yes, indeed. But then if she has no right to any of it, what does it amount to?'

'But she has a right to all of it;—she and her mother between them.'

'I shall never believe it, Frederic—never; and not the less so because they now want to bind you to them by such a compromise as this.'

'I think you look at it in a wrong light, uncle Charles.'

'Well;—well. I will say nothing more about it. I don't see why you shouldn't take it,—I don't indeed. It ought to have been yours. Everybody says that. You'll have to buy land, and it won't give you nearly so much then. I hope you'll buy land all the same, and I do hope it will be properly settled when you marry. As to marrying, you will be able to do much better than what you used to think of.'

'We won't talk about that, uncle Charles,' said the Earl.

As far as the rector's opinion went, it was clear that the offer might be accepted; but yet it was felt that very much must depend on what the Solicitor-General might say. Then Miss Lovel gave her opinion on the matter, which did not

altogether agree with that of her brother. She
believed in Lady Anna, whereas the rector
professed that he did not. The rector and Lady
Fitzwarren were perhaps the only two persons
who, after all that had been said and done,
still maintained that the Countess was an impostor, and that Lady Anna would only be
Anna Murray, if everybody had his due. Miss
Lovel was quite as anxious on behalf of the
Earl as was her brother, but she clung to the
hope of a marriage. 'I still think it might all
come right, if you would only wait,' said aunt
Julia.

'It's all very well talking of waiting, but how
am I to live?'

'You could live here, Frederic. There i;
nothing my brother would like so much. I
thought he would break his heart when the
horses were taken away. It would only be for a
year.'

'What would come of it?'

'At the end of the year she would be your
wife.'

'Never!' said the Earl.

'Young men are so impatient.'

'Never, under any circumstances, would I ask
her again. You may make your mind up to
that. As sure as you stand there, she will marry
Daniel Thwaite, if she lives another twelvemonth.'

'You really think so, Frederic?'

'I am sure of it. After what she said to me, it
would be impossible I should doubt it.'

'And she will be Lady Anna Thwaite! Oh
dear, how horrible. I wish she had died when

she was ill;—I do indeed. A journeyman tailor!
But something will prevent it. I really think
that Providence will interfere to prevent it!'
But in reference to the money she gave in her
adhesion. If the great lawyer said that it might
be taken,—then it should be taken. At the end
of a week the Earl hurried back to London to
see the great lawyer.

CHAPTER XL

No Disgrace at all

Before the Solicitor-General returned to town things had come to a worse pass than ever. Lady Lovel had ordered her daughter to be ready to start to Paris by a certain hour, on a certain day,—giving her three days for preparation,—and Lady Anna had refused to go. Whereupon the Countess had caused her own things to be packed up, and those of her daughter. Sarah was now altogether in the confidence of the Countess, so that Lady Anna had not even dominion over her own clothes. The things were stowed away, and all the arrangements were made for the journey; but Lady Anna refused to go, and when the hour came could not be induced to get into the carriage. The lodgings had been paid for to the day, and given up; so that the poor old woman in Keppel Street was beside herself. Then the Countess, of necessity, postponed her journey for twenty-four hours, telling her daughter that on the next day she would procure the assistance of magistrates and force the rebel to obedience.

Hardly a word had been spoken between the mother and daughter during those three days. There had been messages sent backwards and forwards, and once or twice the Countess had violently entered Lady Anna's bedroom, demanding submission. Lady Anna was always on the bed when her mother entered, and, there lying, would shake her head, and then with sobs accuse the Countess of unkindness. Lady Lovel had become furious in her wrath, hardly knowing what she herself did or said, always asserting her own authority, declaring her own power, and exclaiming against the wicked ingratitude of her child. This she did till the young waiting-woman was so frightened that she was almost determined to leave the house abruptly, though keenly alive to the profit and glory of serving a violent and rich countess. And the old lady who let the lodgings was intensely anxious to be rid of her lodgers, though her money was scrupulously paid, and no questions asked as to extra charges. Lady Anna was silent and sullen. When left to herself she spent her time at her writing-desk, of which she had managed to keep the key. What meals she took were brought up to her bedroom, so that a household more uncomfortable could hardly be gathered under a roof.

On the day fixed for that departure which did not take place, the Countess wrote to Mr. Goffe for assistance,—and Lady Anna, by the aid of the mistress of the house, wrote to Serjeant Bluestone. The letter to Mr. Goffe was the first step taken towards obtaining that assistance from civil authorities to which the Countess thought herself to be entitled in order that her legal dominion over her daughter might be enforced. Lady Anna wrote to the Serjeant, simply begging that he would come to see her, putting her letter open into the hands of the landlady. She implored him to come at once,—and, as it happened, he called in Keppel Street that night, whereas Mr. Goffe's visit was not made till the next morning. He asked for the Countess, and was shown into the drawing-room. The whole truth was soon made clear to him, for the Countess attempted to conceal nothing. Her child was rebelling against authority, and she was sure that the Serjeant would assist her in putting down and conquering such pernicious obstinacy. But she found at once that the Serjeant would not help her. 'But Lady Anna will be herself of age in a day or two,' he said.

'Not for nearly two months,' said the Countess indignantly.

'My dear Lady Lovel, under such circumstances you can hardly put constraint upon her.'

'Why not? She is of age, or she is not. Till she be of age she is bound to obey me.'

'True;—she is bound to obey you after a fashion, and so indeed she would be had she been of age a month since. But such obligations here in England go for very little, unless they are supported by reason.'

'The law is the law.'

'Yes;—but the law would be all in her favour before you could get it to assist you,—even if you could get its assistance. In her peculiar position, it is rational that she should choose to wait till she be able to act for herself. Very great interests will be at her disposal, and she will of course wish to be near those who can advise her.'

'I am her only guardian. I can advise her.' The Serjeant shook his head. 'You will not help me then?'

'I fear I cannot help you, Lady Lovel.'

'Not though you know the reasons which induce me to take her away from England before she slips entirely out of my hands and ruins all our hopes?' But still the Serjeant shook his head. 'Every one is leagued against me,' said the Countess, throwing up her hands in despair.

Then the Serjeant asked permission to visit Lady Anna, but was told that he could not be allowed to do so. She was in bed, and there was nothing to make it necessary that she should receive a visit from a gentleman in her bedroom. 'I am an old man,' said the Serjeant, 'and have endeavoured to be a true and honest friend to the young lady. I think, Lady Lovel, that you will do wrong to refuse my request. I tell you fairly that I shall be bound to interfere on her behalf. She has applied to me as her friend, and I feel myself constrained to attend to her application.'

'She has applied to you?'

'Yes, Lady Lovel. There is her letter.'

'She has deceived me again,' said the Countess, tearing the letter into atoms. But the Serjeant so far frightened her that she was induced to promise that Mrs. Bluestone should see Lady Anna on the following morning,—stipulating, however, that Mrs. Bluestone should see herself before she went up-stairs.

On the following morning Mr. Goffe came early. But Mr. Goffe could give his client very little comfort. He was, however, less uncomfortable than the Serjeant had been. He was of opinion that Lady Anna certainly ought to go abroad, in obedience to her mother's instructions, and was willing to go to her and tell her so, with what solemnity of legal authority he might be able to assume; but he could not say that anything could be done absolutely to enforce obedience. Mr. Goffe suggested that perhaps a few gentle words might be successful. 'Gentle words!' said the Countess, who had become quite unable to restrain herself. 'The harshest words are only too gentle for her. If I had known what she was, Mr. Goffe, I would never have stirred in this business. They might have called me what they would, and it would have been better.' When Mr. Goffe came down-stairs he had not a word to say more as to the efficacy of gentleness. He simply remarked that he did not think the young lady could be induced to go, and suggested that everybody had better wait till the Solicitor-General returned to town.

Then Mrs. Bluestone came, almost on the heels of the attorney;—poor Mrs. Bluestone, who now felt that it was a dreadful grievance both to her and to her husband that they had had anything to do with the Lovel family! She was very formal in her manner,—and, to tell the truth for her, rather frightened. The Serjeant had asked her to call and see Lady Anna Lovel. Might she be permitted to do so? Then the Countess burst forth with a long story of all her wrongs,—with the history of her whole life. Not beginning with her marriage,—but working back to it from the intense misery, and equally intense ambition of the present hour. She told it all; how everybody had been against her,— how she had been all alone at the dreary Grange in Westmoreland,—how she had been betrayed by her husband, and turned out to poverty and scorn;—how she had borne it all for the sake of the one child who was, by God's laws and man's, the heiress to her father's name; how she had persevered,—intermingling it all with a certain worship of high honours and hereditary position with which Mrs. Bluestone was able in some degree to sympathise. She was clever, and words came to her freely. It was almost impossible that any hearer should refuse to sympathise with her,—any hearer who knew that her words were true. And all that she told was true. The things which she narrated had been done;—the wrongs had been endured;—and the end of it all which she feared, was imminent. And the hearer thought as did the speaker as to the baseness of this marriage with the tailor,—thought as did the speaker of the excellence of the marriage with the lord. But still there was something in the woman's eye,—something in the tone of her voice, something in the very motion of her hands as she told her story, which made Mrs. Bluestone feel that Lady Anna should not be left under her mother's control. It would be very well that the Lovel family should be supported, and that Lady Anna should be kept within the pale of her own rank. But there might be things worse than Lady Anna's defection,—and worse even than the very downfall of the Lovels.

After sitting for nearly two hours with the Countess, Mrs. Bluestone was taken up-stairs. 'Mrs. Bluestone has come to see you,' said the Countess, not entering the room, and retreating again immediately as she closed the door. 'This is very kind of you, Mrs. Bluestone,' said Lady Anna, who was sitting crouching in her dressing-gown over the fire. 'But I thought that perhaps the Serjeant would come.' The lady, taken off her guard, immediately said that the Serjeant had been there on the preceding evening. 'And mamma would not let me see him! But you will help me!'

In this interview, as in that below, a long history was told to the visitor, and was told with an eloquent energy which she certainly had not expected. 'They talk to me of ladies,' said Lady Anna. 'I was not a lady. I knew nothing of ladies and their doings. I was a poor girl, friend-less but for my mother, sometimes almost with-out shoes to my feet, often ragged, solitary, knowing nothing of ladies. Then there came one lad, who played with me;—and it was mamma who brought us together. He was good to me, when all others were bad. He played with me, and gave me things, and taught me,—and loved me. Then when he asked me to love him again, and to love him always, was I to think that I could not,—because I was a lady! You despise him because he is a tailor. A tailor was good to me, when no one else was good. How could I despise him because he was a tailor? I did not despise him, but I loved him with all my heart.'

'But when you came to know who you were, Lady Anna——'

'Yes;—yes. I came to know who I was, and they brought my cousin to me, and told me to love him, and bade me be a lady indeed. I felt it too, for a time. I thought it would be pleasant to be a Countess, and to go among great people; and he was pleasant, and I thought that I could love him too, and do as they bade me. But when I thought of it much, —when I thought of it alone,—I hated myself. In my heart of hearts I loved him who had always been my friend. And when Lord Lovel came to me at Bolton, and said that I must give my answer then,—I told him all the truth. I am glad I told him the truth. He should not have come again after that. If Daniel is so poor a creature because he is a tailor,—must not I be poor who love him? And what must he be when he comes to me again after that?'

When Mrs. Bluestone descended from the room she was quite sure that the girl would become Lady Anna Thwaite, and told the Countess that such was her opinion. 'By the God above me,' said the Countess rising from her chair;—'by the God above me, she never shall.' But after that the Countess gave up her project of forcing her daughter to go abroad. The old lady of the house was told that the rooms would still be required for some weeks to come,— perhaps for months; and having had a conference on the subject with Mrs. Bluestone, did not refuse her consent.

At last Sir William returned to town, and was besieged on all sides, as though in his hands lay the power of deciding what should become of all the Lovel family. Mr. Goffe was as confidential with him as Mr. Flick, and even Serjeant Bluestone condescended to appeal to him. The young Earl was closeted with him on the day of his return, and he had found on his desk the following note from the Countess:—

'The Countess Lovel presents her compliments to the Solicitor-General. The Countess is very anxious to leave England with her daughter, but has hitherto been prevented by her child's obstinacy. Sir William Patterson is so well aware of all the circumstances that he no doubt can give the Countess advice as to the manner in which she should proceed to enforce the obedience of her daughter. The Countess Lovel would feel herself unwarranted in thus trespassing on the Solicitor-General, were it not that it is her chief anxiety to do everything for the good of Earl Lovel and the family.'

'Look at that, my lord,' said the Solicitor-General, showing the Earl the letter. 'I can do nothing for her.'

'What does she want to have done?'

'She wants to carry her daughter away beyond the reach of Mr. Thwaite. I am not a bit surprised; but she can't do it. The days are gone by when a mother could lock her daughter up, or carry her away,—at any rate in this country.'

'It is very sad.'

'It might have been much worse. Why should she not marry Mr. Thwaite? Let them make the settlement as they propose, and then let the young lady have her way. She will have her way,—whether her mother lets her or no.'

'It will be a disgrace to the family, Sir William.'

'No disgrace at all! How many peers' daughters marry commoners in England. It is not with us as it is with some German countries in which noble blood is separated as by a barrier from blood that is not noble. The man I am told is clever and honest. He will have great means at his command, and I do not see why he should not make as good a gentleman as the best of us. At any rate she must not be persecuted.'

Sir William answered the Countess's letter as a matter of course, but there was no comfort in his answer. 'The Solicitor-General presents his compliments to the Countess Lovel. With all the will in the world to be of service, he fears that he can do no good by interfering between the Countess and Lady Anna Lovel. If, however, he may venture to give advice, he would suggest to the Countess that as Lady Anna will be of age in a short time, no attempt should now be made to exercise a control which must cease when that time shall arrive.' 'They are all joined against me,' said the Countess, when she read the letter;—'every one of them! But still it shall never be. I will not live to see it.'

Then there was a meeting between Mr. Flick and Sir William. Mr. Flick must inform the ladies that nothing could be done till Lady Anna was of age;—that not even could any instructions be taken from her before that time as to what should subsequently be done. If, when that time came, she should still be of a mind to share with her cousin the property, she could then instruct Mr. Goffe to make out the necessary deeds.

All this was communicated by letter to the Countess, but Mr. Goffe especially requested that the letter might be shown to Lady Anna, and that he might receive a reply intimating

that Lady Anna understood its purport. If
necessary he would call upon Lady Anna in
Keppel Street. After some delay and much
consideration, the Countess sent the attorney's
letter to her daughter, and Lady Anna herself
wrote a reply. She perfectly understood the
purport of Mr. Goffe's letter, and would thank
Mr. Goffe to call upon her on the 10th of May,
when the matter might, she hoped, be settled.

CHAPTER XLI

Nearer and Nearer

So they went on living in utter misery till the month of May had come round, and Lady Anna was at last pronounced to be convalescent.

Late one night, long after midnight, the Countess crept into her daughter's room and sat down by the bedside. Lady Anna was asleep, and the Countess sat there and watched. At this time the girl had passed her birthday, and was of age. Mr. Goffe had been closeted with her and with her mother for two mornings running, Sir William Patterson had also been with them, and instructions had been given as to the property, upon which action was to be at once taken. Of that proportion of the estate which fell to Lady Anna, one entire moiety was to be made over to the Earl. While this was being arranged no word was said as to Daniel Thwaite, or as to the marriage with the lord. The settlement was made as though it were a thing of itself; and they all had been much surprised,—the mother, the Solicitor-General, and the attorney,—at the determination of purpose and full comprehension of the whole affair which Lady Anna displayed. When it came to the absolute doing of the matter,—the abandonment of all this money,—the Countess became uneasy and discontented. She also had wished that Lord Lovel should have the property, —but her wish had been founded on a certain object to be attained, which object was now farther from her than ever. But the property in question was not hers, but her daughter's, and she made no loud objection to the proceeding. The instructions were given, and the deeds were to be forthcoming some time before the end of the month.

It was on the night of the 11th of May that the Countess sat at her child's bedside. She had brought up a taper with her, and there she sat watching the sleeping girl. Thoughts wondrously at variance with each other, and feelings thoroughly antagonistic, ran through her brain and heart. This was her only child,—the one thing that there was for her to love,—the only tie to the world that she possessed. But for her girl, it would be good that she should be dead. And if her girl should do this thing, which would make her life a burden to her,—how good it would be for her to die! She did not fear to die, and she feared nothing after death;—but with a coward's dread she did fear the torment of her failure if this girl should become the wife of Daniel Thwaite. In such case most certainly would she never see the girl again,—and life then would be all a blank to her. But she understood that though she should separate herself from the world altogether, men would know of her failure, and would know that she was devouring her own heart in the depth of her misery. If the girl would but have done as her mother had proposed, would have followed after her kind, and taken herself to those pleasant paths which had been opened for her, with what a fond caressing worship, with what infinite kisses and blessings, would she, the mother, have tended the young Countess and assisted in making the world bright for the high-born bride. But a tailor! Foh! What a degraded creature was her child to cling to so base a love!

She did, however, acknowledge to herself that the girl's clinging was of a kind she had no power to lessen. The ivy to its standard tree is not more loyal than was her daughter to this wretched man. But the girl might die,—or the tailor might die,—or she, the miserable mother, might die; and so this misery might be at an end. Nothing but death could end it. Thoughts and dreams of other violence had crossed her brain, —of carrying the girl away, of secluding her, of frightening her from day to day into some childish, half-idiotic submission. But for that the tame obedience of the girl would have been necessary,—or that external assistance which she had sought, in vain, to obtain among the lawyers. Such hopes were now gone, and nothing remained but death.

Why had not the girl gone when she was so like to go? Why had she not died when it had seemed to be God's pleasure to take her? A little indifference, some slight absence of careful tending, any chance accident would have made that natural which was now,—which was now so desirable and yet beyond reach! Yes;—so desirable! For whose sake could it be wished that a life so degraded should be prolonged? But there could be no such escape. With her eyes fixed on vacancy, revolving it in her mind, she thought that she could kill herself;—but she knew that she could not kill her child.

But, should she destroy herself, there would

be no vengeance in that. Could she be alone, far out at sea, in some small skiff with that low-born tailor, and then pull out the plug, and let him know what he had done to her as they both went down together beneath the water, that would be such a cure of the evil as would now best suit her wishes. But there was no such sea, and no such boat. Death, however, might still be within her grasp.

Then she laid her hand on the girl's shoulder, and Lady Anna awoke. 'Oh, mamma;—is that you?'

'It is I, my child.'

'Mamma, mamma; is anything the matter? Oh, mamma, kiss me.' Then the Countess stooped down and kissed the girl passionately. 'Dear mamma,—dearest mamma!'

'Anna, will you do one thing for me? If I never speak to you of Lord Lovel again, will you forget Daniel Thwaite?' She paused, but Lady Anna had no answer ready. 'Will you not say as much as that for me? Say that you will forget him till I am gone.'

'Gone, mamma? You are not going!'

'Till I am dead. I shall not live long, Anna. Say at least that you will not see him or mention his name for twelve months. Surely, Anna, you will do as much as that for a mother who has done so much for you.' But Lady Anna would make no promise. She turned her face to the pillow and was dumb. 'Answer me, my child. I may at least demand an answer.'

'I will answer you to-morrow, mamma.' Then the Countess fell on her knees at the bedside and uttered a long, incoherent prayer, addressed partly to the God of heaven, and partly to the poor girl who was lying there in bed, supplicating with mad, passionate eagerness that this evil thing might be turned away from her. Then she seized the girl in her embrace and nearly smothered her with kisses. 'My own, my darling, my beauty, my all; save your mother from worse than death, if you can;—if you can!'

Had such tenderness come sooner it might have had deeper effect. As it was, though the daughter was affected and harassed,—though she was left panting with sobs and drowned in tears,—she could not but remember the treatment she had suffered from her mother during the last six months. Had the request for a year's delay come sooner, it would have been granted; but now it was made after all measures of cruelty had failed. Ten times during the night did she say that she would yield,—and ten times again did she tell herself that were she to yield now, she would be a slave all her life. She had resolved,—whether right or wrong,—still, with a strong mind and a great purpose, that she would not be turned from her way, and when she arose in the morning she was resolved again. She went into her mother's room and at once declared her purpose. 'Mamma, it cannot be. I am his, and I must not forget him or be ashamed of his name;—no, not for a day.'

'Then go from me, thou ungrateful one, hard of heart, unnatural child, base, cruel, and polluted. Go from me, if it be possible, for ever!'

Then did they live for some days separated for a second time, each taking her meals in her own room; and Mrs. Richards, the owner of the lodgings, went again to Mrs. Bluestone, declaring

that she was afraid of what might happen,
and that she must pray to be relieved from the
presence of the ladies. Mrs. Bluestone had to
explain that the lodgings had been taken for
the quarter, and that a mother and daughter
could not be put out into the street merely because they lived on bad terms with each other.
The old woman, as was natural, increased her
bills;—but that had no effect.

On the 15th of May Lady Anna wrote a note
to Daniel Thwaite, and sent a copy of it to her
mother before she had posted it. It was in two
lines:—

'DEAR DANIEL,

'Pray come and see me here. If you get this
soon enough, pray come on Tuesday about one.
'Yours affectionately,
'ANNA.'

'Tell mamma,' said she to Sarah, 'that I intend
to go out and put that in the post to-day.' The
letter was addressed to Wyndham Street. Now
the Countess knew that Daniel Thwaite had left
Wyndham Street.

'Tell her,' said the Countess, 'tell her——;
but, of what use to tell her anything? Let the
door be closed upon her. She shall never return
to me any more.' The message was given to
Lady Anna as she went forth:—but she posted
the letter, and then called in Bedford Square.
Mrs. Bluestone returned with her to Keppel
Street; but as the door was opened by Mrs.
Richards, and as no difficulty was made as to
Lady Anna's entrance, Mrs. Bluestone returned
home without asking to see the Countess.

This happened on a Saturday, but when Tuesday came Daniel Thwaite did not come to Keppel Street. The note was delivered in course of post at his old abode, and was redirected from Wyndham Street late on Monday evening,—having no doubt given cause there for much curiosity and inspection. Late on the Tuesday it did reach Daniel Thwaite's residence in Great Russell Street, but he was then out, wandering about the streets as was his wont, telling himself of all the horrors of an idle life, and thinking what steps he should take next as to the gaining of his bride. He had known to a day when she was of age, and had determined that he would allow her one month from thence before he would call upon her to say what should be their mutual fate. She had reached that age but a few days, and now she had written to him herself.

On returning home he received the girl's letter, and when the early morning had come, —the Wednesday morning, the day after that fixed by Lady Anna,—he made up his mind as to his course of action. He breakfasted at eight, knowing how useless it would be to stir early, and then called in Keppel Street, leaving word with Mrs. Richards herself that he would be there again at one o'clock to see Lady Anna. 'You can tell Lady Anna that I only got her note last night very late.' Then he went off to the hotel in Albemarle Street at which he knew that Lord Lovel was living. It was something after nine when he reached the house, and the Earl was not yet out of his bedroom. Daniel, however, sent up his name, and the Earl begged that he would go into the sitting-room and wait. 'Tell Mr. Thwaite that I will not keep him above a quarter of an hour.' Then the tailor was shown into the room where the breakfast things were laid, and there he waited.

Within the last few weeks very much had been said to the Earl about Daniel Thwaite by many people, and especially by the Solicitor-General. 'You may be sure that she will become his wife,' Sir William had said, 'and I would advise you to accept him as her husband. She is not a girl such as we at first conceived her to be. She is firm of purpose, and very honest. Obstinate, if you will, and,—if you will,—obstinate to a bad end. But she is generous, and let her marry whom she will, you cannot cast her out. You will owe everything to her high sense of honour;—and I am much mistaken if you will not owe much to him. Accept them both, and make the best of them. In five years he'll be in Parliament as likely as not. In ten years he'll be Sir Daniel Thwaite,—if he cares for it. And in fifteen years Lady Anna will be supposed by everybody to have made a very happy marriage.' Lord Lovel was at this time inclined to be submissive in everything to his great adviser, and was now ready to take Mr. Daniel Thwaite by the hand.

He did take him by the hand as he entered the sitting-room, radiant from his bath, clad in a short bright-coloured dressing-gown such as young men then wore o' mornings, with embroidered slippers on his feet, and a smile on his face. 'I have heard much of you, Mr. Thwaite,' he said, 'and am glad to meet you at last. Pray sit down. I hope you have not breakfasted.'

Poor Daniel was hardly equal to the occasion. The young lord had been to him always an enemy,—an enemy because the lord had been the adversary of the Countess and her daughter, an enemy because the lord was an earl and idle, an enemy because the lord was his rival. Though he now was nearly sure that this last ground of enmity was at an end, and though he had come to the Earl for certain purposes of his own, he could not bring himself to feel that there should be good fellowship between them. He took the hand that was offered to him, but took it awkwardly, and sat down as he was bidden. 'Thank your lordship, but I breakfasted long since. If it will suit you, I will walk about and call again.'

'Not at all. I can eat, and you can talk to me. Take a cup of tea at any rate.' The Earl rang for another teacup, and began to butter his toast.

'I believe your lordship knows that I have long been engaged to marry your lordship's cousin,—Lady Anna Lovel.'

'Indeed I have been told so.'

'By herself.'

'Well;—yes; by herself.'

'I have been allowed to see her but once during the last eight or nine months.'

'That has not been my fault, Mr. Thwaite.'

'I want you to understand, my lord, that it is not for her money that I have sought her.'

'I have not accused you, surely.'

'But I have been accused. I am going to see her now,—if I can get admittance to her. I shall press her to fix a day for our marriage, and if she will do so, I shall leave no stone unturned to accomplish it. She has a right to do with herself as she pleases, and no consideration shall stop me but her wishes.'

'I shall not interfere.'

'I am glad of that, my lord.'

'But I will not answer for her mother. You cannot be surprised, Mr. Thwaite, that Lady Lovel should be averse to such a marriage.'

'She was not averse to my father's company nor to mine a few years since;—no nor twelve months since. But I say nothing about that. Let her be averse. We cannot help it. I have come to you to say that I hope something may be done about the money before she becomes my wife. People say that you should have it.'

'Who says so?'

'I cannot say who;—perhaps everybody. Should every shilling of it be yours I should marry her as willingly to-morrow. They have given me what is my own, and that is enough for me. For what is now hers and, perhaps, should be yours, I will not interfere with it. When she is my wife, I will guard for her and for those who may come after her what belongs to her then; but as to what may be done before that, I care nothing.'

On hearing this the Earl told him the whole story of the arrangement which was then in progress;—how the property would in fact be divided into three parts, of which the Countess would have one, he one, and Lady Anna one. 'There will be enough for us all,' said the Earl.

'And much more than enough for me,' said Daniel as he got up to take his leave. 'And now I am going to Keppel Street.'

'You have all my good wishes,' said the Earl. The two men again shook hands;—again the lord was radiant and good humoured;—and again the tailor was ashamed and almost sullen. He knew that the young nobleman had behaved well to him, and it was a disappointment to him that any nobleman should behave well.

Nevertheless as he walked away slowly towards Keppel Street,—for the time still hung on his hands,—he began to feel that the great prize of prizes was coming nearer within his grasp.

CHAPTER XLII

Daniel Thwaite comes to Keppel Street

EVEN the Bluestones were now convinced that
Lady Anna Lovel must be allowed to marry
the Keswick tailor, and that it would be expedient
that no further impediment should be thrown in
her way. Mrs. Bluestone had been told, while
walking to Keppel Street with the young lady, of
the purport of the letter and of the invitation given
to Daniel Thwaite. The Serjeant at once declared
that the girl must have her own way,—and the
Solicitor-General, who also heard of it, expressed
himself very strongly. It was absurd to oppose
her. She was her own mistress. She had shown
herself competent to manage her own affairs.
The Countess must be made to understand that
she had better yield at once with what best grace
she could. Then it was that he made that
prophecy to the Earl as to the future success
of the fortunate tailor, and then too he wrote
at great length to the Countess, urging many
reasons why her daughter should be allowed to
receive Mr. Daniel Thwaite. 'Your ladyship
has succeeded in very much,' wrote the Solicitor-
General, 'and even in respect of this marriage you
will have the satisfaction of feeling that the man
is in every way respectable and well-behaved.
I hear that he is an educated man, with culture
much higher than is generally found in the state
of life which he has till lately filled, and that he
is a man of high feeling and noble purpose.
The manner in which he has been persistent in

his attachment to your daughter is in itself
evidence of this. And I think that your ladyship
is bound to remember that the sphere of life in
which he has hitherto been a labourer, would
not have been so humble in its nature had not
the means which should have started him in
the world been applied to support and succour
your own cause. I am well aware of your feelings
of warm gratitude to the father;—but I think
you should bear in mind, on the son's behalf,
that he has been what he has been because his
father was so staunch a friend to your ladyship.'
There was very much more of it, all expressing the
opinion of Sir William that the Countess should
at once open her doors to Daniel Thwaite.

The reader need hardly be told that this was
wormwood to the Countess. It did not in the
least touch her heart and had but little effect on
her purpose. Gratitude;—yes! But if the whole
result of the exertion for which the receiver is
bound to be grateful, is to be neutralised by the
greed of the conferrer of the favour,—if all is to
be taken that has been given, and much more
also,—what ground will there be left for gratitude? If I save a man's purse from a thief, and
then demand for my work twice what that purse
contained, the man had better have been left
with the robbers. But she was told, not only
that she ought to accept the tailor as a son-in-
law, but also that she could not help herself.
They should see whether she could not help herself. They should be made to acknowledge that
she at any rate was in earnest in her endeavours
to preserve pure and unspotted the honour of the
family.

But what should she do? That she should put on a gala dress and a smiling face and be carried off to church with a troop of lawyers and their wives to see her daughter become the bride of a low journeyman, was of course out of the question. By no act, by no word, by no sign would she give aught of a mother's authority to nuptials so disgraceful. Should her daughter become Lady Anna Thwaite, they two, mother and daughter, would never see each other again. Of so much at any rate she was sure. But could she be sure of nothing beyond that? She could at any rate make an effort.

Then there came upon her a mad idea,—an idea which was itself evidence of insanity,— of the glory which would be hers if by any means she could prevent the marriage. There would be a halo round her name were she to perish in such a cause, let the destruction come upon her in what form it might. She sat for hours meditating,—and at every pause in her thoughts she assured herself that she could still make an effort.

She received Sir William's letter late on the Tuesday,—and during that night she did not lie down or once fall asleep. The man, as she knew, had been told to come at one on that day, and she had been prepared; but he did not come, and she then thought that the letter, which had been addressed to his late residence, had failed to reach him. During the night she wrote a very long answer to Sir William pleading her own cause, expatiating on her own feelings, and palliating any desperate deed which she might be tempted to perform. But, when the letter had been copied and folded, and duly sealed with the Lovel arms, she locked it in her desk, and did not send it on its way even on the following morning. When the morning came, shortly after eight o'clock, Mrs. Richards brought up the message which Daniel had left at the door. 'Be we to let him in, my lady?' said Mrs. Richards with supplicating hands upraised. Her sympathies were all with Lady Anna, but she feared the Countess, and did not dare in such a matter to act without the mother's sanction. The Countess begged the woman to come to her in an hour for further instructions, and at the time named Mrs. Richards, full of the importance of her work, divided between terror and pleasurable excitement, again toddled upstairs. 'Be we to let him in, my lady? God, he knows it's hard upon the likes of me, who for the last three months doesn't know whether I'm on my head or heels.' The Countess very quietly requested that when Mr. Thwaite should call he might be shown into the parlour.

'I will see Mr. Thwaite myself, Mrs. Richards; but it will be better that my daughter should not be disturbed by any intimation of his coming.'

Then there was a consultation below stairs as to what should be done. There had been many such consultations, but they had all ended in favour of the Countess. Mrs. Richards from fear, and the lady's-maid from favour, were disposed to assist the elder lady. Poor Lady Anna throughout had been forced to fight her battles with no friend near her. Now she had many friends, —many who were anxious to support her, even the Bluestones, who had been so hard upon her while she was along with them;—but they who were now her friends were never near her to assist her with a word.

So it came to pass that when Daniel Thwaite called at the house exactly at one o'clock Lady Anna was not expecting him. On the previous day at that hour she had sat waiting with anxious ears for the knock at the door which might announce his coming. But she had waited in vain. From one to two,—even till seven in the evening, she had waited. But he had not come, and she had feared that some scheme had been used against her. The people at the Post Office had been bribed,—or the women in Wyndham Street had been false. But she would not be hindered. She would go out alone and find him, —if he were to be found in London.

When he did come, she was not thinking of his coming. He was shown into the dining-room, and within a minute afterwards the Countess entered with stately step. She was well dressed, even to the adjustment of her hair; and she was a woman so changed that he would hardly have known her as that dear and valued friend whose slightest word used to be a law to his father,— but who in those days never seemed to waste a thought upon her attire. She had been out that morning walking through the streets, and the blood had mounted to her cheeks. He acknowledged to himself that she looked like a noble and high-born dame. There was a fire in her eye, and a look of scorn about her mouth and nostrils, which had even for him a certain fascination,—odious to him as were the pretensions of the so-called great. She was the first to speak. 'You have called to see my daughter,' she said.

'Yes, Lady Lovel,—I have.'

'You cannot see her.'

'I came at her request.'

'I know you did, but you cannot see her. You can be hardly so ignorant of the ways of the world, Mr. Thwaite, as to suppose that a young lady can receive what visitors she pleases without the sanction of her guardians.'

'Lady Anna Lovel has no guardian, my lady. She is of age, and is at present her own guardian.'

'I am her mother, and shall exercise the authority of a mother over her. You cannot see her. You had better go.'

'I shall not be stopped in this way, Lady Lovel.'

'Do you mean that you will force your way up to her? To do so you will have to trample over me;—and there are constables in the street. You cannot see her. You had better go.'

'Is she a prisoner?'

'That is between her and me, and is no affair of yours. You are intruding here, Mr. Thwaite, and cannot possibly gain anything by your intrusion.' Then she strode out in the passage, and motioned him to the front door. 'Mr. Thwaite, I will beg you to leave this house, which for the present is mine. If you have any proper feeling you will not stay after I have told you that you are not welcome.'

But Lady Anna, though she had not expected the coming of her lover, had heard the sound of voices, and then became aware that the man was below. As her mother was speaking she rushed down-stairs and threw herself into her lover's arms. 'It shall never be so in my presence,' said the Countess, trying to drag the girl from his embrace by the shoulders.

'Anna;—my own Anna,' said Daniel in an ecstacy of bliss. It was not only that his sweetheart was his own, but that her spirit was so high.

'Daniel!' she said, still struggling in his arms.

By this time they were all in the parlour, whither the Countess had been satisfied to retreat to escape the eyes of the women who clustered at the top of the kitchen stairs. 'Daniel Thwaite,' said the Countess, 'if you do not leave this, the blood which will be shed shall rest on your head,' and so saying, she drew nigh to the window and pulled down the blind. She then crossed over and did the same to the other blind, and having done so, took her place close to a heavy upright desk, which stood between the fireplace and the window. When the two ladies first came to the house they had occupied only the first and second floors;—but, since the success of their cause, the whole had been taken, including the parlour in which this scene was being acted; and the Countess spent many hours daily sitting at the heavy desk in this dark gloomy chamber.

'Whose blood shall be shed?' said Lady Anna, turning to her mother.

'It is the raving of madness,' said Daniel.

'Whether it be madness or not, you shall find, sir, that it is true. Take your hands from her. Would you disgrace the child in the presence of her mother?'

'There is no disgrace, mamma. He is my own, and I am his. Why should you try to part us?'

But now they were parted. He was not a man to linger much over the sweetness of a caress when sterner work was in his hands to be done. 'Lady Lovel,' he said, 'you must see that this opposition is fruitless. Ask your cousin, Lord Lovel, and he will tell you that it is so.'

'I care nothing for my cousin. If he be false, I am true. Though all the world be false, still will I be true. I do not ask her to marry her cousin. I simply demand that she shall relinquish one who is infinitely beneath her,—who is unfit to tie her very shoe-string.'

'He is my equal in all things,' said Lady Anna, 'and he shall be my lord and husband.'

'I know of no inequalities such as those you speak of, Lady Lovel,' said the tailor. 'The excellence of your daughter's merits I admit, and am almost disposed to claim some goodness for myself, finding that one so good can love me. But, Lady Lovel, I do not wish to remain here now. You are disturbed.'

'I am disturbed, and you had better go.'

'I will go at once if you will let me name some early day on which I may be allowed to meet Lady Anna,—alone. And I tell her here that if she be not permitted so to see me, it will be her duty to leave her mother's house, and come to me. There is my address, dear.' Then he handed her a paper on which he had written the name of the street and number at which he was now living. 'You are free to come and go as you list, and if you will send to me there, I will find you here or elsewhere as you may

command me. It is but a short five minutes'
walk beyond the house at which you were staying
in Bedford Square.'

The Countess stood silent for a moment or
two, looking at them, during which neither the
girl spoke nor her lover. 'You will not even allow
her six months to think of it?' said the Countess.

'I will allow her six years if she says that she
requires time to think of it.'

'I do not want an hour,—not a minute,' said
Lady Anna.

The mother flashed round upon her daughter.
'Poor vain, degraded wretch,' she said.

'She is a true woman, honest to the heart's
core,' said the lover.

'You shall come to-morrow,' said the Countess.
'Do you hear me, Anna?—he shall come to-
morrow. There shall be an end of this in some
way, and I am broken-hearted. My life is over
for me, and I may as well lay me down and die.
I hope God in his mercy may never send upon
another woman,—upon another wife, or another
mother,—trouble such as that with which I have
been afflicted. But I tell you this, Anna; that
what evil a husband can do,—even let him be
evil-minded as was your father,—is nothing,—
nothing,—nothing to the cruelty of a cruel
child. Go now, Mr. Thwaite; if you please.
If you will return at the same hour to-morrow
she shall speak with you—alone. And then she
must do as she pleases.'

'Anna, I will come again to-morrow,' said the
tailor. But Lady Anna did not answer him. She
did not speak, but stayed looking at him till he
was gone.

'To-morrow shall end it all. I can stand this no longer. I have prayed to you,—a mother to her daughter; I have prayed to you for mercy, and you will show me none. I have knelt to you.'

'Mamma!'

'I will kneel again if it may avail.' And the Countess did kneel. 'Will you not spare me?'

'Get up, mamma; get up. What am I doing, —what have I done that you should speak to me like this?'

'I ask you from my very soul,—lest I commit some terrible crime. I have sworn that I would not see this marriage,—and I will not see it.'

'If he will consent I will delay it,' said the girl, trembling.

'Must I beg to him then? Must I kneel to him? Must I ask him to save me from the wrath to come? No, my child, I will not do that. If it must come, let it come. When you were a little thing at my knees, the gentlest babe that ever mother kissed, I did not think that you would live to be so hard to me. You have your mother's brow, my child, but you have your father's heart.'

'I will ask him to delay it,' said Anna.

'No;—if it be to come to that I will have no dealings with you. What; that he,—he who has come between me and all my peace, he who with his pretended friendship has robbed me of my all, that he is to be asked to grant me a few weeks' delay before this pollution comes upon me,— during which the whole world will know that Lady Anna Lovel is to be the tailor's wife! Leave me. When he comes to-morrow, you shall be sent for; but I will see him first. Leave me, now. I would be alone.'

Lady Anna made an attempt to take her mother's hand, but the Countess repulsed her rudely. 'Oh, mamma!'

'We must be bitter enemies or loving friends, my child. As it is we are bitter enemies; yes, the bitterest. Leave me now. There is no room for further words between us.' Then Lady Anna slunk up to her own room.

CHAPTER XLIII

Daniel Thwaite comes again

THE Countess Lovel had prepared herself on that morning for the doing of a deed, but her heart had failed her. How she might have carried herself through it had not her daughter come down to them,—how far she might have been able to persevere, cannot be said now. But it was certain that she had so far relented that even while the hated man was there in her presence, she determined that she would once again submit herself to make entreaties to her child, once again to speak of all that she had endured, and to pray at least for delay if nothing else could be accorded to her. If her girl would but promise to remain with her for six months, then they might go abroad,—and the chances afforded them by time and distance would be before her. In that case she would lavish such love upon the girl, so many indulgences, such sweets of wealth and ease, such store of caresses and soft luxury, that surely the young heart might thus be turned to the things which were fit for rank, and high blood, and splendid possessions. It could not be but that her own child,—the child who a few months since had been as gentle with her and as obedient as an infant—should give way to her as far as that. She tried it, and her daughter had referred her prayer,—or had said that she would refer it,—to the decision of her hated lover; and the mother had at once lost all command of her temper. She had become fierce,—nay, ferocious; and had lacked the guile and the self-command necessary to carry out her purpose. Had she persevered, Lady Anna must have granted her the small boon that she then asked. But she had given way to her wrath, and had declared that her daughter was her bitterest enemy. As she seated herself at the old desk where Lady Anna left her, she swore within her own bosom that the deed must be done.

Even at the moment when she was resolving that she would kneel once more at her daughter's knees, she prepared herself for the work that she must do, should the daughter still be as hard as stone to her. 'Come again at one to-morrow,' she said to the tailor; and the tailor said that he would come.

When she was alone she seated herself on her accustomed chair and opened the old desk with a key that had now become familiar to her hand. It was a huge piece of furniture,—such as is never made in these days, but is found among every congregation of old household goods,— with numberless drawers clustering below, with a vast body, full of receptacles for bills, wills, deeds, and waste-paper, and a tower of shelves above, ascending almost to the ceiling. In the centre of the centre body was a square compartment, but this had been left unlocked, so that its contents might be ready to her hand. Now she opened it and took from it a pistol; and, looking warily over her shoulder to see that the door was closed, and cautiously up at the windows, lest some eye might be spying her action even through the thick blinds, she took

the weapon in her hand and held it up so that
she might feel, if possible, how it would be with
her when she should attempt the deed. She
looked very narrowly at the lock, of which the
trigger was already back at its place, so that
no exertion of arrangement might be necessary
for her at the fatal moment. Never as yet had
she fired a pistol;—never before had she held
such a weapon in her hand;—but she thought
that she could do it when her passion ran high.

Then for the twentieth time she asked herself
whether it would not be easier to turn it against
her own bosom,—against her own brain; so
that all might be over at once. Ah, yes;—so
much easier! But how then would it be with this
man who had driven her, by his subtle courage
and persistent audacity, to utter destruction?
Could he and she be made to go down together
in that boat which her fancy had built for them,
then indeed it might be well that she should seek
her own death. But were she now to destroy
herself,—herself and only herself,—then would
her enemy be left to enjoy his rich prize, a prize
only the richer because she would have disappeared from the world! And of her, if such had
been her last deed, men would only say that the
mad Countess had gone on in her madness. With
looks of sad solemnity, but heartfelt satisfaction,
all the Lovels, and that wretched tailor, and her
own daughter, would bestow some mock grief on
her funeral, and there would be an end for ever
of Josephine Countess Lovel,—and no one would
remember her, or her deeds, or her sufferings.
When she wandered out from the house on that
morning, after hearing that Daniel Thwaite

would be there at one, and had walked nearly into the mid city so that she might not be watched, and had bought her pistol and powder and bullets, and had then with patience gone to work and taught herself how to prepare the weapon for use, she certainly had not intended simply to make the triumph of her enemy more easy.

And yet she knew well what was the penalty of murder, and she knew also that there could be no chance of escape. Very often had she turned it in her mind, whether she could not destroy the man so that the hand of the destroyer might be hidden. But it could not be so. She could not dog him in the streets. She could not get at him in his meals to poison him. She could not creep to his bedside and strangle him in the silent watches of the night. And this woman's heart, even while from day to day she was meditating murder,—while she was telling herself that it would be a worthy deed to cut off from life one whose life was a bar to her own success, —even then revolted from the shrinking stealthy step, from the low cowardice of the hidden murderer. To look him in the face and then to slay him,—when no escape for herself would be possible, that would have in it something that was almost noble; something at any rate bold, —something that would not shame her. They would hang her for such a deed! Let them do so. It was not hanging that she feared, but the tongues of those who should speak of her when she was gone. They should not speak of her as one who had utterly failed. They should tell of a woman who, cruelly misused throughout her life, maligned, scorned, and tortured, robbed of her own, neglected by her kindred, deserted and damned by her husband, had still struggled through it all till she had proved herself to be that which it was her right to call herself;—of a woman who, though thwarted in her ambition by her own child, and cheated of her triumph at the very moment of her success, had dared rather to face an ignominious death than see all her efforts frustrated by the maudlin fancy of a girl. Yes! She would face it all. Let them do what they would with her. She hardly knew what might be the mode of death adjudged to a Countess who had murdered. Let them kill her as they would, they would kill a Countess;— and the whole world would know her story.

That day and night were very dreadful to her. She never asked a question about her daughter. They had brought her food to her in that lonely parlour, and she hardly heeded them as they laid the things before her, and then re-moved them. Again and again did she unlock the old desk, and see that the weapon was ready to her hand. Then she opened that letter to Sir William Patterson, and added a postscript to it. 'What I have since done will explain every-thing.' That was all she added, and on the following morning, about noon, she put the letter on the mantelshelf. Late at night she took herself to bed, and was surprised to find that she slept. The key of the old desk was under her pillow, and she placed her hand on it the moment that she awoke. On leaving her own room she stood for a moment at her daughter's door. It might be, if she killed the man, that

she would never see her child again. At that
moment she was tempted to rush into her
daughter's room, to throw herself upon her
daughter's bed, and once again to beg for mercy
and grace. She listened, and she knew that her
daughter slept. Then she went silently down to
the dark room and the old desk. Of what use
would it be to abase herself? Her daughter was
the only thing that she could love; but her
daughter's heart was filled with the image of
that low-born artisan.

'Is Lady Anna up?' she asked the maid about
ten o'clock.

'Yes, my lady; she is breakfasting now.'

'Tell her that when—when Mr. Thwaite comes,
I will send for her as soon as I wish to see her.'

'I think Lady Anna understands that already,
my lady.'

'Tell her what I say.'

'Yes, my lady. I will, my lady.' Then the
Countess spoke no further word till, punctually
at one o'clock, Daniel Thwaite was shown into
the room.

'You keep your time, Mr. Thwaite,' she said.

'Working men should always do that, Lady
Lovel,' he replied, as though anxious to irritate
her by reminding her how humble was the
man who could aspire to be the son-in-law of a
Countess.

'All men should do so, I presume. I also am
punctual. Well, sir;—have you anything else to
say?'

'Much to say,—to your daughter, Lady Lovel.'

'I do not know that you will ever see my
daughter again.'

'Do you mean to say that she has been taken away from this?' The Countess was silent, but moved away from the spot on which she stood to receive him towards the old desk, which stood open,—with the door of the centre space just ajar. 'If it be so, you have deceived me most grossly, Lady Lovel. But it can avail you nothing, for I know that she will be true to me. Do you tell me that she has been removed?'

'I have told you no such thing.'

'Bid her come then,—as you promised me.'

'I have a word to say to you first. What if she should refuse to come?'

'I do not believe that she will refuse. You yourself heard what she said yesterday. All earth and all heaven should not make me doubt her, and certainly not your word, Lady Lovel. You know how it is, and you know how it must be.'

'Yes,—I do; I do; I do.' She was facing him with her back to the window, and she put forth her left hand upon the open desk, and thrust it forward as though to open the square door which stood ajar;—but he did not notice her hand; he had his eye fixed upon her, and suspected only deceit,—not violence. 'Yes, I know how it must be,' she said, while her fingers approached nearer to the little door.

'Then let her come to me.'

'Will nothing turn you from it?'

'Nothing will turn me from it.'

Then suddenly she withdrew her hand and confronted him more closely. 'Mine has been a hard life, Mr. Thwaite;—no life could have been harder. But I have always had something before me for which to long, and for which to hope;—

something which I might reach if justice should at length prevail.'

'You have got money and rank.'

'They are nothing;—nothing. In all those many years, the thing that I have looked for has been the splendour and glory of another, and the satisfaction I might feel in having bestowed upon her all that she owned. Do you think that I will stand by, after such a struggle, and see you rob me of it all,—you,—you, who were one of the tools which came to my hand to work with? From what you know of me, do you think that my spirit could stoop so low? Answer me, if you have ever thought of that. Let the eagles alone, and do not force yourself into our nest. You will find, if you do, that you will be rent to pieces.'

'This is nothing, Lady Lovel. I came here,—at your bidding, to see your daughter. Let me see her.'

'You will not go?'

'Certainly I will not go.'

She looked at him as she slowly receded to her former standing-ground, but he never for a moment suspected the nature of her purpose. He began to think that some actual insanity had befallen her, and was doubtful how he should act. But no fear of personal violence affected him. He was merely questioning with himself whether it would not be well for him to walk up-stairs into the upper room, and seek Lady Anna there, as he stood watching the motion of her eyes.

'You had better go,' said she, as she again put her left hand on the flat board of the open desk.

'You trifle with me, Lady Lovel,' he answered. 'As you will not allow Lady Anna to come to me here, I will go to her elsewhere. I do not doubt but that I shall find her in the house.' Then he turned to the door, intending to leave the room. He had been very near to her while they were talking, so that he had some paces to traverse before he could put his hand upon the lock,—but in doing so his back was turned on her. In one respect it was better for her purpose that it should be so. She could open the door of the compartment and put her hand upon the pistol without having his eye upon her. But, as it seemed to her at the moment, the chance of bringing her purpose to its intended conclusion was less than it would have been had she been able to fire at his face. She had let the moment go by,—the first moment,—when he was close to her, and now there would be half the room between them. But she was very quick. She seized the pistol, and, transferring it to her right hand, she rushed after him, and when the door was already half open she pulled the trigger. In the agony of that moment she heard no sound, though she saw the flash. She saw him shrink and pass the door, which he left unclosed, and then she heard a scuffle in the passage, as though he had fallen against the wall. She had provided herself especially with a second barrel, —but that was now absolutely useless to her. There was no power left to her wherewith to follow him and complete the work which she had begun. She did not think that she had killed him, though she was sure that he was struck. She did not believe that she had accomplished

anything of her wishes,—but had she held in her
hand a six-barrelled revolver, as of the present
day, she could have done no more with it. She
was overwhelmed with so great a tremor at her
own violence that she was almost incapable of
moving. She stood glaring at the door, listening
for what should come, and the moments seemed
to be hours. But she heard no sound whatever.
A minute passed away perhaps, and the man
did not move. She looked around as if seeking
some way of escape,—as though, were it possible,
she would get to the street through the window.
There was no mode of escape, unless she would
pass out through the door to the man who, as
she knew, must still be there. Then she heard
him move. She heard him rise,—from what
posture she knew not, and step towards the
stairs. She was still standing with the pistol in her
hand, but was almost unconscious that she held
it. At last her eye glanced upon it, and she was
aware that she was still armed. Should she
rush after him, and try what she could do with
that other bullet? The thought crossed her mind,
but she knew that she could do nothing. Had
all the Lovels depended upon it, she could not
have drawn that other trigger. She took the
pistol, put it back into its former hiding-place,
mechanically locked the little door, and then
seated herself in her chair.

CHAPTER XLIV

The Attempt and not the Deed confounds us*

THE tailor's hand was on the lock of the door when he first saw the flash of the fire, and then felt that he was wounded. Though his back was turned to the woman he distinctly saw the flash, but he never could remember that he had heard the report. He knew nothing of the nature of the injury he had received, and was hardly aware of the place in which he had been struck, when he half closed the door behind him and then staggered against the opposite wall. For a moment he was sick, almost to fainting, but yet he did not believe that he had been grievously hurt. He was, however, disabled, weak, and almost incapable of any action. He seated himself on the lowest stair, and began to think. The woman had intended to murder him! She had lured him there with the premeditated intention of destroying him! And this was the mother of his bride,—the woman whom he intended to call his mother-in-law! He was not dead, nor did he believe that he was like to die; but had she killed him,—what must have been the fate of the murderess! As it was, would it not be necessary that she should be handed over to the law, and dealt with for the offence? He did not know that they might not even hang her for the attempt.

He said afterwards that he thought that he sat there for a quarter of an hour. Three minutes, however, had not passed before Mrs.

Richards, ascending from the kitchen, found him upon the stairs. 'What is it, Mr. Thwaite?' said she.

'Is anything the matter?' he asked with a faint smile.

'The place is full of smoke,' she said, 'and there is a smell of gunpowder.'

'There is no harm done at any rate,' he answered.

'I thought I heard a something go off,' said Sarah, who was behind Mrs. Richards.

'Did you?' said he. 'I heard nothing; but there certainly is a smoke,' and he still smiled.

'What are you sitting there for, Mr. Thwaite?' asked Mrs. Richards.

'You ain't no business to sit there, Mr. Thwaite,' said Sarah.

'You've been and done something to the Countess,' said Mrs. Richards.

'The Countess is all right. I'm going up-stairs to see Lady Anna;—that's all. But I've hurt myself a little. I'm bad in my left shoulder, and I sat down just to get a rest.' As he spoke he was still smiling.

Then the woman looked at him and saw that he was very pale. At that instant he was in great pain, though he felt that as the sense of intense sickness was leaving him he would be able to go up-stairs and say a word or two to his sweetheart, should he find her. 'You ain't just as you ought to be, Mr. Thwaite,' said Mrs. Richards. He was very haggard, and perspiration was on his brow, and she thought that he had been drinking.

'I am well enough,' said he rising,—'only

that I am much troubled by a hurt in my arm. At any rate I will go up-stairs.' Then he mounted slowly, leaving the two women standing in the passage.

Mrs. Richards gently opened the parlour door, and entered the room, which was still reeking with smoke and the smell of the powder, and there she found the Countess seated at the old desk, but with her body and face turned round towards the door. 'Is anything the matter, my lady?' asked the woman.

'Where has he gone?'

'Mr. Thwaite has just stepped up-stairs,—this moment. He was very queer like, my lady.'

'Is he hurt?'

'We think he's been drinking, my lady,' said Sarah.

'He says that his shoulder is ever so bad,' said Mrs. Richards.

Then for the first time it occurred to the Countess that perhaps the deed which she had done,—the attempt in which she had failed,— might never be known. Instinctively she had hidden the pistol and had locked the little door, and concealed the key within her bosom as soon as she was alone. Then she thought that she would open the window; but she had been afraid to move, and she had sat there waiting while she heard the sound of voices in the passage. 'Oh,—his shoulder!' said she. 'No,—he has not been drinking. He never drinks. He has been very violent, but he never drinks. Well,— why do you wait?'

'There is such a smell of something,' said Mrs. Richards.

'Yes;—you had better open the windows. There was an accident. Thank you;—that will do.'

'And is he to be alone,—with Lady Anna, up-stairs?' asked the maid.

'He is to be alone with her. How can I help it? If she chooses to be a scullion she must follow her bent. I have done all I could. Why do you wait? I tell you that he is to be with her. Go away, and leave me.' Then they went and left her, wondering much, but guessing nothing of the truth. She watched them till they had closed the door, and then instantly opened the other window wide. It was now May, but the weather was still cold. There had been rain the night before, and it had been showery all the morning. She had come in from her walk damp and chilled, and there was a fire in the grate. But she cared nothing for the weather. Looking round the room she saw a morsel of wadding near the floor, and she instantly burned it. She longed to look at the pistol, but she did not dare to take it from its hiding-place lest she should be discovered in the act. Every energy of her mind was now strained to the effort of avoiding detection. Should he choose to tell what had been done, then, indeed, all would be over. But had he not resolved to be silent he would hardly have borne the agony of the wound and gone up-stairs without speaking of it. She almost forgot now the misery of the last year in the intensity of her desire to escape the disgrace of punishment. A sudden nervousness, a desire to do something by which she might help to preserve herself, seized upon her. But there was nothing which she could do. She could not follow him lest he should accuse her to her face. It would be vain for her to leave the house till he should have gone. Should she do so, she knew that she would not dare return to it. So she sat, thinking, dreaming, plotting, crushed by an agony of fear, looking anxiously at the door, listening for every footfall within the house; and she watched too for the well-known click of the area gate, dreading lest any one should go out to seek the intervention of the constables.

In the meantime Daniel Thwaite had gone up-stairs, and had knocked at the drawing-room door. It was instantly opened by Lady Anna herself. 'I heard you come;—what a time you have been here!—I thought that I should never see you.' As she spoke she stood close to him that he might embrace her. But the pain of his wound affected his whole body, and he felt that he could hardly raise even his right arm. He was aware now that the bullet had entered his back, somewhere on his left shoulder. 'Oh, Daniel;—are you ill?' she said, looking at him.

'Yes, dear;—I am ill;—not very ill. Did you hear nothing?'

'No!'

'Nor yet see anything?'

'No!'

'I will tell you all another time;—only do not ask me now.' She had seated herself beside him and wound her arm round his back as though to support him. 'You must not touch me, dearest.'

'You have been hurt.'

'Yes;—I have been hurt. I am in pain, though I do not think that it signifies. I had better go to a surgeon, and then you shall hear from me.'

'Tell me, Daniel;—what is it, Daniel?'

'I will tell you,—but not now. You shall know all, but I should do harm were I to say it now. Say not a word to any one, sweetheart,—unless your mother ask you.'

'What shall I tell her?'

'That I am hurt,—but not seriously hurt;—and that the less said the sooner mended. Tell her also that I shall expect no further interruption to my letters when I write to you,—or to my visits when I can come. God bless you, dearest;—one kiss, and now I will go.'

'You will send for me if you are ill, Daniel?'

'If I am really ill, I will send for you.' So saying, he left her, went down-stairs, with great difficulty opened for himself the front door, and departed.

Lady Anna, though she had been told nothing of what had happened, except that her lover was hurt, at once surmised something of what had been done. Daniel Thwaite had suffered some hurt from her mother's wrath. She sat for a while thinking what it might have been. She had seen no sign of blood. Could it be that her mother had struck him in her anger with some chance weapon that had come to hand? That there had been violence she was sure,—and sure also that her mother had been in fault. When Daniel had been some few minutes gone she went down, that she might deliver his message. At the foot of the stairs, and near the door of the parlour, she met Mrs. Richards. 'I suppose the young man has gone, my lady?' asked the woman.

'Mr. Thwaite has gone.'

'And I make so bold, my lady, as to say that he ought not to come here. There has been a doing of some kind, but I don't know what. He says as how he's been hurt, and I'm sure I don't know how he should be hurt here,—unless he brought it with him. I never had nothing of the kind here before, long as I've been here. Of course your title and that is all right, my lady; but the young man isn't fit;—that's the truth of it. My belief is he'd been a drinking; and I won't have it in my house.'

Lady Anna passed by her without a word and went into her mother's room. The Countess was still seated in her chair, and neither rose nor spoke when her daughter entered. 'Mamma, Mr. Thwaite is hurt.'

'Well;—what of it? Is it much that ails him?'

'He is in pain. What has been done, mamma?' The Countess looked at her, striving to learn from the girl's face and manner what had been told and what concealed. 'Did you—— strike him?'

'Has he said that I struck him?'

'No, mamma;—but something has been done that should not have been done. I know it. He has sent you a message, mamma.'

'What was it?' asked the Countess, in a hoarse voice.

'That he was hurt, but not seriously.'

'Oh;—he said that.'

'I fear he is hurt seriously.'

'But he said that he was not?'

'Yes;—and that the less said the sooner mended.'

'Did he say that too?'

'That was his message.'

The Countess gave a long sigh, then sobbed, and at last broke out into hysteric tears. It was evident to her now that the man was sparing her,—was endeavouring to spare her. He had told no one as yet. 'The least said the soonest mended.' Oh yes;—if he would say never a word to any one of what had occurred between them that day, that would be best for her. But how could he not tell? When some doctor should ask him how he had come by that wound, surely he would tell then! It could not be possible that such a deed should have been done there, in that little room, and that no one should know it! And why should he not tell,—he who was her enemy? Had she caught him at advantage, would she not have smote him, hip and thigh? And then she reflected what it would be to owe perhaps her life to the mercy of Daniel Thwaite, —to the mercy of her enemy, of him who knew, —if no one else should know,—that she had attempted to murder him. It would be better for her, should she be spared to do so, to go away to some distant land, where she might hide her head for ever.

'May I go to him, mamma, to see him?' Lady Anna asked. The Countess, full of her own thoughts, sat silent, answering not a word. 'I know where he lives, mamma, and I fear that he is much hurt.'

'He will not——die,' muttered the Countess.

'God forbid that he should die;—but I will

go to him.' Then she returned up-stairs without a word of opposition from her mother, put on her bonnet, and sallied forth. No one stopped her or said a word to her now, and she seemed to herself to be as free as air. She walked up to the corner of Gower Street, and turned down into Bedford Square, passing the house of the Serjeant. Then she asked her way into Great Russell Street, which she found to be hardly more than a stone's throw from the Serjeant's door, and soon found the number at which her lover lived. No;—Mr. Thwaite was not at home. Yes;—she might wait for him;—but he had no room but his bedroom. Then she became very bold. 'I am engaged to be his wife,' she said. 'Are you the Lady Anna?' asked the woman, who had heard the story. Then she was received with great distinction, and invited to sit down in a parlour on the ground-floor. There she sat for three hours, motionless, alone, —waiting,—waiting,—waiting. When it was quite dark, at about six o'clock, Daniel Thwaite entered the room with his left arm bound up. 'My girl!' he said, with so much joy in his tone that she could not but rejoice to hear him. 'So you have found me out, and have come to me!'

'Yes, I have come. Tell me what it is. I know that you are hurt.'

'I have been hurt certainly. The doctor wanted me to go into a hospital, but I trust that I may escape that. But I must take care of myself. I had to come back here in a coach, because the man told me not to walk.'

'How was it, Daniel? Oh, Daniel, you will tell me everything?'

Then she sat beside him as he lay upon the couch, and listened to him while he told her the whole story. He hid nothing from her, but as he went on he made her understand that it was his intention to conceal the whole deed, to say nothing of it, so that the perpetrator should escape punishment, if it might be possible. She listened in awe-struck silence as she heard the tale of her mother's guilt. And he, with wonderful skill, with hearty love for the girl, and in true mercy to her feelings, palliated the crime of the would-be murderess. 'She was beside herself with grief and emotion,' he said, 'and has hardly surprised me by what she has done. Had I thought of it, I should almost have expected it.'

'She may do it again, Daniel.'

'I think not. She will be cowed now, and quieter. She did not interfere when you told her that you were coming to me? It will be a lesson to her, and so it may be good for us.' Then he bade her to tell her mother that he, as far as he was concerned, would hold his peace. If she would forget all past injuries, so would he. If she would hold out her hand to him, he would take it. If she could not bring herself to this,—could not bring herself as yet,— then let her go apart. No notice should be taken of what she had done. 'But she must not again stand between us,' he said.

'Nothing shall stand between us,' said Lady Anna.

Then he told her, laughing as he did so, how hard it had been for him to keep the story of his wound secret from the doctor, who had

already extracted the ball, and who was to visit
him on the morrow. The practitioner to whom
he had gone, knowing nothing of gunshot
wounds, had taken him to a first-class surgeon,
and the surgeon had of course asked as to the
cause of the wound. Daniel had said that it was
an accident as to which he could not explain
the cause. 'You mean you will not tell,' said
the surgeon. 'Exactly so. I will not tell. It is my
secret. That I did not do it myself you may
judge from the spot in which I was shot.' To
this the surgeon assented; and, though he pressed
the question, and said something as to the
necessity for an investigation, he could get no
satisfaction. However, he had learned Daniel's
name and address. He was to call on the morrow,
and would then perhaps succeed in learning
something of the mystery. 'In the meantime,
my darling, I must go to bed, for it seems as
though every bone in my body was sore. I have
brought an old woman with me who is to look
after me.'

Then she left him, promising that she would
come on the morrow and would nurse him.
'Unless they lock me up, I will be here,' she
said. Daniel Thwaite thought that in the present
circumstances no further attempt would be made
to constrain her actions.

CHAPTER XLV

The Lawyers agree

WHEN a month had passed by a great many
people knew how Mr. Daniel Thwaite had
come by the wound in his back, but nobody
knew it 'officially'. There is a wide difference
in the qualities of knowledge regarding such
matters. In affairs of public interest we often
know, or fancy that we know, down to every
exact detail, how a thing has been done,—
who have given the bribes and who have
taken them,—who has told the lie and who has
pretended to believe it,—who has peculated and
how the public purse has suffered,—who was in
love with such a one's wife and how the matter
was detected, then smothered up, and condoned;
but there is no official knowledge, and nothing
can be done. The tailor and the Earl, the
Countess and her daughter, had become public property since the great trial had been commenced, and many eyes were on them. Before
a week had gone by it was known in every club
and in every great drawing-room that the tailor
had been shot in the shoulder,—and it was
almost known that the pistol had been fired by
the hands of the Countess. The very eminent
surgeon into whose hands Daniel had luckily
fallen did not press his questions very far when
his patient told him that it would be for the
welfare of many people that nothing further
should be asked on the matter. 'An accident
has occurred,' said Daniel, 'as to which I do not

intend to say anything further. I can assure you that no injury has been done beyond that which I suffer.' The eminent surgeon no doubt spoke of the matter among his friends, but he always declared that he had no certain knowledge as to the hand which fired the pistol.

The women in Keppel Street of course talked. There had certainly been a smoke and a smell of gunpowder. Mrs. Richards had heard nothing. Sarah thought that she had heard a noise. They both were sure that Daniel Thwaite had been much the worse for drink,—a statement which led to considerable confusion. No pistol was ever seen,—though the weapon remained in the old desk for some days, and was at last conveyed out of the house when the Countess left it with all her belongings. She had been afraid to hide it more stealthily or even throw it away, lest her doing so should be discovered. Had the law interfered,—had any search-warrant been granted,—the pistol would, of course, have been found. As it was, no one asked the Countess a question on the subject. The lawyers who had been her friends, and had endeavoured to guide her through her difficulties, became afraid of her, and kept aloof from her. They had all gone over to the opinion that Lady Anna should be allowed to marry the tailor, and had on that account become her enemies. She was completely isolated, and was now spoken of mysteriously,—as a woman who had suffered much, and was nearly mad with grief, as a violent, determined, dangerous being, who was interesting as a subject for conversation, but one not at all desirable as an acquaintance. During the whole of this month the Countess remained in Keppel Street, and was hardly ever seen by any but the inmates of that house.

Lady Anna had returned home all alone, on the evening of the day on which the deed had been done, after leaving her lover in the hands of the old nurse with whose services he had been furnished. The rain was still falling as she came through Russell Square. The distance was indeed short, but she was wet and cold and draggled when she returned; and the criminality of the deed which her mother had committed had come fully home to her mind during the short journey. The door was opened to her by Mrs. Richards, and she at once asked for the Countess. 'Lady Anna, where have you been?' asked Mrs. Richards, who was learning to take upon herself, during these troubles, something of the privilege of finding fault. But Lady Anna put her aside without a word, and went into the parlour. There sat the Countess just as she had been left,—except that a pair of candles stood upon the table, and that the tea-things had been laid there. 'You are all wet,' she said. 'Where have you been?'

'He has told me all,' the girl replied, without answering the question. 'Oh, mamma;—how could you do it?'

'Who has driven me to it? It has been you,— you, you. Well;—what else?'

'Mamma, he has forgiven you.'

'Forgiven me! I will not have his forgiveness.'

'Oh, mamma;—if I forgive you, will you not be friends with us?' She stooped over her

mother, and kissed her, and then went on and
told what she had to tell. She stood and told it
all in a low voice, so that no ear but that of her
mother should hear her,—how the ball had hit
him, how it had been extracted, how nothing
had been and nothing should be told, how
Daniel would forgive it all and be her friend,
if she would let him. 'But, mamma, I hope
you will be sorry.' The Countess sat silent,
moody, grim, with her eyes fixed on the table.
She would say nothing. 'And, mamma,—I must
go to him every day,—to do things for him and
to help to nurse him. Of course he will be my
husband now.' Still the Countess said not a
word, either of approval or of dissent. Lady
Anna sat down for a moment or two, hoping
that her mother would allow her to eat and
drink in the room, and that thus they might
again begin to live together. But not a word
was spoken nor a motion made, and the silence
became awful, so that the girl did not dare to
keep her seat. 'Shall I go, mamma?' she said.
'Yes;—you had better go.' After that they
did not see each other again on that evening,
and during the week or ten days following they
lived apart.

On the following morning, after an early
breakfast, Lady Anna went to Great Russell
Street, and there she remained the greater part
of the day. The people of the house understood
that the couple were to be married as soon as
their lodger should be well, and had heard much
of the magnificence of the marriage. They were
kind and good, and the tailor declared very
often that this was the happiest period of his

existence. Of all the good turns ever done to
him, he said, the wound in his back had been
the best. As his sweetheart sat by his bedside
they planned their future life. They would still
go to the distant land on which his heart was set,
though it might be only for a while; and she,
with playfulness, declared that she would go
there as Mrs. Thwaite. 'I suppose they can't
prevent me calling myself Mrs. Thwaite, if I
please.'

'I am not so sure of that,' said the tailor. 'Evil
burs stick fast.'

It would be vain now to tell of all the sweet
lovers' words that were spoken between them
during those long hours;—but the man believed
that no girl had ever been so true to her lover
through so many difficulties as Lady Anna had
been to him, and she was sure that she had never
varied in her wish to become the wife of the man
who had first asked her for her love. She thought
much and she thought often of the young lord;
but she took the impress of her lover's mind,
and learned to regard her cousin, the Earl, as an
idle, pretty popinjay, born to eat, to drink, and
to carry sweet perfumes. 'Just a butterfly,' said
the tailor.

'One of the brightest butterflies,' said the girl.
'A woman should not be a butterfly,—not
altogether a butterfly,' he answered. 'But for
a man it is surely a contemptible part. Do you
remember the young man who comes to Hotspur*on the battlefield, or him whom the king
sent to Hamlet*about the wager? When I saw
Lord Lovel at his breakfast table, I thought
of them. I said to myself that spermaceti

was the "sovereignest thing on earth for an inward wound,"*and I told myself that he was of "very soft society, and great showing.""* She smiled, though she did not know the words he quoted, and assured him that her poor cousin Lord Lovel would not trouble him much in the days that were to come. 'He will not trouble me at all, but as he is your cousin I would fain that he could be a man. He had a sort of gown on which would have made a grand frock for you, sweetheart;—only too smart I fear for my wife.' She laughed and was pleased,—and remembered without a shade either of regret or remorse the manner in which the popinjay had helped her over the stepping-stones at Bolton Abbey.

But the tailor, though he thus scorned the lord, was quite willing that a share of the property should be given up to him. 'Unless you did, how on earth could he wear such grand gowns as that? I can understand that he wants it more than I do, and if there are to be earls, I suppose they should be rich. We do not want it, my girl.'

'You will have half, Daniel,' she said.

'As far as that goes, I do not want a doit*of it, —not a penny-piece. When they paid me what became my own by my father's will, I was rich enough,—rich enough for you and me too, my girl, if that was all. But it is better that it should be divided. If he had it all he would buy too many gowns; and it may be that with us some good will come of it. As far as I can see, no good comes of money spent on race-courses, and in gorgeous gowns.'

This went on from day to day throughout a month, and every day Lady Anna took her place with her lover. After a while her mother came up into the drawing-room in Keppel Street, and then the two ladies again lived together. Little or nothing, however, was said between them as to their future lives. The Countess was quiet, sullen,—and to a bystander would have appeared to be indifferent. She had been utterly vanquished by the awe inspired by her own deed, and by the fear which had lasted for some days that she might be dragged to trial for the offence. As that dread subsided she was unable to recover her former spirits. She spoke no more of what she had done and what she had suffered, but seemed to submit to the inevitable. She said nothing of any future life that might be in store for her, and, as far as her daughter could perceive, had no plans formed for the coming time. At last Lady Anna found it necessary to speak of her own plans. 'Mamma,' she said, 'Mr. Thwaite wishes that banns should be read in church for our marriage.'

'Banns!' exclaimed the Countess.

'Yes, mamma; he thinks it best.' The Countess made no further observation. If the thing was to be, it mattered little to her whether they were to be married by banns or by licence,*—whether her girl should walk down to church like a maid-servant, or be married with all the pomp and magnificence to which her rank and wealth might entitle her. How could there be splendour, how even decency, in such a marriage as this? She at any rate would not be present,

let them be married in what way they would.
On the fourth Sunday after the shot had been
fired the banns were read for the first time in
Bloomsbury Church, and the future bride was
described as Anna Lovel,—commonly called
Lady Anna Lovel,—spinster. Neither on that
occasion or on either of the two further callings,
did any one get up in church to declare that
impediment existed why Daniel Thwaite the
tailor and Lady Anna Lovel should not be
joined together in holy matrimony.

In the meantime the lawyers had been at work
dividing the property, and in the process of
doing so it had been necessary that Mr. Goffe
should have various interviews with the Countess.
She also, as the undisputed widow of the late
intestate Earl, was now a very rich woman,
with an immense income at her control. But
no one wanted assistance from her. There was
her revenue, and she was doomed to live apart
with it in her solitude,—with no fellow-creature
to rejoice with her in her triumph, with no de-
pendant whom she could make happy with her
wealth. She was a woman with many faults,—
but covetousness was not one of them. If she
could have given it all to the young Earl,—
and her daughter with it, she would have been
a happy woman. Had she been permitted to
dream that it was all so settled that her grand-
child would become of all Earl Lovels the most
wealthy and most splendid, she would have
triumphed indeed. But, as it was, there was no
spot in her future career brighter to her than
those long years of suffering which she had
passed in the hope that some day her child might

be successful. Triumph indeed! There was nothing before her but solitude and shame.

Nevertheless she listened to Mr. Goffe, and signed the papers that were put before her. When, however, he spoke to her of what was necessary for the marriage,—as to the settlement, which must, Mr. Goffe said, be made as to the remaining moiety of her daughter's property,—she answered curtly that she knew nothing of that. Her daughter's affairs were no concern of hers. She had, indeed, worked hard to establish her daughter's rights, but her daughter was now of age, and could do as she pleased with her own. She would not even remain in the room while the matter was being discussed. 'Lady Anna and I have separate interests,' she said haughtily.

Lady Anna herself simply declared that half of her estate should be made over to her cousin, and that the other half should go to her husband. But the attorney was not satisfied to take instructions on a matter of such moment from one so young. As to all that was to appertain to the Earl, the matter was settled. The Solicitor-General and Serjeant Bluestone had acceded to the arrangement, and the Countess herself had given her assent before she had utterly separated her own interests from those of her daughter. In regard to so much, Mr. Goffe could go to work in conjunction with Mr. Flick without a scruple; but as to that other matter there must be consultations, conferences, and solemn debate. The young lady, no doubt, might do as she pleased; but lawyers can be very powerful. Sir William was asked for his opinion, and suggested that

Daniel Thwaite himself should be invited to
attend at Mr. Goffe's chambers, as soon as his
wound would allow him to do so. Daniel, who
did not care for his wound so much as he should
have done, was with Mr. Goffe on the following
morning, and heard a lengthy explanation from
the attorney. The Solicitor-General had been
consulted;—this Mr. Goffe said, feeling that a
tailor would not have a word to say against so
high an authority;—the Solicitor-General had
been consulted, and was of opinion that Lady
Anna's interests should be guarded with great
care. A very large property, he might say a
splendid estate, was concerned. Mr. Thwaite
of course understood that the family had been
averse to this marriage,—naturally very averse.
Now, however, they were prepared to yield.

The tailor interrupted the attorney at this
period of his speech. 'We don't want anybody
to yield, Mr. Goffe. We are going to do what we
please, and don't know anything about yielding.'

Mr. Goffe remarked that all that might be
very well, but that, as so large a property was at
stake, the friends of the lady, according to all
usage, were bound to interfere. A settlement had
already been made in regard to the Earl.

'You mean, Mr. Goffe, that Lady Anna has
given her cousin half her money?'

The attorney went on to say that Mr. Thwaite
might put it in that way if he pleased. The deeds
had already been executed. With regard to the
other moiety Mr. Thwaite would no doubt not
object to a trust-deed, by which it should be
arranged that the money should be invested in
land, the interest to be appropriated to the use

of Lady Anna, and the property be settled on the eldest son. Mr. Thwaite would, of course, have the advantage of the income during his wife's life. The attorney, in explaining all this, made an exceedingly good legal exposition, and then waited for the tailor's assent.

'Are those Lady Anna's instructions?'

Mr. Goffe replied that the proposal was made in accordance with the advice of the Solicitor-General.

'I'll have nothing to do with such a settlement,' said the tailor. 'Lady Anna has given away half her money, and may give away the whole if she pleases. She will be the same to me whether she comes full-handed or empty. But when she is my wife her property shall be my property,—and when I die there shall be no such abomination as an eldest son.' Mr. Goffe was persuasive, eloquent, indignant, and very wise. All experience, all usage, all justice, all tradition, required that there should be some such settlement as he had suggested. But it was in vain. 'I don't want my wife to have anything of her own before marriage,' said he; 'but she certainly shall have nothing after marriage,—independent of me.' For a man with sound views of domestic power and marital rights always choose a Radical! In this case there was no staying him. The girl was all on his side, and Mr. Goffe, with infinite grief, was obliged to content himself with binding up a certain portion of the property to make an income for the widow, should the tailor die before his wife. And thus the tailor's marriage received the sanction of all the lawyers.

A day or two after this Daniel Thwaite called
upon the Countess. It was now arranged that
they should be married early in July, and questions had arisen as to the manner of the ceremony. Who should give away the bride? Of
what nature should the marriage be? Should
there be any festival? Should there be brides-
maids? Where should they go when they were
married? What dresses should be bought?
After what fashion should they be prepared to
live? Those, and questions of a like nature,
required to be answered, and Lady Anna felt
that these matters should not be fixed without
some reference to her mother. It had been her
most heartfelt desire to reconcile the Countess
to the marriage,—to obtain, at any rate, so
much recognition as would enable her mother
to be present in the church. But the Countess
had altogether refused to speak on the subject,
and had remained silent, gloomy, and impene-
trable. Then Daniel had himself proposed that
he would see her, and on a certain morning he
called. He sent up his name, with his compliments, and the Countess allowed him to be
shown into her room. Lady Anna had begged
that it might be so, and she had yielded,—
yielded without positive assent, as she had now
done in all matters relating to this disastrous
marriage. On that morning, however, she had
spoken a word. 'If Mr. Thwaite chooses to
see me, I must be alone.' And she was alone
when the tailor was shown into the room. Up
to that day he had worn his arm in a sling,
—and should then have continued to do so;
but, on this visit of peace to her who had

attempted to be his murderer, he put aside
this outward sign of the injury she had inflicted
on him. He smiled as he entered the room,
and she rose to receive him. She was no longer
a young woman;—and no woman of her age
or of any other had gone through rougher
usage;—but she could not keep the blood out
of her cheeks as her eyes met his, nor could she
summon to her support that hard persistency
of outward demeanour with which she had
intended to arm herself for the occasion. 'So
you have come to see me, Mr. Thwaite?' she
said.

'I have come, Lady Lovel, to shake hands
with you, if it may be so, before my marriage
with your daughter. It is her wish that we should
be friends,—and mine also.' So saying, he put
out his hand, and the Countess slowly gave him
hers. 'I hope the time may come, Lady Lovel,
when all animosity may be forgotten between
you and me, and nothing be borne in mind but
the old friendship of former years.'

'I do not know that that can be,' she said.

'I hope it may be so. Time cures all things,—
and I hope it may be so.'

'There are sorrows, Mr. Thwaite, which no
time can cure. You have triumphed, and can
look forward to the pleasures of success. I have
been foiled, and beaten, and broken to pieces.
With me the last is worse even than the first. I
do not know that I can ever have another friend.
Your father was my friend.'

'And I would be so also.'

'You have been my enemy. All that he did to
help me,—all that others have done since to

forward me on my way, has been brought to nothing—by you! My joys have been turned to grief, my rank has been made a disgrace, my wealth has become like ashes between my teeth; —and it has been your doing. They tell me that you will be my daughter's husband. I know that it must be so. But I do not see that you can be my friend.'

'I had hoped to find you softer, Lady Lovel.'

'It is not my nature to be soft. All this has not tended to make me soft If my daughter will let me know from time to time that she is alive, that is all that I shall require of her. As to her future career, I cannot interest myself in it as I had hoped to do. Good-bye, Mr. Thwaite. You need fear no further interference from me.'

So the interview was over, and not a word had been said about the attempt at murder.

CHAPTER XLVI

Hard Lines

At the time that the murder was attempted Lord Lovel was in London,—and had seen Daniel Thwaite on that morning; but before any confirmed rumour had reached his ears he had left London again on his road to Yoxham. He knew now that he would be endowed with something like ten thousand a year out of the wealth of the late Earl, but that he would not have the hand of his fair cousin, the late Earl's daughter. Perhaps it was as well as it was. The girl had never loved him, and he could now choose for himself;—and need not choose till it should be his pleasure to settle himself as a married man. After all, his marriage with Lady Anna would have been a constrained marriage,—a marriage which he would have accepted as the means of making his fortune. The girl certainly had pleased him;—but it might be that a girl who preferred a tailor would not have continued to please him. At any rate he could not be unhappy with his newly-acquired fortune, and he went down to Yoxham to receive the congratulation of his friends, thinking that it would become him now to make some exertion towards reconciling his uncle and aunt to the coming marriage.

'Have you heard anything about Mr. Thwaite?' Mr. Flick said to him the day before he started. The Earl had heard nothing. 'They say that he has been wounded by a pistol-ball.' Lord Lovel stayed some days at a friend's house on his road into Yorkshire, and when he reached the rectory, the rector had received news from London. Mr. Thwaite the tailor had been murdered, and it was surmised that the deed had been done by the Countess. 'I trust the papers were signed before you left London,' said the anxious rector. The documents making over the property were all right, but the Earl would believe nothing of the murder. Mr. Thwaite might have been wounded. He had heard so much before,—but he was quite sure that it had not been done by the Countess. On the following day further tidings came. Mr. Thwaite was doing well, but everybody said that the attempt had been made by Lady Lovel. Thus by degrees some idea of the facts as they had occurred was received at the rectory.

'You don't mean that you want us to have Mr. Thwaite here?' said the rector, holding up his hands, upon hearing a proposition made to him by his nephew a day or two later.

'Why not, Uncle Charles?'

'I couldn't do it. I really don't think your aunt could bring herself to sit down to table with him.'

'Aunt Jane?'

'Yes, your Aunt Jane,—or your Aunt Julia either.' Now a quieter lady than Aunt Jane, or one less likely to turn up her nose at any guest whom her husband should choose to entertain, did not exist.

'May I ask my aunts?'

'What good can it do, Frederic?'

'He's going to marry our cousin. He's not at all such a man as you seem to think.'

'He has been a journeyman tailor all his life.'

'You'll find he'll make a very good sort of gentleman. Sir William Patterson says that he'll be in Parliament before long.'

'Sir William! Sir William is always meddling. I have never thought much about Sir William.'

'Come, Uncle Charles,—you should be fair. If we had gone on quarrelling and going to law, where should I have been now? I should never have got a shilling out of the property. Everybody says so. No doubt Sir William acted very wisely.'

'I am no lawyer. I can't say how it might have been. But I may have my doubts if I like. I have always understood that Lady Lovel, as you choose to call her, was never Lord Lovel's wife. For twenty years I have been sure of it, and I can't change so quickly as some other people.'

'She is Lady Lovel now. The King and Queen would receive her as such if she went to Court. Her daughter is Lady Anna Lovel.'

'It may be so. It is possible.'

'If it be not so,' said the young lord, thumping the table, 'where have I got the money from?' This was an argument that the rector could not answer;—so he merely shook his head. 'I am bound to acknowledge them after taking her money.'

'But not him. You haven't had any of his money. You needn't acknowledge him.'

'We had better make the best of it, Uncle Charles. He is going to marry our cousin, and we should stand by her. Sir William very strongly advises me to be present at the marriage, and to offer to give her away.'

'The girl you were going to marry yourself!'

'Or else that you should do it. That of course would be better.'

The rector of Yoxham groaned when the proposition was made to him. What infinite vexation of spirit and degradation had come to him from these spurious Lovels during the last twelve months! He had been made to have the girl in his house and to give her precedence as Lady Anna, though he did not believe in her; he had been constrained to treat her as the desired bride of his august nephew the Earl,— till she had refused the Earl's hand; after he had again repudiated her and her mother because of her base attachment to a low-born artisan, he had been made to re-accept her in spirit, because she had been generous to his nephew; —and now he was asked to stand at the altar and give her away to the tailor! And there could come to him neither pleasure nor profit from the concern. All that he had endured he had borne simply for the sake of his family and his nephew. 'She is degrading us all,—as far as she belongs to us,' said the rector. 'I can't see why I should be asked to give her my countenance in doing it.'

'Everybody says that it is very good of her to be true to the man she loved when she was poor and in obscurity. Sir William says——'

'—— Sir William!' muttered the rector between his teeth, as he turned away in disgust. What had been the first word of that minatory speech Lord Lovel did not clearly hear. He had been brought up as a boy by his uncle, and had never known his uncle to offend by swearing.

No one in Yoxham would have believed it possible that the parson of the parish should have done so. Mrs. Grimes would have given evidence in any court in Yorkshire that it was absolutely impossible. The archbishop would not have believed it though his archdeacon had himself heard the word. All the man's known antecedents since he had been at Yoxham were against the probability. The entire close at York would have been indignant had such an accusation been made. But his nephew in his heart of hearts believed that the rector of Yoxham had damned the Solicitor-General.

There was, however, more cause for male-diction, and further provocations to wrath, in store for the rector. The Earl had not as yet opened all his budget, or let his uncle know the extent of the sacrifice that was to be demanded from him. Sir William had been very urgent with the young nobleman to accord everything that could be accorded to his cousin. 'It is not of course for me to dictate,' he had said, 'but as I have been allowed so far to give advice somewhat beyond the scope of my profession, perhaps you will let me say that in mere honesty you owe her all that you can give. She has shared everything with you, and need have given nothing. And he, my lord, had he been so minded, might no doubt have hindered her from doing what she has done. You owe it to your honour to accept her and her husband with an open hand. Unless you can treat her with cousinly regard you should not have taken what has been given to you as a cousin. She

has recognised you to your great advantage as
the head of her family, and you should certainly
recognise her as belonging to it. Let the marriage be held down at Yoxham. Get your uncle
and aunt to ask her down. Do you give her
away, and let your uncle marry them. If you
can put me up for a night in some neighbouring
farm-house, I will come and be a spectator. It
will be for your honour to treat her after that
fashion.' The programme was a large one, and
the Earl felt that there might be some difficulty.

But in the teeth of that dubious malediction
he persevered, and his next attack was upon Aunt
Julia. 'You liked her;—did you not?'

'Yes;—I liked her.' The tone implied great
doubt. 'I liked her, till I found that she had
forgotten herself.'

'But she didn't forget herself. She just did
what any girl would have done, living as she
was living. She has behaved nobly to me.'

'She has behaved no doubt conscientiously.'

'Come, Aunt Julia! Did you ever know any
other woman to give away ten thousand a-year
to a fellow simply because he was her cousin?
We should do something for her. Why should
you not ask her down here again?'

'I don't think my brother would like it.'

'He will if you tell him. And we must make
a gentleman of him.'

'My dear Frederic, you can never wash a
blackamoor white.'

'Let us try. Don't you oppose it. It behoves
me, for my honour, to show her some regard
after what she has done for me.'

Aunt Julia shook her head, and muttered to

herself some further remark about negroes. The inhabitants of the Yoxham rectory,—who were well born, ladies and gentlemen without a stain, who were hitherto free from all base inter-marriages, and had nothing among their male cousins below soldiers and sailors, parsons and lawyers, who had successfully opposed an intended marriage between a cousin in the third degree and an attorney because the alliance was below the level of the Lovels, were peculiarly averse to any intermingling of ranks. They were descended from ancient earls, and their chief was an earl of the present day. There was but one titled young lady now among them,—and she had only just won her right to be so considered. There was but one Lady Anna,—and she was going to marry a tailor! 'Duty is duty,' said Aunt Julia as she hurried away. She meant her nephew to understand that duty commanded her to shut her heart against any cousin who could marry a tailor.

The lord next attacked Aunt Jane. 'You wouldn't mind having her here?'

'Not if your uncle thought well of it,' said Mrs. Lovel.

'I'll tell you what my scheme is.' Then he told it all. Lady Anna was to be invited to the rectory. The tailor was to be entertained somewhere near on the night preceding his wedding. The marriage was to be celebrated by his uncle in Yoxham Church. Sir William was to be asked to join them. And the whole thing was to be done exactly as though they were all proud of the connection.

'Does your uncle know?' asked Mrs. Lovel,

who had been nearly stunned by the proposition.

'Not quite. I want you to suggest it. Only think, Aunt Jane, what she has done for us all!' Aunt Jane couldn't think that very much had been done for her. They were not to be enriched by the cousin's money. They had never been interested in the matter on their own account. They wanted nothing. And yet they were to be called upon to have a tailor at their board,— because Lord Lovel was the head of their family. But the Earl was the Earl; and poor Mrs. Lovel knew how much she owed to his position. 'If you wish it of course I'll tell him, Frederic.'

'I do wish it;—and I'll be so much obliged to you.'

The next morning the parson had been told all that was required of him, and he came down to prayers as black as a thunder-cloud. It had been before suggested to him that he should give the bride away, and though he had grievously complained of the request, he knew that he must do it should the Earl still demand it. He had no power to oppose the head of the family. But he had never thought then that he would be asked to pollute his own rectory by the presence of that odious tailor. While he was shaving that morning very religious ideas had filled his mind. What a horrible thing was wickedness! All this evil had come upon him and his because the late Earl had been so very wicked a man! He had sworn to his wife that he would not bear it. He had done and was ready to do more almost than any other uncle in England. But this he could not endure. Yet when he was shaving, and thinking with religious horror of the iniquities of that iniquitous old lord, he knew that he would have to yield. 'I dare say they wouldn't come,' said Aunt Julia. 'He won't like to be with us any more than we shall like to have him.' There was some comfort in that hope; and trusting to it the rector had yielded everything before the third day was over.

'And I may ask Sir William?' said the Earl.

'Of course we shall be glad to see Sir William Patterson if you choose to invite him,' said the rector, still oppressed by gloom. 'Sir William Patterson is a gentleman, no doubt, and a man of high standing. Of course I and your aunt will be pleased to receive him. As a lawyer I don't think much of him;—but that has nothing to do with it.' It may be remarked here that though Mr. Lovel lived for a great many years after the transactions which are here recorded, he never gave way in reference to the case that had been tried. If the lawyers had persevered as they ought to have done, it would have been found out that the Countess was no Countess, that the Lady Anna was no Lady Anna, and that all the money had belonged by right to the Earl. With that belief,—with that profession of belief,—he went to his grave an old man of eighty.

In the meantime he consented that the invitation should be given. The Countess and her daughter were to be asked to Yoxham;—the use of the parish church was to be offered for the ceremony; he was to propose to marry them; the Earl was to give the bride away; and

Daniel Thwaite the tailor was to be asked to dine at Yoxham rectory on the day before the marriage! The letters were to be written from the rectory by Aunt Julia, and the Earl was to add what he pleased for himself. 'I suppose this sort of trial is sent to us for our good,' said the rector to his wife that night in the sanctity of their bedroom.

CHAPTER XLVII

Things arrange themselves

BUT the Countess never gave way an inch. The following was the answer which she returned to the note written to her by Aunt Julia;—

'The Countess Lovel presents her compliments to Miss Lovel. The Countess disapproves altogether of the marriage which is about to take place between Lady Anna Lovel and Mr. Daniel Thwaite, and will take no part in the ceremony.'

'By heavens,—she is the best Lovel of us all,' said the rector when he read the letter.

This reply was received at Yoxham three days before any answer came either from Lady Anna or from the tailor. Daniel had received his communication from the young lord, who had called him 'Dear Mr. Thwaite,' who had written quite familiarly about the coming nuptials with 'his cousin Anna,'—had bade him come down and join the family 'like a good fellow,'—and had signed himself, 'Yours always most sincerely, Lovel.' 'It almost takes my breath away,' said the tailor to his sweetheart, laughing.

'They are cousins, you know,' said Lady Anna. 'And there was a little girl there I loved so much.'

'They can't but despise me, you know,' said the tailor.

'Why should any one despise you?'

'No one should,—unless I be mean and

despicable. But they do,—you may be sure. It is only human nature that they should. We are made of different fabric,—though the stuff was originally the same. I don't think I should be at my ease with them. I should be half afraid of their gilt and their gingerbread, and should be ashamed of myself because I was so. I should not know how to drink wine with them, and should do a hundred things which would make them think me a beast.'

'I don't see why you shouldn't hold up your head with any man in England,' said Lady Anna.

'And so I ought;—but I shouldn't. I should be awed by those whom I feel to be my inferiors. I had rather not. We had better keep to ourselves, dear!' But the girl begged for some delay. It was a matter that required to be considered. If it were necessary for her to quarrel with all her cousins for the sake of her husband,—with the bright fainéant* young Earl, with Aunts Jane and Julia, with her darling Minnie, she would do so. The husband should be to her in all respects the first and foremost. For his sake, now that she had resolved that she would be his, she would if necessary separate herself from all the world. She had withstood the prayers of her mother, and she was sure that nothing else could move her. But if the cousins were willing to accept her husband, why should he not be willing to be accepted? Pride in him might be as weak as pride in them. If they would put out their hands to him, why should he refuse to put out his own? 'Give me a day, Daniel, to think about it.' He gave her the day, and then that great decider of all things, Sir William, came to him, congratulating him, bidding him be of good cheer, and saying fine things of the Lovel family generally. Our tailor received him courteously, having learned to like the man, understanding that he had behaved with honesty and wisdom in regard to his client, and respecting him as one of the workers of the day; but he declared that for the Lovel family, as a family,—'he did not care for them particularly.' 'They are poles asunder from me,' he said.

'Not so,' replied Sir William. 'They were poles asunder, if you will. But by your good fortune and merit, if you will allow me to say so, you have travelled from the one pole very far towards the other.'

'I like my own pole a deal the best, Sir William.'

'I am an older man than you, Mr. Thwaite, and allow me to assure you that you are wrong.'

'Wrong in preferring those who work for their bread to those who eat it in idleness?'

'Not that;—but wrong in thinking that there is not hard work done at the one pole as well as the other; and wrong also in not having perceived that the best men who come up from age to age are always migrating from that pole which you say you prefer, to the antipodean pole to which you are tending yourself. I can understand your feeling of contempt for an idle lordling, but you should remember that lords have been made lords in nine cases out of ten for good work done by them for the benefit of their country.'

'Why should the children of lords be such to the tenth and twentieth generation?'

'Come into parliament, Mr. Thwaite, and if you have views on that subject opposed to hereditary peerages, express them there. It is a fair subject for argument. At present, I think that the sense of the country is in favour of an aristocracy of birth. But be that as it may, do not allow yourself to despise that condition of society which it is the ambition of all men to enter.'

'It is not my ambition.'

'Pardon me. When you were a workman among workmen, did you not wish to be their leader? When you were foremost among them, did you not wish to be their master? If you were a master tradesman, would you not wish to lead and guide your brother tradesmen? Would you not desire wealth in order that you might be assisted by it in your views of ambition? If you were an alderman in your borough, would you not wish to be the mayor? If mayor, would you not wish to be its representative in Parliament? If in Parliament, would you not wish to be heard there? Would you not then clothe yourself as those among whom you lived, eat as they ate, drink as they drank, keep their hours, fall into their habits, and be one of them? The theory of equality is very grand.'

'The grandest thing in the world, Sir William.'

'It is one to which all legislative and all human efforts should and must tend. All that is said and all that is done among people that have emancipated themselves from the thraldom of individual aggrandizement, serve to diminish in some degree the distance between the high and

the low. But could you establish absolute equality
in England to-morrow, as it was to have been
established in France some half century ago, the
inequality of men's minds and character would
re-establish an aristocracy within twenty years.
The energetic, the talented, the honest, and the
unselfish will always be moving towards an
aristocratic side of society, because their virtues
will beget esteem, and esteem will beget wealth,
—and wealth gives power for good offices.'

'As when one man throws away forty thousand
a year on race-courses.'

'When you make much water boil, Mr.
Thwaite, some of it will probably boil over.
When two men run a race, some strength must
be wasted in fruitless steps beyond the goal.
It is the fault of many patriotic men that, in
their desire to put down the evils which exist
they will see only the power that is wasted, and
have no eyes for the good work done. The
subject is so large that I should like to discuss it
with you when we have more time. For the
present let me beg of you, for your own sake
as well as for her who is to be your wife, that you
will not repudiate civility offered to you by her
family. It will show a higher manliness in you
to go among them, and accept among them the
position which your wife's wealth and your own
acquirements will give you, than to stand aloof
moodily because they are aristocrats.'

'You can make yourself understood when you
speak, Sir William.'

'I am glad to hear you say so,' said the lawyer,
smiling.

'I cannot, and so you have the best of me.

But you can't make me like a lord, or think that a young man ought to wear a silk gown.'

'I quite agree with you that the silk gowns should be kept for their elders,' and so the conversation was ended.

Daniel Thwaite had not been made to like a lord, but the eloquence of the urbane lawyer was not wasted on him. Thinking of it all as he wandered alone through the streets, he began to believe that it would be more manly to do as he was advised than to abstain because the doing of the thing would in itself be disagreeable to him. On the following day, Lady Anna was with him as usual; for the pretext of his wound still afforded to her the means of paying to him those daily visits which in happier circumstances he would naturally have paid to her. 'Would you like to go to Yoxham?' he said. She looked wistfully up into his face. With her there was a real wish that the poles might be joined together by her future husband. She had found, as she had thought of it, that she could not make herself either happy or contented except by marrying him, but it had not been without regret that she had consented to destroy altogether the link which bound her to the noble blood of the Lovels. She had been made to appreciate the sweet flavour of aristocratic influences, and now that the Lovels were willing to receive her in spite of her marriage, she was more than willing to accept their offered friendship. 'If you really wish it, you shall go,' he said.

'But you must go also.'

'Yes;—for one day. And I must have a pair of gloves and a black coat.'

'And a blue one,—to be married in.'

'Alas me! Must I have a pink silk gown to walk about in, early in the morning?'

'You shall if you like, and I'll make it for you.'

'I'd sooner see you darning my worsted stockings, sweetheart.'

'I can do that too.'

'And I shall have to go to church in a coach, and come back in another, and all the people will smell sweet, and make eyes at me behind my back, and wonder among themselves how the tailor will behave himself.'

'The tailor must behave himself properly,' said Lady Anna.

'That's just what he won't do,—and can't do. I know you'll be ashamed of me, and then we shall both be unhappy.'

'I won't be ashamed of you. I will never be ashamed of you. I will be ashamed of them if they are not good to you. But, Daniel, you shall not go if you do not like it. What does it all signify, if you are not happy?'

'I will go,' said he. 'And now I'll sit down and write a letter to my lord.'

Two letters were written accepting the invitation. As that from the tailor to the lord was short and characteristic it shall be given.

'MY DEAR LORD,

'I am much obliged to you for your lordship's invitation to Yoxham, and if accepting it will make me a good fellow, I will accept it. I fear, however, that I can never be a proper

fellow to your lordship. Not the less do I feel
your courtesy, and I am,

'With all sincerity,
'Your lordship's very obedient servant,
'DANIEL THWAITE.'

Lady Anna's reply to Aunt Julia was longer
and less sententious, but it signified her intention
of going down to Yoxham a week before the
day settled for the marriage, which was now
the 10th of July. She was much obliged, she
said, to the rector for his goodness in promising
to marry them; and as she had no friends of her
own she hoped that Minnie Lovel would be her
bridesmaid. There were, however, sundry other
letters before the ceremony was performed, and
among them was one in which she was asked
to bring Miss Alice Bluestone down with her,
—so that she might have one bridesmaid over
and beyond those provided by the Yoxham
aristocracy. To this arrangement Miss Alice
Bluestone acceded joyfully,—in spite of that
gulf, of which she had spoken;—and, so accompanied, but without her lady's-maid, Lady Anna
returned to Yoxham that she might be there
bound in holy matrimony to Daniel Thwaite
the tailor, by the hands of her cousin, the Rev.
Charles Lovel.

CHAPTER XLVIII

The Marriage

THE marriage was nearly all that a marriage should be when a Lady Anna is led to the hymeneal altar. As the ceremony was transferred from Bloomsbury, London, to Yoxham, in York-shire, a licence had been procured, and the banns of which Daniel Thwaite thought so much, had been called in vain. Of course there are differences in aristocratic marriages. All earls' daughters are not married at St. George's, Hanover Square, nor is it absolutely necessary that a bishop should tie the knot, or that the dresses should be described in a newspaper. This was essentially a quiet marriage,—but it was quiet with a splendid quietude, and the obscurity of it was graceful and decorous. As soon as the thing was settled,—when it was a matter past doubt that all the Lovels were to sanction the marriage,—the two aunts went to work heartily. Another Lovel girl, hardly more than seen before by any of the family, was gathered to the Lovel home as a third brides-maid, and for the fourth,—who should officiate, but the eldest daughter of Lady Fitzwarren? The Fitzwarrens were not rich, did not go to town annually, and the occasions for social bril-liancy in the country are few and far between! Lady Fitzwarren did not like to refuse her old friend, Mrs. Lovel; and then Lady Anna was Lady Anna,—or at any rate would be so, as far as the newspapers of the day were concerned.

Miss Fitzwarren allowed herself to be attired in
white and blue, and to officiate in the procession,
—having, however, assured her most intimate
friend, Miss De Moleyns, that no consideration
on earth should induce her to allow herself to be
kissed by the tailor.

In the week previous to the arrival of Daniel
Thwaite, Lady Anna again ingratiated herself
with the ladies at the rectory. During the days
of her persecution she had been silent and apparently hard;—but now she was again gentle,
yielding, and soft. 'I do like her manner, all the
same,' said Minnie. 'Yes, my dear. It 's a pity
that it should be as it is to be, because she is very
nice.' Minnie loved her friend, but thought it
to be a thing of horror that her friend should
marry a tailor. It was almost as bad as the story
of the Princesss who had to marry a bear;—
worse indeed, for Minnie did not at all believe
that the tailor would ever turn out to be a gentleman, whereas she had been sure from the first
that the bear would turn into a prince.

Daniel came to Yoxham, and saw very little
of anybody at the rectory. He was taken in at
the house of a neighbouring squire, where he
dined as a matter of course. He did call at the
rectory, and saw his bride,—but on that occasion
he did not even see the rector. The squire took
him to the church in the morning, dressed in a
blue frock coat, brown trousers, and a grey
cravat. He was very much ashamed of his own
clothes, but there was nothing about him to
attract attention had not everybody known he
was a tailor. The rector shook hands with him
politely but coldly. The ladies were more affec-

tionate; and Minnie looked up into his face long
and anxiously. 'He wasn't very nice,' she said
afterwards, 'but I thought he'd be worse than
that!' When the marriage was over he kissed his
wife, but made no attempt upon the brides-
maids. Then there was a breakfast at the rectory,
—which was a very handsome bridal banquet.
On such occasions the part of the bride is always
easily played. It is her duty to look pretty if
she can, and should she fail in that,—as brides
usually do,—her failure is attributed to the
natural emotions of the occasion. The part of
the bridegroom is more difficult. He should be
manly, pleasant, composed, never flippant, able
to say a few words when called upon, and quietly
triumphant. This is almost more than mortal
can achieve, and bridegrooms generally manifest
some shortcomings at the awful moment. Daniel
Thwaite was not successful. He was silent and
almost morose. When Lady Fitzwarren congratulated him with high-flown words and a
smile,—a smile that was intended to combine
something of ridicule with something of civility,
—he almost broke down in his attempt to answer
her. 'It is very good of you, my lady,' said he.
Then she turned her back and whispered a word
to the parson, and Daniel was sure that she was
laughing at him. The hero of the day was the
Solicitor-General. He made a speech, proposing
health and prosperity to the newly-married
couple. He referred, but just referred, to the
trial, expressing the pleasure which all concerned
had felt in recognising the rights and rank of
the fair and noble bride as soon as the facts of
the case had come to their knowledge. Then he

spoke of the truth and long-continued friendship and devoted constancy of the bridegroom
and his father, saying that in the long experience
of his life he had known nothing more touching or
more graceful than the love which in early days
had sprung up between the beautiful young girl
and her earliest friend. He considered it to be
among the happinesses of his life that he had
been able to make the acquaintance of Mr.
Daniel Thwaite, and he expressed a hope that
he might long be allowed to regard that gentleman as his friend. There was much applause, in
giving which the young Earl was certainly the
loudest. The rector could not bring himself to
say a word. He was striving to do his duty by the
head of his family, but he could not bring himself to say that the marriage between Lady Anna
Lovel and the tailor was a happy event. Poor
Daniel was compelled to make some speech
in reply to his friend, Sir William. 'I am bad
at speaking,' said he, 'and I hope I shall be
excused. I can only say that I am under deep
obligation to Sir William Patterson for what he
has done for my wife.'

The couple went away with a carriage and
four horses to York, and the marriage was over.
'I hope I have done right,' said the rector in
whispered confidence to Lady Fitzwarren.

'I think you have, Mr. Lovel. I'm sure you
have. The circumstances were very difficult,
but I am sure you have done right. She must
always be considered as the legitimate child of
her father.'

'They say so,' murmured the rector sadly.

'Just that. And as she will always be con-

sidered to be the Lady Anna, you were bound
to treat her as you have done. It was a pity that
it was not done earlier, so that she might have
formed a worthier connection. The Earl, however, has not been altogether overlooked, and
there is some comfort in that. I dare say Mr.
Thwaite may be a good sort of man, though
he is——not just what the family could have
wished.' These words were undoubtedly spoken
by her ladyship with much pleasure. The Fitzwarrens were poor, and the Lovels were all
rich. Even the young Earl was now fairly well
to do in the world,—thanks to the generosity
of the newly-found cousin. It was, therefore,
pleasant to Lady Fitzwarren to allude to the
family misfortune which must in some degree
alloy the prosperity of her friends. Mr. Lovel
understood it all, and sighed; but he felt no
anger. He was grateful to Lady Fitzwarren for
coming to his house at all on so mournful an
occasion.

And so we may bid farewell to Yoxham. The
rector was an honest, sincere man, unselfish, true
to his instincts, genuinely English, charitable,
hospitable, a doer of good to those around him.
In judging of such a character we find the difficulty of drawing the line between political saga-
city and political prejudice. Had he been other
than he was, he would probably have been less
serviceable in his position.

The bride and bridegroom went for their
honeymoon into Devonshire, and on their road
they passed through London. Lady Anna
Thwaite,—for she had not at least as yet been
able to drop her title,—wrote to her mother

telling her of her arrival, and requesting permission to see her. On the following day she went alone to Keppel Street and was admitted. 'Dear, dear mamma,' she said, throwing herself into the arms of her mother.

'So it is done?' said the Countess.

'Yes;—mamma,—we are married. I wrote to you from York.'

'I got your letter, but I could not answer it. What could I say? I wish it had not been so;— but it is done. You have chosen for yourself, and I will not reproach you.'

'Do not reproach me now, mamma.'

'It would be useless. I will bear my sorrows in silence, such as they are. Do not talk to me of him, but tell me what is the life that is proposed for you.'

They were to stay in the south of Devonshire for a month and then to sail for the new colony founded at the Antipodes. As to any permanent mode of life no definite plan had yet been formed. They were bound for Sydney, and when there, 'my husband,'—as Lady Anna called him, thinking that the word might be less painful to the ears of her mother than the name of the man who had become so odious to her, —would do as should seem good to him. They would at any rate learn something of the new world that was springing up, and he would then be able to judge whether he would best serve the purpose that he had at heart by remaining there or by returning to England. 'And now, mamma, what will you do?'

'Nothing,' said the Countess.

'But where will you live?'

'If I could only find out, my child, where I might die, I would tell you that.'

'Mamma, do not talk to me of dying.'

'How should I talk of my future life, my dear? For what should I live? I had but you, and you have left me.'

'Come with me, mamma.'

'No, my dear. I could not live with him nor he with me. It will be better that he and I should never see each other again.'

'But you will not stay here?'

'No;—I shall not stay here. I must use myself to solitude, but the solitude of London is unendurable. I shall go back to Cumberland if I can find a home there. The mountains will remind me of the days which, sad as they were, were less sad than the present. I little dreamed then when I had gained everything my loss would be so great as it has been. Was the Earl there?'

'At our marriage? Oh yes, he was there.'

'I shall ask him to do me a kindness. Perhaps he will let me live at Lovel Grange?'

When the meeting was over, Lady Anna returned to her husband overwhelmed with tears. She was almost broken-hearted when she asked herself whether she had in truth been cruel to her mother. But she knew not how she could have done other than she had done. Her mother had endeavoured to conquer her by hard usage,—and had failed. But not the less her heart was very sore. 'My dear,' said the tailor to her, 'hearts will be sore. As the world goes yet awhile, there must be injustice; and sorrow will follow '

When they had been gone from London about a month the Countess wrote to her cousin the Earl and told him her wishes. 'If you desire to live there of course there must be an end of it. But if not, you might let the old place to me. It will not be as if it were gone out of the family. I will do what I can for the people around me, so that they may learn not to hate the name of Lovel.'

The young lord told her that she should have the use of the house as long as she pleased,— for her lifetime if it suited her to live there so long. As for rent,—of course he could take none after all that had been done for him. But the place should be leased to her so that she need not fear to be disturbed. When the spring time came, after the sailing of the vessel which took the tailor and his wife off to the Antipodes, Lady Lovel travelled down with her maid to Cumberland, leaving London without a friend to whom she could say adieu. And at Lovel Grange she took up her abode, amidst the old furniture and the old pictures, with everything to remind her of the black tragedy of her youth, when her husband had come to her and had told her, with a smile upon his lips and scorn in his eye, that she was not his wife, and that the child which she bore would be a bastard. Over his wicked word she had at any rate triumphed. Now she was living there in his house the un-questioned and undoubted Countess Lovel, the mistress of much of his wealth, while still were living around her those who had known her when she was banished from her home. There, too often with ill-directed generosity, she gave away her money, and became loved of the poor around her. But in the way of society she saw no human being, and rarely went beyond the valley in which stood the lonely house to which she had been brought as a bride.

Of the further doings of Mr. Daniel Thwaite and his wife Lady Anna,—of how they travelled and saw many things; and how he became perhaps a wiser man,—the present writer may, he hopes, live to tell.

EXPLANATORY NOTES

1 *Keswick*: in Cumberland, in the Lake District, a mining and manufacturing town since the Middle Ages, but also known for the beautiful country surrounding it, and associated with the Romantic poets; it was Southey's home in retirement (see Chapter XXVII.

23 *Solicitor-General*: the legal officer, serving under the Attorney-General, who represents the state or the crown in suits relating to the public interest.

26 *Yorkshire Stingo*: name of an inn (stingo = strong ale).

31 *statesmen*: in Cumberland, small landholders (see *OED* s. v. statesman, 2).

32 *poets of the lakes, who had not as yet become altogether Tories*: alluding to Southey and Wordsworth, who in middle age abandoned their early radical views for conservative ones, and were both duly rewarded with the Laureateship.

35 *More's Utopia, Harrington's Oceana*: classics of utopian political philosophy. Sir Thomas More's *Utopia* was published in Latin in 1516 and in English in 1551; James Harington's romance *The Commonwealth of Oceana* appeared in 1656.

46 *silk*: barrister's robes.

47 *hunters*: fox-hunting horses.

50 *Harrow*: the famous public school where Byron, Sir Robert Peel, Palmerston, Churchill—and Trollope— were educated; in the *Autobiography* Trollope describes his misery as an impoverished day-student there.

51 *there were still Whigs in those days*: The term Whig as a name for the party opposed to the Tories was superseded by Liberal after about the middle of the nineteenth century, 'though Whig was still used to indicate adherence to moderate or outdated Liberal principles' (*OED*).

70 *I'll stand the racket*: I'll take the responsibility.

74 *speaking daggers*: alluding to *Hamlet*, III. iii. 357: 'I will speak daggers to her, but use none.'

75 *as the Jew dealt with the Christians in the play*: In *The Merchant of Venice* Shylock tells Bassanio, 'I will buy with you, sell with

you, talk with you, walk with you, and so following; but I will not eat with you, drink with you, nor pray with you' (I. iii. 31 ff.).

77 *Jupiter Tonans*: Jupiter the Thunderer.

78 *Brasenose*: the Oxford college of Robert Burton and Walter Pater.

131 *Swan and Edgar's,—Marshall and Snellgrove*: stylish London shops.

140 *consols*: securities with no maturity date.

topping: pre-eminent.

Margaux: Château Margaux, one of the greatest Bordeaux wines.

champagne . . . was not yet a necessity: champagne until the latter half of the nineteenth century was a sweet wine, and only became the universally fashionable drink of choice after English dealers marketed a dry variety.

144 *Bolton Abbey*: the ruins of this priory dating from Norman times were famous for their romantic beauty and spectacular setting.

145 *corn of idleness*: properly 'bread of idleness', Proverbs 31: 27.

white doe of Rylston: the local legend told of a white doe which, before the dissolution of the monasteries under Henry VIII, would appear in the Abbey churchyard every Sunday during the service. Wordsworth's poem on the subject, 'The White Doe of Rylston', was published in 1815.

Landseer's picture of the abbey in olden times: the famous painting, an imaginative reconstruction of the Priory before the dissolution, was exhibited in 1834 and acquired by the duke of Devonshire. It is now at Chatsworth.

151 *on the box*: outside the carriage, with the driver.

168 *scouted*: ridiculed.

195 *baronet who dated back from James I*: the rank of baronet, equivalent to a hereditary knighthood, was created by James I in 1610. It was not originally a grand title, having been invented essentially for sale to raise money for the crown, and baronets were outranked not only by the entire peerage, but even by their younger sons. Trollope's second cousin was a

baronet; the title now belongs to Frederic Trollope's Australian descendants.

205 *chaffer*: haggle.

266 *mail*: the daily mail coach.

283 *Brown's Hotel*: This small first-class hotel is still in business in Albermarle Street, though it is now entered from Dover Street.

287 *heir-at-law*: the unquestionable legal heir (what an *heir apparent* becomes after the death of the person he or she is to succeed).

288 *quidnuncs*: gossips, newsmongers (people who are always asking *quid nunc?*, 'what now?').

306 *Reform Bill*: the act, passed after intense and bitter debate in 1832, greatly extended voting rights and removed inequities and abuses in the system of representation.

318 *the Lady of the Strachy . . . yeoman of the wardrobe*: referring to *Twelfth Night*, II. v. 36, Malvolio citing the marriage of a low-born husband to a noble wife as a precedent for his wooing of Olivia (Malvolio's allusion is unexplained).

349 *Chief Baron*: the Lord Chief Baron was the chief justice of the Court of Exchequer; the title was abolished in 1873.

365 *douceur*: little gift, bribe (*OED* 3).

381 *A lover's ears . . .* : *Love's Labour's Lost*, IV. iii. 332–3.

462 *The Attempt and not the Deed confounds us*: *Macbeth*, II. i. 10–11, Lady Macbeth fearing that Macbeth has botched the murder of Duncan.

477 *Hotspur*: in *I Henry IV* King Henry sends 'a certain lord . . . perfumèd like a milliner' to demand the prisoners Hotspur is holding, and Hotspur refuses to give them up (I. iii. 33–6).

Hamlet: in *Hamlet* the elegantly affected Osric, whom Hamlet mocks as a 'water-fly', is sent to propose the terms of the wager Claudius will make on Hamlet's duel with Laertes (V. ii. 82).

478 *spermaceti was 'the sovereignest thing on earth for an inward wound'*: the perfumed lord's recommendation to Hotspur, l. 57; *spermaceti* = ointment.

'very soft society, and great showing': Osric's description of Laertes, V. ii. 102.

a doit: the smallest trifle.

479 *banns . . . licence*: banns are read three times in the local parish
church, publicly declaring the couple's intention to marry;
Lady Lovel is shocked because the practice implies that the
couple are commoners. The licence permits the couple to be
married outside their parish, either more discreetly or (as it
turns out in this case) more grandly.

498 *fainéant*: idler.

THE WORLD'S CLASSICS

A Select List

JANE AUSTEN: Emma
Edited by James Kinsley and David Lodge

WILLIAM BECKFORD: Vathek
Edited by Roger Lonsdale

JOHN BUNYAN: The Pilgrim's Progress
Edited by N. H. Keeble

THOMAS CARLYLE: The French Revolution
Edited by K. J. Fielding and David Sorensen

GEOFFREY CHAUCER: The Canterbury Tales
Translated by David Wright

CHARLES DICKENS: Christmas Books
Edited by Ruth Glancy

BENJAMIN DISRAELI: Coningsby
Edited by Sheila M. Smith

MARIA EDGEWORTH: Castle Rackrent
Edited by George Watson

SUSAN FERRIER: Marriage
Edited by Herbert Foltinek

ELIZABETH GASKELL: Cousin Phillis and Other Tales
Edited by Angus Easson

THOMAS HARDY: A Pair of Blue Eyes
Edited by Alan Manford

HOMER: The Iliad
Translated by Robert Fitzgerald
Introduction by G. S. Kirk

HENRIK IBSEN: An Enemy of the People, The Wild Duck,
Rosmersholm
Edited and Translated by James McFarlane

HENRY JAMES: The Ambassadors
Edited by Christopher Butler

JOCELIN OF BRAKELOND:
Chronicle of the Abbey of Bury St. Edmunds
Translated by Diana Greenway and Jane Sayers

BEN JONSON: Five Plays
Edited by G. A. Wilkes

LEONARDO DA VINCI: Notebooks
Edited by Irma A. Richter

HERMAN MELVILLE: The Confidence-Man
Edited by Tony Tanner

PROSPER MÉRIMÉE: Carmen and Other Stories
Translated by Nicholas Jotcham

EDGAR ALLAN POE: Selected Tales
Edited by Julian Symons

MARY SHELLEY: Frankenstein
Edited by M. K. Joseph

BRAM STOKER: Dracula
Edited by A. N. Wilson

ANTHONY TROLLOPE: The American Senator
Edited by John Halperin

OSCAR WILDE: Complete Shorter Fiction
Edited by Isobel Murray

A complete list of Oxford Paperbacks, including The World's Classics, OPUS, Past Masters, Oxford Authors, Oxford Shakespeare, and Oxford Paperback Reference, is available in the UK from the Arts and Reference Publicity Department (RS), Oxford University Press, Walton Street, Oxford OX2 6DP.

In the USA, complete lists are available from the Paperbacks Marketing Manager, Oxford University Press, 200 Madison Avenue, New York, NY 10016.

Oxford Paperbacks are available from all good bookshops. In case of difficulty, customers in the UK can order direct from Oxford University Press Bookshop, Freepost, 116 High Street, Oxford, OX1 4BR, enclosing full payment. Please add 10 per cent of published price for postage and packing.